MAUD

HEIRS TO A BROKEN AGE

MAUD

HEIRS TO A BROKEN AGE

L. L. JUNIOR

Troubador Publishing Ltd
Unit E2 Airfield Business Park,
Harrison Road, Market Harborough,
Leicestershire LE16 7UL
Tel: 0116 279 2299
Email: books@troubador.co.uk
Web: www.troubador.co.uk

ISBN 978-1-83628-538-0

British Library Cataloguing in Publication Data.
A catalogue record for this book is available from the British Library.

The manufacturer's authorised representative in the EU for product safety is Authorised Rep
Compliance Ltd, 71 Lower Baggot Street, Dublin D02 P593 Ireland (www.arccompliance.com).

Printed and bound by CPI Group (UK) Ltd, Croydon, CR0 4YY
Typeset in 12pt Adobe Jenson by Troubador Publishing Ltd, Leicester, UK

For my parents and my son.

PROLOGUE
MAUD

The cold here is not simply a season – it is a law, unbroken and eternal.

This world is locked beneath an unyielding curse of frost.

The sun exists, somewhere beyond the thick, rolling clouds, but its light has never touched the land – not in living memory.

Here, there is no true day, no true night – only a dimming and a darkening. A ceaseless twilight drapes the world in an eerie, timeless haze, where the only real difference between day and night is how deep the shadows stretch.

All seasons feel the same – icy, muted, unchanging. The bitter winds of winter never fade, the rivers remain half-frozen, their sluggish currents winding like veins of liquid glass beneath thick layers of cracked ice. Snow falls in endless waves, sometimes gently, sometimes in violent storms, but it never ceases. It buries ruins, trees, mountains, even the scars of past wars – a shroud of white that hides the past beneath its suffocating weight.

And yet…

Nature has endured.

Somehow, despite the unrelenting frost, life has found a way.

Not in abundance, not in defiance, but in adaptation.

The forests stand skeletal and twisted, their blackened branches coated in hoar frost, yet they do not wither. Their roots stretch deep beneath the permafrost, feeding off what little the earth still offers, drinking from underground veins of warmth long forgotten by the sky. Their bark is thick, hardened against the cold, and some trees bear glowing veins of blue or violet, pulsing faintly in the dark – a sign of something ancient that lingers within the land.

Plants cling to existence, not by thriving, but by surviving. Low-growing shrubs with leathery, frost-resistant leaves nestle against the rocks, their roots burrowed into the stone for warmth. Some glow faintly, their sap imbued with a pale, bioluminescent shimmer, casting unnatural light in the deepest woods. There are no flowers, no lush fields of green, only the remnants of what was – plants that have learned to drink the cold itself, to grow not by warmth, but by resilience.

The animals of Maud are no less stubborn.

Great, white-furred wolves, their bodies massive, their pelts thick enough to resist even the worst of storms, prowl the forests and valleys, moving in near silence. Their eyes gleam like pale moons, watching from the darkness, intelligent and wary.

Towering elk-like creatures, their antlers twisting like the frozen branches of trees, move through the ice fields, their breath curling into the cold air like smoke. Their hooves are wide, allowing them to traverse the deep snow with ease, and their hides are covered in a thick, silver-tipped fur that glows faintly beneath the twilight.

Smaller creatures skitter through the underbrush – burrowing mammals with thick hides, foxes with tails that flicker like wraiths in the dim light, and birds with feathers so pale they vanish against the snow. Some of these creatures have developed strange, unnatural traits, as if touched by something beyond the natural order – glowing eyes, fur that shifts to blend into the ice, the ability to move without disturbing the snow beneath them.

They do not thrive – they persist.

This is not a world of abundance.

It is a world of survival.

The sky is a swirling abyss of ashen greys and deep blues, a vast, shifting canvas of storm clouds that never part, never warm, never yield. The wind howls like a grieving spectre, tearing through the endless white landscape, carrying with it whispers of a world long forgotten.

A thick, ghostly mist lingers over the frozen ground, moving unnaturally, as though it lives, creeping and curling between frostbitten trees and jagged cliffs of ice. Snow blankets the hills and valleys, yet there is no true stillness here – only the silence of something *waiting*.

The land stretches vast and empty, rolling hills rising and falling like the frozen ribs of a long-dead beast. Each slope is buried beneath thick snow, untouched, pristine, yet heavy with something unseen. The air is sharp, each breath a needle in the lungs, every gust of wind carrying flecks of ice that bite at exposed skin like a warning.

Descending deeper, the hills give way to a forest – a twisted, skeletal place, where trees stand black and gnarled, their limbs coated in frost, reaching skyward like broken fingers desperate to grasp something lost. The brittle remains of silver-tinged leaves cling stubbornly to their branches, unmoved by the ceaseless wind. Beneath the trunks, the ground is split and frozen, laced with eerie veins of pale, glowing fungi, pulsing like the last, feeble beats of a dying heart.

The silence within the forest is thick, oppressive. The snow muffles sound, but beneath it, something unseen shifts. The weight of the air itself changes, as if the world is holding its breath.

Beyond the forest, the land rises into mountains – colossal, jagged peaks, their forms blackened and sharp, vanishing into the storm that rages above them. The wind becomes a living thing here, a relentless force howling through the canyons, tearing through stone and ice with a fury that never fades.

A river winds its way up the mountainside, frozen over, its surface cracked like ancient glass. The sluggish water beneath writhes, trapped yet still moving, never truly still. The path ahead is treacherous, the cliffs sheer, the snowfall unending.

And then... the storm grows worse.

The sky churns, black and violet clouds twisting like an open wound. Thunder growls from within the abyss, an unnatural sound that seems to rattle the very bones of the world. The snow thickens, blinding, suffocating.

A bolt of lightning splits the sky.

Then another.

The storm does not relent – it intensifies, and a cascade of lightning finally hits the top of the mountain.

The storm rages on, the winds howling like a chorus of lost souls, tearing through the jagged peaks of the ancient mountain. Snow and ice batter the cliffs, carried in violent flurries, yet even beneath the unrelenting storm, something has changed.

The impact of the lightning strike, the force that shattered the mountainside, has not only revealed the hidden gateway – it has uncovered something far older.

A balcony of stone, once buried beneath the unyielding grip of ice and rock, now stands exposed.

Carved by hands long forgotten, it stretches outward from the mountainside, its foundations worn by time, but unyielding, as if it had waited ages to be seen once more.

The balcony is massive, hewn from dark stone, its edges lined with towering pillars, each one adorned with intricate carvings – symbols that no modern tongue remembers, their meanings swallowed by history. Some of the engravings have been eroded, lost to time's patient hunger, while others remain sharp, defiant against the centuries.

Though the storm has buried much of the world in frost and ruin, this place still feels untouched by decay. The stone, though weathered, still holds the weight of purpose, as if those who once stood here had never truly left.

Icicles hang in thick clusters from the arches, shimmering like frozen daggers in the dim light, while frost clings to the ancient stone, veining the surface like a living thing. And yet, beneath the ice, something else lingers – a faint, pulsing energy, woven into the rock itself, as if the mountain still remembers what it was meant to protect.

Beyond the balcony's edge, a vast abyss stretches below, a sheer drop into darkness. Far below, the valley disappears into the haze of the storm, the snowfall choking out the land beneath like a ghostly tide.

This was no ordinary stone platform – it was a watchpoint, built near the summit, once overlooking the world far below.

A place where ancient eyes once watched the horizon, standing guard over something greater.

It stands silent, its purpose lost to the centuries, until now.

Behind it, set into the very bones of the mountain, the gateway looms – massive, carved with symbols that still pulse faintly with a forgotten power. The entrance, once buried, now waits once more, yawning open like a maw of shadow, whispering secrets the world has long forgotten. A doorway to something ancient, something cast aside.

A threshold to what was never meant to be forgotten.

The very air vibrates, thick with an unseen force, rippling like heat over ice.

A mist seeps from within, swirling with deep blues and shimmering silvers, whispering in voices that do not belong to the wind.

The world beyond is consumed by the storm, yet here, before this entrance, something else stirs.

Something old.

Something waiting.

THE AWAKENING

The wind outside fades into a distant, muffled wail.

Inside, the air is dense, ancient, untouched. The cold is deeper, thicker, pressing into the bones like an unspoken presence. The scent of old stone lingers, mingled with something faint, something beyond time.

Darkness reigns.

Until…

A flicker.

One by one, torches ignite along the walls – not with natural flame, but with an unnatural blue fire, casting a shifting, ghostly glow. Their light stretches across towering walls, revealing a corridor too vast for mortals to have built, too sacred for time to have erased.

The passage extends forward, leading into something greater, something sacred.

The walls bear carvings, ancient and unreadable, their symbols pulsing subtly with a silent energy. The floor is smooth, worn by time, yet untouched by any living soul for centuries upon centuries.

And at the end of the passage, the space opens up.

A hall, vast beyond comprehension.

The architecture is impossible, shifting beneath the eerie glow, as if the very fabric of reality bends within these walls. The space feels endless, yet contained, sacred and unknowable.

At the centre, an ancient fountain stands – a monolith of ice and stone, frozen in time.

Cracks slither across its surface.

A drip of water.

Then another.

The sound echoes through the chamber, small yet immense, as the frost begins to melt.

The water swirls, no longer still, no longer silent.

And beneath it…

Something awakens.

Six figures lie motionless, each resting upon individual black stone slabs, their forms encased in layers of ice and frost.

Naked. Silent.

Their skin pale – except for the hulking, ebony-skinned warrior and the mighty dwarf lying beside him, their forms imposing even in slumber.

A misty vapour rises from their bodies, a breath returning after an eternity of stillness.

Then…

A twitch.

Fingers, once frozen, move.

A slow breath escapes parted lips, forming a faint cloud in the freezing air.

The fountain trembles, the water now moving in an unnatural current, responding to something unseen.

Then…

A crack.

The ice splits, shattering across their skin.

The six remain silent, their eyes yet to open…

But something deep within them stirs.

They are waking.

A shuddering breath breaks the silence.

The first to awaken is a towering figure – a man built like a force of nature itself. His colossal form, over two metres tall, rises slowly from the frozen slab, steam rising from his thawing skin as if the very ice is reluctant to release him. His muscles, carved from the trials of gods and war, are beyond mortal comprehension – thick cords of raw power stretch beneath his onyx skin, his physique a testament to brute strength and unshaken will. Every motion is slow at first, like a mountain shifting after centuries of stillness, but soon, life surges through him.

His chest, broad as a warhorse, is dusted with thick, coarse hair, a natural mantle of rugged strength. His shoulders are immense, leading to arms that could tear through steel, veins bulging beneath his skin as he clenches his fists, the cracking of frozen joints echoing through the chamber. His hands, large enough to crush a skull in a single grip, flex as he tests his reborn flesh.

His face is a masterpiece of brutal beauty – sharp, angular features chiselled with both grace and might. A strong, square jaw, a proud, slightly broad and curved nose, and piercing eyes that flicker open, glowing faintly with an ancient fire and bright black colour. His short, coarse black hair is damp with melted frost, framing his powerful brow, while a thick, neatly kept beard clings to his jaw, enhancing his raw allure.

As he sits up fully, the ice cracking beneath his sheer weight, his breath comes out in thick clouds, chest rising and falling like a storm-touched sea. He blinks once, twice – then his gaze sharpens, a primal intelligence flickering behind those intense eyes. He does not gasp, nor does he shudder.

He simply wakes, like a beast returning to the hunt. He's Drunnyak.

The chamber hums with unseen energy as another breath stirs the cold air.

The next to awaken is her; a vision of beauty so absolute it defies mortal words, her name – Aneeve. The frost steams away from her flawless olive skin, her body sculpted with an impossible balance of grace and power. She shifts, her form emerging from the ice like a goddess reborn, every movement both delicate and commanding.

Her long, golden hair cascades over her shoulders, damp from the thaw, strands clinging to her high cheekbones and strong, elegant jaw.

It shimmers under the ethereal blue torchlight, every lock falling into place with effortless perfection. Her ears, long and pointed, mark her elven heritage, though she is nothing like the frail, waifish kind sung about in human tales. She is strength. She is desire. She is untouchable, yet irresistible.

Her face is a masterpiece of divine symmetry – eyes sharp and piercing, the colour of radiant gold or the richest amber depending on how the light catches them. Full lips, naturally flushed, part slightly as she exhales her first breath in aeons, the soft sound alone enough to shake the soul of any who might witness it. Her nose is straight, noble, yet faintly upturned at the tip – just enough to give her an edge of playful arrogance, as if she already knows the effect she has on the world around her.

Her body is nothing short of devastating. Strength and femininity intertwine in a perfect dance – her shoulders proud, arms lean yet sculpted with the unmistakable tone of a warrior. Her waist narrows with breathtaking precision, curving into hips that could drive men to madness. Her bosom, full and firm, rises and falls with each slow breath, her skin untouched by time, flawless even in the dim glow of the chamber. And her legs – long, powerful, shaped by the grace of a huntress and the seduction of a goddess – shift as she pushes herself upright.

As she sits, ice cracking and water pooling around her, her golden eyes finally focus. There is no fear, no hesitation – only a slow, knowing smirk that graces her perfect lips, as if she has already decided that the world should bow at her feet.

The stillness in the chamber is broken again.

Two figures stir, their movements perfectly synchronised, as if bound by something deeper than time. The frost peels away from their skin, steam rising like spectres from their reborn forms. As their breathing steadies, their emerald eyes – radiant and piercing, like light shining through deep forest canopies – flutter open, glowing faintly in the dim torchlight.

Though unmistakably twins, they are two halves of the same whole – one carved by peace, the other by war.

The first, the fair one, is a vision of quiet elegance. His long, obsidian-black hair spills over his shoulders like silk, unbound and untamed, yet pristine in its perfection. His features are sharp but smooth, chiselled with an artistry untouched by hardship. His nose is straight and noble, his lips finely shaped, neither too soft nor too severe. His frame is lean, sculpted with a natural grace, each muscle defined but never overwhelming. Strength lies in him, but not the kind that seeks battle. He is the whisper of wind through leaves, the patient hand that coaxes life from the earth. If a blade has ever touched his palm, it was only to carve wood, not flesh.

Beside him, his twin is built from the same divine mould, but hardened for survival. His face, though just as beautiful, bears the marks of battle. His nose, once regal, is now slightly crooked – a permanent reminder of fights fought and won. His jawline is sharper, his expression harder, as though he has faced storms and refused to bow. His body, though just as smooth as his brother's, is heavier with muscle, built not just to move but to strike. His shoulders are broader, his arms thick with the power of a warrior, his chest rising and falling with the steady breath of someone who knows how to kill, but does not seek to.

Both exhale at the same time, mist rolling from their lips, their emerald eyes adjusting to the chamber's dim glow. Their long black hair, sleek and untouched by time, frames their striking features as they sit up, ice cracking beneath their weight. They turn to each other, wordless, understanding already passing between them without the need for speech.

Nashir – the nurturer, the gentle hand, the soul in tune with the world's quiet beauty.

Alentar – the hunter, the protector, the warrior who stands between life and death.

They are awake.

The chamber shudders once more. A deep, rumbling breath echoes through the frozen air as the next to wake is not just a man, but a mountain called Taril.

Ice cracks violently around him as his massive frame shifts, the frost unwilling to let go of something so immovable, so unbreakable. Then, with a mighty inhale, the last remnants of his slumber melt away, and his body, thick as iron and just as unyielding, rises from the ancient slab.

He is the very essence of dwarven strength – stout but powerful, built like the foundation of a fortress. His muscles, compact yet immense, ripple beneath his light brown skin, which bears the hardened texture of stone worn smooth by time and war. His arms, thick as tree trunks, flex as he stretches, joints popping like distant thunder. His hands are broad, calloused, strong enough to crush boulders and gentle enough to wield a craftsman's hammer.

His hair, long and wild, cascades down his back in thick waves, blending seamlessly into his beard – a mighty, untamed mass of braids and coarse strands, each one a testament to age and experience. Silver streaks run through both, not as a sign of weakness but as proof of his endurance, his defiance against time itself. His face is rugged, square-jawed, with deep lines that speak of battles fought, victories won, and losses endured. His brow is heavy, his nose slightly crooked from old fights, but his eyes – fierce, piercing, the colour of molten gold – burn with an intensity that has never faded.

He plants his feet on the cold stone, the impact reverberating through the chamber like a war drum. His breath is steady, measured, as if he has already accepted his return without question. He does not need to understand the why, only the now.

A protector has no need for hesitation.

His gaze sweeps over the others, not with awe or fear, but with quiet certainty. Whatever storm has called them back, whatever force has shaken them from their long rest, he is here to stand against it. Not as a conqueror. Not as a destroyer.

But as a shield.

And no force in this world, or the next, will break him.

The final breath of frost escapes into the cold air as the last figure stirs.

Slowly, the ice that clings to his skin melts away, tracing rivulets of water down the contours of a body forged in its prime. He is neither the towering beast of the first to wake, nor the slender grace of the elven twins – he is the balance between power and refinement, a man in the peak of his strength, as if shaped by the very essence of vitality itself.

He rises, controlled and unhurried, muscles coiling beneath his skin with quiet power. Taller than the elves, yet standing beneath the hulking form of the dark-skinned warrior, he moves with the ease of a man who knows himself, his place, his worth. His body is neither too lean nor overly built, but the perfect fusion of endurance, agility and might – a man shaped not just for battle, but for life itself.

His hair, a deep chestnut brown, is tousled from the thaw, falling just past his ears, a natural ruggedness that complements his thick, short beard, neatly trimmed but far from ornamental. His jaw is strong, his cheekbones sharp yet softened by a warmth in his expression that the others have not yet shown. And then, his eyes – like sapphires kissed by a diamond's light, a rare and mesmerising mix of blue and silver, shining with a depth that holds both wisdom and curiosity.

As he fully awakens, his gaze drifts over his companions – warriors, legends, protectors, each a figure of might and power. But unlike them, his first instinct is not battle or caution. Instead, his lips curl into a soft, knowing smile – a smile that speaks not of dominance or arrogance, but of understanding, of something gentler yet just as strong.

He exhales slowly, shaking away the last remnants of his long slumber. Then, with a simple, almost amused glance around, he takes in the moment before finally speaking.

"Well." His voice is rich, warm, steady. "Anyone know where we are?" Opilkhos asks.

The silence lingers for only a moment before the first voice breaks it.

Drunnyak stretches, rolling his massive shoulders before letting out a deep, satisfied groan. "Well, well… Feels like I've been asleep for a damn eternity." He cracks his neck, then smirks, eyes flicking toward Aneeve. "And yet, first thing I see when I wake up? A muse, a divine vision. Guess fate loves me after all." Licking his lips whilst he watches her every move.

Aneeve scoffs, crossing her arms under her chest with an amused smirk. "Flatter me all you want, big man, but if you think you'll wake up in my arms next, keep dreaming."

7

Drunnyak chuckles, placing a hand on his chest dramatically. "Ouch, right in the heart. At least let me enjoy the view before you shatter my soul." Walking around her and watching every inch of her perfect body.

Taril grunts, rolling his shoulders as he sits up. "You waking up with a soul at all is a surprise," he mutters. His golden eyes scan the room, his expression unreadable. "Where in the name of stone and steel are we?"

"Somewhere ancient." Nashir speaks for the first time, his voice calm but thoughtful. He runs a hand over the now-thawed stone slab he lay upon, eyes scanning the mystical symbols along the cavern walls. "And powerful. I don't recognise the markings, but they hum with something… familiar."

Alentar remains silent, rising to his feet with slow, deliberate movements. His gaze sweeps over the chamber like a predator assessing its surroundings. His fingers twitch slightly, as if longing to hold a weapon, yet he makes no move toward one.

Opilkhos, still seated, exhales, rubbing his temples as if trying to reach for something just out of grasp. "I don't even know my name… no memories to recollect." He looks around at the others, his expression earnest, searching. "And yet, I know I can fight. I know I can wield magic. It's like knowledge without history."

Drunnyak flexes an arm, grinning. "Yeah, well, I don't need a name to know I can punch through a wall." He glances at Taril. "And you, old man, feel like the type who's swung a hammer at more than just an anvil."

Taril exhales through his nose, unimpressed. "You don't need memories to see that I could break you in half, boy."

Drunnyak grins wider. "Now that's a challenge I wouldn't mind testing. Later."

Aneeve rolls her eyes. "Brainless, the both of you. No point in testing our strength if we don't even know why we're here." She looks toward Nashir, her sharp gaze expectant. "You seem like the thinking type. Any theories?"

Nashir nods slightly. "A few. But nothing concrete. What I do know is this – whatever has woken us, it was no accident. We were put here for a reason."

A heavy silence settles over them at his words.

Opilkhos stands at last, his posture steady but his eyes full of questions. "Then we need to find that reason." His gaze falls upon the ancient passage leading deeper into the cavern. Faint, flickering lights dance along its path, as if urging them forward.

Drunnyak stretches one more time, rolling his shoulders. "Well, mystery or not, sitting around ain't solving it. Time to move." He gestures toward the passage. "Ladies first?" He grins at Aneeve.

She smirks back, tossing her golden hair over her shoulder. "Nice try. You go first, brute. That way, if there's something nasty ahead, it'll chew on you first."

Drunnyak laughs, stepping toward the cavern exit corridor without hesitation. "Oh, I like you."

And with that, they take their first steps forward into the unknown.

As they move toward the exit, a deep, grinding noise echoes through the chamber. Stone shifts, dust falls from the ceiling, and with a heavy thud, a hidden door along the wall slides open.

They all turn sharply. Standing beside the open doorway, his hand still resting on an ancient mechanism, is Alentar. His emerald eyes flick between them, and this time, a rare expression crosses his face. His lips curl slightly, and he raises an eyebrow with a smirk, holding his stance just a moment longer than necessary. It's subtle, but unmistakable – he's *showing off*.

Drunnyak lets out a low whistle. "Now that's a welcome gift." Without hesitation, he strides forward, eager hands reaching for the biggest, meanest-looking weapon he can find – a *massive* war hammer nearly the size of Taril himself.

Before he can even lift it, a thick, plated hand slaps his wrist away.

"Nah." Taril shakes his head, standing firm beside the war hammer. "Yer too young to be playing with the grown-ups' toys."

Drunnyak blinks. "What?"

Taril smirks, effortlessly grabbing the war hammer and hoisting

9

it up as if it were nothing, strapping it to his back alongside a shield nearly as big as he is. The clank of his full plate armour echoes through the chamber as he steps past Drunnyak with a satisfied grunt.

The big man crosses his arms, scowling. "That's ageist."

"No, that's *realist*," Taril fires back, adjusting his gauntlets.

Aneeve snickers from the side. "It *is* funny watching the biggest of us get told no by a dwarf."

Drunnyak grumbles but moves on, reaching for something else. His fingers brush against the hilt of a *huge* broadsword. Even broken halfway down the blade, the weapon is still massive, still taller than Taril himself. He lifts it, rolling his shoulders, and gives it a few test swings. It may be shattered, but it *feels* right.

His eyes then drift to his clothing. No finely crafted armour or shimmering metal, no enchanted robes or protective layers – just the thick, rugged leather of a lion, draped over his massive frame. It's stitched together with little care for elegance, raw and untamed, and if anyone stood too close, they'd swear multiple lions had been skinned and sewn together on the spot. It still *smelt* like lions. *A lot* of lions.

Alentar, who had been standing closest to him, wrinkles his nose slightly and takes a step back. "You planning on hunting with that, or attracting more of them?"

Drunnyak grins. "Both."

Alentar, meanwhile, steps toward his own gear. Thick leather clothes, the colour of deep vegetation, mould around his frame. As he moves, the fabric shifts – subtle at first, but unmistakable. His outfit mimics his surroundings, blending seamlessly. He tightens his bracers, slinging a masterfully wrought bow across his back, a quiver of arrows at his hip. Two slightly curved swords slide into their places at his sides, ready and waiting.

Nashir reaches for a long staff, fingers tracing the detailed carvings – branches, vines, flowers, even the faint outlines of animals. It feels like a piece of the very earth itself, humming with quiet power. Beneath his fingers, the wood seems almost alive. He wears a deep green robe, light and flowing, but beneath it, a layer of protective leather keeps him guarded. He spins the staff once, testing its balance, before nodding to himself.

Aneeve steps forward, running her hands over a robe so exquisitely woven it seems otherworldly. Brushing her fingers along the ornate armour shaped for both elegance and war. "At least now I won't have to listen to you brutes drooling over me while I'm naked," she muses as she grabs two perfectly balanced scimitars.

Taril scoffs. "Like steel would change that."

Aneeve smirks. "Oh, I know. But at least it'll make *me* feel less like an object of worship."

Drunnyak grins, fastening a belt around his waist. "Can't blame a man for admiring perfection."

Aneeve's robe shimmers like steel woven into fabric, catching the dim light like diamonds. The way it hugs her form makes it even more impossible to ignore, and she smirks as she fastens the last piece. "Well, well," she purrs, "I'm *definitely* keeping this."

Drunnyak smirks. "Oh, we *definitely* support that decision."

Aneeve rolls her eyes. "Of course you do."

Finally, Opilkhos steps toward the last set of armour – a full silver plate, polished to perfection, glimmering with a faint golden hue. It fits him like it was forged for him alone. A long sword rests in its sheath beside a sturdy shield, both gleaming under the chamber's light. He grips the sword's hilt, feeling the weight of it, and exhales deeply.

There's something about this – about all of it – that *fits*.

Alentar, now fully equipped, leans back against the wall, arms crossed. His smirk lingers. His gaze sweeps over the group before he speaks. "Are you done staring at her arse, or do we plan on actually figuring out where the hell we are?" His voice is quiet but firm, cutting through the chamber with ease.

Silence.

Drunnyak, in mid-buckle, pauses before turning toward him with a slow, amused grin. "You been watching *us*, then?"

Alentar shrugs, adjusting a bracer as if completely unconcerned. His smirk doesn't fade.

Aneeve tilts her head, a smirk of her own forming. "What's the matter, little elf? Feeling left out?"

He lets out a short chuckle, shaking his head as he straps a dagger to his thigh. "Not at all." His voice lowers, a hint of dry amusement in it. "Just figured I'd remind you all that we woke up in an ancient ruin with no memories, and the first thing we're doing is arguing about my chest and your…" He gestures toward Aneeve's lower half, raising an eyebrow again.

Aneeve places a hand over her heart dramatically. "Darling, are you accusing *me* of distracting the group?"

Alentar meets her gaze without hesitation. "I'm accusing *them* of being distracted."

Nashir chuckles softly, fastening his own belt. "He's not wrong."

Opilkhos, now dressed in his full silver plate, shakes his head with an amused sigh. "Let's focus. If these weapons and clothes were left for us, then whoever – or whatever – put us here expected us to use them."

Taril tightens his gauntlets, nodding. "Aye. Best not to keep them waiting."

Drunnyak, now fully geared, stretches his arms before cracking his knuckles. "Fine, fine. No more staring. I'll *try* to keep my eyes on the road." He winks at Aneeve.

She smirks. "Good boy."

Alentar pushes himself off the wall, adjusting the swords at his hip before turning toward the passage. His smirk returns for just a moment, as if he's still pleased with himself.

This time, when they step forward, they do so not as confused souls stumbling in the dark, but as warriors, clothed and armed, walking toward whatever fate has in store.

As they step into the long corridor, the dim glow of the ancient torches flickers against the cold stone walls. Their footsteps echo through the passage, slow and cautious, but steady. At the far end, the cavern finally opens – beyond it, the unknown.

Just as they near the exit, something unseen *grips* them. A rush – not of wind, nor magic, but of something *deeper*.

Emotion.

Memories.

A flood of images, fragments of lives once lived, surging through their minds like a tide breaking free from a dam.

Taril's breath hitches as he sees himself – not as he is now, but before. Sitting by a fire, a massive mug of ale in hand, laughing as Drunnyak claps a hand on his back hard enough to rattle his bones. The two of them, sparring in the snow-covered plains, blades clashing, Drunnyak calling him an old man and Taril swearing he'd knock his teeth out.

Drunnyak grips his temples as memories slam into him. Battles fought side by side with Taril, war cries echoing in the wind. Drinking competitions neither of them ever *really* won. Late-night talks about what lay beyond their lands, about freedom. He remembers gripping Taril's shoulder before their last battle, calling him "brother". His lips curl into a grin – Taril was the only one who could match him in will and wit.

The twins inhale sharply – together, yet separate.

Nashir sees himself alone in a vast forest, hands in the soil, feeling the land breathe beneath his touch. A gentle world, a quiet world. A world where Alentar never belonged.

Alentar sees something different – his own child reflection in the river, bruised, battered. Sparring with Drunnyak, taking punches from Taril, his nose breaking beneath a well-placed strike. He sees Aneeve grabbing him by the collar, scolding him for his reckless nature, but still taking his side in every fight.

Aneeve – Niv, as they used to call her – gasps as the memories hit her hardest. Her memories are loud, full of laughter, of teasing, of protecting. She sees Nashir at her side, quiet, wise, never speaking more than necessary, but always watching, understanding. She sees Alentar, brash and bold, running straight into battle, forcing her to chase after him time and time again. She feels the way her heart always clenched when he got hurt. She remembers gripping a sword so tightly her knuckles went white, standing between him and a foe too strong for him to face alone.

When the wave of memories settles, they all stand frozen, chests rising and falling with heavy breaths.

Then, slowly, they meet each other's eyes.

"Taril." Drunnyak's voice is gruff, rougher than before, but it holds warmth.

Taril smirks. "Aye, lad."

"Niv," Nashir breathes, turning toward her.

She blinks, then grins wide. "*Damn* right, little brother."

Alentar's gaze flickers between them, something hesitant, something raw crossing his face. "You *all* remember?"

"Not everything," Taril grunts. "But enough to know that I'm amongst friends."

Alentar chuckles – low, quiet – and swallows hard. His eyes shift to Drunnyak. "You used to beat the hell out of me."

Drunnyak's grin is all teeth. "And you deserved it, you little cunt."

They all stop for a second, looking at each other, expecting a reaction, before bursting into a loud laugh, even Alentar, who shakes his head before saying, "But I learned from the best."

He glances at Drunnyak and Taril – not with his usual sharp intensity, but with something else. Something almost… *kind.*

Taril and Drunnyak exchange a glance, then, almost as one, they give him a firm nod. No teasing this time. No sarcasm.

Just silent recognition.

A moment of pride.

And then…

Their laughter fades into something warmer, something *earned.*

All at once, as if no time had passed, they're themselves again – friends and brothers-in-arms.

The tension fades as they start saying each other's names – laughing, clapping hands against backs, shoulders bumping, the closeness returning as if it had never left.

But then…

A silence falls.

Their eyes turn, one by one, toward the last of them.

14

Toward *him*.

Opilkhos.

And without knowing why, without hesitation…

They say another name.

"Harinnil?"

The air in the corridor shifts. The name lingers, heavy and unfamiliar, yet spoken with such certainty.

Opilkhos feels his stomach drop. His chest tightens, breath catching in his throat. "I…" His voice comes out hoarse, uncertain. "That's not my name."

They all stare, confusion flickering in their expressions.

"My name is Opilkhos."

The certainty in his tone silences them.

He grips his forehead, trying to force the memories back – but all he sees is two things.

A cabin near the ocean.

And *her*.

Lena.

A gorgeous young woman with dark, flowing hair, eyes like deep amber, and a smile that made his heart race. He remembers her laugh, her touch, the way his lips met hers as the waves crashed beyond their home.

That's all.

Nothing else.

No war, no battles, no friendships forged in blood and hardship.

Just *her*.

He looks up – sees the uncertainty in their faces. The concern.

"I don't know who Harinnil is," he admits, voice steady despite the weight in his chest. "But I know who *I* am."

"Aye," Taril finally says, though there's something unreadable in his expression. "Aye, lad. You do."

And yet, none of them says the name again.

Because now, doubt lingers.

And deep down, somewhere none of them can reach just yet…

Something doesn't *fit*.

The silence is suffocating.

Then…

A voice slithers through the air, low and guttural, crawling like a serpent into their ears. "He can never be Harinnil… because I am him."

A chill runs through the cavern – not the cold they have known since their awakening, but something far worse. A primal, unnatural dread. The torches that had guided their path tremble in the presence of the voice, their flames flickering wildly before dying, one by one.

And then the shadow comes.

Like a living thing, it stretches from the cavern's entrance, devouring what little light remains. It moves like ink spilling over the stone, creeping toward them, its very presence smothering warmth and breath alike.

A figure emerges from the darkness.

Tall, draped in tattered black robes that seem to move as if stitched from the void itself. The air *reeks* – of decay, of age, of something that *should not be*.

But what lies beneath the robes is worse.

A glimpse of armour, the same as Opilkhos is wearing – old, corroded, infested with mould, as if time itself has rejected its existence. Bony hands, half-covered in patches of rotting flesh, protrude from the sleeves. And then, the face – partially skeletal, yet cruelly preserved in places, as if death itself has been unable to finish its work.

And the eyes.

Two orbs of carmine red, swirling with a knowing, sinister gleam.

Despite his wretched form, there is no rage in them.

Only amusement.

And something resembling… *fondness*.

"Ah… my old friends."

His voice drips with eerie warmth, twisting the air itself. Mocking? Sincere? It is impossible to tell.

His gaze lingers, gliding over each of them until it lands on Alentar. And for the briefest moment, something shifts.

Something softens.

A dark, hollow smile plays at the edges of his ruined lips. *Pleased.*

But Alentar – he does not smile back.

His emerald eyes darken with something unspoken. Sadness. Guilt.

The shadowed figure tilts his head, as if reading that expression with ease. A low chuckle rattles in his throat. "Ah, Alentar… You mourn me already?"

Alentar's jaw tightens, his hands curling into fists at his sides. But he says nothing.

The figure exhales slowly – perhaps in amusement, perhaps something else.

Then his attention shifts.

He looks at Opilkhos.

And whatever warmth had been in his voice dies.

"But you…" The cavern feels colder. "You should not be here."

Opilkhos meets his gaze, his body tense, his expression unreadable – but something in his stance betrays unease.

"You walk with an abomination," the figure continues, his voice like a slow, creeping poison. "A false name. A lie made flesh. A mistake that should never have awakened."

The others shift slightly. Taril grips his hammer a little tighter, Drunnyak's fingers twitch near the hilt of his broken blade. Aneeve narrows her eyes, her weight shifting as if preparing for something.

But Opilkhos does not move.

Only his fingers curl slightly into fists.

For a moment, neither of them speaks.

Then… Opilkhos exhales. And when he does speak, his voice is steady. "I am not a mistake."

A beat.

The robed figure's lips curl.

The cavern air remains thick, heavy with something unseen – something oppressive.

Harinnil's crimson eyes linger on Opilkhos for a moment longer, his gaze unreadable, before his lips curl ever so slightly.

"As you shall prove in time."

His voice slithers through the air, carrying something ominous, something final.

Then, without another word, he turns his back to them.

His dark robes ripple as he moves, slow and deliberate, toward the cavern's exit. The flickering torches, long extinguished by his arrival, remain dark as he passes, his shadow swallowing what little light remains. He walks as if the world itself waits for him.

The others hesitate, watching his form retreat into the unknown.

And then, as if drawn by something greater than choice, they follow.

The cavern walls stretch high above them, the air thick with the weight of old magic, of forgotten things. The stone beneath their feet is smooth, untouched by time yet worn by something beyond it. The corridor feels longer now, deeper, as if each step takes them further from the past they once knew and deeper into something *new*.

Alentar moves with more purpose than the others, closing the distance between himself and Harinnil.

Closer.

His emerald eyes flick to Harinnil's profile, searching.

Waiting.

But Harinnil does not look back.

He does not acknowledge Alentar's presence, does not meet his gaze.

And yet, Alentar keeps trying.

His own expression is difficult to place – one of recognition, of longing, of sadness so deep it does not yet have a name. Even he does not understand it.

But it is there.

And for the first time since awakening, the unshakeable warrior does not seem like a warrior at all.

He seems like something else.

Something lost.

The corridor ahead narrows, the path leading ever forward until, finally, it opens.

And they step out onto the balcony.

The cavern is no longer their prison.

The outside world greets them.

And for the first time in a long time, they see it. Maud.

As they emerge into open air, the weight of the world itself crashes upon them.

The air is frigid – colder than the cavern, colder than anything they have ever known. The moment their boots touch the stone platform, a howling wind rips through them, carrying the sharp bite of ice and decay. The storm above rages, thick and unnatural – a mass of swirling dark clouds, suffocating the sky, leaving no trace of sun, no glimpse of warmth.

A relentless downpour – not just rain, but a brutal mix of snow and hail – pummels them, the heavy impact rattling against their armour, their clothing, their very skin. It does not fall gently; it *lashes* at them, striking like a warning, like the world itself rejects their presence.

Harinnil stands at the balcony's edge, unmoved. The wind tangles through his tattered robes, his skeletal hands gripping the stone railing as his burning crimson eyes scan the land before them. He does not react to the storm, to the cold, to the presence of the others.

But Opilkhos does.

He keeps his gaze fixed on Harinnil, his grip tightening around the hilt of his sword. His knuckles whiten beneath the force of it, but he does not draw – he only watches. Searching. *Waiting*.

The others, spread across the balcony, say nothing at first.

Because below them…

The world they have awakened to is *wrong*.

The balcony overlooks a vast valley, carved between mountains that stand like ancient, frozen titans, their peaks lost within the storm's grasp. The land should be thriving, yet it is nothing but a grave of ice and ruin.

Down in the valley, once-green fields now lie buried beneath endless snow, their rolling hills barely visible beneath the suffocating frost. Trees, stripped of their life, stand as blackened skeletons, their branches twisted in agony, reaching for a sky that has long since abandoned them.

And far beyond the valley, sitting atop a distant hill, a forest still lingers – barely. Its trees, though still standing, seem frozen in time, their bark coated in layers of thick ice, their roots strangled beneath an unforgiving frost. There is no colour. No warmth. Just endless, cursed cold.

Beyond the forest, where the land rises into the distant mountains, shadows move. Not the kind cast by light, but something else. Something that *should not be there.*

The wind howls louder.

The storm screams.

And the silence among them breaks.

"What *happened* here?" Aneeve's voice is quieter than usual, lacking its usual playfulness, replaced by something raw. Unease.

No one answers.

Drunnyak exhales sharply, his breath escaping in thick clouds of mist. He runs a hand over his face, wiping away the ice collecting in his beard. "This… isn't what we left behind."

Taril grips the hilt of his war hammer, staring out at the desolation before them. "It's *wrong.*"

Alentar remains still, his sharp eyes focused – not on the land, not on the storm, but on Harinnil. He shifts slightly, moving closer, still searching for something in the man's expression. Still waiting for him to look back.

But Harinnil does not move.

Does not turn.

Finally, it is Nashir who speaks, his voice quiet but firm. "How long have we been gone?"

The question hangs, lingering in the air like a spectre.

And then…

Harinnil laughs.

Low. Slow. *Amused.*

And filled with something *terrible.*

Harinnil exhales, his voice a whisper against the storm. "Too long."

His carmine eyes flicker – not just with power, but with something deeper. Something distant.

The wind howls around him, the storm lashing against his decayed form, but he does not react. His mind drifts, wandering through the shattered remnants of time, reaching for something that has long since slipped from his grasp.

Memories – faint, fractured, elusive.

A world that was not frozen. A sky that was not empty. Laughter that did not echo in his mind like a cruel illusion. The warmth of camaraderie, of purpose, of *life*.

But that world is gone.

Two thousand years.

Two thousand *years* of pain. Of emptiness. Of silence so suffocating it had drowned out the sound of his own name.

A lifetime of watching the world die, of standing among the cursed ruins of what once was, of fighting battles he could never win.

Of being alone.

Always *alone*.

But now...

Finally...

He turns.

Slowly, deliberately, his gaze shifts to the one who has been watching him the entire time.

Alentar.

Their eyes meet – emerald and carmine.

For a long moment, Harinnil simply studies him. As if making sure he is real. As if waiting for this fragile illusion to shatter like all the others before it.

Then...

His lips curve into a small, tired smile.

And, as impossible as it seems, from the corner of his ruined eye...

A single tear falls.

"But it's damn good seeing you all again."

His voice, though weathered, is genuine. Warm. The first trace of life he has shown since his arrival.

His fingers twitch as if to reach out – but they do not.

His smile lingers, even under the weight of the storm.

"Even under the circumstances."

Harinnil's moment of warmth is brief – a fleeting ember swallowed by the abyss.

The single tear dries as quickly as it fell, leaving no trace it was ever there.

Then… he shifts.

His posture straightens, shoulders squaring with a quiet, commanding weight. The air thickens, and the darkness at his feet spreads, curling around the stone like grasping tendrils. The warmth in his expression drains, replaced by something colder.

Something *final*.

His crimson eyes flick back toward Opilkhos, lingering on him with something that is neither curiosity nor hatred – just sheer, unwavering disdain.

"It is good seeing you all again…" His voice is deeper now, the weight of his words pressing into the air like a looming storm. Then, his lips curl – not in warmth, but in disgust. "Apart from this sickening parody that walks among you."

The wind howls louder, and Opilkhos tightens his grip around his sword, his knuckles turning white. But he does not speak.

Harinnil doesn't linger on him. Instead, his gaze sweeps over the others, his tone shifting – darker, heavier. "Make no mistake."

The world seems to hold its breath.

"Next time we meet, it will be as enemies." His carmine eyes land on Alentar once more, and for the briefest moment – just for him – the expression softens. A fraction. But only for an instant. "And I shall not grant you mercy… not even to you, my dear friend."

The words land heavy, laced with something that feels both inevitable and tragic.

The storm rages on, ice pelting against them, as Harinnil steps back toward the edge of the balcony.

"Do what you must. Recover what you have lost." His voice now carries the finality of a closing door, of fate sealing itself into place.

"When the time is right…" He turns, his tattered robes billowing as the shadows at his feet swirl. "We shall see each other again."

And then…

The darkness consumes him.

His form dissolves, unravelling into the storm like a whisper lost to the wind.

And just like that…

He is gone.

The moment Harinnil vanishes into the storm, a heavy silence settles over the group.

Only the howling wind remains, screaming through the mountains, carrying with it the weight of an eternity lost. Snow and ice continue to batter their armour, pelting against steel and leather with an unrelenting rhythm.

No one speaks at first.

Not because there is nothing to say, but because none of them knows where to begin.

Drunnyak exhales sharply, lifting a hand to his face, dragging his fingers across his rough skin, brushing away the frost that has settled thick into his beard. Small shards of ice crackle as they break apart, falling away like brittle glass. His nostrils flare as he releases a long breath, steam billowing into the frozen air. "Well. That was a lovely fucking reunion."

Taril lets out a low grunt, crossing his arms. "Aye. Could've done without the part where he promised to kill us next time we meet." His golden eyes flick toward Opilkhos. "Or the part where he looked at you like he'd rather burn the world down than share the same air."

Opilkhos stiffens, but he says nothing. His sapphire-diamond eyes remain fixed on the place where Harinnil once stood, his grip still tight around his sword. His mind churns, searching for answers that refuse to come.

"I don't get it," Niv mutters, pulling her shimmering robes tighter around herself as if they could shield her from more than just the cold. "Why does he *hate* you so much? I mean, sure, you've got a face that pisses people off—"

Drunnyak snorts.

"—but that was *personal*."

Opilkhos swallows, his throat dry despite the cold. "I don't know." His voice is quiet but firm. "I don't know him. And yet... I feel like I should."

"Not just him," Nashir says, finally breaking his own silence. He turns, scanning the snow-covered landscape with an unreadable expression. "This world. This... *everything*." He clenches his jaw, frustration flickering across his normally calm features. "Why is it that we only get *fragments*? Why do we know who we are, but not what happened?"

Drunnyak tightens his grip around the hilt of his broken broadsword. "Tch. It's like someone gutted our memories and left us with the scraps."

Niv folds her arms, frowning. "Yeah, well, it's *bullshit*. Someone or *something* didn't want us to wake up *knowing*." Her golden eyes narrow as she looks out at the storm. "But why?"

No one has an answer.

The wind screams, as if mocking them.

Alentar stands apart from them all, silent as always.

His form is a dark silhouette against the storm, standing at the very edge of the stone balcony, his weight shifting dangerously as he leans forward.

Watching.

Searching.

He is still, too still, his sharp emerald eyes scanning the world like a predator seeking prey. His breath is slow, steady, despite the storm whipping around him, his thick leather shifting colours subtly as it mimics the stone beneath him.

It is only when Nashir notices how close he is to the edge that he speaks.

"Alentar," he calls out over the wind, "if you plan on throwing yourself off, at least do it somewhere we can reach your corpse."

Niv raises an eyebrow, crossing her arms as she watches Alentar teeter on the edge. Her voice drips with sarcasm, but there's a sharp undercurrent of concern beneath it. "Oh, he wouldn't die from the fall – just break every bone in his body and force us to carry his arrogant arse the rest of the way." She exhales, shaking her head. "And knowing him, he'd still smirk about it."

Drunnyak snorts, rolling his shoulders as he eyes Alentar's reckless stance. "Oh, no doubt. Probably shatter both legs and still expect us to be impressed." He smirks, shaking his head. "Hell, he'd probably call it a 'calculated risk.'"

Alentar doesn't react.

At first.

Then, without moving his eyes from the horizon, he speaks. "Something's out there."

That shuts them up.

Alentar shifts his footing slightly, keeping his balance as he leans forward even more, squinting through the endless storm. His face is unreadable – calm, focused – but beneath that stillness, there is something *tense*, something *wrong*.

Taril steps closer, placing a firm foot on the stone beside him. "What do you see?"

Alentar doesn't answer immediately. He stares, his breath slow, controlled, his entire body honed like a blade – until finally, he exhales. "Figures. Moving together."

That alone is enough to send a ripple through the group.

"Where?" Nashir asks.

"Far." Alentar tilts his head slightly. "Too far."

Niv moves to his side, shielding her eyes from the storm as she squints into the distance. "How many?"

Alentar doesn't blink. "Dozens, maybe. The fog is too thick for me to see through, and I can't hear their heartbeats from here."

Drunnyak frowns. "People?"

"I don't know. Humanoid shapes, for sure."

Nashir steps forward. "Can you make out anything else?"

Alentar's lips press into a thin line. He watches – *waits* – but the blizzard, the snow, the unnatural weight of the storm itself make it impossible. The figures are moving, trudging through the ice in a slow, unified path, but *what* they are, *who* they are… "I can't see them clearly," he admits, frustration barely touching his tone. "But they're heading somewhere."

Taril's grip tightens on his war hammer. "Then we need to know where."

A heavy pause follows.

The storm continues to rage.

Opilkhos finally speaks, his voice low. "Do we follow them?"

Another silence.

The question lingers, but deep down, they already know the answer.

There is nothing behind them – nothing left in the cavern, no past to reclaim.

Only the path ahead.

Only Maud's frozen fate.

Alentar finally steps back from the ledge, his emerald eyes still locked on the distant movement. He exhales once. "We follow."

BEYOND THE EDGE,
INTO THE UNKNOWN

Alentar's emerald eyes linger on the distant figures for just a moment longer.

Then, he turns back to the group – his sharp gaze flicking over their uncertain faces, the storm whipping around them. The weight of the unknown presses on them all.

And yet… he grins.

A cheeky, almost reckless smile, so out of place on his usually stoical face, flickers to life.

Then, without hesitation, he jumps.

No warning. No fear. No flinch.

One moment he is standing at the edge – the next, he is gone.

"*Alentar!*" Drunnyak roars, surging forward.

Taril curses under his breath; something in dwarfish. Nashir's eyes widen in shock. Opilkhos takes an involuntary step forward.

But Niv…

She *laughs*.

A thrilled, delighted laugh, clapping her hands together like a spectator at a performance. "Oh, yes! That's my brother!"

The others whip their heads toward her in disbelief, but Niv just leans against the railing, fully enjoying the spectacle.

And what a spectacle it is.

Alentar plummets through the sky, vanishing into the thick, churning clouds below. But instead of disappearing into the abyss, the moment his body pierces the storm, he moves.

Fast.

The howling winds rip around him, but he plays with them, shifting his body like a bird riding the currents. The storm wants to drag him into chaos – wants to tear him apart – but he moves with it, not against it.

The swirling clouds envelop him, an ocean of white and grey, yet he is untouched. His leather armour shifts, mimicking the tones around him, making him a living shadow amidst the storm.

Then…

He flips.

Once. Twice. The momentum of the wind becomes his weapon, his ally. He dives head first into a thicker part of the storm, letting the gusts spin him violently – then, at the last second, he twists in mid-air, correcting himself with the ease of someone who has done this a thousand times before.

His gloved fingers brush against the thick mist of the clouds, as if feeling the storm itself, before he kicks off nothing but air, propelling himself forward into an even deeper descent.

The world rushes past him.

Jagged cliffs of ice and towering stone formations pierce the sky far below, ready to tear apart anything that falls without caution.

But Alentar…

He does not fear.

He does not hesitate.

He laughs.

The sound is lost in the roar of the storm, but in his heart, he knows – this is freedom. This is his element. This is what he was made for.

Then, far below, an outstretched peak juts out from the mountain range, slick with frost and ice.

Perfect.

He angles his body, shifting slightly as he hovers. His boots barely graze an incoming ledge before he kicks off it, using it to propel himself again, turning his deadly fall into an elegant, controlled descent.

The wind rushes past him as he lands, feet first, on a narrow ledge, barely wide enough to stand on.

He crouches low, absorbing the impact, the ice cracking beneath him – then, without a moment's pause, he pushes off into a perfect forward roll, landing gracefully on another outcropping below.

His feet hit the stone with absolute precision.

He rises.

Tall. Unshaken. Completely unfazed.

A gust of wind sends his cloak whipping around him as he finally looks back up – toward the balcony, toward them.

Above, Drunnyak is gaping like a stunned ox. Taril grips the railing with both hands, looking half a second away from diving after Alentar just to drag him back up. Nashir still hasn't blinked. Opilkhos looks between them, as if unsure if what just happened was real.

And Niv...

Niv is laughing.

Clapping. Proud.

She leans over the railing, shouting, "Show-off!"

Alentar grins.

Then, without another word, he turns his gaze back toward the world below – toward the figures in the distance.

And without hesitation, he moves forward.

As the group above watches in stunned silence, Alentar doesn't stop.

He moves with purpose, each step deliberate, as if the sheer act of walking is an art form only he understands. The storm still rages around him, the wind shrieking, but he weaves through it with ease, his leather shifting in colour as he moves, blending subtly with the icy stone beneath his feet.

Then, without even looking up, he lifts an arm and points.

Farther down, a small plateau juts out from the mountainside, shielded slightly from the worst of the wind – a rare spot of stability in this cursed world. His finger lingers on it for a moment, a silent *there*, before he starts walking toward it.

From the balcony, they watch as he approaches the area, his movements fluid, unhindered by the biting frost beneath his boots.

Then, he stops.

He kneels, brushing away the thick layer of snow covering the stone. The ice resists at first, but with a firm swipe of his gloved hand, the rock underneath is exposed. He studies it for a brief moment, then, with an exhale, he sits.

Back straight, legs casually spread, his arms resting on his knees.

Like he's been waiting for them all along.

Like he *knew* they would follow.

Like none of this – *none of it* – was ever in doubt.

Above, Niv smirks, still leaning over the railing. "Look at him," she muses, voice filled with amusement. "You just owned this mountain."

Drunnyak finally snaps out of his stunned state. "That son of a bitch." His voice is somewhere between admiration and absolute exasperation.

Without missing a beat, Niv smirks, tilting her head as she shoots back, "Well, that would make you long-lost brothers then, wouldn't it?"

Drunnyak whips his head toward her, scowling. "The hell does that mean?"

Niv shrugs, her golden eyes glinting mischievously. "I mean, considering how often you two try to out-stupid each other, you must share the same bloodline of reckless lunatics."

Drunnyak opens his mouth – then pauses, realising she's not exactly wrong.

Taril snorts, Nashir smirks, and even Opilkhos presses his lips together to hide the hint of amusement in his expression.

Below, Alentar, still sitting on the stone, doesn't react. But they *know* – he *heard* it.

And somehow, that makes it even worse.

Taril shakes his head, muttering something about reckless idiots, before stepping back from the railing.

30

Nashir lets out a quiet breath and glances toward Opilkhos. "Guess we're going down."

Opilkhos, still gripping his sword, nods once.

Drunnyak cracks his neck, rolling his shoulders. "Fine." He exhales sharply, watching as Alentar leans back on his hands, completely unbothered by the raging storm around him. "But I'm not jumping."

He looks at Taril, and they laugh out loud after the comment.

And with that, they move.

One by one, they follow.

The descent is long, winding and treacherous.

Yet the storm does not touch them.

The biting cold that should have seeped into their bones, the ice that should have numbed their fingers – none of it affects them. Their bodies move through the elements untouched, as if the frozen world does not dare claim them.

The deeper they go, the darker the night becomes. The heavy clouds above swirl, thick and oppressive, blotting out whatever pale light lingers in the sky. Shadows stretch over the jagged cliffs and steep pathways, the frozen peaks towering over them like ancient sentinels, watching their every move.

Snow drifts lazily now, falling in thick, silent waves, blanketing the rocky terrain in white. It piles high along the slopes, untouched by time, an endless grave of forgotten winters. And yet, beneath the ice, beneath the layers of frost, something feels *alive*.

The wind shifts unnaturally, howling between the cracks in the mountains, whispering through the frozen crevices like voices long since buried. It does not speak in words, but in presence – watching, waiting.

Frozen rivers cut deep through the valleys below, their surfaces thick with jagged ice, barely revealing the sluggish, dark water beneath. The cliffs loom, their edges jagged and sharp, marking the scars of an age long past.

And yet, despite the bleakness, they move together.

Step by step, guided by instinct more than memory. Their footing is sure, their breath steady, their movements practised – as if they have done this before. As if their bodies remember the terrain even when their minds do not.

And finally, after what feels like hours…

They reach him.

Alentar is exactly where they left him – perched lazily atop the stone, arms crossed behind his head, legs casually stretched out.

And…

He's snoring.

Loudly.

Dramatically.

The second they set foot on the plateau, his exaggerated, obnoxious snoring fills the air, deep and comically fake.

They all stare at him for a beat.

Then, without a word, they walk right past him.

Not one of them reacts.

Not one of them gives him the satisfaction.

Niv smirks, but she keeps moving. Nashir doesn't even blink. Taril mutters something under his breath, shaking his head. Opilkhos simply walks forward.

Still Alentar doesn't break character.

The snoring continues, even louder now, as if he's personally offended by their lack of response.

Finally, Drunnyak stops just long enough to glance back at him, a slow grin creeping onto his face. "Show-off. I hope next time you crash that ugly face."

And with that, he turns and keeps walking.

Alentar doesn't move. Doesn't open his eyes. Doesn't acknowledge it.

But they all know.

And then…

Laughter.

Loud, unrestrained, *familiar.*

It echoes through the frozen cliffs, rising above the wind, ringing through the darkened mountains like something untouched by time.

For the first time since their awakening…

They *feel* it.

The rhythm. The energy.

The camaraderie.

The way they move, the way they jest, the way they laugh…

It's as if they never went to slumber at all.

The night deepens as they move, their laughter fading into the silence of the frozen world.

Then… the fog rises.

Thick. Heavy.

It rolls in like an encroaching tide, swallowing the land in pale, shifting veils. Visibility vanishes. The world beyond their immediate steps is gone, replaced by a dense, swirling whiteness. And yet, they do not falter. They do not hesitate.

Their pace remains steady, their movements instinctive, unchanged, unbothered. Even as the fog wraps around them like a living thing, as if whispering secrets long forgotten, they move forward.

Slowly, the jagged cliffs and sharp slopes of the mountains begin to fade behind them. The descent evens out, the terrain shifting beneath their feet, no longer treacherous but untamed.

It feels pure in its solitude, untouched by the footprints of men, elves or dwarves. A land where only nature has ruled, undisturbed, thriving in its own way beneath the endless cold. No roads, no ruins, no lingering signs of civilisations past – just the raw, ancient pulse of the wild.

And then…

They reach a hill.

It rises gently before them, stretching into the unknown, shrouded by fog and shadow. But something is different now.

The snow, which has been relentless since the moment they awoke, begins to lessen.

The flurries that should be piling at their feet do not. Instead, the ground itself absorbs the snowfall, as if drinking in the frozen curse, pulling it deep into the earth.

And beneath the frost, life returns.

Small patches of vegetation peek through the receding snow. Not lush, not thriving, but *present*. Blades of frozen grass, brittle shrubs, even the faint, skeletal remains of once-great trees. It is not much.

But it is something.

And then, just beyond the hill…

The forest.

Dark, vast, impossibly old. The trees loom ahead, stretching high, their blackened branches reaching for the sky like twisted fingers. Their bark is thick with ice, but beneath it, the faintest glow of deep, pulsing green lingers.

At its entrance, a river runs – a contrast of frozen and flowing, one side encased in solid ice, the other barely moving, sluggish but *alive*. The sound of water, even in its slow crawl, is the first true sound of nature they have heard since awakening.

And they are not alone.

Eyes watch them from the distance.

A pack of white wolves.

Their thick coats blend seamlessly with the snow, but their piercing eyes gleam through the fog. They stand atop a ridge overlooking the group, their posture neither aggressive nor fearful – just reluctant.

Cautious.

Curious.

The group slows, tension flickering between them.

But Nashir…

Nashir does not stop.

He sees them. And they see him.

Something in his expression shifts, his emerald eyes softening, his breath coming slower, deeper. He does not see threats. He does not see predators.

He sees beings of this world.

Guardians of the frost.

The moment stretches, long and unbroken, as if time itself has slowed to witness this meeting.

Then, without a word, Nashir kneels.

34

He unlaces his boots, pulling them free, stepping onto the ice-kissed ground barefoot.

The others watch, mesmerised, their voices caught in their throats.

Nashir's staff is placed gently onto the earth. He stands with nothing – no weapon, no shield, no barrier.

Then, with slow, open hands, he *invites* them.

His gaze does not waver. His heartbeat does not quicken.

And the wolves…

They watch him back.

The group watches in silence.

Nashir stands barefoot on the frozen earth, his presence at once calm and commanding. The world itself seems to respond to him – to *recognise* him.

An unseen force stirs, subtle at first. A faint aura radiates from him, barely visible in the mist, like a warm breath against the bitter cold. But it is not warmth in the way fire gives heat – it is *life*.

It coils around him, invisible yet *felt*. It seeps into the ground beneath his feet, melds with the frost-covered earth, touches the trees with reverence.

And the world responds.

The once-brittle blades of grass, suffocated under the weight of endless winter, tremble. The frost coating the thin shrubs cracks, melts. The skeletal trees, once appearing lifeless, seem to shift, breathe, their bark pulsing with the faintest flicker of colour.

The wolves watch, wary but curious, their thick white fur dusted with snow. The lead wolf – an enormous creature, eyes gleaming like pale moons – steps forward first. Its movements are slow, deliberate, but not out of fear.

The air shimmers, hums, as the aura surrounding Nashir grows. It does not burn – it *invites*.

The pack hesitates no longer.

One by one, the wolves step forward, paws pressing into ground that feels softer than before. They close the distance, drawn to him, the snow beneath them receding ever so slightly with every step.

The others watch, mesmerised.

Niv, standing closest to Drunnyak, feels something stir inside her. A recognition. A reminder of what they had once known, once witnessed.

Without a word, she moves closer – softly, without her usual playfulness. She gently wraps her arms around Drunnyak's thick, muscled arm, resting her cheek against it for just a second. A silent acknowledgement of the moment.

Drunnyak glances down at her, and in that brief exchange, there is no teasing.

No sarcasm.

Just an understanding.

A kind glance. A flicker of something familiar.

Because this – *this* – is who Nashir was.

Who he *is*.

Not just one of them. Not just a warrior.

But a part of this world. A bridge between what was and what remains.

And as the first wolf reaches him, standing mere inches away, their eyes lock – emerald to ice.

And time seems to stop.

The giant dire wolf – a creature of ancient blood, its fur thick as winter's breath – steps forward with measured grace.

Its paws press into the softened ground, no longer brittle with frost, but yielding just enough beneath its weight. Its presence is commanding, yet not oppressive. The moonlight catches the sheen of its thick, silvery-white coat, the faintest wisps of steam rising from its breath in the cold night air.

And then, gently, it lowers its head.

Nashir does not move – he simply *exists* in the moment, his emerald eyes unwavering, his hands still extended in offering.

The dire wolf – the alpha – leans in, its cold nose brushing against his fingers, inhaling his scent. Then, with the same tenderness a father would show a wounded pup, it licks Nashir's open hands.

Slow. Deliberate. Warm.

A silent acceptance.

A bond.

The others watch, barely breathing.

The sheer size of the creature should make this moment terrifying. It could tear through flesh with a single bite, crush bones with its massive paws. And yet here, in the glow of Nashir's aura, it is nothing but gentle.

There is *trust*.

A moment passes where nothing else exists – just them.

Then…

The rest of the pack moves.

They step closer, eyes no longer wary, no longer hesitant.

The younger wolves bound forward first, sniffing curiously, brushing against Nashir's arms. Their tails swish, their movements no longer guarded, but playful.

And Nashir…

He *laughs*.

Not a restrained chuckle, not a quiet amusement, but a full, unrestrained sound. A sound that belongs to life.

He falls backward into the softened snow, and the wolves are on him.

Nipping, nudging, rolling against him – playing. The great alpha remains standing, watching, but the younger ones tumble into Nashir as if he is one of their own. He responds in kind, ruffling their thick fur, pushing back playfully, rolling with them in the snow.

A wild dance of kinship.

From the trees above, movement stirs.

A fluttering of wings.

Crows, black as the void, descend, perching on the nearest branches, their heads tilting, observing with sharp, knowing eyes. Owls, silent as spirits, glide in to rest upon the limbs of frozen trees, their gaze heavy with ancient wisdom.

They watch.

All of them.

Not with fear. Not with malice.

But recognition.

As if they know this is how it should be.

The world breathes, just for a moment.

And from the side, the group watches, unspoken warmth filling the space between them.

Niv still holds on to Drunnyak's arm, her golden eyes shimmering as she watches her brother become himself again. Drunnyak, usually loud and brash, only smiles – a slow, knowing grin, as if remembering an old joke from a lifetime ago. Taril, his arms crossed, nods ever so slightly, the weight of something unspoken sitting in his stance. Opilkhos watches, silent, but with something distant in his expression.

And Alentar...

He stands a little further back, eyes half-lidded, his breath calm, his presence at ease.

For the first time since awakening, none of them speak.

Because there is nothing *to* say.

There is only this moment.

A moment of *understanding*.

A moment of *life*.

Nashir's laughter lingers in the cold air, his smile unyielding, untouched by the weight of lost memories or the desolation that surrounds them.

He pushes himself up from the softened ground, his breath steady, his hands brushing gently over the thick fur of the wolves still circling him. Their warmth, their presence – it is not something new.

It is something *remembered*.

He looks toward his companions, his emerald eyes shimmering in the dim light, filled with something deep, something *whole*. He *sees* them.

Then he looks back at the wolves, at the crows and owls perched above, at the whispering trees that now stand a little taller, a little brighter.

And in a voice soft yet resonant, he speaks. "*Amin naa sinome, ionnathamin.*" I am here, my sons.

His words carry in the wind, not loud, not forced – just *known*.

The pack watches him, silent but aware, their keen eyes flickering with something understood.

Then…

With a teasing grin, Nashir reaches down and gives the nearest wolf's flank a firm tap, right at its thick-furred rump.

The beast huffs, shaking out its fur, and nudges him back with an amused growl, almost as if scolding him for his mischief.

The others snicker as Nashir steps away, his grin never fading.

He moves toward the group, reaching down to retrieve his staff, the intricate carvings glinting softly with a new-found vibrance, as if the world itself has given something back to him.

He walks with the ease of someone who belongs – someone claimed not by war, not by memories, but by the very heartbeat of the land itself.

As he approaches, Niv smirks, her golden eyes gleaming. "You've always had a thing for strays, brother."

Nashir chuckles, spinning his staff once before resting it against his shoulder. "We all have our strengths."

Drunnyak snorts. "Tch. I'll take a sword over a pack of oversized mutts."

Taril smirks, adjusting his war hammer. "We'll see how you feel when they save your arse."

The group laughs, the cold around them feeling a little less harsh, the weight on their shoulders a little less heavy.

And with that, they turn back toward the waiting forest, stepping forward together.

Hours pass as they move deeper into the forest, the towering trees stretching endlessly above them like ancient, watching giants.

The deeper they go, the more the cold softens.

Not in temperature – no, the bite of Maud's eternal frost is ever-present – but in *presence*. The oppressive weight that clung to them in the mountains seems to lift, slowly, subtly, as if the forest itself refuses to be claimed by the frozen curse that grips the world beyond.

And at the centre of it all – Nashir.

His every step pulses with quiet resonance, his staff humming with a warmth not felt in centuries. The glow is faint, unseen by the untrained eye, but the forest feels it. The very ground beneath him shifts, absorbing the silent gift he offers.

The trees lean ever so slightly toward him. The frost clinging to their bark cracks, receding just enough to reveal veins of deep green beneath.

The animals – they know him.

Eyes peer from the foliage, silent and cautious. Stags with antlers thick as branches watch from a distance, their breath steaming in the cold. Owls – great, ancient things – follow from the treetops, shifting from branch to branch with spectral grace. Packs of smaller creatures – foxes, wildcats, even a few wary boars – move within the underbrush, not daring to approach, but not fleeing either.

They do not fear Nashir.

They *recognise* him.

The group notices, exchanging quiet glances among themselves as more and more of the woodland creatures begin to follow.

Drunnyak grunts. "You ever feel like you're walking with someone famous?"

Taril huffs, shaking his head. "Can't tell if we're his bodyguards or part of the procession."

Niv smirks, nudging Nashir's side playfully. "I always knew you were special, brother. I just didn't know you had fans."

Nashir chuckles, eyes twinkling, but he says nothing.

The fog, once thick and oppressive, begins to fade. The deeper they move, the clearer their surroundings become, as if the forest itself is allowing them to see.

It is then that they realise…

Alentar is gone.

They stop.

Their eyes dart around, their senses sharpening.

"When was the last time we saw him?" Nashir asks, his voice calm, but carrying an underlying tension.

Drunnyak exhales sharply. "Tch. That sneaky bastard. He was just here."

Niv turns, scanning the trees with narrowed golden eyes. "He does this. We *know* he does this."

Taril grips his war hammer, his expression grim. "Yeah, well, he *usually* comes back before we notice he's gone."

For a moment, only silence.

Then…

A shadow moves.

Above them.

Before anyone can react, something drops from the treetops – fast, fluid, silent as the wind.

In one effortless motion, Alentar lands in a crouch, sliding backward against the bark of a massive tree, his hands bracing against the wood to slow his descent.

They barely register his presence before he straightens, stepping into the dim light.

His face is unreadable, but his emerald eyes burn with urgency.

"Hundreds." His voice is low, sharp as a blade.

The group tenses.

"Hundreds of what?" Drunnyak growls, already tightening his grip on his broken sword.

Alentar turns his gaze forward, past them, into the trees ahead. "Undead."

The word lands heavy.

THE FIRST BATTLE

"They're moving," Alentar continues, eyes flicking between them, watching as the weight of his words sinks in. "Scattered, but together. Not mindless. Searching."

A beat of silence.

"For what?" Opilkhos asks.

Alentar meets his gaze. "Their next meal."

And then…

From the distance, carried on the thinning fog, comes the first sound of them.

A low, rattling groan.

And another.

And another.

Growing.

Spreading.

Moving closer.

Nashir takes a slow, steady breath, his emerald eyes shifting toward the woodland creatures still lingering nearby. In a voice softer than the wind, he whispers in elvish, *"Hide, protect yourselves. We'll deal with them."*

The animals do not hesitate.

The great stag turns first, vanishing into the thickets. The owls and crows take to the skies, their wings slicing through the night in eerie silence. Even the wolves, though reluctant, lower their heads in understanding before slipping into the shadows of the trees, their forms melting into the wild.

The forest belongs to them.

The battle does not.

The group does not speak.

They do not need to.

Instinct takes over.

Each step, each motion is *known* – as if they have done this a thousand times before, even without the memory to recall it. Their bodies, their senses, their very *essence* remembers what their minds do not.

A shift in weight. A steadying of breath. A silent understanding between warriors.

They move forward, deeper into the forest, toward the growing stench of death.

The first signs of the undead appear – shuffling silhouettes, hunched figures dragging themselves from the mist, gathering.

They do not see.

They do not think.

But they *feel*.

Smell.

Their heads snap toward the living.

A deep, guttural hunger drives them forward, twisted limbs stretching toward warmth, toward life, toward flesh.

A shuddering moan breaks the air, followed by another, then another.

More of them appear, their hollow eyes gleaming with need.

And yet...

A light cuts through the darkness.

A golden shimmer, radiant as the first break of dawn.

Opilkhos.

His sword gleams in his grasp, but it is not the blade that shines – it is *him*.

The moment his presence flares, his silver armour catching the glow and magnifying it, the undead stagger.

They shrink back from the light, their bodies burning as they try to approach, their twisted, rotting limbs curling inward as if the radiance itself is scorching them.

But their hunger…

Their hunger pushes them forward.

They burn, yet they move.

They suffer, yet they crawl.

The need to devour is stronger than the pain.

With slow, jerking steps, they lurch toward the group, toward the light, their fingers clawing at the air, their bodies trembling with the agony of each step.

And yet, they do not stop.

They *cannot*.

The battle unfolds. The first wave lunges.

A mass of twisted corpses, some barely more than skeletons, others still clinging to rotted flesh, charge through the mist, driven by hunger alone. Their bodies are weak, brittle – yet they are relentless.

The group does not flinch.

They move.

Opilkhos steps forward, his golden aura blazing against the tide of darkness.

His sword is not just a weapon – it is a beacon.

As the undead rush him, he swings in a controlled, divine arc, the blade cutting through both flesh and shadow. The first creature to reach him is cleaved in two, its form burning into ash before it even hits the ground.

Another lunges, grasping for him with bony fingers. He raises his shield.

The moment the creature touches his armour, the light consumes it, reducing it to smouldering embers.

But still, more come.

They burn, yet they crawl forward.

Opilkhos's stance remains firm, his shield steady, his presence alone forcing the horde back.

To his left, a roar shakes the night.

Drunnyak doesn't wait.

He meets them.

His massive frame moves like a beast in its element, his broken broadsword swinging through bodies with brutal precision. Though the blade is shattered, it does not matter – it still destroys.

A jagged slash tears through a cluster of undead, severing limbs, shattering bones. One leaps onto his back, clawing at him – he grabs it with one hand and hurls it against a tree with such force that its body explodes into pieces.

Another rushes him, shrieking.

Drunnyak grins, a wild, reckless glint in his eyes as the undead lunges toward him, its gaping maw snapping at his arm.

But he doesn't move.

Doesn't dodge.

Doesn't even flinch.

The creature's rotting teeth clamp down on his thick, scarred forearm – only for a sickening crack to echo through the battlefield.

The teeth shatter.

Fragments of blackened enamel and bone rain from its mouth, clinking uselessly against Drunnyak's lion-hide clothes.

For a moment, both of them just stand there – the brute of a man and the mindless corpse – staring at each other in an awkward pause, as if neither had quite expected this outcome.

The undead, despite being an empty husk, tilts its head, its jaw now a toothless, gaping mess.

Drunnyak raises an eyebrow.

The creature's lipless mouth curls slightly – not in a snarl, but in something else entirely.

A smile.

Toothless.

Ridiculous.

And then...

They both laugh.

Drunnyak's booming belly laugh shakes the air, a deep, shameless roar of amusement, while the undead lets out a grotesque, wheezing croak that could almost be mistaken for chuckling – if one ignored the fact that it no longer has any teeth.

Drunnyak pats the creature affectionately on the shoulder, still shaking with laughter. "Tough luck, bonebag. Should've chewed on something softer, like Niv's voluptuous and gorgeous bosoms."

And with one massive punch, he sends the undead flying back into the horde, its grinning, toothless skull still bobbing as it disappears into the chaos.

Blood and rot stain his lion-hide clothes, the stench unbearable to anyone else. But Drunnyak? He laughs, pushing forward as if the battlefield is his playground.

Niv barely pauses, driving her blade through the neck of an approaching corpse before snorting at Drunnyak's remark. "Oh, please," she scoffs, twisting her sword free as blackened blood sprays across the snow. "Even if they did, at least they wouldn't break their damn teeth on solid rock like your thick skull." She sidesteps an incoming swipe, effortlessly slashing across the undead's chest, then tosses a mocking smirk over her shoulder. "Besides," she adds, voice dripping with sarcasm, "you'd kill to get that close, and we all know it." Then, without missing a beat, she kicks a corpse straight into Drunnyak, sending it crashing into him. "Here – since you like 'em soft."

Niv moves like a storm.

Her scintillating robe gleams under Opilkhos's light as she weaves through the battlefield.

Where Drunnyak and Taril break the undead with brute strength, Niv cuts them apart with precision.

A step. A twist. A spin – steel flashes, and three heads fall to the ground before their bodies even collapse.

One screeches as it leaps toward her – she ducks, her blade sweeping upward in one fluid motion, splitting it from stomach to throat.

Another lunges for her back – she doesn't even look, merely stepping aside and letting its momentum carry it straight into Drunnyak's waiting fist.

She laughs as she fights, the thrill of battle awakening something deep in her blood.

This is where she belongs.

Taril fights as he has always fought – like an unbreakable wall.

He stands his ground, his giant war hammer crashing downward, reducing the undead to piles of splintered bone with every devastating blow.

One by one, they charge – he meets them with raw force, sending entire bodies flying back with the sheer power of his swings.

One manages to grab his arm, trying to pull itself up his armour – he spins, using the weight of his shield to crush its skull into the ground.

More come – he meets each and every one.

He does not fall.

Nashir does not strike first – he *commands*.

His staff glows, the aura pulsing in waves, responding to the forest itself. The ground beneath them trembles, roots shifting, vines emerging from the soil.

When the undead get too close, the very trees attack them.

Vines lash out, wrapping around skeletal limbs, ripping them apart before they can reach their prey. The earth opens beneath a cluster of them, swallowing them whole into a pit of twisting roots.

A dying tree, old and withered, suddenly bursts to life beside Nashir. Its once-frozen branches bend downward, impaling a cluster of undead like a spear before lifting them off the ground and hurling them into the distance.

Nashir smiles, his bare feet pressing against the earth, feeling its heartbeat.

The land fights with him.

And then… there is Alentar.

No one sees him move.

He disappears into the shadows, his body melting into the dark as if he is a part of it.

Then…

An undead shrieks – but not because it is attacking.

Because it is dying.

A dagger erupts from the base of its skull, piercing through the rotting flesh – then it's gone before it ever hits the ground.

Alentar reappears behind another, his curved blade slicing through its spine before it even notices his presence.

He moves faster than sight, every attack silent, unseen, untraceable.

And his arrows – they do not go to waste.

He fires into the horde – each shot precise, piercing through skulls, felling them before they even reach the others.

And when his quiver runs low?

He retrieves them.

With effortless acrobatics, he vaults over a fallen corpse, plucking his embedded arrow from its skull in mid-flip before landing perfectly on a thick tree branch. Another corpse twitches near him – he stomps down on its head before yanking his arrow free.

Every movement is efficient, deadly.

A shot. A kill. A retrieval.

And the cycle continues.

His hands move like they remember a dance long forgotten.

AN ENDLESS TIDE

But no matter how many they cut down...

More come.

Hundreds surge forward, crawling, shrieking, their endless hunger unrelenting.

They step over the corpses of their own kind, climbing over their fallen, dragging their broken bodies toward the warmth of the living.

One collapses from Opilkhos's light, only for two more to scramble over its burning remains.

Taril shatters five with one swing – ten more replace them.

Drunnyak tears through an entire row, blood coating his fists, but there is no end.

They do not stop coming.

Not yet.

Not until the night itself decides otherwise.

And then...

From the distance...

Something else moves in the dark.

The battle does not end.

As the group fights, pushing forward with the unrelenting precision of warriors who have done this a thousand times before, they finally see it...

The edge of the forest.

Beyond the thinning trees, the land opens. The horizon stretches far, revealing a colossal mountain standing tall against the darkened sky. And in the distance, scattered torches flicker – not aimless fires, but signs of life.

For the first time since awakening, they are not alone.

But their relief is short-lived.

As the horde seems to thin, their ranks replenish.

More dead rise, crawling from the ice-covered earth, filling the gaps left by their fallen.

And then…

Something different emerges.

From amidst the shambling corpses, five figures rise, standing taller, broader, stronger than the rest. Their bodies are thicker, their flesh not as decayed, but reinforced, hardened, as if something unnatural has shaped them beyond death.

Their movements are different.

They do not lurch mindlessly.

They *observe*.

Their rotting eyes glow with a dark intelligence, watching the battlefield, reading the fight, positioning themselves among the horde as if they are controlling it.

These are not mindless corpses.

These are commanders of the dead.

Drunnyak spits to the side, wiping blood from his lips. "Oh, good," he grunts, rolling his shoulders. "Bigger bastards to break."

Niv flicks the blood from her blade, her golden eyes narrowing as she studies them. "They're different."

Taril adjusts his stance, his war hammer heavy in his grip. "No," he mutters, voice low. "They're *smarter*."

Opilkhos grips his sword tighter, his aura still glowing – but the new enemies do not fear his light. They step forward with purpose, unshaken by the divine energy burning through the others.

Alentar, standing atop a broken tree stump, his bow drawn, sees what lies beyond.

His emerald eyes sharpen.

Beyond the battlefield, beyond the undead tide, he sees movement near the mountain.

And then...

Fire.

A great wall of flame erupts, illuminating the night from afar. A trench carved into the earth separates the dead from something – no, *someone* – on the other side.

And then he sees them.

Living people.

Soldiers.

Arrows rain down upon the undead, streaking from the other side of the chasm, striking rotting bodies with precision. Men atop battlements, hurling burning oil, lighting the corpses aflame before they can reach the other side.

They are defending the path into the mountain.

And the horde is pushing toward it.

Alentar's gaze sweeps across the battlefield, analysing everything, mapping the chaos with a hunter's instinct. "We've got living people ahead!" he calls, voice cutting through the sounds of battle.

The others glance at him, still fighting, still cutting down the endless undead.

"There's a ditch – they're using it to keep the horde out. But they won't be able to hold forever." His voice tightens, his bowstring drawn taut. "And we've got a bigger problem..."

His eyes lock onto the five new undead closing in on them.

The ones who are watching.

Controlling.

Leading.

His fingers flex around the bow.

"This fight just changed."

The battle intensifies.

The five monstrous undead fix their hollow, unnatural eyes on the group, their grotesque forms pushing through the lesser undead with purpose.

They are not here to fight the human soldiers at the mountain.

They are here to stop the group from reaching them.

Alentar is the first to move.

With impossible speed, he leaps onto a tree branch, his body blending into the darkness of the forest canopy. His bow is already drawn before his feet touch the wood. He does not stop.

One arrow. Two. Three.

Each shot finds its mark, clearing the path ahead, striking through the skulls of the mindless undead that swarm before his companions.

Then, with a twist of his body, he launches himself through the air, using the trees as his springboard. He flips, twisting in mid-air, releasing another shot as he sails above his companions.

The arrow pierces through the throat of an undead lunging at Drunnyak.

Before he even lands, another shot – a direct hit between the eyes of one dragging itself toward Opilkhos.

Then his feet touch another branch, and he launches again.

He is a phantom in motion, moving like the wind, opening the way forward with each shot.

But the five new enemies do not fall like the others.

They do not falter.

And now, they move.

Faster than anything the group has faced, they charge.

One rushes straight for Niv.

She braces, blades drawn, ready to meet the attack…

But Taril is already there.

He steps in front of her, his massive shield slamming into the charging creature, stopping it in mid-motion. The impact is thunderous, the force so strong that the earth cracks beneath his feet.

The beast snarls, its thick, rotting skin barely dented, but it is forced back.

Niv does not hesitate.

She moves around Taril's defence, using his bulk to her advantage – she spins, her blade slashing into the creature's side, striking the one place Taril's shield left exposed.

It howls, but it does not die.

Instead, it lunges again, faster.

Taril's arm moves before Niv can react – his shield knocks the beast's claw aside, pushing it away from her.

And for a moment…

It happens.

As Niv turns, preparing for her next attack, her eyes meet Taril's.

Something inside her pulls.

And then…

A memory strikes like lightning.

A fireplace, warm and safe, the crackling of flames filling the air.

A young girl, golden-haired, laughing, curled up on a massive armoured lap, her small arms wrapped around the thick chest of a dwarf who'd never let anything harm her. "Tell me another, Taril!"

A deep chuckle, a voice softer than she ever remembered it being. "Haven't I spoiled you enough with stories, lass?"

She giggles, nuzzling into his thick beard. "Never. You're the best at them."

Another laugh, gentler this time, followed by a strong, steady hand patting her head. "Aye, then. Just one more."

The memory collapses back into the present, but the warmth remains.

The battle still rages.

The enemy is still before them.

But in that one heartbeat of a moment, Niv doesn't think.

She acts.

She leans in and kisses Taril's cheek.

It's brief, but the meaning lingers.

Taril blinks, his entire body momentarily stunned. He has faced wars, monsters, horrors beyond reckoning – but this?

This disarms him.

Niv smirks, stepping past him. "Still the best at keeping me alive."

Taril, for once, has no words.

But a slow, knowing smile touches his lips.

And then the enemy strikes again, and the fight resumes.

The battle moves in perfect balance.

Each of them a piece of a greater whole, each movement calculated, instinctive – a rhythm of war rediscovered.

Opilkhos stands like a radiant wall, his golden light burning away the darkness, shielding the others as they press forward.

Taril and Niv fight as one, steel and hammer moving in perfect harmony, his shield blocking every strike she does not see, her blade finding every opening he creates.

Alentar rains death from above, his arrows unceasing, retrieved and reused in an endless cycle, each shot carving open a path forward.

Nashir moves with the earth, his staff humming with life, roots and vines snapping up from the ground to ensnare the undead, twisting through their bodies like living chains, breaking their charge.

They are warriors of another time.

But then…

Drunnyak changes. Something snaps inside him.

The battlefield is carnage, bodies strewn across the snow, the air thick with frost and blood. The fight rages on, but Drunnyak no longer fights – he destroys.

His pace shifts. Faster. More brutal.

A roar bellows from deep within his chest, so thunderous that the very mountain trembles, loose ice and rock cascading from the cliffs above. It is not human. It is a force of nature, something raw and untamed, something that has been unleashed.

The others feel it before they see it.

His eyes turn white.

Vacant. Empty.

Like his mind is gone, replaced by something else – something primal, something unchained.

He lunges forward.

His jagged broadsword cleaves through three at once, their bodies splitting apart like wet parchment. Another leaps at him – he catches it in mid-air, his massive hands closing around its torso.

A moment of stillness.

Then...

A sickening twist.

The body is torn in half.

For the first time since they crawled from the frozen ground...

The undead hesitate.

But Drunnyak does not.

He charges deeper, moving without restraint, without fear, as though the weight of his own body no longer matters.

Another lunges – he meets it in mid-motion, grabbing it by the throat, lifting it as if it weighs nothing.

Its claws scratch at him, raking his skin, but... nothing.

Drunnyak doesn't feel it.

With one monstrous heave, he hurls it into the horde, its body crashing through its kin, breaking others apart like brittle bones beneath a war hammer.

Another monstrous undead comes for him – one of the five that led the horde.

Its blade comes down toward him – but he does not block.

He steps forward into the strike, letting it glance off his thick hide, the blade barely nicking his skin.

His fist slams into its chest – the impact alone shatters its ribcage, splintering bone outward as it crumples into the snow.

Another swings for his neck – he ducks, steps in, drives his sword into its gut, and rips upward, cleaving it clean in two.

The last two remain.

One charges from behind – he hears it, but he doesn't turn.

Instead, he reaches back, grabs it by the head, and squeezes.

The skull shatters like dry bark.

The final one leaps high, aiming to land on him, to take him down...

But Drunnyak is faster.

He catches it in mid-air, slamming it downward with such force that its spine snaps on impact.

And then...

The battlefield is his.

The trench looms ahead – the last barrier between them and the living.

But the undead still pour from below, climbing over each other, grasping, reaching, so close to breaking through.

Drunnyak does not slow, and he leaps.

The soldiers had heard the battle, the roars in the distance, the tremors of war, but they had never seen the ones fighting it.

Not until now.

A roar.

Not the wail of the undead. Not the cry of a man.

Something else. Something primordial.

The sound shook the air itself, a thunderous bellow that sent vibrations through the frozen ground beneath them.

An immense figure leaping from the darkness from a distance so far that they couldn't believe their eyes. Descending like a force of nature, his silhouette a blur against the storm-choked sky.

Drunnyak hit the ground with the force of an avalanche, the impact splitting the ice beneath his feet, sending cracks racing outward.

Two of the undead were in his grasp – one in each massive hand.

The soldiers froze.

For a moment, the battle itself paused, as if the world itself did not know what to do with the thing that had just dropped into their midst.

Then...

Drunnyak moved.

With a guttural growl, he clenched his fists, crushing the throats of the undead in his grasp, their bodies twisting, writhing, before snapping with wet, sickening crunches.

And then, with a feral grin, he hurled them into the horde, sending the broken corpses barrelling into their own ranks.

Some of the soldiers stared in horror. Others – the younger, the fearful – broke.

They turned, running for their lives, scattering from the trench like frightened animals.

"What in all the hells…?"

"By the gods, what is that?!"

"*Run!*"

But not all fled.

A handful of warriors held their ground, though their hands trembled on their weapons.

Not because of the undead.

But because of him.

Their captain did not run. He stood, blade in hand, watching the titan of a man tear through the battlefield as if he had been born to it. "Hold the line!" he bellowed, his voice cutting through the fear.

The remaining soldiers snapped to attention, rallying behind their captain as their eyes remained fixed on the monster in their midst.

A monster who fought for them.

And as they held their ground, as they watched him carve his path through the cursed, a realisation took hold – they might survive this night.

Drunnyak did not care for the ones leaving or the ones standing beside him.

His white-hot fury is fading, the fog of rage lifting.

His breath slows.

And suddenly, his hands shake.

His chest rises sharply, his heart pounding in his ears.

And then… he feels it.

The pain.

It floods into him all at once.

The cuts, the slashes, the claws that raked his skin but never broke it before – now, he feels all of them.

The weight he never noticed before crushes him all at once.

His knees buckle, his vision swims, and for the first time…

Drunnyak feels mortal.

"What…?" The word barely escapes his lips.

His fingers twitch, his hands trembling in front of his own eyes.

The trench full of writhing undead, their bodies piling up, climbing, nearly breaking through.

The soldiers bracing for another wave, unaware that this warlord who just leaped from the heavens is falling apart before their eyes.

And then... a single drop of blood touches the snow.

Then another.

And then blood pours from him.

Drunnyak stares down at himself, at the deep crimson trailing from his nose, from his mouth, from wounds that never even opened. "I..." His voice is weak.

Drunnyak looks up, fear etched across his face – not for the undead, nor the soldiers, but for himself.

At what is happening to him.

And then everything goes black.

A GIANT FALLS UNCONSCIOUS

The earth is still shaking from Drunnyak's landing, the echoes of his monstrous roar still trembling through the mountainside. But now...

He does not rise.

The unstoppable warlord, the raging beast who tore through the horde like a force of nature itself, now lies still.

Amidst the carnage, amidst the screams and clashing steel, the living and the dead continue their fight – but the soldiers' eyes remain fixed on Drunnyak.

Not on the trench.

Not on the undead still clawing their way upward.

But on the giant who has fallen.

A legend in the making, brought to his knees.

Their faces are a mixture of awe, fear and confusion. They watched him fight like he was more monster than man, an unstoppable warlord of raw destruction.

And yet now, he looks human.

His massive chest rises unevenly, his skin pale beneath the moonlight, his fingers twitching as if grasping at something unseen. Blood trails from his mouth, crimson spilling across the snow – proof that whatever protected him before is now gone.

And still, the battle rages on.

The undead do not care for fallen warriors.

They keep coming.

A new wave claws its way over the trench, dragging broken limbs and hollow eyes toward the living.

And that's when he appears. A wee boy.

No more than eight years old, small and fragile, dressed in fake wooden armour, a tiny sword crafted from bark and twine strapped to his side – a child who has no place on a battlefield, yet here he is.

And he is running toward the giant.

His legs kick up frost, his breath sharp and uneven, his face a mix of terror and unwavering courage.

The soldiers see him too late.

"Caelan, no! Get back!"

But he doesn't stop.

He leaps, throwing himself over Drunnyak's massive body, shielding him with his tiny frame, his small arms wrapping around the warlord's unmoving chest.

His voice small, shaking, yet loud enough for all to hear. "Please, Mr Drunnyak, don't die!"

The words shattered the chaos.

The captain's breath caught. His sword arm stiffened.

Drunnyak.

The name hit like a war drum in his skull.

It wasn't an unfamiliar name. It belonged to stories he heard when he was the same age as the boy, to legends whispered in the dim light of The Stubborn Goat, spoken over cups of ale by old men who swore they had heard it from someone who heard it from someone else.

A name that never should have belonged to the flesh-and-blood warrior who had just torn through the battlefield like a force of nature.

His eyes snapped to the giant lying in the snow, to the massive chest that, against all odds, still rose and fell.

Drunnyak.

The captain had seen monsters. He had seen heroes.

But this?

This was something else.

And as the boy clung to the fallen titan, as the soldiers around them whispered, some in reverence, some in disbelief, the captain's grip on his blade tightened.

Because if the legends were true...

Then the world was about to change forever.

The clashing steel, the roaring undead, the shouts of warriors – they all faded into nothing.

The group, still fighting, all hear it.

The boy's voice cuts through the noise, through the chaos, through the very essence of war itself.

And one thought claws into their minds.

He called him by name.

How does he know him?

Their chests tighten, but there is no time to question it.

Because while the living hesitate, the dead do not.

A grotesque undead figure pulls itself over the trench, its jagged fingers digging into the frozen dirt, its empty sockets locked onto the child.

A sickening hunger radiates from it, its jaw snapping open, eager to tear through the warm, beating heart that does not belong in this fight.

The boy doesn't see it.

Drunnyak does not move.

The group is too far away.

And yet...

A sharp whistle cuts through the air.

Then a single, perfect shot.

The undead jerks violently as a black-feathered arrow pierces through its skull, the force snapping its head back, its rotting body tumbling lifelessly into the snow.

The soldiers barely register what happened before their eyes, and are already drawn to where the shot came from, but they can't see due to the distance and the darkness.

Hundreds of metres away, standing atop the distant ruins of a collapsed tower, bow still raised, emerald eyes sharp and unyielding...

Alentar.

His face is unreadable, his expression unwavering, but his body is still as a hunter at the end of his hunt.

The wind whips through his long black hair, his cloak billowing behind him, his stance calm, unshaken – because he never misses.

And he did not miss now.

The undead drops, the child still clutching Drunnyak, still whispering, still holding on to something far greater than a fallen warrior.

Nashir stands still.

His emerald eyes take in the scene before him – Drunnyak collapsed, bleeding, vulnerable in a way they have never seen before. The small boy still clutching him, a fragile soul amidst warriors and monsters.

The undead still pour from the trench, dragging themselves upward, nearly breaking through.

The soldiers – the living – stand on the edge of hope and oblivion.

It is time to end this.

"Cross the trench," Nashir commands, his voice calm, steady, unchallenged. "Protect the living. Protect Drunnyak."

The others do not hesitate.

They do not question.

Alentar meets his gaze from afar and nods once, understanding.

The rest move, breaking into action without another word, as if they have done this before, as if their bodies remember something their minds have yet to recall.

Nashir, left alone before the trench, exhales slowly.

The soldiers can finally see the giant's companions, so they rally to their captain.

Then...

He lifts his staff.

And the world listens.

A deep, resonant pulse spreads through the earth, rippling outward like a heartbeat. The wind stills, the snowfall slows, and the very air

62

changes – charged with something ancient, something that has not stirred in thousands of years.

Nashir closes his eyes, his fingers curling against the wood of his staff, and he calls out.

Not with words, but with his soul.

And the land answers.

A tremor shudders through the frozen ground.

A low, groaning sound, like the earth itself is awakening.

Then…

The trench erupts.

Roots, thick and blackened with age, lunge from the soil like great serpents, coiling around the undead in a crushing grip.

Vines explode from the ice, snapping forward like whips, wrapping around skeletal limbs, yanking them back into the abyss.

The ground splits open, jagged cracks racing through the battlefield as the very land devours the dead.

The undead struggle, but there is no escape.

Their broken bodies are dragged down into the earth, their shrieks muffled as the soil closes over them, burying them in the very land they once crawled from.

Some try to climb, their clawed hands digging into the ice, desperate…

But the roots constrict.

The vines tighten.

Bones snap like brittle twigs.

Flesh bursts beneath the crushing pressure.

The trench becomes their tomb.

And then…

Silence.

The battlefield stands still.

The undead that had nearly climbed free are now motionless, tangled in a web of roots and soil, buried in the land that refused to let them rise again.

The soldiers and their captain stare in shock, breathless, unable to process what they have just witnessed.

The group – standing now among the living, among those they have just fought to save – watches their brother.

Nashir lowers his staff.

The pulsing energy fades, the ground settling once more.

He looks to them, his emerald eyes still bright, victorious…

And then he grins.

A knowing grin.

Like Drunnyak before him.

And then his legs give out.

The pain hits him all at once – his wounds, the exhaustion, the sheer weight of what he has just done.

He stood as if he were untouchable – but he is still flesh. Still mortal.

His body trembles, his vision darkens.

And before he can take another breath…

Nashir collapses.

His body finally yielding to the toll of his power. His staff slips from his grasp, landing in the bloodstained snow beside him. His breath is ragged, his once-glowing presence dimming, no longer the radiant force that just commanded the land itself.

And yet…

Even though the battle is over, even though the undead have fallen…

The battlefield still feels wrong.

Alentar moves instantly, leaping from stone to stone, dodging broken weapons and torn bodies as he rushes to his twin's side. But just as he reaches Nashir, he stops.

So does everyone else.

Something is happening.

The battlefield, once thick with broken bodies, shattered bones, and coagulated blood, begins to shift.

The dead – what remains of them – begin to disappear.

Their flesh crumbles.

Their bones wither.

The blood pooled in the snow dissolves, turning to nothing but greyish dust.

Slowly, steadily, as if the earth itself is swallowing them whole, the remnants of battle fade into the frozen land.

The group watches, silent, their exhaustion momentarily forgotten in the face of something they do not understand.

Taril, still gripping his war hammer, his stance unshaken despite the battle, speaks first. His voice is calm but edged, rough with suspicion. "Was this Nashir?"

Alentar kneels beside his twin, pressing a hand to his chest, feeling the rise and fall of his breath, ensuring he is still alive, but his gaze flickers back toward the battlefield, toward the vanishing dead.

Niv frowns, gripping the hilt of her blade. "If it was him, why would he collapse first?"

Taril shakes his head. "It wasn't Nashir. It wasn't any of us."

The group exchanges glances.

A powerful force has been unleashed here tonight.

And none of them know what caused it.

"Then what in the hells…?" Niv starts, but before she can finish…

A voice answers. "Morning came."

The words are gruff, weary, but firm, spoken by a man approaching from the side.

The group turns sharply, hands instinctively hovering over their weapons as they meet the gaze of one of the humans they have just saved.

A man – older than most here, strong despite the wear of time, his weathered face lined with battle and command. His armour, though scratched and battered, still bears the markings of leadership.

The leader of these soldiers. Eldric, their captain.

He stops a few paces away, eyeing them not with fear, but with something else – something like disbelief. "The undead return to the earth at sunrise," he continues, his sharp gaze sweeping over them. "They'll be back at night. Again. And again. As they always do."

Silence.

The group does not speak.

They look at each other – not just confused, but disturbed.

Because they did not know this.

They fought this war as if it could be won, as if their blades, their power, their will alone could end the tide.

But the humans speak of it as if it is inevitable.

A cycle.

A curse.

They do not question it, do not fear it as something unknown – because to them, it has always been.

The realisation settles over them like a thick, suffocating fog.

Niv's fingers tighten around her sword's hilt, her golden eyes darkening. "You say that like it's normal."

The man doesn't flinch. "Because it is."

Taril exhales slowly, rolling his shoulders, his expression darkening. "And yet we know nothing of it."

The man watches them carefully. "Why wouldn't you?"

None of them have an answer.

Because they don't know why.

They don't know why the world is like this.

They don't know why they don't remember.

And for the first time since awakening, none of them have words.

Alentar breaks the silence.

His expression unreadable, he gently moves Nashir, lifting his brother from the frozen ground with ease. His movements are careful, deliberate – not just a warrior carrying another, but something far more personal.

Without looking back, without asking more questions, he steps forward – toward the group – and crosses the trench with the same agility as before, using his skills.

As Alentar carries Nashir closer to the group, they are silent, burdened not just by exhaustion, but by the weight of what they have just learned.

They still don't understand.

Not the world. Not themselves.

Not the curse that has shaped this land into a never-ending battlefield.

And yet, as they step forward, something catches their attention.

The child.

Still kneeling beside Drunnyak's massive form, his small hands still clinging to the warrior's unmoving arm. He hasn't let go. Hasn't left his side.

But it isn't his presence that holds their gaze.

It's the object tied to his belt.

A statue – small, worn, carved from dark stone.

The likeness is unmistakable.

Even in its weathered state, even in its crude but careful craftsmanship, the shape of the muscular figure, the broad shoulders, the fearless stance, the distinct scars carved into its stone surface...

It is Drunnyak.

A prayer idol. A token of devotion.

The realisation settles in like a cold hand gripping their spines.

The boy's voice echoes in their minds – the way he cried out Drunnyak's name before anyone had spoken it aloud.

They glance at each other – Taril, Niv, Alentar, Opilkhos – uncertainty flickering in their gazes.

How does this child know Drunnyak?

How do any of them have statues like this?

None of them speak.

Not yet.

But as they step forward, as Alentar adjusts Nashir's weight over his shoulder, as they move toward whatever answers await them beyond this battlefield...

One thing is certain.

At least one person besides Harinnil remembers them.

Even if they do not remember themselves.

A SURVIVOR'S WORLD

In the hours before our heroes stirred from their long slumber, the villagers they would soon meet had done as they always had – enduring the night, holding the line, and surviving, as their forefathers had before them.

This is but a fragment of their tale, a glimpse into the world as it stood before fate began to stir.

Dawn stirs beyond the veiled sky, but to the weary soldiers, it remains unseen.

Beyond the eternal grey veil of clouds, the sun struggles to rise, but its warmth never touches the land.

No golden hues spill over the mountains.

No brilliant sky marks the passing of another cursed night.

Only the shifting of shadows, the wind growing still, and the unnatural silence that follows.

And the only way they know that morning has come is when the undead begin to disappear.

It begins as it always does.

The battlefield, once thick with moving corpses, begins to shift.

Flesh shrivels, bones crumble to dust, and the stench of decay starts to fade, as though it was never there.

The frozen blood pooled in the snow seeps away, vanishing without a trace – not absorbed, not melted, simply gone.

The earth trembles, drinking in the last remnants of the night's horror.

And just like that, the dead vanish again.

The living remain.

Breathing.

Surviving.

For one more day.

The soldiers stand in hollow silence, weapons hanging loose in exhausted hands.

Not because they are victorious. But because they know this is not the end.

It never is.

They fought with everything they had, and tonight, they will do it again.

A soldier wipes blood from his face – his own, or another's, he doesn't know or care.

Another leans on his sword, his chest heaving, his legs barely holding him upright.

Some tend to the wounded, binding cuts, whispering quiet prayers to an unknown being, hoping for a better life.

No one speaks.

Because what is there to say?

They survived. That is all that matters.

Captain Eldric, his armour dented and cracked, his face lined with age and too many nights like this, exhales sharply, rolling his shoulders. "It's over." His voice is rough, flat, as if speaking the words will make them real. "For now."

No one cheers.

No one celebrates.

They simply breathe.

And in the heavy silence that follows, a sound cuts through the morning frost.

A soft, stifled sob.

Eldric turns his head…

And sees young Caelan.

Caelan watched the battle, as he's done every night since his father left.

He watched from behind the broken wagons, gripping the edges of the wood, peering out with wide, terrified eyes as the men fought for their lives against the unrelenting night.

He clutched his wooden sword, as if the brittle piece of bark and twine could protect him.

He prayed.

And when his hands shook too much, when his breath hitched with silent sobs, he turned his fingers to the one thing that always brings him comfort.

The small statue of Drunnyak – worn and rough, carved from dark stone, tied securely to his belt.

He gripped it tightly, his cold fingers tracing the old grooves, the deep ridges of the massive warrior's figure.

"Please, please, please…" He prayed to the one who did not break, did not fall, did not fear, as his father told him in many tales before. To Drunnyak, the warlord, the warrior of unshaken strength. "Please make them strong. Make them win. Please don't let them die."

Tears blurred his vision, his chest a tight knot of fear and helplessness.

He wanted to fight, like the men and his father.

He wanted to stand tall. Make his father proud.

But he wasn't strong.

He was just a boy.

And he was afraid.

So he held the statue tighter, and watched.

Watched as the soldiers held the line, as they pushed back the monsters of the night.

Watched as the cursed horrors crumbled at dawn, fading into the ground, claimed once more by the eternal cycle.

And as the battlefield fell silent, as the warriors lowered their weapons, exhausted, broken, but alive…

Caelan's fingers finally loosened from the statue. He exhaled.

Morning had come. They had survived.

But then… His breath hitched.

His small body froze, his mind locking in place, unable to comprehend what he was seeing.

Because among the fading corpses, one did not vanish yet, and caught his attention.

One still stood.

She stood at the edge of the battlefield, motionless, her head tilted slightly, as though listening for something distant.

But she did not hear.

She did not see.

She did not breathe.

Her hair, once flowing and dark, now hung in tangled strands, limp and lifeless. Her skin, once warm, once kissed by the firelight of their home, was now a sickly shade of grey, stretched too thin over bones that should not be moving.

But she did move.

Not with the mindless hunger of the others.

Not with rage.

With hesitation, and Caelan knew why. Because she was his mother.

He believed that a part of her, even in this wretched, cursed form, still knew him.

"Mama?"

The word barely left his lips, but it was loud enough to slice through the frozen air like a blade.

The soldiers flinched, as if the sound of it hurt them too.

Her clouded eyes shifted, but she did not lunge.

She did not snarl. She paused.

For the briefest moment – a second, a heartbeat, a flicker of something almost human…

It looked like she remembered.

Caelan sobbed, his small hands shaking, his feet moving on their own. "Mummy, it's me!"

His tiny arms reached for her, as if he could pull her back from whatever abyss had swallowed her soul.

And then… A soldier moved.

A sword rose – a reflex honed by years of survival.

And the boy… Threw himself forward.

"No! Don't! Please!"

But the soldier did not hesitate.

Because he knew, as they all did…

Morning had come, but she could still be a threat to young Caelan. The dead will belong to the earth once more.

A single, precise strike. Steel pierced her skull.

Her body jerked, shuddered – then fell limp in the snow.

Dead again. For now.

Caelan did not move. Did not blink.

His hands were still reaching, still trembling in the empty space where she had just stood.

Eldric watched him carefully, his chest tightening, but he said nothing.

Because there was nothing to say.

The soldiers did not move, because they understood.

They had all lost someone to the night throughout their lives.

They had all wanted to believe, just for a moment, that the dead could still remember them, but none of them had remembered before, and this naive belief always added more corpses to their side.

The battlefield was quiet now.

Only the living remained, but even they felt like ghosts, moving through the aftermath like shadows of themselves.

The soldiers gathered, tending wounds, replacing shattered weapons, whispering prayers for those who would never return home.

But the battlefield itself was empty.

No corpses, no rotting flesh, no remnants of the horrors they had fought through the night.

Only the scars of battle remained – the deep slashes in the frozen earth where bodies had collapsed, the patches of disturbed snow where blood had been spilled but left no stain.

Soon, even those marks would be erased.

The wind would rise, the frost would settle again, and there would be no proof that anything had happened here at all.

But Eldric's wounds told a different story, and so did his nephew.

Caelan still knelt in the snow, motionless, his small hands curled into fists, his breath ragged with the weight of grief too large for a child to bear.

Eldric's joints ached as he lowered himself to one knee beside him, his armour groaning under the weight of exhaustion. His rough, battle-worn hand rested on the boy's trembling shoulder.

"Your father left you under my care," Eldric said, his voice rough but gentle. "You should be resting, protecting your little cousins, not running into the middle of battle."

Caelan didn't move.

Didn't look up.

Eldric exhaled, glancing at the place where Elise had fallen. There was no body now – only the imprint of where she had been. The wind was already starting to fill it in. "I know you miss her," he said softly. "But you have to understand…" He hesitated, choosing his words carefully. "Whatever she was… she ain't no more."

For a moment, there was nothing.

Then Caelan moved. His small shoulders tensed, his breath hitching. His voice, when it finally came, was thin, fragile, but laced with something deep, something broken. "You don't understand, Uncle." He lifted his face, his tear-streaked cheeks flushed with cold, his eyes raw from crying, but filled with something deeper than grief… Desperation. "I know she wasn't the same – I know she was… wrong." His lips quivered, his fingers gripping at Eldric's sleeve like a drowning child reaching for a lifeline. "But she stopped, Uncle. She stopped when she heard me." His chest heaved. "She knew me."

Eldric's heart clenched because he had seen it too.

That awful, fleeting moment where Elise had paused, where her rotting hands had hesitated, where the hunger in her lifeless eyes had flickered with something else – something almost human.

And that was the worst part.

Not that she had risen.

Not that she had turned into one of the countless horrors they faced every night.

But that some part of her had still been there. Still been Elise.

Eldric sighed, his fingers tightening on the boy's small shoulder. "Maybe she did," he admitted, his voice quieter now, weighted with a sadness he rarely let himself feel. "Maybe some part of her still knew you." He looked away for a moment, toward the distant horizon, where the sky remained a perpetual shade of grey, where morning never truly came. "But it wouldn't have lasted, Caelan." His tone was firm, not unkind, but unyielding. "It never does."

Caelan's lips pressed together, his small hands clutching at the wooden armour he still wore. "Then why?" His voice broke. "Why does it have to be like this, Uncle? Why do they come back just to suffer? Why do we have to kill them again and again? Why?!" Caelan cried out to the heavens, his voice raw with despair.

Eldric had no answer because there was no answer. Not one that would bring the boy peace. Not one that would bring any of them peace. "I don't know," he said honestly, looking at his nephew's eyes.

Caelan shook his head, hot tears spilling onto the ice, dripping onto the small stone statue still tied to his belt. "I hate it," he whispered. "I hate this world."

Eldric closed his eyes for a moment, taking in a slow breath.

Then, without a word, he reached forward, wrapping his arms around the boy, pulling him close.

Caelan did not resist.

The child buried his face into his uncle's shoulder, his tiny fingers gripping onto his battered cloak, holding on as though afraid that if he let go, the last warmth in the world would disappear.

"I know, lad," Eldric murmured, pressing a hand against the back of Caelan's head. "I know."

For a long moment, they stayed there, kneeling in the frost, surrounded by the marks left behind by the battle.

No bodies.

No proof.

Just the faint depressions in the ice where people had once stood, fought, died, and vanished.

Soon, even those would be gone.

The wind would cover them.

Just like it did every morning.

Eldric's bones protested as he finally rose to his feet, but he ignored them, lifting his nephew with him, cradling the boy in his arms as he had when Caelan was much younger, before the world had taken too much from him. "Let's go home."

Even as exhaustion settled into his body, even as the ache in his wounds became unbearable, he carried his nephew through the battlefield, toward their village, toward whatever rest they could still grasp before night came again.

And Caelan – for the first time since she had fallen – closed his eyes and slept.

A long walk, made even longer by the weight of battle. The captain, nestling his weary nephew, and his soldiers, dragging their exhausted bodies, trudged through the hidden passage between the mountains, each step carrying them closer to the fragile warmth of home.

Tucked between towering cliffs and jagged peaks, hidden in the folds of the merciless mountains, lay a village that should not exist.

And yet – it stood.

A place carved not by nature, nor by gods, but by the hands of those who refused to break.

Here, in the shadow of the frostbitten world, among the endless grey of Maud's skies, life persisted.

It was not untouched by the cold. The winds still howled, the frost still clung to the earth, and the ever-present weight of night's curse loomed over them like a spectre, but within these walls, the suffering did not rule constantly.

Here, warmth existed – not just in flames and hearths, but in the quiet resilience of those who called it home.

The village was not large, nor grand, but it was clever.

Nestled between the mountains, the homes were built into the rock itself, using the natural formations as protection from the cruellest storms.

Some dwellings stood along the valley floor, small stone houses with wooden roofs, patched over the years with whatever could be salvaged. Others clung to the mountainside, built on narrow ledges, their wooden balconies jutting out like nests suspended over the world.

Bridges of thick rope and sturdy planks connected the levels, swaying slightly in the ever-present wind. The people had learned to move with them, never against them.

It was a village of odd shapes and winding paths, built wherever space could be claimed. No two homes were alike – some had rounded stone walls, others tall chimneys, and some were so tightly tucked between rock formations that their roofs were made of pure, unbroken stone.

And at its heart, the village square.

A fountain stood at the centre, its basin cracked with age but still flowing – not with crystal-clear water, but with something stranger.

The liquid had a faint luminescence, its surface rippling with a deep blue hue, giving the square a soft glow even in the dimmest hours.

They did not know where it came from, only that it never froze, even in the worst winters.

A tavern stood close by, squat and sturdy, its wooden sign hanging crookedly, but proudly called The Stubborn Goat.

It was a place of laughter, of warmth, of whispered fears and drunken boasts.

A place where soldiers and farmers sat side by side, where the weight of the world could be drowned in ale and quiet company.

Where the fire always burned, and no one drank alone.

Beyond it, a small trading post stood, its stalls arranged haphazardly, offering everything from dried meats to battered tools, from simple cloth to old, well-worn books. A scavenger's market, but a necessary one.

And around it all, life moved.

A blacksmith's forge glowed faintly, its chimney sending thin tendrils of smoke into the sky.

A leatherworker tanned hides near the eastern path, the scent strong but familiar.

And scattered throughout, children played in the snow, their laughter ringing against the stone, a sound that defied the cruelty of the world beyond their walls.

Just outside the village, where the earth was slightly more forgiving, small patches of frost-kissed farmland clung to life.

They were not vast fields of golden wheat, nor sprawling orchards heavy with fruit.

They were humble plots, where only the hardiest crops grew – root vegetables, thick-skinned squash, bitter greens that could withstand the biting cold.

Each plant was a battle won.

At the mouth of a well-lit cavern, more delicate greenery thrived – herbs, mushrooms, vines carefully cultivated in the safety of the stone.

This place was tended by those who understood life better than war, who knew the land not for what it had taken, but for what it could still give.

And among them, animals stirred.

Furred mountain goats, their thick coats protecting them from the frost, moved within fenced enclosures built against the cliffs.

Small coops housed hardy fowl, their feathers ruffled against the cold.

Even a few pigs and dogs could be seen – creatures that should not thrive here, and yet they did.

Because the people had made it so.

This village, this fragile place of firelight and stone, was not a kingdom, nor a fortress.

But it was theirs.

And while the curse of Maud loomed over them, while the undead still rose and fell with the turning of time, while the cold never truly relented…

They had found a way to hold on.

To carve something warm out of the frozen world.

To exist in defiance of the dark.

And for now, that was enough.

The path to the village was steep, winding its way up through the narrow pass between the mountains, where jagged cliffs loomed like silent sentinels. The wind still carried the bite of frost, but here it was gentler – as if the mountains themselves shielded those who called this place home.

As Eldric and his weary companions trudged up the well-worn trail, they saw the next shift of watchmen gathering near the outer defences.

They were not men, not yet.

Boys – lean and sharp-eyed, their faces still soft with youth but hardened by a world that had forced them to grow too soon.

Their weapons were light, their armour patched together, and though they held bows and spears, they were mostly watchers, not warriors.

Their duty was to observe, to warn, to stand at the edge of the trench and at the hidden pass that led into the village, ensuring that nothing reached their people without being seen first.

Among them, one stood slightly apart, his stance firmer, his gaze sharper.

A boy just shy of sixteen, tall for his age, though his frame had not yet filled out. His dark hair was cropped short, likely self-cut with a knife, and his sharp hazel eyes missed nothing.

Edric.

Named after Eldric himself, though the boy seemed to carry the weight of it uneasily.

He had always been serious beyond his years, but there was an undeniable fire in him, a quiet pride in his duties.

As Eldric passed, still carrying his nephew in his arms, he slowed, stopping before the young watchman.

"If you see any sign of my brother," Eldric said, his voice low but steady, "run to me. I'll be at home."

Edric nodded once, no questions, no hesitation. "Aye, Captain."

The lad had always been one to obey first, think later – a quality Eldric admired and feared in equal measure.

With that, he moved on, his boots crunching softly against the snow-dusted path, his weary breath visible in the cold air.

Eldric's arms ached, but he did not loosen his hold on Caelan.

The boy had buried his face in his uncle's chest, exhaustion having stolen his strength, his tiny hands gripping the edge of Eldric's cloak as if afraid to let go.

The child had lost too much, too soon.

And he would lose more.

But not today.

Today, he would sleep in warmth, with a roof over his head and his uncle's arms to protect him.

So as they climbed closer to home, Eldric hummed.

A deep, low tune, rough from years of shouting commands and breathing in the bitter cold, but steady.

An old song, from before the world had fallen to frost and waking death.

A soldier's lullaby.

Oh, my son, the road is long,
The night is dark, the wind is strong,
But the fire still burns, the stars still shine,
And in my arms, you'll rest tonight...

The melody drifted softly through the cold air, words barely more than a murmur, but enough.

Enough to bring a small comfort to a boy who had cried all he could cry.

Enough to remind the men who followed Eldric – bruised, battered, but alive – that they still had something to return to.

A place that was not just stone and fire...

But home.

Eldric's home stood not far from the village centre, a modest but sturdy dwelling nestled between two large stone formations that shielded it from the worst of the wind.

The exterior was built of thick wooden beams, reinforced with stone at its base, ensuring the cold could never truly claim it. A small garden, now dusted with frost, rested against the side, where his wife grew what little herbs could survive the endless winter.

The door creaked softly as he pushed it open, stepping inside as quietly as his heavy boots would allow.

And immediately, warmth embraced him.

The air smelled of roasting meat and spiced broth, of woodsmoke and dried lavender tucked into the beams.

A fire crackled in the hearth, its golden glow stretching over the stone walls, casting soft shadows that danced along the wooden furniture.

The home was small but welcoming, filled with the touches of a family that had built a life together despite the world's cruelty.

A quilt lay draped over a rocking chair, half-stitched with a pattern of small animals and mountains.

Simple carvings decorated the wooden beams – not grand designs of warriors and gods, but tiny things. A flower, a tree, a rabbit. The delicate work of a woman who wanted to make a home not just for survival, but for living.

And at the centre of this warmth, two little figures rushed toward him.

"Papa!"

Two small forms collided with his legs, their arms wrapping around him as best as their little bodies allowed.

His daughters – Isla and Norah.

Isla, the older one at six years old, had golden-brown hair like her mother's, always tangled from her endless adventures around the house. Her freckled nose scrunched as she grinned up at him, her little hands grasping at his coat as if checking he was still real.

Norah, just three years old, clung to him tightly, her chubby hands fisting into his tunic, her dark curls a mess from sleep. She buried her face in his knee, her small voice muffled as she giggled.

"You were gone forever!" Isla declared dramatically.

"Forever!" Norah echoed.

Eldric let out a soft chuckle, though his body ached with exhaustion, and his heart ached even more. "Aye," he murmured, kneeling just enough to press a kiss against each of their foreheads, holding them close. "It felt that way for me too."

Footsteps approached softly, and Eldric looked up, meeting the eyes of the woman who kept him whole.

Marianne.

She stood near the hearth, her hazel eyes filled with quiet relief, though her hands – still dusted with flour from whatever she had been preparing – were clasped tightly, betraying the worry she always tried to hide.

Her honey-brown hair, now loosely tied back, framed a face that carried both softness and strength.

She was not a warrior, but she fought in other ways.

Through every meal she cooked, through every wound she bandaged, through every quiet, unwavering moment of love she gave to this family.

And he loved her for it.

"You're late," she said softly, stepping closer, resting a gentle hand against his cheek. "More than usual."

Eldric leaned into her touch for just a moment, closing his eyes briefly, letting himself feel something other than the cold. "It was a long night," he admitted. "And a hard one."

Marianne's gaze flickered down, just now noticing the small, sleeping form in his arms. "Caelan," she whispered, her voice filled with quiet understanding.

Eldric nodded.

"He's exhausted," Eldric said, his voice softer now, almost pleading. "Please, let him rest."

Isla and Norah immediately quieted, their wide eyes watching as their father moved with the careful steps of a man who had spent years cradling a child who deserved peace.

Marianne led the way to a small room off to the side, where a low wooden bed sat close to the fire, already layered with thick fur blankets.

Eldric knelt down, gently easing Caelan onto the bed, his strong hands tucking the fur around him, ensuring not a single draught could reach the boy.

Even in sleep, Caelan's small hands gripped the edge of Eldric's cloak, as if afraid to let go.

Eldric stilled, his throat tightening for a moment. "You're safe now, lad," he murmured, his rough fingers gently brushing Caelan's dark curls away from his face. "Sleep."

Caelan did not stir, only burrowing deeper into the warmth.

Marianne watched from the doorway, her arms wrapped around herself, her expression unreadable.

She understood what was not being said.

She knew what it meant when Eldric returned home with haunted eyes.

And so, she simply whispered, "Come. You need rest too."

But Eldric lingered a moment longer, watching over the boy as if ensuring that sleep had truly claimed him.

Then, at last, he rose – and stepped into the warmth of his home, where love still existed, where his family waited for him.

And for the first time that day, he let himself breathe.

The weight of battle was not just in Eldric's bones, but in every strap of his armour, every dented plate, every piece of leather stiffened by frost and blood.

And like every morning he returned home, his family helped remove it, piece by piece...

Not just to relieve him of its burden, but to remind him that he was still a man beneath it.

Marianne unbuckled the pauldrons at his shoulders, her fingers gentle but practised, lifting away the battered steel with a quiet sigh.

Isla, ever eager, worked at the straps on his forearm guards, her little hands fumbling but determined. "You should teach me how to do this right, Papa," she said, her brow furrowed in concentration.

Eldric chuckled, despite the weariness in his limbs. "I'll make a shieldmaiden of you yet, lass," he teased.

Norah, the youngest, was given the simplest task – one she had done on many mornings before. She waddled over carefully, carrying a small wooden bowl filled with warm water, a clean rag floating inside. She set it down in front of him with great importance, her tiny face serious. "Clean," she declared proudly.

Eldric smiled, reaching out to ruffle her dark curls. "Aye, my love, clean indeed."

She giggled, stepping back to let her mother take over.

Marianne dipped the rag into the water, wrung it out, and gently pressed it against the dried blood along his temple.

The warmth eased the stiffness in his face, and for a moment, he simply closed his eyes, letting himself exist in this moment of peace.

A moment where there were no swords. No curses. No cold.

Only his family.

And the quiet blessing of being home.

But peace never lasted long.

As Marianne worked, her voice softened. "Any word of him?"

She didn't need to say his name.

They all knew who she meant.

Garric.

Caelan's father.

Eldric's older brother.

The man who'd practically raised him alone after their parents died.

A warrior, a leader – the backbone of this village.

If Eldric had learned how to hold a sword, how to stand tall, how to endure, it was because of Garric.

Where others saw a hardened man, Eldric saw his brother, standing over him in the dead of night when he was just a boy, telling him to stop crying, that he had to be strong, because no one else would protect them.

A lifetime of scars, each one telling a story of sacrifice.

Where others feared, Garric walked forward.

Where others hesitated, he struck first.

The village stood because he willed it to stand.

And now, he was gone.

Eldric exhaled slowly, eyes opening, his expression growing heavier. "No word," he admitted.

Marianne paused, soaking the cloth in the water again, her lips pressing into a thin line. "It's been too long, Eldric."

"I know."

"You should send men to look for him."

"And risk more lives?" Eldric ran a rough hand through his greying hair, his frustration mounting. "I understand the need for trade, but the journey south is too dangerous. The cold alone could take them. And the undead..." He stopped himself, shaking his head. "And it's not just them any more," he muttered.

Marianne's brows furrowed. "What do you mean?"

Eldric leaned back against the chair, rubbing a tired hand over his face. "The last time we heard from him, he spoke of giants."

Marianne's face paled slightly.

Isla, sitting at his feet, perked up. "Giants?" she whispered, eyes wide with curiosity rather than fear.

Eldric sighed. "Aye, lass. Not like the stories, though. These are not the old, wise giants of legend. They are hunters. Bigger than any man, faster than they should be for their size." He looked up at Marianne again, his voice quieter now, more grim. "And if they were truly seen on the southern pass... then the roads are worse than we thought."

Marianne's hands tightened around the rag, as if gripping something unseen. "If he's still out there," she said carefully, "he won't make it home alone."

Eldric knew that.

He had known it for days now.

But to admit it? To voice that fear in front of his daughters?

Instead, he reached down, pulling Isla into his lap, letting her lean against his chest.

"Your uncle is a stubborn man," he said. "More stubborn than me, if you can believe it."

Isla giggled, nodding.

"He'll come home," he continued, his voice steady, convincing – maybe for them, maybe for himself. "And if he doesn't, I'll go find him myself."

Marianne looked at him sharply, but said nothing.

Because they both knew what that would mean.

That if Garric had not returned by now, he may never return at all.

But for today – for the sake of their daughters, for the sake of the little boy sleeping in the next room – they did not speak that truth aloud.

Today, they held on to warmth.

On to hope.

On to each other.

Because the night would come again.

And when it did, they would have to fight once more, but as the story goes, they wouldn't be alone in the next fight.

AN UNEXPECTED MEETING

Back to where the story left off. The battlefield stood silent. The morning had claimed the undead, swallowing them into the earth, leaving behind only their scars.

But the land had not forgotten.

Where the cursed had risen and fallen, the ground bore the wounds of battle.

Blood had left no stain, but the earth remembered.

The trench, once a desperate defence, was now eerily silent, its depths lined with the remnants of struggle. The crushed remains of weapons, shattered shields, and the ghostly imprints where bodies had collapsed, only to be reclaimed by the morning's curse.

The wind howled softly through the clearing, a haunting reminder of what had transpired just hours before.

And at the centre of it all...

Two figures lay motionless.

But they were not dead.

Drunnyak, the titan of a man, his massive form sprawled amidst the ruins of the battlefield, breathed deeply, steadily, but did not stir. His body bore no open wounds, yet exhaustion had claimed him, his muscles twitching as if reliving the battle even in unconsciousness.

And Nashir…

His robe, once vibrant with the life of nature, now dulled, his body curled as if the very earth had tried to shelter him. His breathing was slower, but strong, his fingers twitching slightly against the soil.

For the first time in centuries…

They had fallen… but not for long.

The first voice to break the silence was a whisper. "The boy and Borgrim weren't so crazy after all."

A murmur passed through the gathered soldiers as they cautiously stepped forward, eyes wide, unbelieving.

"Caelan always spoke of Drunnyak," another muttered. "Said he would come back. We thought it was just the foolish hope of a child."

A few men exchanged looks, as if daring each other to step closer.

But then…

"Taril."

The name hung in the air, spoken in hushed awe.

A younger soldier, barely more than a boy, turned to one of the veterans. "Taril? You mean… from the stories?"

The older man nodded slowly, his voice barely above a breath. "Aye. Borgrim told the tales at The Stubborn Goat… but not just of Taril – of him and Drunnyak."

Another soldier leaned in, his voice low and reverent. "The war-forged dwarf and the mountain of a man. The two titans who stood together when the world still had kings. It's said that before the world turned to ice, before the cursed nights, there was a war unlike any other… and they were in the heart of it."

The veteran continued, his voice turning almost reverent as he recited the old tale. "Borgrim said Taril was the unbreakable shield, the warrior who stood where no one else could. That when the greatest warlords fell, he alone held the line. And Drunnyak," he swallowed, "was the storm that followed. If Taril was the mountain, then Drunnyak was the avalanche that crushed all in its wake."

The men listened in silent awe.

"They were more than warriors. They were forces of nature. Shoulder to shoulder, no enemy could break them. They waged war with gods, laughed in the face of death, and when the world burned—"

"They did not fall," another soldier murmured.

The legend lingered in the cold air, thick with reverence.

Then...

A deep, gravel-like voice cut through the quiet. "He still can. For I am he."

The soldiers turned sharply.

Taril stepped forward.

His stance was unshaken, unbothered by the weight of the legend they whispered.

He planted his massive shield into the earth, its surface scarred, dented, worn, but unbroken.

His eyes, as old as the mountains, burned with something deep and absolute.

And in that moment, the soldiers saw it...

The truth in the legend.

Because Taril was still standing, and his war was not over.

The name hung in the air like an unsheathed blade, sharp and undeniable.

"Taril Ironborn."

For a moment, no one moved.

Then, as if something ancient had been set into motion, the reaction rippled through the gathered soldiers.

Some cheered, their voices raw with disbelief and awe.

Others stood frozen, gripping their weapons as if the weight of their reality had just shifted beneath their feet.

A few took a step back, fear creeping into their eyes – not fear of battle, not fear of death, but fear of standing in the presence of something that should not exist.

Because they had seen the battle.

They had watched these warriors carve through the undead as if they had done so for centuries.

And now, they stood before them – not just men, but myths given form.

Eldric's breath was steady, but his heart hammered against his ribs.

He had spent his life fighting, leading men, carving out survival in a world that sought to end them every night.

But this?

This was different.

He could still hear his older brother's voice, low and reverent, telling stories of a time before the frost, before the curse, of a war that tore the heavens and sundered the land: *When the world still had kings, Taril stood where no other could. And beside him, an avalanche of a man – Drunnyak the Unrelenting.*

He had thought them stories.

Tales meant to keep restless boys entertained, meant to make old men feel like the past had once been greater than the present.

And yet…

Here they were.

And then, a child's voice rose above the murmurs. "My father was right!" The boy's words struck the silence like a spark to dry tinder. "Borgrim was right!" Caelan's voice trembled with excitement, his small fists clenched at his sides. "He told me stories! My father did too! They said you'd come back one day! They said you would save us!"

His breath caught, his eyes locking onto Drunnyak, filled with something deeper than belief.

Validation.

Taril exhaled through his nose, his expression unreadable, but his grip tightened on his shield.

The soldiers did not move closer.

Not out of fear of an enemy – but out of reverence.

They had heard tales of men who had held back the tides of war.

They had heard whispers of warriors who had once defied gods.

And now…

They stood before them.

Legends, walking once more.

As Eldric approached their saviours, he noticed that Caelan had never moved.

Even after the battle ended, even as the undead crumbled away with the morning, even as the soldiers had whispered uncertain prayers over the fallen, he never left Drunnyak's side.

The boy had wrapped his small arms around the massive warrior's unmoving form, shielding him with his own frail body, as if his warmth alone could pull Drunnyak back to life.

Even when the soldiers tried to gently pull him away, he had clung tighter, shaking his head.

"No," he had whispered, his voice raw from exhaustion and grief. "He's not dead. He just needs to wake up."

And so, they had let him be.

Eldric stepped forward, closer to Taril. His presence was commanding – even in weariness, the weight of leadership settled across his broad shoulders. His piercing gaze swept over the unconscious warriors, taking in their unusual attire, their strange but unmistakable presence. "I am Captain Eldric," he said, his voice firm, yet lacking hostility. "Leader of this village's watch."

He looked toward the others, measuring their reaction.

A pause settled between them, heavy, deliberate. The standing warriors exchanged glances, unspoken words passing in the silence.

Then, at last, Taril stepped forward, resting his massive shield on the ground. His presence was immovable – like the mountain itself. "Pleasure to make your acquaintance, Eldric."

Taril looked to his companions, and through his eyes they understood the message.

No mention of their awakening.

No mention of Harinnil.

For now, they would listen. For now, they would learn.

Because something in this world was wrong.

And the first step to understanding it was to let the living tell their side of the story.

The moment hung thick in the frozen air, the only sound the soft whisper of the wind sweeping through the remains of battle.

Then – a sudden gasp.

A sharp intake of breath.

Drunnyak twitched.

Drunnyak grunted, rubbing the back of his neck, casting Taril a sideways glance. "Hells," he muttered under his breath, "seems we've got a fan club."

A shudder rippled through his massive frame, his fingers curling slightly, his chest rising with a sudden, sharp inhale.

Caelan froze.

For a breath, nothing moved.

Then, with a strained groan, Drunnyak's eyes snapped open.

Pale, piercing. Alive.

And the first thing he saw was the boy, still clutching his tunic with everything he had, his face pressed into his chest, his breath uneven with quiet sobs.

Drunnyak's brow furrowed slightly as he blinked, his mind sluggish, his body aching as if he had fought the entire world and barely crawled out alive. "Hells, kid." His voice came, rough as stone. "You been cryin' on me all night?"

Caelan sniffed sharply, his small hands tightening their grip, unwilling to let go.

Drunnyak let out a deep sigh, his massive hand coming to rest gently on the boy's back. "All right, all right," he muttered, his voice quieter now. "I'm here, lad."

He forced himself upright, his muscles screaming in protest, as if his own body had not yet decided if it would let him live.

But he was Drunnyak.

His body did not get a choice.

Nearby, another form stirred. A shallow breath.

Fingers twitching against the frozen earth. A shift in the air.

The subtle, unmistakable hum of something deeper than flesh waking.

Nashir's eyes fluttered open.

For a moment, all he saw was the sky.

The swirling, clouded, sunless sky of Maud.

He inhaled slowly, feeling the ache of his bones, the weight of something deeper than exhaustion pressing against his body.

His magic had drained itself to the very root, and it was unfamiliar.

Not the kind of depletion that came from pushing too far, reaching beyond his limits.

No, this was something else.

As if the world itself had taken something from him.

As if it had demanded more than he was willing to give.

His fingers curled into the dirt. It felt different.

Not the same world he once knew, even though he didn't remember everything.

His chest rose sharply as he finally pushed himself up onto his elbows.

A soldier let out a sharp curse as he did, stumbling back.

All eyes turned to him.

And Nashir, still blinking against the ache in his limbs, smiled faintly. "Well," his voice was hoarse but amused, "I suppose I should be thankful you didn't bury me yet."

Drunnyak let out a short, rough laugh, still seated where he had woken, his arm around Caelan. "Would've," he grumbled, "if I could lift your skinny arse."

The moment Nashir sat up, Drunnyak let out a deep exhale, rubbing a massive hand over his face.

"By the gods," he muttered. "Did we win or just get our arses handed to us?"

"Hard to say," Nashir replied, rolling his shoulders with a groan. "Depends on whether you call passing out in the middle of battle a victory."

Drunnyak squinted at him, then huffed. "I don't remember you standing by when I woke up, twig."

Before Nashir could retort, a strong arm wrapped around Drunnyak's massive shoulder and pulled him in.

Taril.

The dwarf's grip was unyielding, his broad form pressing against Drunnyak's side in an embrace that was half reunion, half restraint.

"Yer still breathin', ya thick-headed fool," Taril grumbled, his voice somewhere between relief and reprimand. "That's all that matters."

Drunnyak let out a low chuckle, clasping a massive hand around the back of Taril's neck in return. "Takes more than a thousand rotting bastards to put me down," he muttered.

Then, another force crashed into him.

Small arms, but a grip like iron.

Caelan.

Still hugging him, still clutching at his tunic like he never planned to let go.

Drunnyak sighed, resting his chin on the boy's head, squeezing his shoulder gently. "Didn't scare ya too bad, did I, lad?"

Caelan shook his head furiously against his chest, sniffling. "You better not do that again."

Drunnyak chuckled, ruffling his hair. "Aye, I'll try not to. But you know me, lad. I love my naps."

That earned a small laugh from the boy, muffled but real.

Then…

"Naps?" Niv's voice rang through the air, sharp with mockery.

Drunnyak glanced up just in time to see her and Alentar making their way toward them, her golden eyes glinting with mischief.

"Is that what we're calling fainting now?" she teased.

Drunnyak scowled. "I didn't faint."

"You fell like a sack of potatoes," Alentar cut in smoothly, smirking as he stepped closer. "Hardly made a sound. I'd call that fainting."

Niv grinned, stepping around to lean against Taril's shoulder. "I've seen virgin maidens last longer on their wedding nights."

Drunnyak groaned loudly, rubbing his face. "You know, I preferred you lot when you weren't talkin'."

"We preferred you when you weren't faintin," Taril muttered under his breath, earning a snort from Nashir and a chuckle from Alentar.

The whole group descended into laughter, the weight of battle, of their exhaustion, momentarily lifted.

The soldiers around them, however, watched in stunned silence, mesmerised by their presence.

They had fought alongside these warriors.

They had seen them carve through the horde like legends come to life.

But now they bickered, they laughed, they embraced as if they had not just survived an impossible battle, but as if they had known each other for lifetimes.

And, in a way, they had.

Eldric cleared his throat, stepping forward, drawing their attention.

The laughter settled, but the warmth remained.

Drunnyak, still grinning, turned to the village captain, nodding. "Captain Eldric," he rumbled. "Seems I owe you and your men my thanks."

Taril inclined his head as well. "Aye. We're grateful for the aid – and the company."

Nashir, still sitting but looking more alert, offered a small, appreciative nod. "Without your men holding that line, this might've been a very different battle," he added.

Eldric studied them for a moment, as if still trying to understand exactly what they were. Then he gave a slow nod. "You fight well," he admitted. "And I'd rather have you on my side than against me."

Drunnyak smirked, cracking his knuckles. "Aye, that's usually how it goes."

Niv rolled her eyes. "And on that note, where's our shadow?" she muttered, looking around.

The group followed her gaze, scanning the battlefield.

Alentar was gone again.

"Damn him," Drunnyak grumbled, shifting to his feet, wincing as his body protested. "We just woke up, he was here just a few seconds ago, and he's already off scouting."

"He's always watching," Nashir murmured.

"Aye," Taril agreed, glancing up toward the higher rocks. "And I'd wager he's not far."

And they were right.

Because when they turned their eyes upward…

They found him.

Alentar stood high above them, perched atop a jagged rock formation that loomed over the battlefield.

His dark cloak billowed slightly in the cold wind, his stance effortless, balanced, like he belonged there, like the mountain itself welcomed him.

His emerald eyes scanned the horizon, sharp, calculating, ever searching.

For movement.

For threats.

For whatever came next.

He didn't need to look down to know they had seen him.

He simply raised one brow, smirking slightly, before returning his gaze to the vast, frozen landscape.

Because even though the battle was over…

The fight was far from finished.

The laughter lingered, the warmth of camaraderie still fresh in the cold air, but as the group settled, as the weight of exhaustion returned, Drunnyak felt something tug at his tunic.

A small hand, hesitant but firm.

He looked down. Caelan.

The boy's wide eyes, still damp from earlier, shone with something deeper now.

Not just relief. Not just admiration.

Reverence.

The kind of unshaken belief that could bend steel and break men.

The belief of a child who had never let go of hope.

Slowly, Caelan unclasped something from his belt and held it up.

Drunnyak stared.

It was not wood.

Not some child's carving.

It was stone, smooth and cold, etched with time, with devotion, with belief.

A small idol, barely the size of the boy's palm, sculpted with careful precision, showing the unmistakable form of a warrior, broad-shouldered and fierce.

It had weathered age and handling, its edges smoothed by years of being held, prayed to, carried as if it were a part of the boy himself.

Drunnyak could see small scratches, a faint crack near the base – proof that it had fallen, been dropped, yet never abandoned.

This was not a simple trinket. This was a relic.

Something passed down, or perhaps made in desperate hope, a tether to something greater.

And Drunnyak, for all his strength, for all his battle-tested resolve, had no idea what to do with it.

"I always believed in you," Caelan whispered.

Drunnyak's jaw clenched, unreadable emotions swirling beneath his gruff exterior.

Caelan swallowed hard, gripping the figurine tighter. "When my father left, I prayed to you to bring him back. When the nights got too long, I held on to you. When I was scared, when I thought we wouldn't make it, I told myself that you were coming." The boy's voice quivered, but his eyes never wavered. "And you did."

A moment of silence stretched between them.

The world felt smaller.

The wind faded into the distance.

Only the boy and the giant of a man that did not yet know he was one remained.

Drunnyak, for all his strength, for all his battle-tested resolve, could not speak at first.

He stared at the idol, at the child who had held his name in his heart long before he had even woken.

Then, slowly, his massive hand reached out.

He took the idol – carefully, as if it were something fragile.

Turned it over in his rough fingers. The weight of it was real. Solid.

The stone was cold, but the warmth from Caelan's hands still clung to it.

This was not just belief. This was faith.

Drunnyak, for the first time in his long and brutal life, had no idea how to carry that weight. "I ain't a saviour, kid," he finally muttered, voice gruff but low. "I ain't a god."

Caelan shook his head. "You don't have to be."

Drunnyak blinked.

Caelan took a deep breath, his small chest rising and falling as he spoke with certainty. "You're Drunnyak! That's enough."

The words hit something deep inside Drunnyak.

Something he didn't understand. Something he wasn't ready to face.

So he did what he always did.

He grunted, shoved the idol back into the boy's hands, and ruffled his hair – perhaps rougher than necessary.

"Keep it," he said, forcing a smirk. "Might be worth something someday."

Caelan smiled through his tears, gripping it like a treasure.

And for the first time, Drunnyak realised…

Maybe to the boy, it was.

A voice broke the silence, brimming with energy. "Come with us!"

Drunnyak turned, his body still heavy from exhaustion, to find Eldric grinning – a rare sight for a man who had spent his life fighting through endless nights.

The captain no longer looked like a commander assessing a battlefield.

He looked like a man who had just witnessed a legend come to life.

"You need food, shelter," Eldric gestured widely, a laugh escaping him, "and, hells, we need to hear your story! Borgrim will want to be the first to throw a mug in your hands, and the whole village will have your names on their lips before night falls!"

The tension that had gripped the soldiers finally broke.

Some clapped each other on the back, their excitement spreading like wildfire, murmuring in half-dazed wonder.

"Taril Ironborn. Drunnyak the Unrelenting. They're real."

"They fought with us. By the gods, they fought with *us*!"

Even the younger ones, those barely more than boys, grinned in wide-eyed awe, their shoulders no longer weighed by fear but lifted by something else – hope.

"Come on," Eldric urged, stepping forward, voice filled with a new-found warmth. "You've given us more than a victory tonight. You've given us a story we'll tell for generations. The least we can do is offer you a warm fire and a feast worthy of warriors."

The group glanced at one another.

Taril huffed, amused. "Didn't expect a welcome like this."

Drunnyak smirked, cracking his knuckles. "Can't say no to food, ale, and a bit of admiration."

Niv arched a brow, smiling. "I do like an audience."

Nashir, still weary, but watching the scene unfold with quiet amusement, murmured, "It would be rude to refuse such enthusiasm."

Drunnyak looked down at Caelan, who was beaming up at him, clutching his idol like a holy relic.

"Well, lad?" Drunnyak asked, ruffling his hair. "Think your village is ready for us?"

Caelan nodded so hard it was a wonder his head stayed on his shoulders. "Now they'll see, Mr Drunnyak! They'll all see I wasn't crazy!"

Eldric laughed heartily, waving his men forward. "Then let's not keep them waiting any longer!"

With cheers, with renewed spirits, the soldiers rallied around their long-awaited heroes.

A cheer broke through the air, unbidden, raw with excitement.

"To the village!" one soldier shouted, raising his blade.

Another clapped his comrade's back. "Aye! The Goat's gonna have a story to tell for years!"

The wave caught like fire, spreading among them.

Forgetting exhaustion, forgetting pain, the soldiers moved like men who had won more than just survival.

They had fought beside something greater than myth.

And now they would celebrate it.

Soldiers whispered, some in hushed reverence, others in giddy disbelief.

Even after the horrors of the night, they could not contain their excitement.

Because for the first time in longer than any of them could remember…

It felt like the world had given something back.

The soldiers gathered their gear, adjusting weapons, tightening belts, murmuring among themselves as they prepared to return to the village.

Yet their movements were distracted – their eyes flickering constantly toward the newcomers.

They whispered, half in awe, half in disbelief, throwing glances at Drunnyak, at Taril, at Nashir…

At legends who walked among them.

But it was not just their strength and presence that unsettled the men.

It was her.

Niv.

She moved with effortless grace, her form draped in the scintillating robe that shimmered like woven steel and clung in ways that did nothing to conceal the fullness of her figure.

And the soldiers noticed.

They were warriors, men who had spent their nights surrounded by death, fighting the endless tide of the cursed.

But now…

Now, they were standing in the presence of something else entirely.

More than a woman.

Something unnatural.

Something perfect.

One soldier nearly stumbled over his own feet as he caught sight of her, earning a quick jab to the ribs from a comrade.

Another, barely older than a boy, visibly swallowed, as if trying to steady himself from whatever spell had just been cast upon his senses.

A veteran near the front sighed quietly, shaking his head. "The stories never mentioned this part," he muttered.

"What stories?" his companion whispered back.

"The ones about Taril and Drunnyak," the man replied. "Didn't think they walked with an elf goddess, too."

Niv arched a perfectly shaped brow, catching their stares with a flick of her golden gaze.

Then...

She smirked.

And the soldier who had been staring too long tripped over his own boots.

Drunnyak let out a bark of laughter, shaking his head as he stretched out his shoulders. "Happens every time," he muttered under his breath.

Taril grunted. "Hmph. Bloody fools," he said, but there was a hint of amusement in his rough voice.

Nashir, ever the observer, watched with quiet amusement, but said nothing.

As for Niv, she sighed dramatically, twirling a golden strand of hair between her fingers. "What?" she mused, her voice light, teasing. "I thought warriors were supposed to have more discipline than this."

Drunnyak smirked. "They fight the undead every night, lass. They ain't built for this kind of danger."

The men quickly looked away, some clearing their throats, others pretending to adjust their weapons – but the glances did not stop.

And so, amidst whispers, stolen looks, and legends stirring back to life...

As the group made their way up the mountain path, flanked by their new-found comrades, the air pulsed with a rare and unshaken energy.

For the first time since awakening, they weren't just warriors in a broken world.

They were part of it, and for now, that was enough.

THROUGH THE GATES
OF THE LIVING

The mountain winds howled, but Eldric walked ahead, unwavering, his presence alone commanding those at the next watch to hold their ground but ask no questions.

The hidden path, narrow and treacherous, wove between towering cliffs of rock and ice, a lifeline carved over generations to keep the village safe from threats both seen and unseen. Few outsiders had ever set foot upon it. Even fewer had been welcomed.

But as they approached the checkpoint, figures emerged from the shadows.

The young watch.

Barely older than sixteen winters, these were not yet men, but not boys either. Their hands gripped spears and bows with the weight of duty, their eyes sharp, trained, disciplined. The next generation of warriors, learning to defend the only home they had ever known.

Yet as they stood their ground, they weren't looking at the returning soldiers.

They were staring at something they had never seen before.

Among the young warriors, one figure stood taller, more seasoned than the rest.

Edric.

He had been descending toward the trench with his team, as he did every morning, preparing to check the remains of the night's battle.

But now he had stopped in his tracks.

Because what was walking toward them was not just returning soldiers.

It was something out of firelight stories.

Drunnyak, a mountain of muscle, his sheer size an overwhelming presence, as if a force of nature had learned to walk.

Taril, armoured head to toe, his shield broad enough to cover most of a man's body, his war hammer slung over his back like it weighed nothing.

And then... the elves.

The young watch stiffened.

Eyes widened. Hands tightened on weapons, though not in aggression, but in stunned awe.

Because elves did not exist – at least, they had never seen one.

And yet...

Here they were.

Niv, ethereal, unnatural, her golden hair glowing even in the dull torchlight, her perfect features almost too flawless to be real.

Nashir, his emerald eyes sharp and knowing, his presence humming with a quiet power that made the very air feel different.

Alentar, his movement too precise, too fluid, like a predator that had never lost a hunt.

They looked ageless, untouched by the weight of years, their beauty an unsettling contrast against the world's harsh reality.

The young soldiers – boys who had grown up only knowing hardship, frost and death – had never seen anything like them.

"Captain Eldric... who are they?" Ronan, the eldest among them, barely managed to find his voice.

Eldric didn't slow his stride. "They walk with us."

The younger soldiers exchanged frantic looks.

Some stared in disbelief at the elves, their minds struggling to reconcile what they had been told their whole lives – that such beings were long gone.

Others focused on Drunnyak and Taril, their minds flashing back to whispered tales of warriors who once stood against the darkness.

But it was Caelan who spoke next. "See?! I told you!" His voice rang through the checkpoint like a war cry. He stepped forward, gripping his idol so tightly his knuckles turned white, his entire body trembling – not from fear, but from sheer vindication. "You all thought I was crazy! But look at them! They're real!"

Silence.

Every young warrior turned to Eldric, as if waiting for him to correct the boy, to tell them it was all a misunderstanding.

But when the captain gave a slow, steady nod...

The air shifted.

Some of the younger watchmen gasped, their spears lowering slightly as they processed the truth.

One lad, no older than fourteen, took a hesitant step back, as if the sight of the elves alone had shaken something inside him.

Another whispered under his breath, "Elves... I thought they were just stories."

"By the gods..." another murmured, eyes darting between Taril and Drunnyak.

One of the soldiers said, "They fought the cursed like they were nothing."

Even Edric, who had seen horrors beyond his years, rubbed a gloved hand over his mouth, exhaling slowly. "Hells, Borgrim's never going to let us hear the end of this."

Drunnyak, watching the sheer disbelief on their faces, grinned and crossed his arms. "Guess we've got a bit of a reputation."

Taril huffed, adjusting his war hammer. "Seems we do."

Niv, her golden eyes watching the stunned soldiers with amusement, smirked. "You'd think they'd never seen something beautiful before."

One of the younger boys turned scarlet, his wide eyes locked onto Niv as if he had just glimpsed something otherworldly, beyond mortal reach.

She noticed.

Without a word, she tilted her head ever so slightly, golden strands of hair cascading over her shoulder, catching the dim torchlight like liquid fire.

Then, with a slow, deliberate grace, she lifted two fingers to her lips – and with the barest flick of her wrist, she sent the faintest, most effortless kiss into the cold night air.

It was barely a movement, but it unravelled the poor lad instantly.

His knees buckled slightly, his breath caught in his throat, and if not for the soldier beside him grabbing his arm, he might have actually collapsed where he stood.

The other men stared, some swallowing hard, others pretending not to notice the way their own gazes had lingered just a little too long.

"For god's sake, boy, keep your feet!" one of the older guards muttered, clapping the lad on the back hard enough to nearly send him face first into the snow.

Niv only smiled, turning forward once more – graceful, untouchable, and entirely too pleased with herself.

Alentar said nothing, his sharp gaze watching the reactions with his usual quiet intensity.

Nashir, ever composed, simply murmured, "The world remembers, even when we do not."

The young soldiers still stood frozen, stuck between awe and reverence.

But Eldric wasn't about to let them linger. "Move aside and get on with your watch," he ordered, his voice carrying the tone of a man who had long accepted the impossible and had no time for hesitation. "We're going home."

Ronan blinked, then slowly nodded. He turned to his men, voice steady but tinged with something more – awe. "Stand down. Let them through."

The young watch stepped aside, parting like a tide, their gazes never leaving the figures walking past them.

As the group continued up the path, the murmurs of disbelief still echoed behind them.

And Caelan?

He walked taller than ever, grinning like he had just won the greatest battle of his life.

Because now, for the first time, the whole village would see the truth.

He had been right all along.

The closer they came to the village, the more the air changed.

At first, it was subtle – a few wandering villagers glancing up from their morning routines, hands pausing over firewood, tools and baskets. They expected returning soldiers, tired but alive.

What they didn't expect was this.

Then the first soldier broke away from the group, stopping at the mouth of a narrow street, his voice rising with disbelief and excitement. "It's them."

Another soldier turned, blinking. "Who?"

The first one didn't answer. He just stared. And then, he ran.

The word raced through the village like wildfire.

Life paused.

Shopkeepers abandoned their stalls. Blacksmiths left the forge in mid-swing, molten iron forgotten. Farmers at the cavern entrance dropped their tools, animals scattering in confusion. Chickens squawked as children darted past, laughter bubbling with excitement as they ran to see the commotion.

The heroes, who had known nothing but the battlefield since awakening, found themselves stepping into something… alive.

The village wasn't just surviving.

It was living.

Though carved into the harsh mountains, it pulsed with warmth. A place of resilience, where homes had been built into rock and wood, where people fought against the cold, against the curse, and refused to let the world take their humanity.

The scent of woodsmoke, cooked meat, and burning oil filled the air.

Torches lined the streets, their glow pushing back the ever-present grey.

And above it all, the sound of children laughing, merchants calling, hammers ringing against anvils.

The group slowed, taking it in.

Drunnyak breathed deeply, his chest rising as he took in the mingling scents. "This…" he muttered, rubbing his chin. "This is good."

Taril nodded once. "Better than I expected."

Nashir said nothing, only watching. Not just the people, but the earth itself. The way plants fought through the frost, how nature itself had adapted, endured.

Alentar, sharp as ever, observed the pathways, the defences, how the village had carved itself into survival. His eyes flicked to hidden watchpoints, places where an ambush could be laid. They were prepared.

Then – a sudden shriek.

Small feet pounding against the frozen stone.

Eldric barely had time to react before two tiny bodies slammed into him – his daughters.

"Papa!"

He let out a surprised grunt, barely catching them in time, their little arms wrapping around his waist with all their strength.

Behind them, Marianne hurried forward, her face a storm of emotions – relief, worry, love.

She met his gaze, and without a word, he pulled her into an embrace.

The scene rippled outward.

Other soldiers, hesitant at first, then overcome, found themselves in the arms of waiting families.

Wives ran to husbands, children clung to fathers they had prayed would return.

One woman sobbed into a soldier's shoulder, gripping him like she never planned to let go.

A man clutched his brother's arm, shaking with laughter and tears.

Their world was never safe, never certain, but today, they had made it home.

The newcomers watched, silent.

Drunnyak's grin softened. "Huh."

Niv, watching a mother kiss her husband's forehead, sighed. "You almost forget what it's like, don't you?"

Nashir only nodded.

Alentar, usually detached, lowered his gaze, a flicker of something unreadable in his emerald eyes.

Even Taril, who had never been one for sentiment, found himself watching the reunions a little longer than necessary.

And then, as if drawn by something deeper than curiosity, their gazes landed on the elves.

Silence.

Their expressions shifted from shock to awe. To something far more profound.

Because elves did not exist.

And yet – here they were.

Niv's golden hair caught the light like something out of a dream, her sharp, knowing gaze sweeping over them with the kind of presence that made men both weak and reverent.

Nashir stood still, watching them back, studying them like a scholar reads an ancient text.

Alentar remained poised, unreadable, but his presence alone felt like a blade waiting to be drawn.

Villagers shifted uncomfortably, some clutching charms, some whispering old prayers.

Then someone finally spoke. "Who... who are they?" A single voice. Small, hesitant.

And then another. "They look like... but no... that's not possible..."

The murmurs rose again, frantic, disbelieving.

And then...

Caelan stepped forward. Still clutching the small idol at his belt, his breath shaky, but his voice strong. "They're the ones we've been waiting for."

Silence fell over the village.

All eyes turned to Eldric.

Waiting for confirmation.

The captain, still holding his daughters close, gave a single nod.

Then, a shadow passed over them.

Not from the sky.

From the doorway of The Stubborn Goat.

A familiar stocky figure stepped into the light, wiping his hands on his apron.

Borgrim.

His grumbling voice was already forming some sharp remark – until he saw them.

The glass slipped from his fingers, crashing against the ground.

The tavern fell silent behind him.

His bushy brows shot up so high they nearly disappeared under his thick forehead.

His mouth opened, then shut.

Then opened again.

"By the gods..."

His wide-eyed stare locked onto Taril first, then Drunnyak, then Nashir.

The shock on his face wasn't just from recognition – it was from something deeper.

Something passed down.

Borgrim's gaze fell upon Taril's armour – specifically, the engravings upon his breastplate.

An ancient symbol.

A towering mountain split down the middle, a river of molten gold flowing between its jagged peaks. Beneath it, two crossed war hammers, their heads inscribed with celestial runes, encircled by a ring of broken chains.

It was a crest long lost to history.

A crest that still lingered in Borgrim's blood, because he was wearing it too.

Hanging from a thick leather cord around his neck, barely noticed before, was an amulet bearing the very same emblem – worn, battered, but unmistakable.

The moment Taril saw it, something deep inside him stirred.

Memories – distant, fractured – flashed in the back of his mind.

A great hall, carved into the heart of a mountain. The glow of forges, the sound of steel on anvil. A people built from stone and fire, strong and unyielding.

And among them, his own bloodline.

The ones who swore fealty, loyalty and kinship to him.

Borgrim's lips parted as realisation struck him. His breath hitched, his hands shook.

He knew.

With slow, trembling steps, Borgrim moved forward.

Each step felt like it carried the weight of centuries.

Then, as he stood before Taril, his legs gave out.

The stocky dwarf fell to his knees, gripping whatever he could – Taril's gauntlet, the edge of his armour – as if grounding himself in the impossible truth.

His voice, when it came, was barely above a whisper – hoarse, reverent, filled with something deeper than faith. "My King… my creator… you have returned. The legends were true."

Borgrim's voice carried through the square like a thunderclap, yet he had barely whispered.

And the world stood still.

A hush fell over the village, so complete it felt as if the wind itself had stopped.

Soldiers who had fought alongside Taril only moments ago, warriors hardened by the horrors of endless nights, now stood frozen, their breath stolen from their chests.

Villagers who had murmured in curiosity now stood in silence, eyes shifting between the kneeling dwarf and the man he swore fealty to.

Even those too young to understand felt the shift.

A little girl, barely past five winters, tugged at her father's sleeve, pointing with wide, wondering eyes. "Papa… is he a king?" she whispered.

Her father, a strong, weathered man, had no answer.

Taril looked down at Borgrim, at the amulet around the dwarf's neck – the same symbol that marked his own armour.

His gloved hand brushed the engraving on his chestplate.

He had worn it without thought. It had always been there, and yet, only now did it feel like something more than metal.

His brow furrowed, his throat tightening with something he did not understand.

"I…" His voice, deep and steady, wavered. He should have known. But he didn't. Not yet. He reached down, grasping Borgrim's arm – not to push him away, but to steady him. "Rise."

Borgrim hesitated.

But when Taril's grip tightened, strong and unwavering, the dwarf finally obeyed.

Borgrim's breath trembled, but his voice did not break. "You are back, My King."

Drunnyak, towering as ever, grinned, his sharp teeth flashing as he stepped closer, clapping Taril on the back with enough force to make even the armoured dwarf shift. "Well, damn, old man. Seems you had yourself a whole damn people waiting for you," he chuckled. His voice carried warmth, a rare moment of pure sincerity. He crossed his arms, looking at Borgrim, then back at Taril. "And you know what? If anyone deserves that, it's you."

For once, there was no jest, no sarcasm. Just pride.

Taril looked up, meeting his gaze.

Drunnyak nodded once, solid and firm.

A gesture that said, *We've fought together, bled together. If you have a home in this world, you can be damn sure we'll defend it with you.*

Then came Niv. She stepped forward, arms still lazily crossed, a teasing smirk playing at her lips, but her eyes were soft. "A king, huh?" she mused. Her golden gaze swept over Taril, as if seeing him in a new light. "I suppose that suits you." She shifted closer, placing a gentle hand on his shoulder. "It's good to see you find a piece of yourself, Taril."

Her voice, though playful, held no mockery.

Only genuine warmth.

Taril looked at her, then at Drunnyak, and then at all of them.

111

Nashir, standing slightly behind, his staff held loosely in his hand, gave a small, knowing nod.

Alentar, quiet and watchful, said nothing — he didn't need to.

Because even he, the most cautious of them, did not need to question if Taril deserved this moment.

He did.

The moment between Taril and Borgrim was the spark that set the village ablaze – not with fire, but with something deeper.

Recognition.

Belief.

Hope.

The murmurs spread like ripples through water, quiet at first, then growing, swelling into something none of them could control.

"Did you hear what he called him?"

"King. He called him a king."

"A creator."

"By the gods, it's true. The stories were true!"

Some villagers stumbled back, hands to their mouths, overwhelmed. Others fell to their knees, their eyes wide with something between reverence and disbelief.

The elders of the village – those who had spent decades whispering old stories, speaking of the past like a distant myth – stood in silent awe.

One of them, a woman with silver-threaded hair, her face lined with years of hardship, pressed a trembling hand to her chest. "The Ironborn has returned," she whispered.

Others nodded, as if saying it aloud solidified the impossible truth before them.

The warriors, those hardened by endless battles against the night, looked to each other.

They had bled and fought for survival for countless winters.

But never before had they stood in the presence of something greater than themselves.

Something legendary.

One of the men – a soldier who had fought at Eldric's side for years, his face streaked with dried blood and exhaustion – let out a breath he hadn't realised he'd been holding. "I thought these were just stories," he muttered.

"They were," another soldier said, his voice barely above a whisper. "But no story ever fought like they did."

Their gazes shifted – not just to Taril, but to all of them.

This wasn't just about Taril's past.

The village was looking at more than warriors. They were looking at legends.

For the first time in their weary lives, they saw something they had never dared to hope for.

A better future.

The night had always come.

The undead had always risen.

The fight had always been theirs alone.

But now… it wasn't.

A young boy, no older than ten, stepped forward hesitantly, his eyes locked onto Taril. He had no memory of the world before, no understanding of who these warriors once were – only the stories passed down.

And yet, he did the only thing his heart told him to do.

He dropped to one knee.

A second later, another villager followed.

Then another.

Then another.

It wasn't an act of worship.

It was an act of belief.

They had stood alone for so long.

Now, they weren't alone any more.

Eldric, watching the unfolding moment, closed his eyes briefly, exhaling as if part of the weight had been lifted from his shoulders.

For the first time in years, the village was not just surviving. It was awakening.

Something had changed, and whether they were ready or not, they were about to see just how much.

The village was already reeling.

Taril's name had shaken their understanding of history. The weight of something ancient, something once thought lost, had settled over them like the first breath of a long-forgotten storm... and then, another shift.

A rustling through the crowd. Heavy, staggering steps.

Boots dragging against the frozen earth.

Heads turned, conversations cut short, murmurs fading into silence.

Young Edric, one of the day watch, came first – his breath laboured, his face pale, his arms braced beneath the massive weight of a man who should not be standing.

Behind him, two more soldiers struggled under the burden, their expressions a mixture of exhaustion and urgency.

And between them, Garric.

The titan of the village.

The warrior who had left unshaken, unbreakable, unrelenting.

Now a ruin of himself.

His face was barely recognisable beneath dried blood and swelling bruises. His once-unyielding frame was slashed and beaten, armour dented, torn in places, exposing deep wounds along his arms and torso.

Each step was agony. Yet he did not fall.

Not Garric.

Not the man who had bled for this village, who had shaped it with his own two hands.

And when Eldric saw him, everything else ceased to exist.

His daughters still clung to him, but his arms around them loosened.

His eyes, wide with disbelief, locked onto his brother.

He did not move. Not at first.

Because for weeks, he had prepared himself for this moment.

But in his mind, Garric was supposed to return standing tall or not at all.

Unshaken.

Unbreakable.

And yet the man before him was barely holding on.

A sharp intake of breath. A tiny blur of movement.

Caelan.

His small frame darted from Eldric and Drunnyak's side, running faster than his feet could carry him, stumbling in his rush, but never stopping.

Wide, tear-filled eyes locked onto his father's battered, broken form. "Daddy!"

The sound pierced the air like a blade.

The village fell silent once more. They did not know how to react. Not to this.

Not to seeing Garric – their strongest, their most unshakeable – reduced to this state.

Not to the sight of the child running toward the man they had thought lost.

Not to the weight of the unknown now pressing upon them all.

Even the new warriors – the ones who had fought through the trenches, who had witnessed the impossible – stood still.

They had seen battle. They had seen monsters.

But this was something different.

A man returning from the edge of death, carrying answers none of them had yet dared to ask.

Their gazes flicked toward each other, unspoken thoughts rippling between them.

All except for one.

Opilkhos.

He did not look at Garric. He did not look at the village.

His gaze was distant, lost, as if he was remembering something.

His fingers clenched at his sides, white-knuckled, as if holding on to something unseen.

As if he too should remember something. Something just beyond reach.

The village did not notice.

His companions did not notice, but within him, a battle of a different kind was stirring.

The village was holding its breath.

Garric had returned – broken, battered, but alive.

Caelan clung to him, his tiny arms wrapped tightly around his father's leg, refusing to let go.

Eldric's mind was still reeling, caught between relief and the raw reality of his brother's wounds.

The soldiers, the villagers – they were all frozen, caught in the weight of the moment.

But not Opilkhos. Something was stirring inside him. A memory – not whole, not clear, but sudden and undeniable. His breath shallowed. His lips parted, and before he even realised he was speaking, the name escaped. "Garrents…"

It was barely more than a whisper.

Soft. Faint.

But his companions heard it.

Drunnyak's head tilted slightly.

Niv's golden eyes flicked toward him.

Taril, Nashir and Alentar shifted their attention, watching him carefully.

They recognised the change. The way his posture stiffened.

The way his expression shifted – not in confusion, but in recognition.

Then…

Opilkhos fixed his gaze upon Garric. His eyes widened.

Because the face before him – the battered, bloodied warrior barely standing – was the spitting image of the vision that had just flashed through his mind.

The same strength. The same presence.

The same feeling of something greater than a man standing before him.

His voice came stronger this time – unshaken, but filled with disbelief. "Ian Garrents."

The name landed like a hammer striking stone, and the reaction was immediate.

Borgrim's eyes snapped toward him, his mouth slightly agape.

Eldric turned sharply, his expression shifting from concern to outright shock.

And Garric – even through the pain, even through the exhaustion – lifted his head fully.

His stare locked onto Opilkhos.

He ignored the pain, the wounds screaming through his body.

He ignored the weight of Caelan still clinging to him.

Because nothing – not even his suffering – could have prepared him for what he had just heard.

"How do you know the name of our forefather?"

His voice was hoarse but firm, carrying the weight of generations.

The village fell completely silent.

The moment stretched – held between disbelief and something deeper.

Because that name was not one to be spoken by strangers. Even most of the villagers had never heard the name.

And yet Opilkhos had spoken it as if he had known it his entire life.

THE ECHO OF A NAME

Garric was a man of unyielding strength, a warrior whose body carried the weight of a lifetime of battles. Even now – broken, bloodied, nearly shattered by the horrors of his journey – he refused to falter.

The moment Opilkhos spoke the name, something in Garric reignited.

The exhaustion in his limbs, the pain clawing through his ribs – all of it became secondary.

With a sharp breath, he tore himself away from the soldiers supporting him.

Their protests meant nothing.

The fire in his chest burned hotter than his wounds.

He stood tall, unwavering, defiant.

Despite the agony in every step, he walked straight toward Opilkhos.

His shoulders remained squared, his jaw tight, his gaze locked onto the one who had spoken the name of a man long gone.

"How do you know our forefather's name?"

His voice, though strained from his injuries, carried the weight of history.

A voice that demanded an answer.

Eldric, still standing near, moved quickly. "Garric, wait." His tone urgent, his hands reaching out as if to steady his older brother. "Look at them!" he insisted, motioning toward the warriors at Opilkhos's side. "Do you not see who stands before you? Taril. Drunnyak. They are here."

Garric's breath hitched.

His eyes, glazed with pain and exhaustion, snapped toward the two figures Eldric had named, and for the first time since he had returned, uncertainty crossed his face.

For all his pain, for all his wounds, he had not been prepared for this.

His chest rose and fell sharply. His body – his very soul – seemed to battle itself.

A part of him wanted to doubt, but another part – the part of him that had lived through horrors, that had walked through an abyss and survived – knew that this was no ordinary trick of the mind.

They were real.

Drunnyak.

Taril.

The names he had grown up hearing in stories. The myths whispered in the dark, standing before him.

Garric's knees buckled, his body swaying.

The pain that had been ignored – that had been overshadowed by sheer will – was taking its toll.

His vision blurred, the edges of the world darkening. He was falling.

Before he could collapse, a firm grasp caught him.

Opilkhos.

The moment his hands touched Garric, the air shifted, and then a gasp rippled through the crowd.

A golden glow, warm and strong, erupted from Opilkhos, spiralling outward like an unseen force awakening for the first time.

It was unlike anything anyone had ever felt before.

Not a power of destruction.

Not an energy that threatened, but a warmth that embraced.

Like the first light of dawn breaking through eternal clouds.

The villagers stepped back in shock, their voices rising in awe and disbelief.

The soldiers felt it course through them – gentle, but powerful.

Then, the light grew.

From Opilkhos's armour, the radiance expanded, illuminating the entire square with a brilliance so strong that none could look upon it directly.

Eyes squeezed shut.

Hands raised instinctively to shield faces.

A golden explosion burst forth – not of force, but of light – washing over the entire village.

And as it passed, it left something behind.

Relief.

Healing.

Strength.

Every wound that had been carried, every ache from the battle, simply ceased to be.

Garric, whose body had been on the verge of death, stood straight once more.

Eldric and his soldiers, who bore the scars of the previous night's battle, felt their strength return in full.

Even Drunnyak, whose body had endured beyond its limits, flexed his fingers as the deep exhaustion vanished.

Nashir, who had pushed himself far beyond the natural, exhaled deeply, feeling the balance within him restored.

The villagers stared at one another, muscles feeling refreshed as if they had just woken from the most restful sleep.

And at the centre of it all, Opilkhos.

Still holding Garric, his golden aura flickering like the last embers of a dying flame.

His eyes met those around him. The faces of a people renewed.

He gave a small, soft smile.

Then his strength gave out. He collapsed, knees hitting the frozen earth.

The aura faded.

The light dimmed, and Opilkhos fell into unconsciousness.

The silence that followed was absolute. The village stood still.

For no one – not even his own companions – knew what they had just witnessed.

The golden light had faded, but its presence lingered in every breath, in every glance, in every heartbeat of the village.

The people stood in quiet astonishment, still reeling from what had unfolded before their eyes. The impossible had become real, and yet life had to continue.

Garric knew this.

Despite the rawness of his return, despite the pain he had felt only moments ago, he was still their leader, and a leader had to lead.

He exhaled, steadying himself before addressing his people.

"Listen well," he called, his voice cutting through the air like a blade – not harsh, but strong; commanding, yet measured. "What we have seen today – what we have felt – it is unlike anything we have ever known."

The murmurs rippled through the crowd again, but his firm tone steadied them.

"I know you are all shaken, mesmerised and curious about our visitors, but our work does not stop here. The village must stand, the watch must hold. We will speak of this, we will make sense of it." His gaze swept across the faces of his people, ensuring they felt included, that they felt part of this moment. "But later. Not now. Not while the day still belongs to us."

A few nods of acknowledgement spread through the crowd.

They trusted him.

They always had.

"Return to your homes, your posts. Tonight, when the fires are lit, I will share all that I know."

There was a beat – a hesitation. Then, like the shifting tide, the village began to move once more.

Farmers turned back toward the sheltered fields. Blacksmiths whispered to one another before returning to their forges. Soldiers regrouped, adjusting their gear, ready to relieve their shift.

The world kept turning, even in the wake of a miracle.

But before Garric turned toward his next task, his eyes found his brother.

Eldric.

His younger sibling who had borne the weight of his absence.

Eldric, who had fought, who had kept this village strong in his stead.

His face softened, if only for a moment.

Garric watched as Eldric walked toward his family, his hands already reaching for his wife.

Marianne stepped forward, her eyes filled with emotion, understanding everything that words could never say.

Eldric cupped her face and kissed her – deeply, fully.

Not just the kiss of a husband, but the kiss of a man who had fought another night, lived another day, and found the world changed by morning.

When he pulled away, he knelt.

His daughters – small, innocent, untouched by the horrors their parents carried – watched him with wide, expectant eyes.

"Go home, my loves," he said softly. "Stay inside until I return."

They nodded, trusting him without hesitation, wrapping their arms around him before running back to their home.

Caelan, however, did not move.

For the first time since he had been small enough to cling to Eldric's leg, he stood apart.

His shoulders squared. His chin lifted.

His father – the warrior, the leader, the man he had spent weeks praying for – was standing again.

Caelan did not need to be told. He would not go home.

He would stand, and so he did.

Tall. Proud.

By his father's side.

Garric watched this, saw it unfold with silent understanding, with a proud but discreet smile.

Then, at last, he turned toward the warriors that had emerged from legend itself.

Garric stepped toward Opilkhos's unconscious form.

The warriors around him tensed instinctively.

Even Taril – stoical and steady – shifted slightly, as if prepared to intervene if needed.

Drunnyak, usually so quick with a sharp remark, narrowed his eyes, and though they had seen Garric's moral strength first-hand, Opilkhos was one of them.

Garric, however, did not hesitate.

With one strong motion, he knelt and lifted Opilkhos onto his back, as if the unconscious warrior weighed nothing.

A ripple of tension passed through the group.

Then Garric nodded.

Not to them – but to two men in particular.

Borgrim and Eldric.

Borgrim, who had not spoken a word since the healing light had touched him, let out a slow breath, gripping the amulet around his neck tightly, as if grounding himself.

Then he met Garric's gaze.

And without hesitation, he turned toward his tavern.

The Stubborn Goat. The heart of the village.

His gaze swept across Drunnyak, Taril, Nashir, Alentar, Niv – finally resting on Opilkhos, still unconscious in his grasp.

His lips twitched slightly – not into a smile, but into something close.

Respect.

"We have much to discuss," he said, his voice strong, steady, but now edged with something else. Something curious. Something undeniably intrigued. Then, with a sharp nod toward the tavern, he gestured forward. "Shall we?"

The words hung in the air, and just as the weight of the moment threatened to settle too deeply, Niv spoke. "Finally," Niv sighed, stretching lazily as if shaking off the weight of the moment. A slow, teasing grin curved her lips as she rolled her shoulders, golden eyes gleaming with mischief. "I was starting to think you'd never ask," she mused, then tilted her head, smirking. "And since you're the one doing the inviting… that means you're paying the tab."

With a playful wink, she strode past him, sauntering toward the tavern as if she had already won.

Drunnyak let out a low chuckle, shaking his head.

Taril simply exhaled, his presence as steady as the mountains.

Alentar remained unreadable, but there was a knowing glint in his emerald gaze.

And Nashir – his eyes flickered with quiet amusement.

Garric smirked, if only for a fraction of a second.

Then, without another word, he turned and strode toward the tavern, still carrying Opilkhos.

Borgrim pushed open the heavy door to The Stubborn Goat, stepping inside first.

Eldric followed his brother.

The rest of the group exchanged glances, then followed.

The heavy wooden door swung shut behind them, and outside, the village, shaken but alive, kept moving.

The world had changed, and inside that tavern, they were about to understand just how much.

The Stubborn Goat had never held a moment like this before.

The scent of freshly baked bread and roasted meats, and the promise of ale filled the air as Borgrim barked orders. "Lorin, Myra, get moving! We need food on the tables! And break out the ale! If there's ever been a reason to drink, it's today!"

Lorin, the young man with dusty brown curls, scrambled to clear the tables, while Myra, fiery-haired and swift, disappeared into the kitchen to fetch steaming loaves of bread, seasoned stews, and thick cuts of meat, the best the village could offer.

Yet, despite the warmth of the hearth, despite the promise of food and drink, no one spoke.

The weight of what had just happened was still settling.

Garric strode through the tavern, Opilkhos's unconscious form cradled in his arms as if the weight of him was nothing.

He laid him carefully upon an old, worn-out sofa by the fire, his movements unexpectedly gentle for a man of such strength.

For a moment, he looked down at the unconscious warrior, then, with a slow breath, he turned away and walked toward his son.

Caelan stood rigid, his fists clenched at his sides.

For hours, for days, for weeks he had held himself together.

A boy who had fought against doubt, against whispers, against his own fear that maybe, just maybe, he really had been wrong, but now his father stood before him.

Whole. Alive.

For a moment Caelan didn't know how to breathe.

Garric sank to one knee, levelling himself with his son. "Caelan—"

The name was barely out of his mouth before the dam broke.

With a choked, heart-wrenching cry, Caelan lunged forward, colliding into his father's chest with the force of a storm. His small fists pounded against Garric's armour, weak but relentless, his body trembling with unfiltered grief. "You left me!" His voice cracked with every word. "You left! You said you'd come back, but you didn't!" He punched again – small, desperate blows that barely registered against Garric's broad frame. "I waited!" Caelan sobbed, his fists slowing, his shoulders shaking. "I waited every day, but you never came!" His legs gave out. His fingers clutched at his father's tunic, gripping it as if letting go meant losing him again. "I thought you were dead." The words barely made it past his lips. "I thought... I thought you were never coming back."

The entire tavern held its breath.

All of them stood in silence, even the visitors – Drunnyak, Taril, Niv, Alentar, Nashir. All watched, feeling the depth of the moment settle over them like an unshakeable force.

Because this was not a battlefield, this was something greater.

Something more painful, more real, more raw.

Garric let his son hit him.

Let him cry.

Let him feel every ounce of grief that had built up inside his small body, let him release it into his father's chest because there was nowhere else it could go.

Then, at last, Garric moved. His arms wrapped around Caelan, pulling him close, holding him tight, pressing his chin against the boy's hair as if anchoring him to the world. "I know, my son," he murmured. His voice was deep, rough – not from authority, but from something far heavier. "I know."

Caelan shuddered against him, gripping him even tighter. "You shouldn't have left."

"I know."

"You should've come home sooner!"

"I know, Caelan."

The boy hiccupped through his sobs. "You should have been here!"

Garric closed his eyes, pressing his forehead against his son's. "I should have." A pause. A silence so full of emotion that it felt suffocating. Then, "I'm here now, my son."

Caelan sniffled, his tears soaking into his father's tunic. "I hate you for leaving."

Garric let out a rough, breathy chuckle, pressing a hand to the back of Caelan's head. "That's fair," Garric murmured, his voice rough with emotion. "But know this – through every step, through every battle, through every moment I thought I wouldn't make it," he pulled Caelan closer, pressing his forehead against his son's, "it was my love for you that kept me going. That was my strength. And I'm sorry, my son… I'm so sorry."

For a long moment, they just held each other.

Father and son.

A man who had left.

A boy who had waited.

A love that had never faded.

The room was so quiet that even the fire in the hearth seemed to crackle softer, as if honouring the moment.

Somewhere in the back of the tavern, a cook wiped at his face, pretending it was just sweat in his eyes.

Borgrim, usually the loudest man in the room, cleared his throat, rubbing at his beard in discomfort – not because he didn't care, but because he cared too much.

Even Drunnyak, who could find humour in anything, simply folded his arms and exhaled, watching with quiet respect.

Niv crossed her arms, but her sharp golden gaze softened.

Taril, silent as ever, simply watched.

Nashir's fingers touched his staff, as if grounding him in something deeper.

And Alentar, from where he leaned against the wall, lowered his eyes slightly – not in shame, but in understanding.

Then…

Garric took a breath, lifting his head.

His gaze shifted, searching for one man in particular.

Eldric.

He found his younger brother standing nearby, still watching, his own emotions carefully concealed.

For all the years that had passed, for all the battles fought, Garric didn't need words to communicate.

Eldric met his eyes, and Garric gave him an order. Not with his voice, not with a command, but with a simple, firm nod. *Make them welcome.*

Eldric understood immediately.

His lips pressed together in silent acknowledgement before he turned to their guests.

Borgrim, who had been watching the exchange, let out a deep breath and clapped his hands together. "Right, then!" he barked, shaking off the weight of the moment. "Let's get some food in our heroes, and for the love of all the gods, get some ale flowing!"

The energy shifted once more.

Not back to normal – because things would never be normal again – but to something new. Something whole.

Garric lingered in the embrace for a moment longer, holding Caelan close, grounding himself in the warmth of his son's small frame. Then, with slow, careful movements, he lifted the boy into his arms and stood. "Come on," he murmured, his voice warm, strong, whole. "Let's go sit at the table with our guests. We have a lot to talk about."

A LEGACY UNEARTHED

The Stubborn Goat had never been this quiet before.

The fire crackled, its glow flickering across wooden beams and worn stone walls. The warmth of the tavern was there, but it did nothing to thaw the weight of the past pressing down on the room.

Plates sat untouched. Mugs of ale were forgotten in hands that no longer gripped them for drinking, but for something else – something heavier.

At the head of the table, Garric Garrents sat tall, his face unreadable, though his fingers curled subtly against the wooden table – not from nerves, but from something close to it.

Beside him, Caelan sat stiffly, small but unflinching, his young eyes wide, filled with the raw weight of witnessing something far greater than himself.

Eldric sat to Garric's right, watching carefully, his presence a quiet force.

And Borgrim – Borgrim stood behind the bar, his hands gripping the counter as though it was the only thing holding him upright.

Across from them, the warriors – the ones who had walked out of legend itself – remained still.

Drunnyak sat forward now, his fingers idly tapping against the side of his mug, his expression unreadable.

Taril sat like the mountain he was, his arms crossed, sharp eyes locked onto Garric –unblinking, unyielding.

Niv, golden eyes glinting in the firelight, studied Garric with quiet calculation, her usual smirk absent.

Alentar leaned back slightly in his chair, but his gaze was locked onto Borgrim.

Nashir's staff rested beside him, his fingers curled over it in quiet contemplation, as if sensing the weight of something yet to be spoken.

And then, at last…

Garric spoke. "I am Garric Garrents." The words came slow, as if the name itself had grown foreign on his tongue. "I haven't used my family name in so long that I almost forgot it existed. Until now." He exhaled. "I apologise if I sounded rude and unwelcoming before. As you saw, I could barely hold myself when I returned, and for that, I apologise once more. The reason why I returned in that state is of urgency, and we'll get to that later, but first we need to address other things."

He looks at the visitors with kinder eyes now. Not the eyes of a leader defending his family, his village, but as someone who idolised the stories he heard as a child, even though the world had been so rough that he couldn't believe those stories to be real. His breath calms down as if he's trying to get to the right spirit.

"What I know of my family, I learned from my parents before they died. Fragments of truth passed between whispers, between lessons, between stories told beside the fire. Before my brother was even old enough to understand, I was told the story of how this village came to be. I clung to every word, not knowing that one day, I would be the one to pass it forward." His eyes flickered briefly to Eldric, then back to the table. "Some of what I know, I learned from Borgrim himself."

The dwarf visibly stiffened, his breath faltering for just a moment.

Garric continued, his voice steady. "This village was built over a hundred years ago. My forefather, Ian Garrents, was its founder, but he didn't do it alone." He turned slightly, his gaze settling on Borgrim, whose knuckles were white against the bar. "Ian had a friend. A young dwarf who should have died in the mines of slavers, beaten, starved, left to rot in chains."

Borgrim's grip on the wood tightened.

The warriors remained still.

Garric didn't falter. "Borgrim and him gathered as many survivors as they could on their way to what we call home now. A few families, scattered, trying to survive our daily struggle with this harsh weather and the undead that rise every night."

A heavy silence fell over the room.

Taril's sharp gaze locked onto the dwarf.

Not with anger.

Not with suspicion.

But with recognition.

Borgrim had not moved.

He stood, his fingers curled so tightly against the bar that his nails dug into the wood.

Then, slowly, he moved.

His boots echoed against the wooden floor as he walked forward.

His wide, tired eyes locked onto Garric and Eldric, filled with a sadness that made him look older than he was.

And then Borgrim did something he had never done before. He bowed his head, and in a voice that had never wavered before, he whispered, "Forgive me, lads."

Garric stiffened.

Eldric's brow furrowed slightly, confusion flickering in his eyes.

Borgrim swallowed hard. His throat worked as he forced the next words out. "I made a promise." His hands curled into fists. "A promise to Ian himself long ago." He exhaled shakily, voice rough as he continued. "I swore to him, before he left, that I would never tell the full truth. Not unless his brothers…" His voice caught. His eyes lifted and landed on the warriors before him. "The gods in flesh returned."

The air thickened.

The fire crackled, the only sound in the weight of the revelation.

No one spoke.

No one moved.

Then, as if dragged by an invisible force, Borgrim turned – slowly, carefully – his gaze sweeping over each of them. And one by one, he called their names. "Drunnyak, the First Warrior. Creator of all men."

Drunnyak's grin was slow, sharp – but his eyes were unreadable.

"Niv, the Silver Flame Sorcerer. Mother of the elven kind and first of all three elves."

Niv's eyebrow arched, but she exhaled softly through her nose, as if recognising something distant.

"Alentar, the Shadow of the Wilds. The first hunter. The first ranger."

Alentar's expression did not shift, but there was something in the way his fingers twitched against the table.

"Nashir, Keeper of Nature. Creator and carer of all flora and fauna."

Nashir's grip tightened around his staff, though his face remained composed.

"Taril, the Unbroken Shield. Father of the dwarven kind."

Taril's jaw tensed, but he did not look away.

And then…

Borgrim's breath shook slightly.

His body turned toward the farthest end of the room. To the warrior lying unconscious on the old, worn sofa.

The golden one.

The one who had healed them all.

Borgrim took a slow, steady step forward.

The firelight flickered against Opilkhos's armour, casting a soft glow over his still face.

Another step.

Another, and then… Opilkhos stirred.

A breath escaped his lips, slow and deep, as if awakening from something far heavier than sleep.

His fingers twitched.

His body tensed, and finally, his eyes opened.

Slowly, they flickered across the faces in the room.

Confusion.

Then recognition.

Then, as his gaze settled on Borgrim…

Something else.

Something shattered.

And then Borgrim spoke the name. "Harinnil."

The room froze.

Drunnyak, Taril, Nashir, Niv, Alentar – all of them tensed, but Opilkhos…

Opilkhos did not. He just stared.

The name hit him like a blade, tearing through something deep, something fragile, something buried beneath centuries of silence.

His breath hitched.

His fingers curled into his palms, nails pressing into flesh, grounding himself in the present, in the now – because the past was clawing at him.

His shoulders stiffened. His entire frame seemed to shrink beneath the weight of a truth he did not know.

And then his expression changed.

Not to shock, not to anger, but to grief.

Deep, aching, shattering grief, because for the first time, the past had called him by name.

Borgrim shook his head. "No," he muttered, his voice low, uncertain, but firm. He took a breath, exhaling slowly, as if steadying himself against the words he was about to say. Then his eyes – haunted, burdened with something none of them could yet understand – lifted to meet Opilkhos's. "You should be the one known as Harinnil, and yet somehow, you're not him."

A pause. A heartbeat stretched too thin.

"You can't be him."

Opilkhos flinched.

Borgrim's hands trembled slightly at his sides, but his voice did not waver. "I met him." His words were not a question. They were not a theory. They were the truth. "Long ago, he came. One night, in the dead of winter." His breath shuddered. "He looked just like you. A spitting image. The same armour, the same eyes, but the darkness followed him." Borgrim's throat tightened. "The shadows moved differently around him. They did not cling to him as they do to a man.

They recoiled, twisted…" He swallowed. "And then, for just a moment, I saw it." Borgrim's voice grew quieter. "His true face." The flickering fire reflected in his wide eyes, but it was not the flames he saw. "It was like the undead, but… different. Not just rotting, not mindless, but… hollow. Something stolen from him. Something… missing." He exhaled sharply. "I don't know what trickery it was, but whatever stood before me that night," his gaze hardened, "it was not you."

Opilkhos's breath shook.

Something inside him shattered further.

Because Borgrim had just confirmed what Opilkhos had always feared – that he was not whole, and that he and Harinnil were more than connected.

That he was missing something. Something that he could almost grasp, yet was still unreachable somehow.

That a piece of him, a part of his very existence had been taken, and he had no memory of it.

The Stubborn Goat trembled.

Not from footsteps.

Not from voices.

Not from anything the villagers could understand.

It was something greater.

Something older.

Something that had been waiting.

The very air in the tavern shifted, thickened, as if the weight of the past had come crashing down upon the present.

Then the wind came.

A violent gust howled from outside, slamming against the doors with an unseen force.

The wooden shutters creaked, banged against the walls, groaning under pressure.

Then, with a deafening roar, the doors burst open.

The wind rushed inside, a storm of biting cold and swirling frost, snuffing out every single flame in the room.

Candles flickered – gone.

Lanterns swayed – darkness fell.

The fire in the hearth – extinguished in an instant.

Yet there was still light.

Not from flame.

Not from torches.

From them.

The warriors.

The ones Borgrim had called gods.

One by one, they began to glow.

Auras of gold, silver, emerald, deep crimson, and the faintest whisper of shadow rose from their bodies, shifting, pulsing, wrapping around them like threads of energy woven from another world.

Their eyes blazing.

Their bodies connected.

And then they stopped seeing the tavern.

Their bodies remained, seated, unmoving – but their minds...

They were no longer here.

Not in this place.

Not in this moment.

They were somewhere else.

Watching, but not watching.

Dreaming, but not dreaming.

They were remembering.

The mortals could do nothing but watch and wonder in awe what was happening.

Garric stood frozen, his fingers twitching as if reaching for a weapon, yet instinct told him this was beyond steel, beyond battle, beyond anything he had ever faced.

Eldric's hands went to his sword hilt, but he did not draw.

Caelan gasped – the warmth in his cheeks drained, his wide eyes locking onto the unnatural glow wrapping around the warriors.

Garric reacted first. "Stay close to me!" he barked, voice hard, commanding, filled with something deeper than fear – something primal.

Caelan stumbled backward, but his father was there.

Eldric, without hesitation, shielded the boy, pulling him close, standing firm before him like an unmovable force.

The light pulsed.

The wind howled, shaking the very foundations of the tavern, dust spilling from the wooden beams above, chairs trembling, the mugs on the tables rattling against the wood.

And then a voice, deep, strong and familiar, shook them all.

"Welcome, brothers. I've been expecting you for a while."

A GLIMPSE FROM THE PAST

Borgrim's heart stopped.

His breath hitched – shallow, uneven, caught between shock and something deeper.

A sound escaped his throat – a choked sob, strangled before it could fully form.

He knew that voice even after all these years.

Even after a lifetime had passed.

Even after he had buried it beneath the weight of time, of duty, of survival…

He knew it.

"Ian…" The name fell from his lips like a prayer.

And then… he wept.

Not softly.

Not in silence.

A raw, guttural cry tore through him – a man no longer in control, no longer a tavern keeper, no longer the dwarf who had built walls around his heart to keep the pain out.

In that moment, he felt like a child again.

A boy, torn from the mines.

A boy, saved from certain death.

A boy, given a life by a man who had vanished before his time.

A boy who had never stopped waiting to hear his friend's voice again.

He staggered forward, one hand reaching toward the glowing forms of the warriors – but they did not see him.

They were gone. Lost to their past and to their memories.

To the truth that had been waiting for them all this time.

And all Borgrim could do – all any of them could do – was wait.

A blinding light.

The mortal world was gone. The Stubborn Goat, the village, the cursed world they had awakened in – all of it disappeared.

Suddenly, they were there again in a time they all had lived.

Back at the end of the war, where the world itself was breaking apart.

The sky torn open, bleeding gold and silver light, black storms writhing through the cracks of heaven. Divine lightning split across the horizon, scorching the ruins of a once-great kingdom.

The land beneath them fractured, shifting, crumbling under the weight of the gods' final battle. Mountains that had stood since creation now trembled, breaking apart into the abyss below.

A great war had been fought here. A war between gods and their father.

Now only a handful remained standing.

Harinnil stood in the centre of it all, inside the same fountain they'd seen when they woke up recently. His golden armour dented and cracked, his body worn but unyielding.

The sacred waters of the Fountain of Creation swirled around his ankles, glowing with divine energy, whispering with the voices of the fallen.

Before him – beyond an impenetrable barrier of light – stood her.

Lena.

The goddess of life.

The one he loved.

The one he needed.

Her hands were pressed against the barrier, radiant and trembling, her form flickering between strength and fading light.

Their fingers were inches apart. So close. So painfully close.

But their father – the All-Father, the first god – stood above them, his fractured form barely holding together.

He should have been dead.

He should have fallen like the others.

Yet his power – his will – remained absolute.

And with the last of his strength, he held the barrier firm.

A hurricane of divine fury tore through the battlefield, winds howling between them, tearing stone and bodies from the ground.

This was not just wind.

This was his father's will.

A force meant to keep them apart.

Harinnil braced himself, his boots digging into the shifting stone, his grip tightening around his broken blade – Drunnyak's own sword, shattered yet unyielding.

He swung forward, cutting through the air, through the invisible force pressing against him. Again. Again.

Lena did the same, her palm radiating golden light as she pressed harder against the barrier, her power pushing against their father's will.

Their eyes met.

Desperate. Determined.

Fate was a cruel thing.

But they refused to bow to it.

"Lena!" Harinnil's voice was raw, torn against the howling storm.

"Harinnil!" she cried, her voice breaking with something deeper than pain – love, loss, the knowledge that this might be the end.

He had absorbed the power of every god that had fallen, his brothers.

He was the only one who could end this.

But without her – without Lena – he wasn't strong enough.

They had to be together. They had to complete the ritual.

But the barrier held.

Their father's burning gaze bore down upon them. His final strike was coming.

139

And then…

A gasp.

A hoarse, broken breath.

Alentar.

From the bloodstained ground, a lone figure rose.

His body wounded, barely holding together.

His vision blurred, the world spinning, broken, collapsing.

His trembling fingers found his last arrow.

The last one he had.

His body screamed against him. His soul cracked under the weight of the choice before him.

But he knew.

Harinnil needed to reach her. He needed to touch her, and there was only one way.

A single tear slid down Alentar's cheek.

Lost in the storm.

Lost in the chaos.

Lost to everything but this moment.

His hands shook and his breath was uneven.

He pulled the arrow back.

It felt impossibly heavy in his grasp, and yet it was the lightest thing he had ever held.

The tear struck the shaft, and for a fleeting moment – a heartbeat – the arrow pulsed.

With his love.

With his devotion.

With his very essence.

And then he let go.

As the arrow left his fingers, Alentar collapsed, lifeless.

His final act could not be stopped.

The wind did not slow it.

The storm did not stop it.

The weight of fate did not bend it.

It cut through the chaos, sharp as destiny itself.

It struck Lena's back.

A breathless gasp.

Her body jolted forward, blood spilling from her lips.

Harinnil's eyes widened, horror and disbelief flooding them as the arrow's fletching protruded from her back.

But then... Something miraculous happened.

The barrier shattered.

Lena stumbled forward, her strength failing, her knees buckling.

Harinnil caught her.

The arrow – Alentar's arrow – pierced them both.

Binding them together.

Her warmth flowed into him.

Her essence became one with his.

Their hands clasped. Foreheads pressed together.

Golden light surged between them with the energy of creation itself.

Tears streamed down their faces.

No words were needed.

She smiled. Through the pain. Through the end.

He wept. As he held her. As he felt her fading into him.

Above them, their father roared.

The fury of a dying god, the final wail of a king who had ruled for eternity, now watching his own downfall.

But it was too late.

Harinnil lifted his gaze in rage as he felt her last breath.

His golden armour – once shattered – now burned with celestial power.

He was complete.

His soul intertwined with Lena's and her light within him.

His sorrow, his love, his rage – all became one.

He held her lifeless body as gently as he could, carefully sliding her free of the arrow that had pierced them both – leaving its jagged shaft still buried in his own flesh.

With words of love lost in the thunderous scenery, he laid her inside the fountain.

The energy of his brothers surged through him – fierce, unrelenting, alive. With their strength in his veins, Opilkhos turned to face his father.

With a final, world-shattering strike, the All-Father was no more.

A cataclysmic explosion erupted, swallowing the battlefield in radiant light.

The heavens cracked.

The mountains crumbled.

The very fabric of existence trembled.

His body was thrown back like a meteor to his love's side. Blood pouring from all his wounds, but his will unshaken. He crawled with whatever strength he had left towards her.

As he reached her, he slowly brought her closer, and in the last moments before everything faded, all that remained were two figures.

Their hands entwined.

Their tears lost in the light.

The blinding light faded.

The battlefield was gone.

The sky, once torn apart by divine war, was whole.

The world, once trembling beneath the weight of gods, was at peace.

And in its place – a different kind of eternity.

Gentle waves kissed the shore, their rhythm unbroken, eternal. The sea stretched into the horizon, endless and golden with the first light of morning.

Birds sang from the trees, their melodies soft, carried by the warm, salty breeze.

A cabin stood nestled against the cliffs, its wooden walls worn by the sea air, but strong, steady. A home untouched by time.

And within it – love without memory.

Lena's fingers traced lazy patterns across his bare chest, her touch feather-light, as if she were memorising him.

Her head rested against his shoulder, golden strands of hair tangled in the soft linen of their bed.

The morning light spilled through the open window, casting a warm glow over them, over the crumpled sheets, over the small world they had made for themselves.

A world without war.

A world without gods.

A world where they were just two souls.

She sighed, content, shifting slightly, her lips curling into a small, teasing smirk as she looked up at him. "You know what?" she murmured, her voice thick with the warmth of morning, with the ease of love.

He hummed in response, his arm tightening around her, pulling her closer.

"Since we can't remember anything, and we seem to be blessed with this place all to ourselves…" Her fingers brushed against his jaw, tilting his face toward her. "I shall name you."

His lips twitched, amused. "Oh?"

She grinned, eyes shining like the sun reflected on the ocean. "Yes. A strong name. A noble name." She ran a hand through his dark, tousled hair, then tapped his nose with the lightest touch. "Sir Opilkhos."

His brows lifted, a chuckle rumbling from his chest. "Sir?"

"Of course." She grinned, nudging his side. "You look far too powerful to be anything less than a knight. And Opilkhos… it sounds right, doesn't it?"

She said it like it was a truth written in the stars.

Like it had always been his name.

Like it had always belonged to him.

Something in him stirred.

A flicker of something deep, something lost.

He had no past.

No name before this.

But here, with her, in this untouched paradise, he didn't need one.

"Opilkhos." He tested it, rolled it over his tongue, felt the way it settled into his soul like it had always been waiting for him. And then… he smiled. "I like it."

Her arms wrapped around his neck, her laughter like the waves against the shore. "Good. Then it's settled."

No past.

No future.

Just this moment.

Just them.

And as the sun rose higher, bathing them in golden light, he kissed her – because words would never be enough.

The warmth of the sun. The scent of the sea. The sound of her laughter.

And then… it was gone.

The golden light faded, unravelling like mist in the morning air.

The waves became echoes. The warmth became a ghost upon their skin.

And when the memory dissolved completely, they were back.

Back in The Stubborn Goat.

Back in the present.

But something wasn't right. The world felt slower.

The crackling of the fire, the shifting of chairs, the murmurs of the humans – all muffled, distant, as if they were standing in water, just out of reach of the waking world.

They looked at each other, tears shining in their eyes, breaths uneven, hands trembling with the weight of what they had just seen – what they had just remembered.

They had all seen her. They all remembered her.

Lena.

A name once lost to time, now carving itself back into their souls like an unshakeable truth.

Her kindness.

Her warmth.

Her soul, gentle as a spring breeze, strong as the roots of the earth.

The weight of who she was, of what she had meant to them, crashed over them like a tidal wave, leaving them breathless.

Drunnyak was the first to break.

His massive hands, which had torn through armies without hesitation, now trembled in his lap.

His small sister.

His sunshine.

The girl who had once sat on his shoulders, giggling as she braided flowers into his wild hair, who had never feared his size, his strength, because she knew he would never hurt her.

The one who had always believed in him, even when he hadn't believed in himself.

His throat worked, but no words came.

Because there were no words for this kind of pain.

For a love lost.

For a soul torn from their world.

For a sister who had been stolen from them all.

Niv's breath hitched, her golden eyes flickering in the dim light.

For the first time since their awakening, she felt small.

Because even she – the Silver Flame, the woman who could twist hearts with a single glance, the one who had always known her own beauty, her own power – had felt small next to Lena.

Not because of vanity.

Not because of jealousy.

But because Lena shone in a way no one else could.

Not only with beauty, but with spirit.

With a light so pure, so effortless, so infinite that standing beside her had always made the rest of the world seem dimmer.

"Gods…" she whispered, her voice breaking, her fingers brushing the tears that spilled down her cheeks.

Alentar sat frozen, hands clasped tight, his entire body wound like a bowstring ready to snap.

Nashir exhaled a shaking breath, his fingers clutching his staff like it was the only thing tethering him to this moment.

Taril's broad shoulders barely moved.

And Opilkhos?

Opilkhos felt like he had lost her twice.

His hands pressed against his chest, over his heart, as if trying to feel the warmth of her still there, as if she had never left.

But she had.

Lena.

Their light.

Their guide.

Their friend.

A name stolen from history.

A love taken from them all.

And yet…

She had never truly left them.

She was in every act of kindness.

She was in the laughter of children, in the quiet of the morning, in the gentle brush of wind upon their skin.

She had been with them even when they had forgotten her.

And now…

Now they would never forget again.

They knew now.

They knew.

Opilkhos was Harinnil and Harinnil was not Opilkhos.

Something had happened in that final battle. Something unnatural.

A split.

The warrior who had fought to the end, who had absorbed the power of gods, who had sacrificed everything – his body had not endured it.

The pure soul. The brother who had tried to save them all – he had been severed.

One half left behind, rotting, corrupted, festering in darkness throughout countless years.

The other reborn, lost, stripped of memory, left wandering a world that no longer knew him.

Harinnil was not whole.

Opilkhos was not whole.

But standing here, as they returned to the mortal world, as the tavern around them slowly came back into focus...

They knew which of them had been left behind in the dark and which of them had walked into the light.

The voices of the humans filtered back into existence – but still, they felt distant.

As if the gods who had once stood together on that battlefield, who had been willing to die for one another, who had held the fate of the world in their hands, had just awoken as strangers.

They turned slowly, all of them, their eyes landing on Opilkhos.

Not with suspicion.

Not with fear.

But with something heavier.

Recognition.

Acceptance.

Grief.

Because he was their brother, but the Lich they'd met earlier was as well.

Drunnyak let out a long breath, running a hand down his face, exhaling sharply. "Fuck."

It was the only word he could manage.

Niv's arms wrapped around her own body, as if she had to physically hold herself together. Her golden eyes shimmered – not with pain for herself, but for him. "Opilkhos..." she whispered. Not Harinnil. Never again.

Alentar, silent, barely breathing, barely moving.

He was shaken because he was the one who had fired the arrow.

He was the one who had sealed their brother's fate.

He had done what had needed to be done, and now he could barely stand under the weight of it.

His hands shook at his sides.

Not from fear, but from memory.

From the feeling of that last shot leaving his fingers.

The one that had destroyed their father.

The one that had broken their brother.

Nashir's breath was deep, measured, controlled – but his grip on his staff was too tight.

Taril rubbed his thumb against the pommel of his war hammer, his expression unreadable.

And then Opilkhos spoke. "I… remember."

His voice was not strong.

Not commanding.

Not filled with the weight of a god reclaiming his past.

It was soft. Unsteady.

It was a man lost in his own existence.

And they knew he was not whole.

None of them were, but as he looked around, as his blue-and-diamond eyes met each of them, one by one, the smallest flicker of something else passed between them.

A truth stronger than the weight of their grief.

He was not alone. Not any more.

None of them spoke.

Not at first.

The fire in The Stubborn Goat had returned, flickering weakly, casting shadows against the walls.

The tavern stood still.

Not with the easy stillness of a tavern at rest, but with something deeper – a silence thick with awe, with uncertainty, with fear.

The villagers had seen great warriors before – leaders, champions, men who had held back the endless tides of the dead – but they had never seen this.

As they returned from whatever realm of memory had stolen them away, something about them had changed.

They stood differently.

Taller, heavier – not just in form, but in presence.

Like men who had walked through time itself and returned bearing the weight of eternity.

The very air in the room felt charged, as if the world itself recognised that gods had awakened in their midst.

The flickering firelight seemed to stretch toward them, the shadows behind them pulling away, bending, unsure of whether to embrace or retreat from what had returned.

The people in the tavern didn't move.

Garric stood like a statue, his battle-hardened eyes narrowing, assessing what now stood before him.

Eldric's fingers tightened against his belt, a soldier's instinct to grip his weapon, even if he knew he wouldn't use it.

Caelan's breath hitched, his small frame half-hidden behind his father, but his eyes never left them – wide, unblinking, shining with something between fear and the kind of wonder only a child could still have.

And Borgrim?

The dwarf exhaled, slow and quiet, his grip loosening on the bar as if he had been holding on to it for support.

But they – the gods reborn – felt something else entirely.

For all the power thrumming through their veins, for all the strength still coiled in their bodies… something was different.

Drunnyak flexed his fingers, rolling his shoulders, expecting to feel the unbreakable might that had once defined him.

He still felt strong.

But not immortal.

Niv's golden gaze flickered over her hands, the same hands that had once commanded men and shattered mountains with a whisper.

She could still feel the fire inside her, but she also felt her pulse.

Alentar, silent, eyes shadowed, rested a hand against his bow, his heartbeat steady – too steady.

It had never been something he had needed to notice before.

Nashir lowered his gaze, exhaling as if listening, waiting for the whisper of the wind, for the hum of life that once had bound him to nature itself.

It was there. But not like before.

And Opilkhos – Opilkhos looked down at his hands.

They had once been unbreakable. They had held Lena. They had held creation itself.

And yet, for all the golden radiance still clinging to his form, for all the power still in his soul…

He could feel himself.

He could feel the weight of his own body, the ache of existence, the burden of being something less than what he had been before.

They were gods, but they were not as they once were. They all wondered what had happened that had forced them to fight their own creator, their father. Why they had to endure all this pain and feel his wrath.

In that fleeting moment, as the silence stretched between them and the ones in the tavern who watched them with reverence, they felt the doubt creeping into their bones.

THE AFTERSHOCK OF POWER

The first scream was enough to make their hearts stop.

Then another, and another.

A chorus of despair.

The gods moved as one, their bodies reacting before their minds could catch up, their instincts driving them toward the chaos beyond the tavern doors.

The moment they stepped outside, they froze.

The village – their newest sanctuary, their last beacon of warmth in a cursed world – was in ruins.

The very land bore the scars of their awakening.

The sky, formerly just a blanket of endless grey, swirled in unnatural chaos, thick storm clouds churning violently, twisting as if something had torn the balance apart.

The wind roared, carrying with it the wails of the suffering, the broken, the terrified.

Where sturdy homes had stood proud along the mountainside, many now lay collapsed, their roofs caved in, wooden beams splintered like brittle bones.

The market stalls, once arranged neatly in the village centre, were shattered, their goods buried beneath snow and rubble.

The great stone fountain, the heart of the village, now lay fractured, a jagged wound splitting its once-proud structure, water spilling over the frozen ground like blood.

The inner watchtowers, meant to protect them from the dangers of the night, had crumbled, crushed beneath fallen rocks loosened from the cliffs above.

Avalanches had torn through the pathways leading up to the trench, burying homes on the outskirts, suffocating lives beneath layers of ice and debris whilst blocking their access in and out of the village.

The stables, once filled with the warmth of livestock, now stood half-destroyed, the panicked cries of animals piercing the air, hooves kicking against broken wood as they tried to escape their ruined pens.

Fires flickered in the wreckage, their orange glow a cruel contrast against the cold destruction.

And the people? They lay scattered.

Some half-buried beneath the wreckage.

Some bleeding from fresh wounds, their cries of pain filling the air.

Some simply standing in shock, staring at the devastation with hollow eyes, unable to comprehend what had happened.

Mothers screamed for lost children.

Fathers dug through debris with bloodied hands.

The elderly clung to one another, whispering prayers into the frozen wind.

And the children? The children sobbed, shivering, clutching their parents, their dolls, their wooden swords – because they didn't understand why their world was falling apart.

The gods stood there, their breath caught in their throats.

They had fought monsters.

They had battled hordes of the undead, but this – this was different.

This was their doing.

The power that had surged through them, that had brought back their past, their purpose, had come at a cost.

Drunnyak's massive hands clenched into shaking fists, his usual confidence stripped away.

Niv pressed a hand to her lips, her golden eyes darting from the wounded to the broken homes, her usual wit lost in the face of tragedy.

Alentar stood rigid, his sharp gaze scanning the destruction, calculating, searching – not for enemies, but for how to fix what they had broken.

Nashir inhaled deeply, the weight of the land's pain pressing into him, his fingers curling around his staff as if to anchor himself.

Taril gritted his teeth, his broad frame heaving with the quiet realisation that even his strength could not undo this.

And Opilkhos – Opilkhos felt it all.

Every cry.

Every wound.

Every life on the brink of being lost.

His hands shook at his sides.

He had once healed the world; now he had helped break it.

The humans had no idea.

They didn't know that the very ones who had stood beside them, who had fought to save them from the horrors of the night, were the ones who had just unleashed a new kind of destruction upon them.

Drunnyak exhaled sharply, his voice hoarse, barely more than a growl. "We did this."

Niv's throat bobbed as she swallowed, her voice quieter. "What have we done?"

The wind howled, carrying the cries of the suffering into the mountains.

And then, without a word, they moved.

Not as gods.

Not as warriors.

But as the ones responsible, and the only ones who could put it right.

The chaos of the village raged on.

The wounded wept.

The broken cried out.

The strong did what they could to pull survivors from the wreckage, to comfort the suffering, to hold together what little they had left.

Garric, Eldric, Borgrim – they all tried to help.

They rushed to the fallen, lifting beams, holding sobbing families, barking orders to keep their people from falling into full despair.

But the gods did not hesitate.

They did not speak.

They did not look at each other for direction.

They simply knew.

And in that moment, for the first time since their return, they became what they were meant to be.

Nashir took a deep breath.

A whisper in elvish, and the land answered.

His staff struck the ground, and the air around him shifted.

Vines burst forth from the broken earth, weaving through the ruins of collapsed homes, lifting fallen beams, and cradling the wounded in gentle, living arms.

The broken trees from the avalanche trembled – and then moved, bending, reshaping, forming into bridges, into shelter, into warmth for those trapped beneath the snow.

The villagers gasped as the very land came alive beneath their feet, responding to Nashir's presence as though it had merely been waiting for its master to return.

Where Nashir's power was the embrace of the earth, Niv's was the fire that defied the cold.

She lifted her hands, fingers glowing with ethereal light, and the air around her ignited, but it did not burn.

It did not rage.

It warmed.

The ice that had trapped people beneath its frozen grasp melted in an instant. Frostbitten fingers, trembling from the unnatural cold, found warmth again.

A child, curled up beneath a collapsed stall, blinked through his tears as the cold was replaced with golden heat, a gentle flame flickering above him like a guardian star.

Niv smiled down at him, soft, reassuring, divine. "You're safe now, little one."

Drunnyak let go a low growl as he watched a deep rumble of an avalanche ready to fall.

And then – stone shattered beneath his grip.

He moved like a force of nature, tearing through fallen debris as if it were nothing more than dried leaves.

His massive hands lifted entire beams from collapsed homes, pulling people from the wreckage as if they weighed nothing.

A man, trapped beneath a boulder, gasped in shock as Drunnyak dug his fingers beneath it and lifted.

The earth trembled beneath his strength.

The villagers stared.

"No man is that strong," one whispered.

"He's not a man," another murmured, eyes wide. "He's something else."

Above, a house teetered on the edge of collapse.

A woman clung to the broken frame, sobbing, unable to climb down as the structure beneath her cracked and swayed.

And then – a blur.

A figure moving faster than the wind itself, scaling the walls as if gravity did not exist.

Alentar moved with inhuman grace, flipping, twisting, his boots barely touching the walls before he was suddenly beside her. "Hold on."

She barely had time to gasp before he grabbed her, twisting in mid-air, kicking off the splintering wood – and they fell.

Not uncontrolled. Not recklessly.

He landed as softly as a feather touching the ground.

As he looked up, his sharp eyes caught movement – two children, high above, stumbling along the crumbling ledge.

They slipped.

Screams tore through the air as their small bodies plummeted downward.

Alentar moved.

His bow was in his hands before thought could catch up.

Two arrows loosed in a heartbeat – straight through the loose fabric of their tunics.

The arrows pinned them in mid-air, their clothing catching against a sturdy wooden beam jutting from the rubble.

They hung there, unharmed, wide-eyed, gasping.

Alentar leapt, moving faster than seemed possible, his fingers grasping the ledge, pulling himself up in a single motion.

The villagers below screamed – not in horror, but in astonishment.

He was gone.

And then he reappeared, holding both children in his arms.

Landing without a sound.

The villagers stared, breathless.

"H-he-he ran on the walls – did you see that? Did you?"

But Alentar was already gone, leaping back into the ruins, saving the next one.

Taril walked through the destruction with purpose.

Where others saw ruin, he saw how to rebuild.

His war hammer struck the ground, and stone obeyed.

The earth shifted, realigned, forming pathways where none had been before.

The cliffs, weakened from the avalanche, strengthened beneath his presence, reinforcing themselves, stabilising before the next disaster could strike.

A man, gasping in terror as the ground beneath him began to crumble, felt solid earth rise beneath his feet. He turned, staring at Taril, his voice caught in his throat. "He commands the very mountains…"

Opilkhos walked to the centre of it all.

Where the great fountain had cracked, where the heart of the village lay broken, he knelt.

His hands pressed against the fractured stone.

His eyes closed.

And then… A pulse.

Not of fire.

Not of stone.

Not of wind or ice or nature itself.

A pulse of life.

A golden light burst from him, rippling outward in waves, filling the village like the warmth of the rising sun.

The wounded gasped as their pain faded.

The weary felt strength return to their limbs.

A man who had collapsed from exhaustion blinked in shock, his body replenished, his breath no longer laboured.

A child covered in cuts and bruises watched in awe as her wounds vanished before her eyes.

It did not change what had been destroyed.

It did not undo their suffering, but it gave them hope.

It gave them strength.

It reminded them they were not alone.

For a long moment, no one spoke.

The villagers – men, women, children – stood in utter silence.

They had seen great warriors.

They had seen leaders, fighters, survivors.

But this… this was not that. This was something else.

And then – a whisper. A murmur, hesitant, filled with awe. "They're not like us. They are gods."

Another voice, stronger – not in fear, but in reverence. "The gods really exist."

And then, like wildfire, the words spread. "The gods have returned!"

Some wept. Some raised their hands in praise.

Others simply stared, unable to process what they had witnessed.

Borgrim, still standing at the tavern doors, felt his breath catch.

He had known. He had always known.

But now they all did.

No one would ever question it again.

The gods had returned, and the world would never be the same.

The wind finally settled.

The skies, once torn by chaos, began to still, the unnatural rage in the heavens softening, giving way to something calmer.

And then the rain came.

Soft at first, a whisper against the broken earth, then stronger, a cleansing cascade from above.

It washed away the dust, the blood, the echoes of suffering.

It ran down the shattered rooftops, soaked into the cracks in the earth, cooled the fires that still smouldered.

The villagers stood together at the heart of their wounded home, their breath still heavy with the weight of survival, their eyes fixed on those who had saved them.

And the gods…

They stood among them, not separate, not above – but as part of it.

Drunnyak, his body streaked with dust and sweat, stood like a mountain, his hands still curled into fists as if he needed to keep holding the weight of the world.

Niv, golden flames still flickering softly at her fingertips, watched the villagers not with pride, but with something deeper – something unspoken.

Alentar, breathing heavily from his constant movement, kept his gaze on the people they had saved, watching their expressions shift, their understanding forming.

Nashir, his hands pressed to the earth, felt the land breathing again beneath his touch, the roots speaking softly, calming.

Taril, his war hammer now at rest, exhaled, watching the rain clean the wounds from the stones, the broken paths, the weary hands of the survivors.

And Opilkhos, with his golden aura still lingering like a warmth that refused to fade, stood in the centre of it all, his gaze unreadable, his heart full of something none of them could name.

Then Garric moved.

The proud warrior, the leader of these people, the unshakeable foundation of their village, stepped forward.

His boots echoed against the soaked stone as he walked, slow and deliberate, toward the gods.

His face – no words could describe it.

He was a man who had stood against the horrors of the night.

A man who had fought, bled, sacrificed.

A man who had seen his people suffer, had seen them rise, had seen them fall – but had never seen this.

He stopped.

He turned, looked at his people, his warriors, his family.

And then he knelt.

A slow, deliberate motion.

One knee pressing into the soaked ground, his head bowing not in submission, but in something greater.

Reverence. Respect. Devotion.

A moment passed.

Then another.

And then the first voice rose. "All hail our saviours."

Another joined. "All hail our gods."

And then the cry erupted. A chorus, raw with emotion, rising into the storm-washed sky. "*Hail! Hail! Hail!*"

It was not just gratitude. It was recognition.

It was a people who had suffered, who had endured, who had held on to hope for so long that they had nearly forgotten what it looked like...

Finally seeing it standing before them.

Garric lifted his head, his voice carrying over the storm. "Let us hail those who have returned to us! Let us honour those who have stood beside us, not as rulers, but as our own! Let us cry their names into the wind, so the heavens may know that the forsaken have come home!"

He threw his arms wide, his voice breaking into a fierce war cry, one of gratitude, of triumph, of unity.

And the people – they roared with him.

The rain poured down, soaking them, washing away the pain, the suffering, the doubt.

And in its place, only faith remained.

A faith that had been lost to time.

The gods stood still.

The chants of the villagers echoed around them, voices rising like a storm's final cry, raw and full of fierce devotion.

They hadn't expected thanks. They hadn't needed praise.

They had caused this.

The avalanche. The destruction. The suffering.

It was their power that had surged through the world, tearing through the balance of nature, breaking this fragile place apart.

A simple thank-you would have been too much. And yet here these people were, kneeling before them, hailing them as gods, as saviours, as something they had never once thought themselves to be.

Drunnyak was the first to shift. His massive arms crossed, his face contorted, eyes flickering from one villager to the next. "They should be cursing us," he muttered under his breath.

His chest felt lighter as he took a deep breath, watching everyone safe.

His hands, once meant to crush and tear through enemies, had instead lifted, saved, rebuilt.

His body was made for war, but today it had been used to protect and save lives.

His shoulders relaxed – just slightly.

Maybe, just maybe, he could get used to this.

Niv tilted her head, golden eyes narrowing, a soft smirk playing at her lips, but there was no teasing in her voice when she whispered, "They really think we're worthy of this?"

Yet, even as she questioned it, she didn't deny how warm it felt.

How right it felt.

She let her hands drop to her sides, the golden flames in her palms finally flickering out, but the warmth remained.

Alentar stood rigid, as if still trying to assess a battlefield that no longer needed him.

His sharp eyes flicked to the villagers, then to his companions, then back again.

It was foreign.

It was strange.

But for the first time since he had awoken, he did not feel like he needed to run.

Nashir exhaled deeply, fingers brushing against the soil beneath him.

It had been so long since he had felt nature respond to him like this.

Not out of duty.

Not out of fear, but out of faith.

Out of belief.

His lips curved into a small, tired smile.

Taril remained silent, his steady presence unmoving, unshaken, yet somehow softer.

He had never asked for recognition.

He had never needed words of gratitude.

And yet seeing these people look at them not with fear, but with admiration…

His grip on his war hammer loosened.

A nod. Barely noticeable, but full of understanding.

Opilkhos stood in the centre of it all.

Watching.

Feeling.

Breathing.

A name had been spoken, shouted in devotion – his name.

Not Harinnil.

Not a memory of a war long lost.

Not a fractured remnant of a past he could barely hold on to.

His name.

And for the first time, he accepted it.

A slow breath. A small smile.

Not because they were gods.

Not because they had been hailed.

But because, for the first time in an eternity, they had a place.

They were not just warriors.

They were not just remnants of a forgotten past.

They belonged.

And as the villagers continued to cry out in worship, in gratitude, in sheer unwavering belief…

The gods stood among them – not above, not apart, but as part of something greater than themselves.

161

THE AWAKENING OF THE DIVINE

As the villagers cried their names, as faith surged through the air like a wildfire catching on to dry wood, something shifted. A tremor, unseen but deeply felt.

A ripple that did not shake the earth, but their very beings.

The warmth of reverence wrapped around them, not in chains, not in burdens, but in pure, undeniable belief.

And then, their glow returned.

It started as little more than a flicker – faint, uncertain – a ghost of the power that had once surged through their veins.

Suddenly, it roared.

Drunnyak's veins pulsed, a deep, smouldering crimson flickering across his skin like the embers of a firestorm, his eyes glowing white-hot, as if the very might of the mountains had woken inside him.

Niv shuddered, her golden aura reigniting, flowing like liquid flame around her form, her very presence radiating heat, not burning, but empowering, intoxicating, divine.

Nashir's glow was soft, deep green, vibrant as life itself, as though the very land recognised him once again as its master.

Alentar's aura flared in a spectral silver, flickering like the light of the moon, elusive, untouchable, his form almost seeming to fade in and out, as if he belonged to the wind itself.

Taril stood firm, his body wreathed in an earthen bronze, his feet rooted as if he and the land had become one, as if stone and god had finally remembered each other.

Opilkhos – he was light.

Not just gold.

Not just radiance, but pure, undeniable presence.

The very air hummed around him, his divine essence pouring through his veins like molten starlight, his form shining so brightly that even the storm clouds above seemed to retreat.

They breathed in, and they felt it.

Stronger.

Clearer.

More whole.

The memories.

The power.

The connection to something far greater than the bodies they wore.

Their mortal vessels had been limiting them.

But now – now something had shifted.

The faith of these people, their belief, their worship – it had called to them, and their divinity had answered.

They looked at one another, seeing themselves not just as warriors, not just as survivors…

But as what they once were.

What they were meant to be.

The people stared in awe.

Some fell to their knees, hands clasped over their mouths in disbelief.

Others wept, trembling, overwhelmed by the sheer presence before them.

Even the soldiers, hardened men who had fought through countless nights of horror, now stood motionless, watching, unblinking.

Eldric clutched the hilt of his sword, not in fear, but in sheer reverence.

Borgrim, for the first time in his long life, felt the breath leave his lungs in stunned silence.

Caelan – wide-eyed, hands trembling – whispered, "I knew it… I always knew it."

Garric stood still. Not kneeling. Not bowing. Watching. Taking in every detail, every pulse of power. His eyes narrowed – not in doubt, but in understanding. "They're not just warriors. They're not just legends. They are gods."

And as the realisation settled across the entire village, as every man, woman and child finally understood the truth…

The gods felt something else.

A whisper in their bones.

A distant call.

They were not whole yet, but they were walking toward it.

And soon they would truly awaken.

The air was alive with power.

The villagers stood in awe, their breath stolen, their hands trembling, their voices silenced by the sheer magnitude of what stood before them.

And in the heart of it all, Opilkhos stepped forward.

His golden aura flickered and surged, an ethereal warmth radiating from his very soul.

Not blinding.

Not overwhelming.

But comforting.

Like the first light of dawn after the longest night.

He turned his gaze to the people, his eyes – a mixture of sapphire and diamond – shimmering not with superiority, but with gratitude.

And then he spoke. "You call us gods… but hear me now. We are not your kings. We are not your rulers. We are no masters of your fate. We are your brothers. Your sisters. Your kin." He looked to each of them, his voice carrying not just power, but sincerity. "You who have suffered, who have fought, who have endured, you are the reason we stand here today. We have forgotten ourselves, lost to the frozen grip of time… but you… You have never forgotten how to fight." His hand clenched around his sword's hilt, raising it high, its polished silver reflecting the firelight, the moonlight, the power that pulsed within him. "And so, I swear to you, by the very breath I take, by the steel I wield, by the life that has been returned to me, I will be worthy of your faith. I will stand with you, fight beside you, bleed for you, and if I must, I will die for you. Not as a god, but as your shield. As your sword. Above all else, as one of you."

The wind howled, but it did not drown him out.

The villagers watched with wide, teary eyes.

And then...

A voice joined him.

Drunnyak stepped forward, his deep voice like thunder. "What he says is true." He clasped his fist against his chest, his smirk softer, but no less fierce. "You fight like warriors. You endure like gods. And if you'll have me, I will fight beside you until my last breath."

Niv grinned, the fire in her golden eyes glowing brighter. "And I promise to make it very, very clear to anything that threatens this village that they'll have to go through us first."

Nashir, his voice quieter, gentler, but no less powerful, stepped beside them. "This land... it has suffered long enough. I will see it thrive again. I will see *you* thrive again."

Taril, the rock of the group, let out a low breath before placing his massive hand against the nearest broken pillar. "Stone can be broken... but it can be rebuilt. And so can we."

Alentar's voice was the last. "I have watched from the shadows for too long." He scanned the faces before him, their admiration, their awe. For once, he did not feel the need to disappear. "But I see you now. And I swear, I will never turn away from you."

The air was thick with emotion, with power, with something greater than words.

Then Garric, still kneeling, slammed his fist against his chest. "Then we shall stand together!"

The villagers erupted. A cheer, a cry, a war chant that shook the very earth beneath them. "*With you! With you! With you!*"

And in that moment, the gods were no longer just legends.

They were no longer just memories.

They were part of this world again.

The weight of the moment gave way to something greater.

Joy. Relief. Laughter.

For the first time in what felt like ages, the village was filled not with fear, not with suffering, but with life.

The villagers, once kneeling in reverence, rose in celebration.

Children rushed forward first, their small hands wrapping around legs they could barely reach, clutching at the gods like they were family.

Drunnyak – massive, unshakeable, a brute by all appearances – froze as a cluster of little ones clung to his knees, tugging at his furs, laughing as if he were some great, gentle beast rather than a warrior forged in battle.

He huffed, rolling his eyes, but there was no mistaking the ghost of a smile on his lips as he patted their heads with hands that had once torn armies apart.

Niv knelt down to a wide-eyed girl, brushing a strand of silver hair from her face. "Well now, aren't you the bravest one here?"

The girl giggled, and before Niv could react, tiny arms wrapped around her neck.

A hug. Small. Warm. Unshaken by fear, full of pure love.

Something tightened in Niv's chest.

She – a goddess, a warrior, a flame of destruction – felt soft for the first time in an eternity.

She hugged the child back.

Alentar watched from the side, his expression unreadable, but when a boy no older than seven reached up toward him, eyes full of curiosity, he surprised even himself by kneeling and allowing the child to touch the leather of his bracers, as if making sure he was real. A slow smile touched his lips. "Yeah, kid. I'm real."

Nashir, standing beside them, felt it differently.

The earth whispered beneath his feet, the energy of the people intertwining with the land, with the trees, with him.

He didn't need words.

They accepted him.

They accepted all of them.

And that was enough.

But among the joy, Taril did not celebrate yet, as he and Alentar heard a cry from beyond the rubble.

His sharp eyes scanned the ruined pathway leading toward the trench – the place where they had once fought, where the mountain itself had buried the only safe passage out.

He felt the stone beneath his hands, ran his fingers along the fractures, studying, calculating.

And then, he exhaled.

"We need this path."

Drunnyak, still carrying a few children clinging to his arms, grunted. "You don't say?"

Taril turned to Nashir. No words were needed.

The nature-bound god nodded, planting his staff into the ground.

The earth trembled in response, as if the mountain itself had awoken to his call.

Vines twisted through the cracks, weaving themselves into the broken stone, holding it firm.

Taril raised his war hammer, his aura pulsing with energy.

The villagers watched in stunned silence as he lifted the hammer high, its weight undeniable, the force of a thousand lifetimes behind it.

And then...

He struck.

The echo rippled through the village, through the mountain itself.

The blocked path shuddered, then cracked, then splintered apart.

A deep, thunderous groan filled the air as the massive stones shifted, moving as if commanded by a force beyond mortal strength.

The villagers gasped, some taking steps back, clutching each other.

And then the rubble gave way, tumbling downward, revealing an open passage once more.

Nashir stepped forward, placing both hands on the ground.

Where once there had been only dust and ruin, a great arch of vines, the broken stones and thick branches took shape, forming a natural threshold to mark the restored path.

The wind carried a sigh, as if the very land itself was relieved.

Drunnyak moved last, stepping toward the remaining unstable rocks.

His massive arms flexed, his breath steady.

With one final strike, he knocked the last loose stones aside, ensuring nothing could collapse again.

He turned back toward the crowd, grinning. "Now it won't kill any of you. You're welcome."

The villagers stood frozen.

They had seen battle.

They had seen hardship.

They had seen the cruelty of the world.

But this – this was divine.

"They…" someone whispered. "They commanded the mountain…"

Borgrim, who had been silent, stepped forward, placing his hand on one of the newly placed stones. His fingers trembled. "The land obeyed them."

A hush fell over the people.

It wasn't just belief any more. It wasn't just faith.

It was undeniable.

The young watchers rushed from their post through the new threshold – breathless, wide-eyed, pale from fear and cold.

They had been trapped, left behind after the avalanche, wondering if they'd lost everything. Convinced the village was gone, but what they saw now – Taril, Drunnyak and Nashir standing beneath the living arch, surrounded by villagers cheering, embracing, alive – left them speechless.

They froze, stunned.

"What… what is this?" one of them whispered.

Villagers rushed to greet them, clapping backs, pulling them in, laughing and crying all at once.

"They did it," someone said, pointing to the gods. "They opened the way – moved the mountain. Brought it to life!"

Another added breathlessly, "You saw it too, didn't you? The path – how it bloomed?"

Drunnyak waved lazily from the side with his natural grin. "Welcome back, lads. Hope you didn't piss yourselves."

Nashir offered a serene smile. "You made it through. That's what matters."

The young watchers, still reeling, looked at the threshold behind them, then at the gods before them.

As the crowd began to settle, basking in joy and disbelief, a young soldier came sprinting down the path, breathless and wide-eyed. "You… you have to come…" he gasped, nearly stumbling.

Everyone turned as he shouted again, louder this time, voice cracking with awe.

"Beyond the trench – something's happened! You have to see it! Now!"

His urgency silenced the murmurs.

The joy faded to curiosity, then concern, and once again they moved, following the boy toward whatever waited beyond the stone and vines.

They rushed.

Villagers, soldiers, young watchers, even the gods, drawn by the urgency in that boy's voice.

No one spoke, there was only the sound of boots on stone, breath catching in anticipation.

And then they saw it.

Just beyond the trench, where once there had been lifeless frost and barren soil, the land had changed.

The ground was green.

Not patches. Not hints.

But vibrant, living green stretching far and wide, farther than their eyes could follow.

Trees were rising – some small saplings, others already stretching skyward, their roots cracking the frozen ground with ancient strength.

Birds of every colour flew overhead, singing, circling, landing gently upon the newly formed branches.

Stags and foxes, wolves and elk, even creatures unseen for generations stepped forward from the distant mist.

Not as invaders, but as if returning home.

The trench, once a scar of war, now marked the edge of something reborn.

No one spoke. Not even the gods.

They all simply turned, eyes falling upon Nashir.

He stood a step behind them, silent.

Eyes glistening. His staff gently pulsing with life.

Niv reached out, touching his arm softly.

Drunnyak gave a small nod, quiet for once.

Even Alentar's guarded stare softened.

Taril stepped closer, resting a hand on his shoulder.

And Nashir... smiled.

Eyes full of wonder.

Full of tears.

As awe swept across the trench, no one could look away.

Villagers wept.

Children laughed.

Soldiers stood frozen in reverence.

Even Garric, Eldric and Borgrim shared glances of disbelief and pride, watching as gods and mortals stood side by side, witnesses to something no story could do justice.

It was perfect.

Until... a sound.

Snorts. Grunts. Shuffling through the undergrowth.

A sounder of wild dire boars – thick, plump and oblivious – wandered out from the trees, drawn by the warmth of the new life.

Dozens of them.

Taril raised an eyebrow, slowly turning his head, expression calm – but his eyes betrayed it: surprise mixed with a dash of hunger.

Alentar, already crouching with a hand on his quiver, grinned like a thief in the moonlight.

His eyes sparkled, full of mischief and intent.

They both turned to Drunnyak, who simply raised his shoulders in a silent *Well?* and cracked his knuckles.

No words were spoken – but none were needed.

Then… thwip-thwip-thwip!

Three arrows.

Three clean shots.

Three unlucky boars.

Later, back in the heart of the village, the day dipping low behind the mountains, the air now filled with music, laughter, and the unmistakable smell of roasted meat.

A great fire crackled at the centre, and three wild boars spun slowly on spits, golden and sizzling, their scent intoxicating.

Villagers danced, drank and feasted, the joy of survival and miracle thick in the air.

Eldric raised a mug, Borgrim sang with slurred vigour atop a table, Garric chuckled as Caelan fell asleep with a chicken leg still in hand.

And in the midst of it all, Nashir stood with arms crossed, glaring.

Taril, Alentar and Drunnyak sat nearby with mugs in hand and plates piled high, not the least bit remorseful.

"You three are unbelievable," Nashir muttered, shaking his head.

Drunnyak grinned with his mouth full. "They were wild and fat. That's nature's way of saying, 'Enjoy your meal.'"

Alentar smirked, raising a perfectly roasted slice. "Balance, brother. We give to the land, it gives back."

Taril nodded solemnly, tearing into his portion. "Besides, it would've been rude not to share with the village."

Nashir sighed, pinched the bridge of his nose, then grabbed a plate. "One of you better have kept the liver."

The fire roared, laughter rose, and the village celebrated not just the return of gods…

But the return of a life they'd never witnessed before.

The meat sizzled over the fire.

Laughter echoed through the air, wrapping the village in a blanket of warmth and celebration.

Near the centre, nestled against his father's side, young Caelan stirred awake, rubbing his eyes and smearing grease across his cheek from a half-eaten drumstick he never finished.

His hair was a mess, his face still drowsy – but his curiosity was already back at full strength.

He sat up, blinking at the gods gathered nearby, and then looked across the fire at Drunnyak, who was laughing with a group of soldiers, a mug in one hand and a boar rib in the other.

Caelan leaned toward Borgrim, who was happily nursing a third mug of ale and humming off-key to himself.

"Hey, Borgrim?" Caelan whispered loudly – because his whispering had never once been quiet. "Is it true? Drunnyak is the god who made humans?"

Borgrim, already a bit flushed and halfway through a hearty belch, blinked. "Eh? Yeah, boy. That's what the old tales say. Shaped 'em from dust and sweat and kicked life into 'em."

Caelan looked back at Drunnyak, then down at his own pale arms, then at the other villagers.

Then back at Drunnyak.

And again at himself.

And then, finally, to the crowd gathered around the fire, in the dead silence of a lull in conversation, he asked, "Then how come he's so dark... and we're all so pale?"

The question lingered.

Forks froze, halfway to their mouths.

Ale nearly spilled, but didn't.

Even the fire seemed to quiet for a second.

Dozens of villagers turned slowly toward Drunnyak.

He stopped chewing.

Slowly, he turned his head – deadpan expression, eyes locked on Caelan.

The kid stared back, innocent as snow.

A long, heavy pause.

Then Drunnyak erupted into a belly laugh, slapping his thigh hard enough to make nearby plates jump. "By the stars, I did wonder!" he bellowed between laughs. "When I made you lot, the damn sun was out! I must've tanned up while you all stayed indoors for a couple thousand years!" He wiped a tear from his eye. "Poor sun ain't been seen since – no wonder you turned into snowflakes!"

The entire village burst into roaring laughter.

Niv leaned into Taril, laughing so hard she snorted.

Borgrim nearly fell off his bench, wheezing into his mug.

Even Garric cracked a rare, wide grin.

Caelan grinned, triumphant, puffing out his chest. "So it's the sun's fault! Or better yet, the lack of it, right?"

Drunnyak raised his mug toward the sky. "Come back, sun! I want my people to stop looking like uncooked bread!"

Laughter echoed down the mountain that night – not from gods, not from warriors, but from people who, for a fleeting moment, felt whole again.

The fire still burned bright at the heart of the village, and laughter still echoed, but the warmth began to fade – not from exhaustion, but from the slow encroachment of night.

The clouds above remained thick and unmoving, a familiar grey ceiling that had never once parted.

No stars. No moon.

Just the growing chill that warned of what came after dusk: the dead.

A young soldier approached Garric and Eldric, hesitating, reluctant to disturb the joy that had, for once, returned to the village. "The sky's darkening," he said quietly. "We should prepare the trench. Light the fires… in case they come again."

Before either brother could answer, Nashir stepped forward, calm and centred, like the earth itself in human form. "Let them rest tonight," he said softly. "The dead will not cross the trench. Not while I stand."

Both captains turned to him, surprised – but the certainty in Nashir's voice left no room for doubt.

He turned his eyes toward his companions.

Taril. Niv. Alentar. Drunnyak. Opilkhos.

Each gave him a nod – not just of support, but of trust.

Whatever he would do, it would be enough.

Garric breathed out slowly and turned to the soldier. "Call off the watches. Let the people sleep."

As the soldier jogged off to deliver the message, a small tug at Garric's side made him pause.

He looked down to see Caelan – wide-eyed, jaw tight, clearly holding something in.

His small hand clung to Garric's cloak, his chest rising and falling too fast for comfort.

Garric knelt immediately. "What is it, my son?"

Caelan's voice shook. Not with fear, but with memory. "I saw her, Daddy."

Garric froze.

His heart missed a beat.

"When the dead came," Caelan whispered, voice cracking, "I saw her... Mummy. I know it was her. She looked at me. Her eyes..." He clenched his fists, trying not to cry. "She knew me. Even like that, she remembered me."

Garric swallowed hard, his throat tight, his hands trembling as he placed them on his son's shoulders.

Before he could answer, a shadow shifted behind him.

Eldric.

He stood silent, one hand resting on the hilt of his blade, the other pressed tightly to his chest, as if trying to keep his own emotions from spilling out.

His eyes were on Caelan, and in them was no doubt.

He had seen it too.

He had recognised her.

When Caelan looked to him, Eldric gave the smallest nod – a solemn, painful truth exchanged without a single word.

Garric looked back to his son, voice low, strained by a hundred battles but never this one. "I believe you." He pulled Caelan into a tight, protective embrace, as if trying to shield him from the weight of that truth. One hand cradled the back of his son's head, his eyes shut tight, jaw clenched as he whispered, "I'm sorry you had to see that... but I believe you."

And behind them, Eldric turned away, his face hardened, not to hide weakness, but to carry strength.

For them both.

For his nephew.

For his brother.

The fire flickered.

The wind grew colder.

But between them, wrapped in love and sorrow, they held each other like lifelines.

The sounds of celebration faded behind him – the clinking of mugs, the laughter, the music drifting like echoes across the mountains.

But Nashir walked in silence, guided not by revelry, but by purpose.

His path led him to the edge of the trench – the line between the living and the cursed.

Soldiers nearby turned at his approach, their expressions wary, respectful.

Before they could offer words or questions, he raised a hand, calm and certain.

"Go," he said gently. "Tonight is not for war. Tonight is for joy. Let the village be whole."

They hesitated for only a breath – then obeyed.

When he was alone, Nashir stepped to the edge of the trench, lowered himself to one knee, and placed his hand upon the cold earth. He whispered in the ancient tongue of the woods: *"Lle úva auta sina omentien." Nothing shall pass here tonight.*

The staff in his hand pulsed.

The earth stirred.

Roots surged upward.

Vines snapped into place.

Brambles twisted together like an army forming rank – a living barricade.

The trench transformed before his eyes – spears of bark, thorned shields of vine, thick enough to stop anything, even death.

And beyond, through the haze of falling snow, he saw them.

The undead.

Drawn by instinct. Hunger. Curse.

They staggered toward the barrier, eyes dull with deathlight...

And were repelled.

Nature lashed out – binding, spearing, throwing them back.

The wall of life did not yield.

And slowly, they began to turn away.

Not defeated.

But denied.

A long breath escaped Nashir's chest, and for the first time since the gods awakened, he allowed himself to rest.

He sank to the ground, the grass welcoming him like an old friend.

His staff rested at his side, still faintly glowing.

Nashir lay back, gazing up at the cloud-choked sky, remembering the stars shining a long time ago.

He exhaled slowly, closing his eyes.

And around him, they came.

Deer with wide, watching eyes.

Foxes, curious and unafraid.

Snow owls above in the trees, silent sentinels.

A family of wolves lay near his feet, tails curling in comfort.

Even the smallest creatures – rabbits, field mice, birds of every colour – gathered in quiet reverence.

Not because he summoned them.

But because they knew. He was one of them.

Their protector. Their kin.

Their god.

The wind brushed through the trees.

The roots hummed beneath him.

And as Nashir breathed deep the scent of life, he smiled – peaceful, surrounded, and at last, he felt at home.

The fire still glowed faintly at the centre of the square, reduced now to smouldering coals and the occasional spark, drifting like fireflies into the night. The laughter had faded into quiet conversation, and many villagers remained – too full, too warm, too grateful to bring themselves to leave.

Garric and Eldric sat on a low stone bench, the weight of the night – and the days before it – hanging heavily on their shoulders.

Between them, Caelan slept peacefully, his head resting against his father's chest, one small hand still clutching a bit of his father's cloak.

Marianne approached with slow, tired steps, their two daughters asleep against her shoulders. Eldric stood to meet her.

"Go ahead and take them," he said softly, placing a kiss on her brow. "I'll be along shortly."

She smiled, brushed Caelan's curls gently with her fingertips, then turned to head home, leaving the brothers alone under the cold, dark sky.

For a while, neither spoke. Only the sounds of wind, distant laughter, and the crackle of embers filled the quiet.

Then Garric exhaled and spoke, his voice low, rough from memory. "You remember that man we met? Months ago, near the trench?"

Eldric nodded slowly. "The one who wandered in from the south. Nearly froze to death. What was his name again?"

"Theron," Garric said. "Said he came from the hills, a place weeks from here on foot. He'd been searching for his son and granddaughter. Said they left their own village hoping to find others. Start something bigger — maybe even a trade route. Said they had dreams of a world that wasn't so broken." He paused. "He didn't find them."

Eldric looked down, remembering the old man's shaking hands, the frost still clinging to his beard, the grief carved into every line of his face.

Garric continued. "He told us about the crops they had. Fruit trees, root vegetables, fresh water from the stream. Even said they had dried meats, honey, medicinal herbs. It sounded too good to be true." He gave a tired smile. "And it was."

Eldric turned to him fully now, quiet.

"After Theron died in our village… I couldn't let the story end there. I needed to know if his people were real. If the son and granddaughter were alive. That's why I left – alone – and asked you to take care of Caelan. I wasn't going to risk more lives if it was all a lie, and to be fair, I needed the walk after Elise." He leaned back, running a hand across his tired face. "I found the village. It was there, just like he said. Nestled between hills. Looked peaceful. Too peaceful." He paused. "But then they locked their gates."

Eldric's brows drew tight. "What happened?"

"Giants." Garric's voice turned to steel. "A small warband. They'd been working with the villagers in secret. The ones the elder loved so much had made a deal with monsters."

Eldric sat forward, stunned.

"The giants had taken his son and granddaughter. Used them to control the village. Told them to send Theron to find more people to lure into traps – other villages, other lives. Fresh blood for slavery. They were ashamed, but fear made them liars. I found out too late." Garric rubbed his side, where his ribs still ached. "They tried to keep me. Question me. Find where I came from. I escaped after days of imprisonment. Barely. I was lucky they didn't kill me outright." His gaze drifted to Caelan, fast asleep in his lap. "I swore I'd never tell the villagers what really happened – not until I knew we were strong enough to protect ourselves. To protect others, too."

Eldric stared into the fire, his face cold and unreadable. "And now we are?"

Garric gave a slow nod and looked at their new friends. "Now we are."

They looked up at the faint glow rising from the village's heart – the laughter, the singing, the gods among them.

"We could build something real here, El. Something that connects people. But it has to be protected. This world… it doesn't give second chances."

Eldric placed a hand on his brother's shoulder. "Then we make this one count."

And together, in the warmth of fading firelight, two brothers sat beneath the frozen sky – one with a child in his arms, the other with duty in his bones – and a quiet promise between them to build a future the world had forgotten to hope for.

The celebration was winding down into a warm, sleepy joy.

Fires burned low, casting soft orange hues on stone and snow. Laughter drifted in gentle waves. Some villagers swayed to quiet tunes played on makeshift flutes and drums, others simply sat close, drinking in the company and warmth.

In the square's centre, Niv danced freely, the fire catching in her hair like sunlight reborn. Her golden eyes sparkled, and the soldiers who followed her steps looked both bewitched and breathless.

Near the edges of the crowd, Opilkhos leaned in quiet reflection, his hand resting calmly on his sword. Despite his distant presence, a few villagers – particularly a pair of blushing women – hovered nearby, casting admiring glances and unsure whispers. He seemed not to notice.

At the heart of the square, Garric and Eldric sat with Caelan curled asleep in Garric's lap, wrapped in a fur cloak. The two brothers shared quiet words, their shoulders heavy with exhaustion and memory.

From the shadows, Alentar watched them – steady, calculating. He caught Drunnyak's gaze, then Taril's. A subtle nod passed between them.

As the three approached, Drunnyak clapped Borgrim's shoulder in passing, who gave a grunt and nodded knowingly, already watching.

Reaching the fire's edge, Drunnyak called out, his voice cutting through the soft revelry. "Niv. Opilkhos. Come."

Niv, in mid-spin, laughed breathlessly and tossed her hair back. She winked at her flushed dance partner before stepping away with feline grace.

Opilkhos drifted toward the group like a shadow returning home, silent and composed, though his eyes were sharp with thought.

But before anything more could be said, the earth shifted, and the animals came.

Wolves, foxes, deer and birds emerged from the treeline, walking without fear. A white elk lingered near the fountain. Children gasped, wide-eyed, while villagers stepped back in awe. No one screamed.

Nashir appeared among them – his robes swept in snow and moss, his staff glowing with a quiet green pulse. He walked barefoot, his presence peaceful and powerful.

Alentar turned as he arrived, his voice calm but insistent. "Before anything else… tell the tale again. I want all of us to hear it."

The gods all gathered, forming a circle around the fire with Garric, Eldric and Caelan at its centre. The fire popped, casting long shadows on their faces.

Garric looked up, surprised by the formality – but nodded. He began slowly, voice gravelled by wear, but steady. "It was almost two months ago," he began quietly. "A morning like any other – cold, grey, the stench of rot still fresh in the air after the night's end. An old man came to us. Skin cracked from frost. Voice weak, but his words… carried fire. Said his name was Theron. He had wandered for weeks, searching for someone to believe him."

Eldric picked up, voice low and certain. "He spoke of a village, far south. A valley cradled between white cliffs. Said it was untouched by the worst of the storm winds. Claimed the ground there was fertile, the weather softer. They grew crops no one here had seen in decades."

Garric continued, now louder. "He spoke of fields of golden barley, green orchards bearing crisp apples, and tart blackberries. Vines of beans thick as a man's arm. Honey. Mushrooms that grew from the shade of silver trees. Salt harvested from steaming caverns. And fish – gods, they had fish! Caught from rivers that hadn't frozen in decades."

Murmurs rippled through the villagers. Even the gods exchanged looks.

"His son and granddaughter went ahead to forge trade. He was trying to reach them. But he was dying. Died in my arms. Said someone had to carry the dream forward. So I did." He looked down at Caelan, then back to the fire. "I went alone. Quiet. Fast. I didn't want to risk anyone else, and after my wife's passing, I promised myself that I would try to give Caelan the best I could, whilst blood ran in my veins. I made it… and it was all true."

The gods leaned in. Taril's brow lowered, Alentar's fingers flexed, Opilkhos's eyes narrowed with concern. Niv tilted her head, her usual grin gone.

"But the village…" Garric's voice faltered, darkened. "It wasn't theirs any more. The giants had taken it. They weren't beasts – they were conquerors. Towering brutes, smart enough to organise, cruel enough to dominate. They controlled everything. Every harvest. Every home. The villagers worked like slaves. The giants grew fat on their labour while the children starved behind hollow doors." His fist clenched. "I tried to leave. One of them caught my trail. I fought, but…" He stopped for a moment, breathing. "They took me. Imprisoned me. Tortured me. Not to kill me – but to break me. They wanted to know where I came from. How far I travelled. If there were others like me."

The gods remained silent, but the firelight danced in their eyes.

Garric finally looked up. "They never got a word from me. Not one."

Silence.

The gods looked at him not as a soldier, not as a man…

But as an equal.

A survivor.

It was Nashir who broke the silence, stepping forward between the firelight and the gods. "You needn't fear the trench any longer," he said. "The land lives. The roots know the shape of death. The air will carry warnings. The wolves will speak through silence. And I… will feel them, long before they come." He tapped his staff. The ground gave a hum like breath held. "If something stronger comes, we'll know. We'll be ready."

Drunnyak turned then, eyes blazing, and stepped up onto the raised stone near the fountain. "Then it's settled." He pointed to Alentar, firm and sure. "You and I leave at first light. We'll find this village. See if the kin the elder spoke of are alive – and whether this place can be reclaimed… or buried." To Taril, he turned next. "You and Nashir stay. This village stands because of you two. Build it stronger. Make it breathe. Raise crops. Purify water. Reinforce it not with fear, but with growth." Then, to Niv and Opilkhos, his voice steady, cutting through doubt. "And you two — don't just patrol walls. Study every ridge, every blind spot, every inch of weakness. Use your magic, your cunning. Ward it, trap it, seal it tight. I want alarms in the wind, traps in the stone. I want this village to spit out the night itself."

Niv raised an eyebrow, her lips curling. "Traps *and* fire? Now you're speaking my language."

Opilkhos said nothing — but there was purpose behind his silence.

A flame danced in Drunnyak's eyes. He stepped onto the stone fountain's edge and looked at each of his companions in turn, saying nothing but speaking everything. Then he turned to Garric. "You stood alone, and you didn't fall. You honoured that old man's final wish, and you carried his fire." He turned to the villagers now — all watching with rapt eyes — and lifted his voice until it echoed through the mountains. "From this night forth, this land is no longer nameless."

The people froze. Soldiers paused in mid-drink. Children stopped even their laughter.

"Let it be known as Garrents. Named for the man who believed in life. Named for the man who refused to be broken. Named for those who stood against the impossible. A village born of sacrifice. Raised by love. Forged in frost — and now rebuilt by fire and will." He lifted his mug high. "Let this be the first of many feasts. The first of many nights not just survived, but celebrated. And I swear on my soul — as long as I live, every one of my sons and daughters shall know joy in this new-found life!"

The roar that followed could have brought down the cliffs, but in fact raised their spirits beyond anything they could ever dream.

BEFORE THE NEXT STORM

A new day rose over Garrents.

The skies above remained shrouded in their eternal veil of grey, with no golden sun to pierce the cold horizon, but even so, something was different.

The air felt… calmer.

The cold was still there, but it no longer sank its teeth so deeply.

It simply existed, like the quiet breath of something ancient that had, for once, decided not to bite.

The villagers, worn from celebration and joy, had slept long and well. For the first time in living memory, they didn't sleep or wake to fear.

Inside the heart of the village, within the worn walls of The Stubborn Goat, the gods stirred. They had found places to lie – against stone, near the hearth, across benches and floors – where warmth lingered from the night before.

They had rested.

Not just their bodies, but something deeper.

And though the sun remained hidden beyond the thick canopy of cloud, it felt like morning.

Outside, the village breathed in rhythm. Animals – wolves, stags, wild hounds and birds – moved beside the people, helping them clean scraps, clear frost from stones, even fetching tools and water as if they had always belonged.

It was harmony — not forced, not tamed. Shared.

Within the tavern, Drunnyak tightened the straps on his broken broadsword, the familiar weight settling across his back. He grabbed the final pack of dried meat and hardened bread from the table and gave it a sniff before tossing it toward Alentar, who caught it without looking.

Alentar was already prepared – leathers layered, blades secured, bow slung across his back. His posture was the same as always: sharp, unreadable, watching through the window as the mist rolled over the village's edge.

By the door, Garric stood. Weather-worn, arms crossed, he eyed the pair with a pride that he didn't try to hide. "I left Caelan with my brother," he said simply. "I shall be your companion for this travel – after all, you'll need someone to guide you there, right?"

Drunnyak let out a low chuckle and motioned toward Alentar with his thumb. "Oh, we'll be fine. I've got my sniffing dog with me."

Alentar's eyebrow twitched. "I can backtrack your steps" he replied flatly. "The snow forgets what I remember, and after all, your smell should help me find our way."

Garric smirked. "He talks more than I expected."

"Don't get used to it," Alentar muttered, tightening a buckle.

Drunnyak gave a playful shove to Garric's shoulder, a show of respect more than jest. "While we're out chasing giants and picking up on what you left behind," he said, "you use this time to help them. Taril, Niv, Nashir... they know power. You know people. You know how to build, shape, guide. Help them make something better than this snow-choked life you've all been crawling through, and above all else, you deserve some quality time with your boy."

Garric nodded, the weight of those words hitting him in the chest. "I will," he said. "You have my word."

Drunnyak pulled his lion-fur-lined cloak over his shoulder and stepped toward the open door. Alentar followed, silent and sure.

Together, they walked out into the frozen light of the new morning – one made for war, one hunter with the eyes of the world, and the future of a village on their shoulders.

Behind them, Garric remained – no longer the one carrying the fire forward, but now the one helping to shape where it would burn.

And far above, in the still grey clouds, the frost held its breath.

As they made their way to the trench, even Drunnyak, for all his cynicism, paused at the crest of the newly formed threshold and gave a low, impressed whistle.

The barricades of root and stone had changed since the night before. Where once there was only frost and blood-soaked soil, there was now life – vivid and defiant.

Vines as thick as a man's leg twisted through the rocks like sleeping serpents. Flowers had bloomed, impossibly, their petals glowing faintly with warmth in the freezing air. Trees had begun to rise – slow, but steady – as if responding to some unseen song beneath the earth. Birds flitted from branch to branch, and soft animal tracks broke the snow's surface like whispers of peace.

Nashir's gift. Nashir's promise.

"Well, I'll be damned," Drunnyak muttered. "Looks like nature's been busy."

Alentar knelt near one of the roots, running his fingers over a cluster of warm moss thriving in a bed of frost. His eyes narrowed, green and sharp, tracing the pattern as if reading something ancient carved into bark. "He made this place remember," Alentar said softly. "The earth knows what it is now."

"Then let's make the rest of it remember too."

They moved forward – no more hesitation, no more words.

They crossed the trench in silence.

Drunnyak looked behind, out across the trench, watching the path leading to the threshold and the village, then moved his gaze to where the other side of the world waited – still frozen, still cursed, untouched by Nashir's breath.

Where mortals would have staggered, they advanced, swift and tireless. Their steps made no apology to the land beneath them. Snow crunched under their weight. Wind swirled around their cloaks like ghosts reaching for old gods.

Their pace was relentless.

Their purpose clear.

Two titans of forgotten age, striding into the breath of Maud's wilderness like it owed them answers.

Drunnyak, the relentless warrior. His lion-skin cloak trailed behind him like the mane of some ancient beast. His broadsword, chipped and brutal, hummed against his back like it hungered.

Alentar, the tracker. His movements were sharp, fluid, each step blending with the terrain as if he were born of it. Where Drunnyak left footprints like stone cracks, Alentar left none.

The air grew colder as they pushed deeper into the hills, but it did not matter. These were no ordinary men. They were carved from war, tempered in silence, and made for paths no one else could walk.

They followed no roads, only instinct.

Only the lingering direction passed down from Theron, the elder whose dying words had spoken of a village that they now knew was bound in chains, and Garric's footsteps guiding their way.

Drunnyak's voice broke the quiet after a time. "You sure Garric's tracks can guide us to the edge?"

Alentar didn't turn. "I don't need the boy's tracks. I can smell the way he walked."

Drunnyak smirked, amused. "My little sniffing dog," he teased.

Alentar glanced over his shoulder, unamused. "Say it again, and I'll leave you in a snowdrift for the wolves to mate on." Giving a smirk, he added, "I'll even make it easier for them, tying you up with no clothes to wear."

The laugh that erupted from Drunnyak shook snow from the branches.

It was the kind of laugh that had echoed through battlefields and feasts alike. Old. Loud. Alive.

They continued up the pass, cliffs rising like jagged blades on either side. In the distance, the first outline of massive stones appeared – markers carved by hands that once believed in peace.

Somewhere beyond them they'd find the village with giants, lies, and chains to be broken, but for now, it was just two brothers, bound not by blood, but by everything that came after it – fighting, hunting, and the promise to never stop walking forward.

And the world, still shivering from the gods' return, began to listen.

CAMPFIRE IN THE FROZEN VALE

They had walked nearly the entire day – what had taken Garric four days alone, they crossed in one.

The wind bit harder now. The land had grown meaner, wilder. The cold no longer whispered – it hissed. Frost clung to their hair and brows, and the distant howls were constant now, rising and falling like the land was remembering to scream.

But they were not bothered.

By twilight, they found shelter within the remains of an ancient watchpost – a half-collapsed stone circle built into the side of a cliff, overgrown with ice and forgotten roots. Alentar, always silent, traced the ancient etchings along the stones – markings that once belonged to their kind. Drunnyak dropped their satchels, took one long breath, and got to work.

The fire was small, but its light pushed back the cold like a challenge, not that they needed it, but it brought a feeling of their past.

Drunnyak sat with his back against a stone slab, legs sprawled out in front of him, a chunk of dried meat in one hand and his blade resting nearby. The flames danced across his bare chest, rising with the heat of laughter.

Alentar leaned just close enough to warm his hands, still half in the shadows, eyes narrowed with quiet amusement.

Beyond the ridge, undead roamed.

Not a horde, not organised – just cursed things, shambling toward the heat, the life, the flame they couldn't reach. They slammed into the wards Alentar had carefully laced into the ground – woven runes carved in an ancient tongue, twisted with vine and ash. The moment they touched them, they burned – silent, clean and final.

Drunnyak watched one such creature burst into blue fire, then flicked a bone toward the flame like it was a pebble. "Ugly bastards," he muttered. "Still desperate, even in death. Can't blame 'em. If I had to smell myself, I'd walk into fire too."

Alentar glanced toward the edge of the protective ring. "Three tried the ward before you finished your meal," he said drily. "You losing your edge?"

Drunnyak snorted and tore off another bite. "Nah. Just giving them a chance."

"Merciful god," Alentar muttered, shaking his head.

They sat like that for a while – the fire crackling, snowflakes drifting past like ash, the silence settling comfortably between them.

Then, after a beat, Drunnyak leaned his head back against the stone, eyes half-lidded, a crooked smile forming. "You know," he said, "it feels good. You and me. Moving and fighting. Like we used to."

Alentar didn't look at him, but his voice softened. "Feels right."

Drunnyak chuckled. "Last time I remember this feeling, you stabbed a troll in the eye with your damn hairpin."

"That was not a hairpin," Alentar snapped. "It was a ceremonial spike."

"You screamed like a girl when it bit your leg." Drunnyak laughed.

"He bit me – I was practically dripping with venom," Alentar replied.

"You almost cried," said Drunnyak.

"It paralysed my lungs. I was just a wee boy, you fucking cunt." Alentar looked seriously to Drunnyak.

A sudden silence, soon to be broken as they both burst out laughing, deep and raw. The sound echoed down the cliffside, bouncing off the stone like a war drum.

The wind howled back – but it couldn't reach them.

Alentar smirked, reluctantly amused. "It's strange."

"What?"

He finally looked at Drunnyak. "We've lost everything. Our names. Our time. The world we knew. But I sit here, next to you – and nothing feels different."

Drunnyak stared into the fire for a long moment. Then he grinned. "That's because nothing *is* different, brother. We fight. We survive. We laugh at death – and when we're done, we piss on it for good measure."

Alentar gave a small, silent nod. "Then let's finish what we started."

The fire crackled between them.

Out in the darkness, death waited, but it would not find them tonight.

The second day was colder.

The snow was thinner now, replaced by crusted frost and jagged ice clawing up from the soil. The trees stood closer together – taller, older – like guardians of a forgotten realm. This land hadn't felt warmth in centuries, and the silence was deep, broken only by the occasional cry of a distant bird, or the crunch of boot against ancient snow.

They walked without pause.

The road narrowed into deer trails, then into nothing at all, and yet Alentar led without question, as if the ground still remembered him. Drunnyak followed, sure and steady, his wide gait breaking through snowbanks like he'd done a thousand times before.

That's when they saw it.

A tree – an old ironwood sentinel – scarred by a symbol.

At first glance, it looked like time had chewed it down, weather and wind biting into bark. But Alentar stopped in mid-step. His hand snapped out, fingers brushing against the carving.

A symbol, half-swallowed by lichen.

A rune shaped like a sweeping arc and three points.

He stared.

Drunnyak came to his side. "Trouble?"

Alentar didn't answer. Not immediately.

He pulled back the fur of his bracer, revealing a mark identical to the one on the tree.

His mark. His signature.

Not just any etching – it was the symbol he gave to his students. The few worthy enough to be called Rangers of the Wyrdwood.

Drunnyak's brow furrowed. "That's yours."

Alentar's voice was distant. "Not mine." He traced the edge with one gloved finger, reverent. "It belonged to Alanteas."

Drunnyak stepped back a little, giving him space.

Alentar looked around, eyes sharper than before, as if seeing through the veil of snow and age. "This was his route. His patrol line." Alentar's throat was tight. His breath visible, shaking slightly in the cold. "My first disciple. The first I marked as a Wyrdwood Ranger." He paused. "I trained them to watch the borders… to be unseen protectors. I remember that when the world began to fall, I sent them out. Told them to watch the lines of the forest, to protect the last roots of nature." His voice broke slightly. "I never saw them again."

Drunnyak's gaze softened.

"I thought they all died," Alentar admitted. "In the war. Before… before we fell into slumber. That final battle. I was sure of it."

He stepped back, eyes scanning the forest like it might peel itself open and reveal an answer.

Drunnyak looked around as well – more trees, all ancient and weary, but suddenly different. Like they had been watching, waiting for someone to return.

Alentar turned to him slowly. "If this is here, if Alanteas made it… it means some of them survived. It means someone carried on."

"You trained them well," Drunnyak said quietly. "Seems one lived long enough to become more like you."

Alentar was taken back for a glimpse of a moment.

He was younger then – not in age, but in presence. His movements still sharp, but not yet worn by sorrow.

The woods of his memory were vibrant, golden green with sunlight speckled through branches.

191

A young elf, lean and determined, stood before him with a bow of whitewood, trembling slightly.

"You must earn the mark," Alentar had said.

The boy nodded. "I will." And he did.

Through storms and beasts, battle and silence, Alanteas earned it. When Alentar carved the mark into his bracer and placed it upon the youth's wrist, he spoke only four words: "Now you never lose."

The world returned in a rush of cold air and falling snow.

Drunnyak was still nearby, arms crossed, not pressing. He had seen the look before – when gods remembered things that hurt more than they healed. "Do you think he lived?" Drunnyak asked quietly.

Alentar looked back to the tree, fingers resting once more on the mark. "I think…" he whispered, "someone wanted me to find this."

That night, they made camp near a cliff overlooking a dead riverbed. The fire cracked low between them. The wind howled above, but the protection Alentar carved again in stone and soil was perfect. The undead came – but never crossed. Their bones burned, one by one, outside the warded circle.

Drunnyak tossed another log on the fire. "You ever think," he said, eyes half-glazed, "that we're not remembering… but reliving?"

Alentar, who had sat for hours in near silence, looked at the flames. "Memory is just the past… reminding us we were never done."

"Sounds like Nashir." Drunnyak grunted.

"Sounds like truth."

Drunnyak took a swig from his flask, wiped his mouth, and stared into the fire. "That boy of yours… Alanteas. If he's still out there, what would he be now?"

Alentar didn't blink. "A legend, I believe."

They both sat still for a moment.

Then, out of the woods, an owl hooted once and flew low across the firelight.

Alentar watched it pass, and without Drunnyak noticing, he smiled, looking at the horizon.

Alentar sat upright, alert as ever, though his eyes weren't watching the forest now.

They were lost in the past.

"He wasn't just a student," Alentar said finally, voice low. "Alanteas was… more like a brother, but someone very different from Nashir. A reflection. I taught him everything I knew – how to speak to the trees, how to become the wind. He was the first I trusted with my secrets."

"And now he might be out there," Drunnyak said, his voice soft but steady. "Or left something behind."

Alentar nodded once. Then, after a long silence, he spoke again. "When the war came, when we marched to face the All-Father, I told them to stay hidden. To protect the weakest ones, but part of me always knew…" His jaw clenched. "They wouldn't just watch. They would fight. They would die."

Drunnyak leaned back and stared up at the frozen stars above. "We all lost people."

Alentar's voice trembled slightly. "I told myself that what we did was necessary. That we gave our lives so others could live." He looked back at the tree, just visible on the ridge, glowing faintly as if under the moonlight. "But maybe… they were the ones who truly stayed behind and I abandoned them."

Drunnyak didn't offer comfort. He never did. But he reached into the firelight and passed Alentar the flask.

Alentar took it, wordless.

Together they sat – brothers in arms, in silence, surrounded by the woods that might still remember their names.

And above them, a snowy owl landed on a nearby branch and watched them closely.

Alentar met its gaze, and for a brief moment, he felt something familiar staring back.

SHADOWS BEHIND THE HILLS

The hills crested like the backs of great beasts, layered in white and jagged with time. The further they travelled, the more unnatural the terrain became – the land warped by centuries of cold, isolation and fear. Trees leaned inward like gossiping elders, heavy with snow and silence.

As they reached the final ridge, Alentar slowed.

Below them, nestled in a shallow bowl of stone and snow, lay the village – a hidden pocket of warmth carved into an otherwise merciless land.

The sky remained a swirling veil of ash and silver, the sun obscured as always, yet something about the air felt... *different*. As if the world paused for a heartbeat, holding its breath.

Smoke curled gently from chimneys, rising like whispered prayers. The homes were clustered tightly together, many built into the mountainside itself, half-buried and insulated by stone and earth, shaped more by necessity than beauty – but they endured. This village endured.

Encircling the settlement, a formidable wall of timber, stone, and sharpened stakes loomed high – clearly designed to withstand more than the cold. The gates, wide and heavily fortified, looked built to withstand monsters – and to hold them back.

And within the walls, movement stirred.

Not just villagers. Giants.

Too slow, too heavy, and too tall to be men, these stone giants moved between the homes – not as guests, but as enforcers. Their presence hung heavy, like a shadow that had grown roots.

Drunnyak's brow darkened.

Alentar squinted, focusing beyond the oppressive structure, beyond the patrols, as if looking for a truth buried deeper. And then came Garric's voice, echoing from memory, soft but clear. "He spoke of fields of golden barley," Alentar murmured aloud, as if the words themselves unlocked what the eye could not yet fully grasp.

His keen eyes flicked to a terraced ridge within the village walls – and there it was.

Beneath a sheet of morning frost, golden stalks bent with winter's weight, still clinging to life. Orchards hugged the southward slope, their branches dormant but unmistakable in shape – apple trees, twisted and patient. A grove beyond that shimmered with silver bark.

"Green orchards bearing crisp apples, and tart blackberries…" Drunnyak added, almost in disbelief.

And further still, glimpses of wonder hidden in the mundane.

Trellised vines, their roots thick and clinging. The edge of a cavern, where faint steam rose like breath from a sleeping beast. The glint of water not frozen – a river alive.

This was no lie.

What Garric had described… *was here.*

"Honey. Mushrooms grown in the shade of silver trees. Salt from steaming caverns," Drunnyak said, voice low with reverence. "And fish… gods, they had fish."

But all of it – *all of it* – chained.

Guarded. Controlled.

The bounty of the land bent beneath the heel of giants.

Alentar's gaze sharpened.

Drunnyak's hands closed into fists.

What they saw now was a land that had survived somehow.

What they remembered was what it could become, and now it was theirs to reclaim from its captors.

The giants towered above the buildings, wrapped in hides, with limbs like tree trunks and skin the colour of stone. Others sat near fires, idly watching humans carry crates, pull sleds, or grind grain under heavy wheels.

The villagers moved like ghosts – silent, coordinated, heads down, expressions blank with survival. They had learned how to live, but not how to be free.

Alentar crouched on the ridge, hidden by thickets and snow. His eyes sharpened, taking in the patrols, the distance between buildings, the movement of guards and beasts alike.

Drunnyak, standing just behind him with arms crossed, cracked his knuckles and grunted. "Well, they sure know how to make friends."

Alentar didn't move. "It's worse than I thought. They're embedded. Organised."

"Which means more bones to break."

Alentar turned slightly, his tone calm but cold. "If we charge in and fail to end it quickly, people will die. Families. Children. This isn't like old times, Drunnyak. These are simple people trying to live in a world that forces them to be more than just alive."

Drunnyak frowned, jaw clenching, fists tightening.

Alentar stood slowly and adjusted his bow on his back. "Give me time," he said. "Let me scout, find the cracks. If we strike, we do it right. No blood spilled unless it must be."

The brute grumbled, muttering something about how "a fight solved most things back in the day", but he nodded. Reluctantly. "I'll wait," he said. "But if one of those oversized bastards so much as sniffs me wrong, I'm cracking something."

Alentar's lips curled in the faintest smirk. "I wouldn't expect anything less." Before parting, he crouched beside Drunnyak, voice low and clear in the swirling dusk. "If you see an arrow with red fletching arcing high into the sky… attack. No restraint. No mercy. And if I light a single green flame on the eastern watchtower," he added, "approach the gate like a lost traveller. No blades drawn. No threats. Just questions."

Drunnyak grunted, clearly preferring the first option.

With that, Alentar vanished, melting into the hills, his cloak already shifting to match stone and snow. His steps left no mark. Not even the cold dared betray him.

Drunnyak exhaled slowly, crouching down near a boulder, watching the village with narrowed eyes.

Below them, the world continued unaware – a place of quiet chains and tired breath, waiting for salvation... or destruction.

The night clung tightly to the land as Alentar stood just beyond the last ridge, eyes fixed on the faint glow of torchlight ahead. The village lay hidden in a fold of the hills, its defences crude but clever – earth mounded into walls, reinforced with stone and wood, built for defence rather than beauty.

Now, the wind whispered around Alentar's form as he weaved through sparse tree cover and snow-covered stones, his presence nothing more than a fleeting shimmer. His body moved with practised elegance, his cloak adjusting in subtle hues to match rock, frost and shadow. To any onlooker, he was simply part of the night.

The outer perimeter of the village was subdued. Two guards – humans – stood near the gate. They looked tired, underfed, but not cruel. Villagers. Survivors.

Alentar bypassed them with ease, scaling the outer stonework and landing silently atop a narrow rooftop.

From above, he took in the structure of the place.

Stone-walled homes hugged the inner hills, many carved halfway into the slopes like burrows. Their chimneys spat thin trails of smoke into the sky, too careful, too small to be for comfort alone. It was survival heat – just enough to cook, not enough to call attention.

The streets between homes were narrow, well worn by foot, and lined with torchlight wrapped in frost-glass – an alchemical trick to keep the flames burning low and steady even in heavy wind. The undead would never breach this place easily. No, something else kept these people shackled.

Further in, he moved along a row of connecting rooftops, lightly leaping between buildings with a quiet grace. His keen eyes scanned the corners.

And there they were.

Giants.

Not many — not in the village proper. Two, massive and half-armoured, sat near the village square around a pit of coals, lazily watching humans stack crates and carry baskets of root vegetables and dried meats. These weren't guards. They were collectors. The humans didn't flinch near them, but they did not meet their eyes either.

Alentar narrowed his gaze. *Garric said he came freely*, he thought. *Met the villagers before they showed their chains.*

This village had been a place of welcome once, perhaps. Maybe the horror didn't live in the village before the captors.

Alentar's gaze shifted further. He slipped through a crevice between buildings, climbed higher up a sloping ridge that crowned the village — and saw it.

Between two converging hills, where the wind howled colder and stronger, lay a mountain unlike the rest. Its stone was darker, smoother — carved by old tools, likely dwarven once, but now corrupted.

A massive gate, built into the mountain, loomed at the far end of a frozen path. Wide enough for giants, tall enough to swallow a tree whole. Massive torches burned blue and green. Movement stirred beyond the gates — shadows as tall as buildings.

A fortress built into the stone.

There, at the base of the slope leading toward it, humans not in chains, pulling sleds and crates uphill toward that gaping maw.

No chains around their wrists, but it was clear in their gait — in the way they kept their heads down, their movements cautious, rehearsed. These were not villagers living freely. They were slaves, working in quiet desperation beneath the eye of giants.

Alentar watched from above, his sharp eyes following them as they hauled barrels of apples, ripe and crisp. Others pushed carts of grain — golden barley, now to be turned into rations for their captors. He saw children carrying baskets of mushrooms plucked from the roots of those silver-barked trees, once described with reverence, now just another quota to meet.

They were surrounded by abundance – rivers that hadn't frozen, hills thick with vines, honeycombs glistening with nectar – and yet not one face showed joy.

Only silence. Only fear.

They lived in a land of plenty, yet starved for freedom.

Alentar's jaw tightened. "Blessed land, cursed lives," he whispered, vanishing into the shadows once more.

Alentar crouched on the ridge, eyes tracking every movement, every patrol. Unlike the more relaxed brutes in the village, the giants at the castle entrance wore armour. Purpose. Rank. They barked orders, shoved the sleds forward, and herded the humans like cattle.

He took note of everything: the number of guards, the rotations, the route from the village up to the castle.

Then he lowered his body, pressing his ear against the cold earth. From the depths, he felt it – a resonance, like a drumbeat buried deep in the stone. Machinery? Or something older?

Whatever ruled this place, it was worse than what Garric saw.

He didn't light the green flame.

Not yet.

A WHISPER OF NAMES

The night was silent, but Alentar could feel the tension as clearly as if it hung from the rooftops.

He moved like breath between shadows, scaling rooftops, vaulting from beam to beam with barely a whisper to mark his passage. His eyes – sharp as an eagle's even in this lightless night – locked onto a flicker of movement below.

There, just beyond a crumbling barn, between a broken wall and a frost-split silo, stood a mature, stocky man with ginger hair, and two stone giants. The man's face was hollowed by years of silent defiance, but his back was straight. In his weathered hand, he clutched a knife – a pitiful sliver of resistance held firm against the impossible.

The giants stood opposite him.

One leaned lazily on a massive timber beam, chewing something stringy and meat-red between his yellow teeth, lips curled into a cruel grin.

The other stood silent, arms crossed, face grim – not cruel, not pleased either. Watching.

"You shouldn't have spoken or defied," the grinning one said, voice a slow, mocking rumble. "You knew what the price was, and now you lost your wife for nothing. Your granddaughter belongs to him now. She's been chosen."

Eamonn's voice shook, but he didn't back down. "She's just a young woman, barely bled," he hissed. "She was promised to be spared. You swore!"

The mocking giant gave a sharp laugh, stepping closer. "Swore? You think oaths mean anything here, old man? He wanted her. So we gave her."

Eamonn took a step back, his knuckles white on the knife. "Then you'll die before you touch another."

The giant raised a brow, amused. "Will I?"

He stepped forward, cracking his neck.

The silent one shifted his weight, clearly uncomfortable.

"Enough," Eamonn spat. "You've taken everything."

The taunting giant growled. "I should crush you just for speaking."

He lunged, arm swinging.

But the silent giant moved, grabbing the other's forearm in mid-strike. "He's no threat. He's broken. Leave it."

The first giant snarled. "Are you telling me how to discipline my meat?"

And then he struck.

A heavy backhanded blow sent the silent one reeling, crashing against a stone wall, cracking it with the force.

Eamonn flinched, bracing for the end as the giant leaped towards him – when suddenly, it was like time stopped.

From the darkness above, a sound like silk tearing through wind.

Thunk.

Thunk.

Thunk-thunk-thunk.

Two arrows buried deep into the giant's eyes, snuffing out his mocking sneer in an instant.

The other three drove into his chest, marking where his heart should be in a tight triangle – precision only one hand in a thousand lifetimes could deliver.

The giant staggered, eyes wide with the shock of death. His body twisted, knees folding.

But before he could hit the ground, he was caught.

A blur descended from the shadows above. Cloak trailing, body weightless.

Alentar.

He landed silently, catching the giant's collapsing form with impossible grace, slowing its fall, guiding it gently to the ground like laying down a broken memory.

His golden eyes flicked to Eamonn.

Silent. Burning.

Alentar's foot sank deeper into the snow as he braced himself, the full weight of the giant draped across his shoulder like a fallen monument. Muscles taut, breath steady, he shifted the massive form with one arm – controlled, effortless. His other hand rose slowly to his lips, fingers gloved in dark leather, and with a calm, deliberate motion, he pressed a single finger there.

His eyes locked with Eamonn's. A silent command. *Quiet*, his gaze seemed to say, steady as stone. And then, barely a whisper, barely a breath, "Shhh."

Alentar lowered the giant's corpse with quiet precision, letting its bulk settle into the snow like a fallen boulder. The breath of the mountain held still, the wind itself hesitant to move.

His eyes scanned the surroundings, sharp, calculating.

There.

A rocky hollow just beyond the edge of the path, partially veiled by a crooked outcrop and a thicket of thorn-laced brush. Perfect.

He moved.

Gripping the giant's leg with one hand, he began dragging the immense body through the snow, boots silent as ghosts upon the frozen earth.

That's when he heard it.

The heartbeat.

Slow at first – dull and off rhythm.

Then faster.

Stronger.

Behind him, the fallen giant – the one who'd tried to protect Eamonn – stirred with a groan, his massive hand twitching against the ground.

Alentar froze in mid-step, head turning just enough to catch the motion with his peripheral vision. His gaze narrowed.

Eamonn, crouched low in the shadow of the ruined stable, looked from the twitching giant to the silent hunter dragging his kin like firewood. His mouth opened slightly, words caught between wonder and terror.

The snow crackled beneath Alentar's foot as he adjusted his grip.

Still calm.

Still measured.

He gave Eamonn a single glance – cool, composed – before resuming the drag, unfazed by the shifting hulk behind him.

The second giant's breath came quicker now. A groan escaped his cracked lips as he lifted his head groggily.

And then… Alentar was gone.

Not a sound.

Not a shimmer.

Only wind and stillness.

Eamonn blinked, heart pounding, eyes darting between the awakening giant and the empty patch of snow from where the other one had vanished. His breath caught in his throat.

Then…

A whisper behind him. Warm. Dangerous.

"Do you trust him?" Alentar's voice curled through the dark like smoke. "Or should I add another giant to my tally?"

Eamonn flinched, but didn't turn. A slow exhale escaped him. "He tried to stop it." Eamonn's voice was quiet but firm. His breath steamed in the cold air. "He's not like the others," he continued. "Only arrived a few days ago. Doesn't laugh when they hurt people. Doesn't speak much either. I've seen him give bread to starving kids when the others weren't looking. His name's Drokan."

Behind them, Drokan groaned.

The giant's massive body shifted, thick arms twitching, fingers curling in pain. His head turned slowly, eyes blinking at the overcast sky above as if trying to remember where – or who – he was. A grimace spread across his cracked lips, and his brow creased beneath his tangled hair. His skull throbbed from the earlier strike.

He tried to sit up – stiff, sluggish – and then froze.

Alentar was standing right in front of him.

Out of nowhere.

One moment, nothing but snow and shadow.

The next, a figure so still, so composed, so deadly that Drokan nearly cried out from sheer instinct.

Alentar's cloak shifted subtly in the wind, blending with the stone, the snow, the dark. It was more than stealth – it was presence, a thing honed sharper than any blade. He gazed into the giant's eyes. Calm. Patient. Dangerous. Then he spoke. "Do you want to live?"

The words were soft. Measured.

But they struck Drokan like a hammer to the chest.

The giant didn't answer – not right away. He couldn't. His jaw trembled. He wasn't sure if he'd pissed himself, but something deep inside him recoiled in ancient fear. This wasn't a simple elf.

This was a predator.

Eyes green as precious emeralds focused entirely on him. Watching. Measuring.

Eamonn didn't dare move.

Didn't blink.

The moment hung, tight as a drawn bowstring, until Alentar, without looking back, tilted his head just enough to speak. "Calm your heart, old man. I can hear your blood running wild."

Eamonn swallowed hard.

Drokan managed a tiny nod – barely more than a flinch – but it was all the answer Alentar needed.

He stepped back just slightly, not lowering his guard, but giving the giant room to breathe. The weight of death still lingered in the air.

But – for now – it held.

Alentar extended his hand.

Drokan hesitated – just for a breath – but then reached out, his massive, trembling fingers closing around Alentar's much smaller palm. With surprising strength, the elf pulled him to his feet, and Drokan rose, unsteady but upright. The moment held a strange dignity – an ancient warrior offering a hand not just in alliance, but in mercy.

Then Alentar lifted his other hand.

A breeze stirred – soft at first, barely more than a sigh. Then it gathered, swirling gently around them, curling over the snow-covered ground. Dust and frost, scattered leaves and disturbed earth – all began to smooth out. The tracks... vanished.

The wind wasn't just nature.

It understood.

Drokan and Eamonn both turned their heads as the wind settled. And when they looked back...

Alentar was gone.

Not a sound.

Not a shadow.

Only the faint shimmer of disturbed air, like a mirage, rippling in the corner of their vision.

Then... his voice. A whisper. Sharp as a blade's edge, soft as falling snow. "Here."

They turned toward a narrow alley between stone buildings, now darker than the others. Shielded. Hidden.

He was there again, only visible when he willed it, half wrapped in shadow, half in light, crouched like a wraith waiting to strike – but calm, composed, beckoning.

"Quickly," he said, with a glance over his shoulder. "We don't have much time."

And they followed, silent and wide-eyed, hearts racing, into the dark.

Alentar turned, his emerald eyes catching the faintest glint of light, pinning the giant with a look that cut through fear and hesitation alike. "Drokan," he said evenly, and the name hit like a hammer.

The giant flinched. Not from pain, but from recognition.

He hadn't spoken his name aloud. Hadn't offered it. Yet the elf knew. Knew *him*.

Alentar then turned his gaze to the older man, who still stood with one hand clenched at his side, the other twitching toward a blade no longer needed. "And you?" Alentar asked, gentler now.

The man blinked, as if waking from a trance. "I… It's… it's Eamonn, sir, Eamonn Dunlea," he stammered, the name falling from his lips with more shock than pride.

Alentar offered the faintest nod of approval, and something in his stance eased – shoulders drawing back as calm settled into his frame. "I am Alentar," he said.

The words weren't loud. They didn't need to be.

They rang in the bones.

In Drokan's breath.

In Eamonn's soul.

The name of a legend told when Eamonn was just a young boy.

A name older than the fall of cities.

The silence that followed wasn't awkward.

It was reverent.

Even the wind dared not speak.

Drokan and Eamonn exchanged a glance – one made of disbelief and something far deeper, something that hummed in the marrow.

Even though they shared no lineage, no culture, no blood between them…

They both knew the name.

A name passed in whispers beneath hearth-smoke.

A name buried in stone and soil, remembered only in fragments of dreams and dying lullabies.

"Alentar," Eamonn breathed again, his voice quivering with awe. "We… we sang your name once. Not as warriors, but in songs." His hand hovered over his chest, as if trying to still the tremor in his heart. "My grandmother, she used to sing of *Alanteas*. The first ranger of the high glade. Said he came from the mountains, with golden eyes and arrows that flew faster than breath itself. Said he left marks on trees so the lost could find their way."

Drokan's expression tightened, not in anger, but in memory. "I heard it too," he rumbled, his voice low and hushed. "In the stone-deep hollows, long before the fire giant came. My mother whispered it when she thought I slept." He blinked, staring at Alentar, not with fear now, but in reverence. "As if... you were never just an elf."

Alentar's gaze softened only slightly, but he didn't deny it. Didn't bask in it. He simply looked at the two of them, his voice as steady and ancient as the trees. "I left a legacy once," he said. "And now I've returned for those still brave enough to protect one."

Eamonn's eyes filled. Drokan lowered his head.

The wind rustled through the darkened streets like an old friend returning home.

Eamonn's face twisted – grief carved fresh across skin already worn by years of sorrow. His voice cracked as he clutched the fabric over his heart, shaking his head in helpless rhythm. "They killed my wife..." His breath caught, like the words themselves refused to leave him. "My children." The next came as a whisper. "My granddaughter... she's only a girl. Barely a woman... They took her. Into the deep."

Beside him, Drokan lowered his head. Even his massive frame seemed to shrink beneath the weight of the truth. "All who go into the mountain, into *his* hall... they don't return," the stone giant said, voice low and hollow. "We knew it. We watched it happen."

There was no malice in him, no defiance – only shame.

Alentar stood still.

Eamonn's fists clenched as tears welled in his eyes. "She's just a child, Alentar," he said, voice hoarse with grief. "My granddaughter. I can't sleep knowing she's in there. You don't know what they do to them..." He broke off, chest heaving, as if even breathing the truth would damn them both. "Please," he begged, stepping forward, his shoulders trembling. "If you can save her, even just her, I'll give you my life. I'll follow you into whatever madness comes next. Just don't leave her there."

Alentar held his gaze, and for a moment – just a breath – there was something else behind those green eyes. Not strategy. Not calculation.

Grief.

Memories.

The weight of lives lost, centuries deep.

"I do know," Alentar said quietly. He placed a hand on Eamonn's shoulder, strong but steady. "And if I move too soon – if I go in for one and draw the fire of all the giants – I lose her. I lose you. I lose every soul still holding on to hope inside this place."

Eamonn's lips trembled, but he didn't speak. He only looked at the man before him, this legend made flesh.

Alentar's grip tightened slightly, anchoring the moment. "You have my word," he said, voice like the calm before a storm. "When the time is right, I'll try. I'll do more than try." He let go, stepping back into the dark once more. "But first," he said, turning just enough to meet Eamonn's eyes one last time, "gather who you can. Pass the word. Quietly. Hide until my signal if you can." His emerald eyes burned, catching the faintest glint of frost as he added, "When you see a single flame – green, burning atop the eastern watchtower – that's how you'll know. You're no longer alone." He stepped back toward the alley, pausing only once more to look over his shoulder. "I'm not alone," he said, the words like iron sheathed in silk. "And when the undead return to the ground... we'll be waiting." Then his gaze shifted, falling cold and direct onto Drokan. "Hide."

The single word made the ground feel thinner beneath the giant's feet.

Alentar's smirk flickered, dry and knowing. "Drunnyak won't show you mercy if he sees you first. He doesn't do reasoning well."

He gave a soft laugh, more breath than sound, but it was enough.

Drokan froze. His massive frame quivered as the name fell like a thunderclap across his mind.

Drunnyak.

The brute.

The monster-slayer.

A name passed between giants like a ghost story, spoken only when fires burned low and weapons lay within reach. A name that made even the cruellest of them lower their voices.

Drokan's eyes widened. His hands trembled. He fell back against the stones, his voice a choked stammer. "P-please," he gasped. "I'm not like them. I didn't hurt anyone, I swear it." His breath came fast now, panicked. "I'm a slave too, just like the humans. Just like *them...*"

Alentar did not move, only watched.

Silent. Calculating. Like the winter itself deciding whether it would let something live.

Then he nodded, almost imperceptibly, and disappeared into the night once more.

Eamonn stood breathless, knife limp at his side, the weight of what he'd just heard pressing down on him like the mountain above. Tears shimmered in the corners of his eyes, not from fear, but from something deeper. A glimmer of hope laced with the agony of restraint.

Across from him, the giant – Drokan – remained still, hunched in the falling snow, his massive form trembling beneath the layers of stone-worn skin. He didn't speak. He didn't have to. Shame sat heavy in his eyes, like someone who had witnessed horrors and survived, only to carry them.

Their gazes met. Man and giant. Prisoner and warden. Victim and reluctant accomplice.

"I didn't know about your family," Drokan rumbled at last, voice low as shifting earth. "But I know what they do. I've heard the screams."

Eamonn's jaw clenched. His fingers curled tight around the knife's hilt – but he didn't raise it. Not this time. "You tried to stop them," he said, almost to himself. "That's more than most."

Drokan nodded slowly, then lowered his head. "I'll hide. Just like he said. And I'll wait for that flame. You have my word."

Eamonn sheathed his knife, the motion slow and deliberate. He took a step back, then another, his eyes never leaving the giant. "I'll do the same," he murmured. "I'll find the quiet ones. The ones still holding on." He glanced up at the distant tower, now just a silhouette against the endless dark. "When the green light burns, we'll be ready."

And for a long moment, the two just stood there in silence – two strangers bound by a single promise and the memory of a whisper in the snow.

Then they parted, wordlessly.

One vanished into the bones of the mountain, where even giants could hide.

Eamonn turned toward the alley, toward the frost-laced corners of the village, and vanished to deliver the message that would ignite everything.

THE HUNTER AND THE BEAST

The wind howled low through the canyons of rock and ice as Alentar descended the slopes with steps as light as breath. The little light hidden behind the thick grey clouds gave no guidance – but he didn't need it. He *was* the dark.

Down in the hollow where they'd agreed to wait, Drunnyak sat on a boulder, hunched over a fire that barely dared flicker in the cold. His broadsword, dull and jagged, lay across his lap, his massive arms crossed, eyes closed – but Alentar knew better than to think him asleep.

So, naturally, he crept up behind him and whispered, just above his ear, "Boo."

In a blur, the giant leapt to his feet with a roar, firelight flashing in his eyes as he snatched up his blade. But the moment his eyes adjusted to the shadows, he saw the lean figure of Alentar leaning casually against a frost-covered tree with a smug smirk on his lips.

Drunnyak growled. "One day, little snake, I *will* crush you for that."

Alentar chuckled as he stepped into the light, a glint in his eyes. "You've said that every time since I figured out how to sneak up on you."

"And one day," Drunnyak grinned, "you'll blink too loud."

They shared a beat of brotherly silence. Then, Alentar's tone shifted – calm, but purposeful. "I've seen the heart of the village. The giants aren't the worst thing there, it seems."

Drunnyak's smile faded.

Alentar knelt by the fire and began drawing lines in the frost-covered dirt – paths, buildings, routes. The castle. The patrols. The villagers. "They've turned this place into a feeding post," he said. "The real power… it lives inside the mountain."

Drunnyak's jaw tensed. "So we kill it."

Alentar nodded, but his hand paused in the dirt. "Yes. But not yet." He looked up, meeting his companion's eyes. "There are innocents. Families. Children. The elder's kin are being held within the fortress walls. If we strike too soon, they'll die screaming, just to spite us."

Drunnyak grunted, shifting uncomfortably. "You want patience."

"Just a little," Alentar said, raising a brow. "Enough time for my contact to warn the quiet ones. To scatter the children. To hide what can't be saved with steel."

A long pause stretched between them.

Then Drunnyak exhaled like a dragon cooling its breath. "Fine," Drunnyak rumbled, cracking his knuckles. "But I get first blood."

Alentar smirked, eyes twinkling with mischief. "You always do." He said it with the ease of an old comrade, but behind the grin, he was already laughing, because one giant had already fallen, and Drunnyak didn't even know it yet. He stood, dusted off the frost, and slung his bow across his back. "Give me until the morning," he said. "Then we bring the storm."

Drunnyak raised his blade and let it rest on his shoulder. "Until the undead rest, you mean," he agreed. "But then I stop holding back."

Alentar gave a short, sharp nod. "Then make sure your blade is ready and your heart is steady," Alentar said, his voice calm but sharp as the wind. He turned to leave, but paused with a sly glance over his shoulder. "Oh – one more thing. There's a stone giant named Drokan. Big, slow, sort of shaped like a crumbling boulder with legs. Smells like moss and bad decisions."

Drunnyak raised an eyebrow.

Alentar continued, smirking, "He's not like the others. Tried to protect a villager earlier. Leave him breathing if you can. He might be useful."

Drunnyak groaned. "Ugh, come on. You always give me the broken ones to spare."

Alentar shrugged. "Well, if it helps... he did soil himself when I mentioned your name."

That got a grin out of Drunnyak. "He's already weak, then. That's a mercy killing."

"Spare him, you brute." Alentar chuckled. "If nothing else, we can use him to scare the rest."

Drunnyak sighed dramatically, hefting his massive sword over one shoulder. "Fine. But if he so much as sneezes in my direction, I'm planting him in the snow."

Alentar grinned. "Fair enough. Just don't make me carve his name on your conscience later."

Drunnyak gave a toothy smirk. "You think I've got room left on that thing?"

The two warriors shared a rare, quiet laugh – just enough to break the tension before the storm to come.

Then, like a breath through pine, Alentar vanished once more.

A STORM TICKING

The wind whistled low and bitter across the barren ridge where Drunnyak stood. His frame, towering and unmoving, was etched in the snowfall like a carved monument. The snow gathered on his broad shoulders, melting before it could stick. He was a mountain of stillness, yet his eyes – those storm-dark eyes – were alive, following every flicker of motion below.

Down the slope, far across the snow-blind plain, the village sprawled like a trapped breath held between the cliff walls and the mountain's shadow. From this distance, the fortress at its heart looked less like a man-made structure and more like a wound carved into the earth – a monstrous scar of stone and steel, crowned by the jagged peaks of what had once been a dwarven stronghold, now blackened by fire and time.

Drunnyak could just make out the towering gates. Giants stood sentry there, their massive silhouettes barely shifting, like grotesque statues. Beyond those gates, life crawled under the yoke of tyranny, and Alentar moved through it all like smoke.

The elf god's steps were weightless, his form a shifting silhouette in the shallow light. Where stone met snow, he passed unseen. Where giants lumbered or bellowed, he remained shadow. He had learned the cadence of patrols, the lazy discipline of creatures too sure of their dominance.

The outer village pulsed with cruel routine. Fires burned low in makeshift pits as villagers toiled under the eyes of their captors. They bent over crates of food – barley, mushrooms, roots grown under silver trees – stacking supplies destined for the fortress above. The very bounty Garric once described, now guarded and hoarded like spoils of war.

Alentar climbed a slanted roof and crouched beneath the shelter of a crumbling archway, his breath misting as he observed.

Children carried buckets of icy water. Women with hollow eyes passed bags of dried beans up to wagons. Men, strong from survival, now looked broken – backs bent beneath the weight of their harvest.

Giants barked orders in low, thunderous grunts. One raised a club lazily when a man stumbled, and the others laughed as if it were a game.

But Alentar didn't flinch.

His gaze swept beyond the village, tracing the heavy iron pipes leading into the hillside, the slave roads that vanished behind stone gates and spiked fences. That was the heart of it. The lair. That was where the kin of Theron were chained.

He reached toward the bracer at his forearm, fingertips brushing the worn markings etched there – the old language of his rangers. It steadied him.

Not yet.

The signal would come later.

For now, he waited.

Watching.

Hunting.

And in the distance, high on the ridge, Drunnyak waited too – a storm held on a leash, waiting for the first crack of thunder to break.

The snow muffled all sound as Alentar reached the edge of the fortress gate, hidden beneath the shelter of a jagged ledge. What had once been the stone-sealed, concealed entrance of a dwarven hold had been ripped wide open, reshaped to accommodate the egos and bodies of giants.

Where once there might've been a simple arch etched with dwarven runes – hidden behind clever stonework and defended by layered traps

– there now stood a massive arched gate, ten men high, lined with iron slabs bolted into the mountain face like crude armour. Spikes jutted from the base, a clear deterrent to siege beasts, though none had likely ever dared approach.

The dwarves had built for function – tucked into the bones of the earth, close to the warmth of stone. But the giants had forced the mountain to display its submission. They had carved pride where once there had been prudence, raising ceilings and splitting hallways wider, cracking what had once been a secret refuge into a monument of brute force.

Alentar slipped through a collapsed side breach, a crumbled dwarven watch-hole now used for refuse. The scent of blood, rot and smoke clung to the walls like a second skin.

Inside, the contrast was even more jarring.

Dwarven halls, once narrow and intricate – designed for compact movement, tight defences, and masterwork craft – had been gutted and reshaped. Ancient runes were scraped off the walls, replaced by crude etchings in Giant-Tongue. Stone columns had been widened, sometimes broken and replaced by ironwood beams. Torches burned with black smoke, illuminating the once-sacred halls with a dirty, wavering glow.

The stone floors, once masterfully tiled with geometric patterns, now bore deep gouges from giant feet, blood smears, and signs of struggle.

Further in, Alentar watched from the shadows as humans carried crates – vegetables, meats, sacks of flour, and dried mushrooms – into the fortress proper. They moved without speaking, trained into silence. Each crate was placed on a massive wooden platform – once a dwarven cargo lift, now a crude elevator – and lowered into the bowels of the fortress by chains as thick as a man's leg.

Giants stood nearby, laughing and mocking the humans as they passed. One slammed a fist into a post to signal the descent. The old mechanisms groaned, and the elevator slowly lowered, taking its burden into the blackened depths.

Alentar followed above, leaping from beam to ledge like a shadow. As he moved deeper, the air thickened. The sounds grew fewer – but heavier.

He passed through a chamber where a dozen giants lounged, their weapons scattered carelessly around them. Half of them were asleep, others tossing dice made from bone, the flickering torchlight glinting off gold jewellery stolen and repurposed.

And beyond that… he saw it.

The main descent – a massive stairway carved straight into the heart of the mountain, widened and scorched from the giants' passage. It led down to where the throne would be. The old dwarven throne room, once the pride of craftsmen and kings, now buried in firelight and tyranny.

Alentar's jaw tightened as he crouched near the overlook, breathing steadily.

This was once a place of something majestic.

Now it reeked of conquest, but not for much longer.

He moved deeper into the shadows, the scent of heat and iron thick in his lungs, the air vibrating with the pulse of something far worse than stone and muscle.

He was getting close.

Very close.

Alentar crouched above the throne room, hidden behind the twisted ribs of the old ventilation arches, high above torchlight and towering beasts. He'd timed everything. Every patrol. Every breath.

A few hours before the morning. That's what he gave himself – and now the sand in his hourglass was almost gone.

Below, a girl sat quietly on a torn cushion beside the throne. Probably fifteen years young, with braided black hair, ashen cheeks, and a stubbornness carved into her brow like the stone walls around her. She watched everything. Especially the giants.

Her father, a man in his forties, leaned back against the cold stone wall, wrists bound in chains as thick as his forearms. He was bruised, but not beaten. Not yet.

They didn't speak. But they stayed close. Every day. Every hour.

Alentar's emerald eyes scanned the chamber again. Only three giants remained. One already dozing near the far wall.

The time had come.

He moved.

Silent as breath, he dropped from the rafters, landing behind a massive tapestry with a muffled thump. He took a moment, listened. Nothing.

Then he slipped into the throne chamber's dark corners.

When the dozing giant grumbled and shifted, Alentar vanished behind a pillar, pressing his back to the stone. The torchlight flickered again.

Now.

He darted forward, his feet barely kissing the floor. A flash of silver – his curved knife – cut the first chain in silence. The man startled. The girl's eyes widened.

"Quiet," Alentar whispered, his voice calm but urgent. "I'm here to get you out."

The man hesitated – then nodded once.

He knew enough to move.

One more slice. The iron shackle slipped free with the barest sound – a muted clang, caught mid-drop by Alentar's quick fingers.

Two freed. No sound.

"Stay low. Keep close. We go out together. The moment I give the signal, you run. Don't look back."

They nodded, and for the first time, Alentar saw it – hope in their eyes.

A few minutes later, he moved through the outer corridor, the freed prisoners following at a distance, staying in the shadows he had already cleared. A few doors unlocked, hallways empty – Alentar had prepared everything in advance.

He left them tucked safely behind the ruined smithy outside the keep, nestled beneath a blanket of snow-covered hides.

"You stay. I'll bring the storm."

He turned toward the cliffside, where the wind was howling low and sharp like a wolf's cry.

The world was ready.

And now, so was he.

Alentar reached the edge of the fortress gate, stepped onto the outer parapet, and raised one hand skyward. His bow glimmered faintly under the pale night.

HOPE SPREADS

Beneath the broken stone ribs of the old silo, where frost crept like fingers through the earth-packed walls, Eamonn stumbled into the shelter, his boots slick with half-melted snow and his breath tearing from his chest.

The gathered villagers looked up – tired, cold, some with children clutched in their arms, all with eyes dulled by too many winters of waiting.

But Eamonn's voice… his voice carried something they hadn't heard in a long time. Fire. "An elf came," Eamonn said, voice rough, trembling as he stepped into the torchlight. "A hunter. Tall as any man, eyes sharp as winter steel. He moved like shadow – and held the weight of a giant over his shoulder like it was nothing."

Murmurs flickered through the crowd – some startled, others disbelieving.

"He found me in the dark," Eamonn continued, his breath still ragged. "Two stone giants had taken my granddaughter earlier on tonight… I was ready to die trying to stop them. And he… he watched from the shadows. Waited. Then, when one of them moved to strike, he unleashed death like it was breath itself."

All sound drained away, leaving only silence and staring eyes.

"I saw him hold that monster's corpse on one shoulder not even a second after killing him, silent as falling snow, not even breaking stride.

And with the other hand, he told me to hush." Eamonn mimicked the gesture, finger to lips. "As calm as you please. Like death was a song he'd sung before."

Gasps. Fear. Wonder.

A younger woman stepped forward, voice shaking. "So we should believe this elf… is supposed to stop all of this?"

Eamonn's eyes blazed. "He's not just an elf. He said his name." He let it fall like a stone in still water. "Alentar."

The name rippled through them. A few older voices whispered it like a forgotten prayer. A man dropped his cup.

An old woman with silver-threaded braids clutched her shawl tighter. "The ranger? From the songs? From the elders' stories?"

Eamonn nodded. "The Bow of the Wild Dawn. He's real. I saw him. I spoke with him. He said he came because Garric told him what was done to us."

"And the giant?" someone asked quietly, almost afraid.

"He spared one," Eamonn said. "A younger one – Drokan. Different from the rest. I saw it in his face. Shame. Grief. That one helped me once before, and Alentar, he let him live."

That stunned them. Giants were monsters, but the story was shifting.

A shiver ran through the gathered villagers, a name pulled from half-remembered tales written in old books and sung in fireside songs long forgotten.

But Eamonn wasn't finished. "And he's not alone."

The villagers turned to one another, startled. Whispers stirred like wind through dry leaves.

"He walks with another," Eamonn said. "A mountain of a man. Drunnyak."

The name meant nothing to most – but one voice cracked the silence like lightning.

"That can't be true!" rasped an old man near the back, bent nearly in half with age, his eyes wide with a blend of awe and fear. His cane slipped from his hand, clattering to the ground as he pushed himself upright. "You said… *Drunnyak?*"

Eamonn nodded, cautious.

The old man's hands trembled. "I heard that name when I was a boy. My grandfather swore it over his deathbed. Said there was once a warrior – not a man, not even a god, but something more – who hunted giants. Who crushed those who preyed on the weak." He stepped forward, his voice growing stronger with each word. "He told me of a time when a fire-wyrm – an elder dragon – ravaged the southern cliffs. Burned villages for weeks. No one could stop it."

The villagers leaned in, held captive by the tale.

"He said a lone warrior walked up the mountainside, without armour, with a giant broadsword and a grin on his face. They say he brought the beast down with his bare hands and roasted its heart over the flames it left behind."

A wave of disbelief rippled through the crowd.

"A dragon?" someone scoffed. "Come on…"

"A bedtime tale," muttered another. "A broken memory from an old man."

But others didn't speak.

They were remembering the fear in Eamonn's voice. The reverence.

And the way the old man trembled – not from frailty, but from awe. "I thought it was a legend," he whispered. "A warning evildoers told their young to keep them humble."

Eamonn's voice was steady now. "Then let them remember their warnings. Because he's real. And he's coming. And then," Eamonn said, his voice softer, "Alentar looked to the east. He said when we see a single green flame atop the eastern watchtower – then we'll know," he pointed toward the snowy ridge where the stone tower loomed, barely visible in the dark, "that we're not alone."

Silence wrapped around them like a heavy blanket. Breath and disbelief, mixing with the stirrings of something buried too long.

Hope.

"What did he ask of us?" the same elder woman finally asked.

Eamonn swallowed, blinking past the tears at the corners of his eyes. "To choose. To hide our children. To warn our neighbours, and if the flame rises," he paused, breath catching, "to take back what's ours." He looked across the gathering, voice low but ringing with quiet fury. "No more chains. No more stolen daughters. No more silence."

And then the older woman – bent from labour, but not broken – raised her chin. "If that flame rises," she whispered, "then by the gods, my children won't see another night beneath these beasts."

A beat.

Then others joined her.

No cheering. No roaring.

Just stillness.

Like a breath drawn before the scream.

Like frost before the thaw.

The kind of silence that makes tyrants shudder.

And then, as if bound by something greater than courage, they turned to go, each slipping into the dark, ready to pass the word – to mothers cradling babes, to old men hiding what pride they had left, to children who had never known a world without fear.

The message was clear.

The reckoning had begun.

The ripple began with whispers – nothing loud, nothing reckless.

Just a subtle shift in posture, a glance passed between hands calloused by stone and frost. Eamonn's words echoed from one mouth to another, carried not by voice but by trust. A mother at the well paused as an old man leaned near, nodding once. A boy tending a fire slipped through a back alley, touching shoulders and passing signals like in a game he'd played before the cold took everything fun away.

It spread like thawing ice, silent but unstoppable. Heads turned, fingers pointed without motion. Doors closed softer than usual. Tools were laid down without sound. A quiet preparation – like trees bracing for a coming storm, but this time, not out of fear.

And above them all, Alentar stood in shadow, perched upon the crumbled ledge of what was once a dwarven parapet, now widened and cracked by hands too large for finesse. His emerald eyes swept across the village – eyes that missed nothing, like an eagle watching its prey.

The giants laughed nearby, crude and lazy, their thunderous steps shaking the old stonework. They saw nothing. They never did.

But *he* did.

From his vantage point, Alentar caught a nod exchanged between two women hauling produce. Saw a man stop to 'tie his bootlace', only to whisper something to another crouched behind barrels. Children moved like birds between crannies, not playing, but delivering invisible messages in the same rhythm they used when pretending not to exist.

He exhaled, a breath slow and steady.

This... this was the beginning.

A thousand battles might be won in flashes of steel, but revolutions began in silence.

His hand gripped the edge of the stone.

"They're ready," he whispered to himself. "Even if they don't believe it yet."

Then, with a faint smile playing at the corners of his lips – proud, solemn, and burning with purpose – Alentar turned toward the fortress's heart, vanishing once more into its dark, winding arteries.

The signal was not far now, and neither was the reckoning.

From the shadows of the far ridge, where night light barely touched stone, a sudden flicker broke the stillness.

A single flame – unnatural and vivid – blazed green atop the eastern watchtower.

Silent. Stark. Impossible to miss.

It didn't dance like ordinary fire. It stood straight and sure, like a spear of emerald light piercing the night sky, casting long shadows over the fortress walls.

To the villagers who had been watching, their breaths caught.

This was it.

To those hidden in homes, in cellars, and under floorboards, the glow was a whisper of hope.

To Drunnyak, it was time to crack some skulls.

The storm was coming.

The cold bit deep at the edge of the world, where broken road met ancient stone. Two giants stood guard atop the crumbling outer gate, draped in furs and arrogance, spears resting across their broad shoulders. Their eyes squinted through the snow, spotting a lone figure trudging through the blizzard.

Drunnyak.

He walked with a heavy limp, dragging his cracked broadsword behind him like a man too tired to carry the burden of war.

From atop the jagged battlements, the two giants loomed in the gloom, their forms half-silhouetted by the sickly torchlight behind them. One squinted into the dark, then snorted.

"Another stray." He nudged the other with a meaty elbow. "Poor bastard doesn't even know where he's walking."

The second leaned forward, eyes narrowing as he watched Drunnyak stumble and sag into the drifting snow.

"Why do they always come at dawn?" the first giant muttered, his voice rough as gravel. "You'd think they'd wait until the damn things were gone."

The other scratched his thick neck, squinting down the winding path that led to the gates. A lone figure approached, staggering with each step. "Think it's worth the trouble?"

"Might be," the first answered, cracking his knuckles. "Could've followed the wrong tracks. Could've come looking for someone." He shrugged, unconcerned. "Either way, the master'll want names. We've got lucky like this before."

Below, Drunnyak trudged through the remnants of snow, patches of frost still clinging to the rocks. Around him, the last of the undead collapsed into the ground, dust and bone slipping back into the earth as the sun, hidden behind heavy clouds, marked the day's grim beginning.

Drunnyak paused just outside the reach of the gate, his shoulders sagging, breath laboured. His blade hung from one hand like dead weight. He dropped to one knee. "Help..." he rasped, voice hoarse with strain. "Please... open the gate..."

One giant leaned over the battlement, spitting into the wind. "Pathetic," he scoffed. "Didn't even get eaten."

The other laughed. "Should've shown up earlier – could've saved us some trouble."

They turned away, already losing interest.

And that's when it happened.

Drunnyak stopped shaking.

His body stilled, his breath evened.

And then…

He smiled.

Not with hope. Not with joy.

With something primal.

Something terrible.

A predator's grin.

He rose slowly, shoulders pulling back, spine straightening. The exhaustion melted away like snow in fire. He rolled his neck with a crack, his knuckles with a flex.

The giants heard the shift.

They turned.

Drunnyak looked up at them – not with pleading eyes, but with calculation. With promise.

The promise of violence.

And for the first time, they didn't laugh.

Hundreds of metres away, high above the village carved into the base of the mountains, Alentar stood atop the fortress wall, unmoving as a statue. His eyes, like an eagle's, pierced through storm and distance. He saw everything.

The flicker in Drunnyak's stance. The subtle shift in his shoulders.

Now.

Alentar moved like a shadow breaking from stone. His hands blurred – pulling levers, cutting ropes, severing cords. Across the fortress interior, bells cracked before they could ring, signal horns dropped silently to the floor, their guardians never seeing the arrows that ended them.

He vaulted from rooftop to rooftop, striking down patrols with a blade in each hand – visible to any human watching.

A blur of death in motion.

Back at the outer gate, Drunnyak exploded into motion.

He stood straight, towering, unshaken.

With a roar that split the air like thunder, he lifted his broken broadsword and swung once.

The giants stood surprised. "What in the…?"

Too late.

Drunnyak charged at the gate.

One leap. Two strides. And then… he jumped.

Over the wall and onto them.

His blade struck first, caving in the skull of the first giant. The second barely had time to raise his spear before Drunnyak tackled him off the parapet, the two of them falling like meteors.

They landed with a quake – Drunnyak on top, sword through the giant's chest.

Within the village below, humans peered from windows and cellars, drawn by the sound.

And they saw it – up on the rooftops: a cloaked figure dancing between chimneys, blades flashing like silver fire.

Giants fell, one by one, to Alentar's precision, their blood steaming in the snow. He struck from impossible angles, vanished into shadow, and reappeared to kill again.

"He's alone," one villager whispered.

"No," said another. "He's not."

Outside the village, a roar tore through the mountains again.

Drunnyak had entered the streets.

A beast unleashed.

The village still simmered with cold dread as smoke rose from scattered chimneys. But above it all, there came a cry – not of fear, but of command.

From a sloped rooftop near the heart of the settlement, Alentar's voice rang out sharp and clear. "To the gates! Move now – your chains are broken!"

From the shadows beneath a crumbled archway, the elder's son emerged, clutching his daughter close. Her black hair clung to her cheeks, her eyes wide with fear and disbelief. But the voice – that voice – cut through it all.

Alentar didn't wait for thanks.

He leapt from the rooftop, landing on a narrow beam, spun in mid-air, and kicked off a crooked pillar to vault across a frozen alley. Every stride, every jump was perfect, as if the very village bent itself to his movement.

Behind him, villagers stirred. First the brave. Then the cautious. Then the desperate.

One called out, "He's leading us!"

Another, "To the gates – go!"

The elder's kin ran ahead, moving with renewed strength. More villagers followed in silent awe.

Alentar moved faster.

Across ledges, down tight corridors, over rusted rooftops. His breath visible, his focus locked. He could see it now.

The gate.

Still intact.

Still closed.

And on the far side, through the flurry of snow, standing among the broken bodies of giants…

Was Drunnyak.

He had leapt the gate not long before, barrelling into the enemy before they could react. He kept the horde behind him, the wall and the gate shielding the village.

Drunnyak stood there now, broad-chested, cloak torn, steam rolling off his skin like smoke from a forge. One giant lay sprawled beside him, its head caved in. Another twitched in the snow, half-crushed beneath Drunnyak's blade.

He hadn't moved.

He was waiting.

Alentar dropped from above, landing beside him in a crouch. He stood and sheathed his blades.

Their eyes met.

"Took you long enough," Drunnyak muttered, a smirk creeping in.

"Had to clear the rooftops," Alentar replied. "Some of us enjoy the scenic route."

Behind them, villagers spilled from alleys, from back doors, from cellars and barns, gathering at the inner side of the gate, eyes wide, voices hushed.

They saw Drunnyak standing like a wall, and Alentar beside him like a blade. They knew something had changed.

The gate still stood, but now, so did they.

The villagers froze near the gate, eyes wide, breath caught.

They had expected battle. Blood. Screams.

But instead, they saw two figures.

Just two.

Drunnyak stood like a mountain of war – blood-slicked blade resting against his shoulder, giant corpses steaming at his feet. Beside him, Alentar, sharp and silent, a shadow with eyes like polished emeralds.

They had done the impossible, and now they looked back.

The villagers clustered near the inner gate, hesitant, uncertain.

Drunnyak stepped forward.

Not toward the fortress.

Toward them.

Snow crunched under his boots. His presence didn't feel mortal – it felt like thunder waiting to break. His towering frame cast a long shadow, his face unreadable but fierce.

He stopped just before them, eyes sweeping over the crowd. Mothers clutching children. Old men with trembling hands. Young boys gripping rusted tools like weapons.

And yet...

He didn't smile. He didn't boast.

He just lifted his sword and planted it in the snow at his side with a dull, deliberate thunk.

Then he spoke – only once. His voice low, steady, absolute. "No more chains." He looked at a man who hadn't yet dropped the firewood he'd been carrying. "Get your families to safety." To another, standing frozen near the stables, "No one stays behind." Then finally, to the whole of them, his voice rising only slightly, "You move when he tells you to," he said, nodding to Alentar. "We end this tonight."

And that was all.

He turned back to the fortress, tightening the straps of his cloak.

He didn't wait for cheers.

He didn't need them.

But behind him, the villagers began to move.

Still scared, but with purpose.

Because for the first time, they weren't moving out of fear.

They were moving with hope.

The villagers had begun to move – quietly, swiftly – gathering their children, the injured, their elders. They slipped between the buildings like ghosts, dragging bedding and crates, finding shelter near the gate. No one dared speak loudly.

But eyes – hundreds of them – watched the two figures walking calmly toward the heart of their prison.

Drunnyak and Alentar.

The giant's corpse outside the gate still smoked in the frost, but neither man looked back. Drunnyak dragged his blade once, then lifted it, cleaning the gore from its edge with a sweep across his own cloak-covered arm. The cloth shredded, but he didn't care.

He turned slightly toward Alentar. "No more games."

Alentar just nodded, casually checking the feathers of an arrow.

They advanced.

Far ahead, just outside the main fortress entrance, a giant ambled lazily along the path, chewing something enormous, leathery and twitching.

It took the villagers a second to realise…

It was a horse's leg.

Mid-bite, the giant stilled, blinking at the uncanny sight – two figures, side by side, drawing near. His jaws moved slower. A furrow etched itself across his heavy brow.

And then…

Thunk.

Thunk.

Two arrows slammed into his eyes, piercing deep with such force that the giant swayed on his feet like a toppled tree.

He collapsed backward with a ground-shaking crack, the half-chewed leg flying from his hand and splatting against a wall.

The villagers gasped. Some shrieked, others ducked, hearts clutched in frozen terror.

Drunnyak never flinched.

He just turned his head slowly toward Alentar – who hadn't even stopped walking, bow still raised, fingers relaxed.

Alentar smirked.

Drunnyak grunted and shook his head. "Show-off."

Alentar gave a one-shouldered shrug. "Just making sure you don't steal *all* the attention."

Drunnyak snorted and adjusted his grip on the sword. "You're lucky I like you, bird-legs."

They walked on – stone-calm, unshaken – heading toward the fortress like two storms in quiet conversation.

And the villagers – still hidden, still hushed – didn't cheer.

They couldn't.

They were too stunned, too breathless.

Because what they were seeing wasn't just courage.

It wasn't even just power.

It was freedom, plain and fierce – walking upright, daring the world to try and stop them.

The silence that followed the giant's collapse didn't last long.

The echo of his fall roared down the stone corridors of the fortress like a warning bell made of bone. From within, heavy footsteps thundered, voices bellowing in guttural Giant-Tongue.

"Who's out there?"

"Sound the alarms!"

"To the gate! To the gate!"

But when one of them yanked the chain to the main bell, nothing happened. He pulled again – nothing.

Then his eyes widened.

There was no bell.

Only the frayed rope swinging in the wind, and blood pooling around the lever's base.

From above, the body of the bell guardian fell past him, landing with a wet crunch.

Alentar had already passed through.

And left no room for sound.

Drunnyak and Alentar stood at the mouth of the entrance, two lone figures against an oncoming wall of death.

Eight giants.

Snarling. Armed. Ready for war.

The first came forward with a roar, swinging a jagged axe the size of a cart.

Drunnyak didn't dodge.

He stepped into the swing, caught the axe by the handle with one massive hand, and used the force to pull the giant down into his rising blade.

Split open from hip to shoulder, the giant gurgled and dropped.

Drunnyak wrenched the axe from the dying brute's hands. "This'll do."

A second giant charged, spear raised.

Thwish. Thwish.

Two arrows struck him – one in the eye, one under the chin. He dropped before he even reached them.

Alentar stood atop the archway, bow still warm, already nocking another arrow. "Six."

Two more giants rushed in tandem.

Drunnyak flung the stolen axe like a spinning comet, catching one in the throat and sending him crashing backward.

The second swung a club – but never finished the motion.

Alentar had dropped behind him, twin blades flashing.

Hamstrings sliced. Spine opened.

The giant screamed and fell to his knees.

Drunnyak walked up and punched through his skull with a gauntleted fist. "Four," he grunted.

The last four came at once – an organised line. Shields, hammers, formation.

Alentar dropped to Drunnyak's side.

They exchanged a look and charged.

Drunnyak met them like a battering ram, blades swinging in wide arcs, smashing through the first shield and driving steel into bone.

He ducked under a hammer, lifted a giant off his feet, and threw him into another, collapsing both into a wall.

Alentar ran along the wall, kicked off a support beam, flipped, and landed behind the final two.

One turned too slow. Blade to spine. Down.

The last swung wildly.

Alentar rolled beneath, stabbed behind the knee, then the throat.

Still standing, the brute clutched his neck until Drunnyak's thrown axe – retrieved in mid-fight – split his head like fruit.

Silence returned.

Eight giants dead. Blood steaming in the snow.

Alentar wiped a smear of crimson from his cheek. "They don't make them like they used to."

Drunnyak rolled his shoulder. "They never did."

Behind them, the villagers hidden within the far edges of the outer village looked on, silent, stunned.

And then one child whispered, "Are they... winning?"

A mother pulled her close, her eyes wide. "No. They're not winning. They've already won."

A WORTHY SACRIFICE

Below the fortress, moments earlier, the elevator chains groaned faintly overhead as Eamonn descended, his wiry frame trembling with both effort and fear. The lift itself had long since fallen into ruin, used only to send crates and produce to the depths. But he didn't ride it. Not truly. He had wrapped his hands in cloth, gripping the ropes, climbing downward – silent, desperate. His boots scraped against the rock wall, the air colder, fouler the deeper he went.

He had seen them. The warriors. The impossible ones. Slaughtering giants like myths walking in flesh, so he made his way to save her. As he approached the fortress, he heard the girl's scream – his granddaughter, his beloved Annah – echoing from the depths.

He would not wait.

Would not fail her too.

At the base of the shaft, Eamonn slipped from shadow to stone, darting past a yawning sentry distracted by the chaos above. The giant scratched his head, clueless, as the old man vanished into the darkness behind a stack of barrels.

He moved fast.

Faster than he should've.

Down corridors carved by dwarves and widened crudely by giants. Past cracked statues of stone kings and rusting braziers. Until he reached it – the great hall below.

The chamber blazed in red-orange light. Torches flickered along the walls of molten rock and black stone. The long table still sagged under the weight of untouched food: bones picked clean, platters of steaming meat, goblets full of blood-wine.

And there...

At the foot of the throne of magma and obsidian, she knelt.

Annah.

Barely fifteen. Her wrists bound in iron, her dress torn. Her eyes still defiant, still *her*, but full of terror.

The young fire giant – hulking, sneering – stood before her, gloating. The Fire Giant King himself loomed nearby, licking grease from his fingers as if she were another course to devour.

And they laughed.

The stone giants around them jeered, slapping tables, stomping their feet in rhythm. All of them so consumed by cruelty, so high in their delusions of power...

That they didn't see Eamonn until he stood in the centre of the chamber.

Chest bare, axe in hand.

Voice like iron against flame. "*Enough!*"

The laughter stopped.

Annah's head jerked up.

The giants blinked.

The Fire Giant King cocked his head, curious. Amused. "Another rat?" he said lazily, waving a hand. "Didn't we squash them all?"

The young fire giant chuckled. "No. This one reek of piss and desperation."

Eamonn stood his ground, breathing heavily, sweat freezing on his skin. "Touch her and you'll lose the rest of your teeth," he spat, eyes locked on the Prince.

Gasps. Then more laughter. Louder now. Crueller.

The Prince took a step forward, towering, half a mountain wrapped in heat and hatred. "You bring *that?*" he sneered, nodding at Eamonn's axe. "To fight *this?*" He flexed his arm, thicker than Eamonn's chest.

235

"I bring the only thing you've never known," Eamonn growled. "*Sacrifice.*"

The Prince bared his teeth. "I should burn you just for speaking."

"Do it," Eamonn snapped. "But let her go. Take me instead."

The Fire Giant King raised a brow. "A trade?" Mocking Eamonn's words with great sarcasm.

Eamonn didn't blink. "My life for hers. That's all I have left to give."

The giants laughed again. But slower. Uneasier.

The Prince leaned forward, grinning. "No, old man. We'll take both. But you… you get the honour of watching."

And with that, he struck.

The backhand sent Eamonn flying across the chamber, his axe skittering away.

Pain flared. Something cracked. Blood spilled from his mouth as he hit the stone floor, gasping.

But he got back up.

Again.

And again.

The giants jeered as they beat him. Stomping on his hands. Twisting his arms. Breaking ribs like twigs.

Until the Fire Giant Prince gripped him by the scalp and dragged him upright, lifting him like a rag doll. "Now," he hissed, forcing Eamonn's bloodied face toward Annah, "*watch.*" He hurled Eamonn's shattered form towards his father at the throne, who caught him in mid-air, applying more pressure to his already broken body.

Annah screamed.

Eamonn cried out, straining, every bone on fire – but he couldn't break free.

The Fire Giant King twisted Eamonn's head by the hair, forcing his shattered, bloodied face to stare forward. "Now," the beast hissed, "*watch.*"

Annah sobbed, bound and trembling, unable to look away, unable to understand why her grandfather was here, why he'd come alone. Her voice broke on a whisper. "Grandfather… why?"

Eamonn didn't answer.

He couldn't. His jaw was broken. His vision blurred. His body barely held together.

But his eyes…

They were kind as the tears rolled whilst looking at her.

They found her through the pain, full of love, *pride*… and peace.

Because in that final moment, through the haze of agony, he saw what she could not.

Not yet.

Steel glinting on the edge of shadow. A shape at the mouth of the hall. A silhouette with a bow.

A figure that didn't belong to this world of filth and fire – but had come for it anyway.

So, Eamonn smiled. It was barely a twitch of his lip. A flicker beneath blood and bruises.

But it was there.

He had bought the time.

He had made it matter.

He had kept her alive long enough.

He turned his head slightly, slowly, toward the hall's entrance, and there, in the dim red torchlight, stood Alentar.

Eyes like starlight through a storm.

A silent god carved in ice and fury.

Their gazes met – just once – and Alentar nodded.

A wordless vow passed between them. One of blood and fire. Of vengeance. Of thanks.

Eamonn's final breath rattled in his chest, but his soul rested.

He had done the impossible.

He had saved her.

THE RECKONING

J ust a few minutes after the fight with the eight giants, the inner chamber opened like a wound beneath the mountain.

Here, the stone bled heat.

Here, the air choked with smoke, sweat, and the copper tang of death.

Drunnyak and Alentar moved with grim purpose, descending deeper, passing beneath a carved archway where dwarven symbols had long since been scratched out, defiled, and replaced with grotesque marks of dominion and excess.

What had once been a dwarven throne hall had become something else. Something sick.

The ceiling stretched high again, lost in smoke and shadow. Molten light pulsed along the black stone veins carved through the walls, the glow illuminating every corner in a flickering orange haze.

Heat poured out – thick, heavy, laced with the stench of rot and roasted meat. Smoke curled around the stone pillars, dancing with shadows cast by flickering torchlight and magma veins that pulsed through the walls like a beating heart.

Drunnyak stepped in first. Behind him, Alentar moved like a breath caught between tension and fury.

At the centre stood a massive, desecrated feast table, stacked high with rotting meat, bones, and half-chewed limbs – animal and human alike. Flies buzzed lazily through the air. Goblets of thickened wine spilled onto the stone, running dark as dried blood.

And what they saw made the air taste like iron.

Three young women lay crumpled near the far end of the hall, barely more than figures in the dirt. Their clothes were torn, blood trailing from mouths, legs, backs – eyes empty, distant, or worse, flickering with what remained of their awareness.

One of them weeping and sobbing, trying to keep as quiet as possible, so the giants didn't focus on her again.

Her body convulsed with every sob, her hands bound, her head tilted to the side – watching, unable to reach…

A man.

Old. Broken.

Eamonn being held by the head like a rag doll in the hand of a monstrous figure.

His chest barely moved.

Alentar's jaw tightened.

His eyes didn't move. Didn't blink. Just watched.

He had seen death.

He had delivered it.

But this – this was different.

Across the hall, as the firelight danced on broken stone and bloodied flesh, Eamonn's eyes met his.

Even from across the chamber, battered and fading, the old man's look held…

Not fear.

Not pain.

But purpose.

A silent message passed between them.

This was the moment.

The seconds Eamonn had bought with his life.

Alentar's hand moved slowly to his bow, and beside him, Drunnyak's knuckles cracked.

A dozen stone giants filled the room. Some lounged at a long table piled with food – bones, steaming meat, barrels of ale. They laughed between bites. Some ignored the scene entirely. Others watched the torment unfold with bored cruelty.

At the back, the Fire Giant King and his son towered.

One seated on a throne of obsidian and flame, runes etched across his molten skin.

The other, younger but no less twisted, stood over the broken girls, licking his lips, fists clenched in anticipation.

Their laughter echoed.

The King grinned, and Drunnyak stopped breathing.

For the first time in years, his hands shook.

Alentar's eyes didn't move. Didn't blink.

Watched the girl sobbing as her grandfather's body was mocked for giving his life for her.

Drunnyak stopped at the edge of the hall.

His expression was stone.

His eyes flame.

The giants didn't yet see them.

The heat shimmered around them, warping the air like a curtain of rising smoke.

Alentar crouched in the shadows above the feast hall, bowstring tight, fingers trembling – not from fear, but from restraint.

Then he felt it.

A shift in the air.

A slow, deep breath.

Then came the sound.

A roar.

Deep, primal, earth-shaking.

Not of pain. Not of fear.

But of dominion.

A sound like a hundred lions claiming their ground, rolling through the ancient stone like thunder from the bones of the mountain itself.

Laughter died.

Tankards froze in mid-air.

The fire giants turned first, their grins stiffening.

Then the others followed…

All eyes drawn to the figure emerging from the darkened archway.

Ebony-skinned. Massive.

His bare chest streaked with soot and blood, muscles corded like braided steel.

Eyes like coals, burning with cold intent.

Drunnyak walked slowly, deliberately, whilst removing his lion-fur clothing.

The fire giants burst into cruel, thunderous laughter; a wall of mockery and heat echoing through the cavern.

The stone giants followed. Uneasy and offbeat.

Their chuckles more reflex than mirth.

Fear wrapped in pretence, but the tremble in their knuckles betrayed them.

They were shaken.

The Fire Giant King rose with a sneer and, with a flick of disgust, hurled Eamonn's broken body across the chamber – a final insult. A discarded life.

And then – wind screamed.

A blur tore across the room.

Faster than thought. Faster than fear could take root.

Alentar.

He caught the old man in mid-air, the force of it cracking the wind around him, and yet he landed softly – a shadow carried by grace, cradling the lifeless form with reverence.

His eyes rose, a green glow sharp, locking onto the giants.

Predator's eyes.

The kind no prey forgets.

The giants flinched. Just a breath. Just a blink.

The fire giants laughed louder, masking the crack in their confidence.

The others joined, strained and hollow, as if laughter might drown the creeping truth — that something in this room had changed and they were no longer the hunters.

Drunnyak turned his head, meeting his brother's gaze. "Go," he said, voice low. Not a command, but something heavier.

Alentar's brows furrowed. "You shouldn't face this alone."

Drunnyak didn't blink. "They need to know they're safe. Make sure they are. Please... leave me be."

It was the 'please' that landed hardest.

Alentar's jaw clenched.

He looked one last time, the rage still raw in his emerald eyes. But he knew.

This was Drunnyak's storm to unleash.

He gave a slow nod. "Make them suffer."

Without a word, Alentar stepped forward, embracing Eamonn's body with solemn grace.

He laid the old man gently against a pillar – his back straight, hands folded, as if placing a king in eternal rest – and then... he moved.

A blur. A wind. A strike of divine purpose.

Before breath could be drawn, before muscle could twitch, he was among the giants.

Not sneaking. Not skulking.

Present. Standing. Glaring.

One by one, his eyes locked with theirs. Unblinking. Unshaken. Unapologetic.

As if daring them to move.

As if already knowing they wouldn't.

His movements were a blur – one arm encircling Eamonn's granddaughter, lifting her with a grace that defied the moment, while the other reached for the second broken woman. The third lay still, death claiming her just heartbeats before.

Their pain met with his silence, and then... he vanished again.

Gone from their midst, already back at the pillar, setting the women down beside Eamonn's body with the same gentleness he'd used to lay him to rest.

A whisper of wind. A blink of movement.

The giants stood stunned, because the predator hadn't attacked.

He'd simply taken back what was his to protect and none of them had stopped him.

None of them even breathed.

The young Fire Giant Prince, still reeling from the blur that had torn his prey from under his nose, let out a guttural roar – humiliation twisting into rage.

He grabbed the massive axe at his feet – an enormous slab of jagged black iron – and hurled it across the chamber like a thunderbolt of death, aiming straight for Alentar's spine.

But Alentar never turned. He didn't flinch.

One hand still resting gently on Eamonn's chest, the other bracing the wounded women, he lifted his arm – calmly, cleanly – and caught the axe in mid-air.

The steel groaned in his grip.

Slowly, deliberately, he turned his head, eyes gleaming like a wolf's under moonlight.

His gaze swept to the Prince, then to Drunnyak, who grinned back like a lion waiting for the signal to pounce.

Alentar smirked. "You don't know what's waiting for you, scum."

The room fell into silence.

The crackling of the hearth sounded like thunder.

The stone giants trembled, their massive chests heaving, wide eyes fixed on the hunter in elf's skin.

They had seen war.

They had seen monsters.

But this? This was something else, and none of them dared breathe.

Before they could process what was happening, Drunnyak was alone.

He stood still for a moment, breathing.

Then, slowly, he reached behind him and drew his broadsword – not to fight, but to leave it behind.

He walked to the nearest wall and drove the blade into the stone.

It sank in so deep, the only thing left visible was the hilt, pulsing with the fury of its master.

The sound rang through the chamber like a war drum.

The laughter stopped.

All heads turned.

The fire giant on the throne squinted, then chuckled again – a cruel, rumbling sound.

Beside him, his grotesque son wiped his hands, adjusted his belt, and sneered, kicking the dead woman near him.

Drunnyak began to walk.

Each step echoed across the stone like the ticking of a divine countdown.

The heat didn't touch him.

The stench didn't move him.

The giants flinched.

He wasn't roaring.

He wasn't posturing.

He was calm, and that calm terrified them.

Because this wasn't rage like before – this was something deeper. Something ancient.

His muscles tightened, the veins across his arms rising like carved stone. His shoulders stretched like a mountain shifting before collapse. His eyes – those dark, molten eyes – no longer blinked.

They were fixed on the throne.

On the monsters.

On the crime.

The Fire Giant King leaned forward on his lava-forged throne, lips curling with amusement. "Another small human come to die in my hall," he said. "After I'm done with you, I'll make the elf pay for his insolence."

Drunnyak said nothing.

He passed the feast table, where the stone giants parted instinctively, as if their bones remembered something their minds had forgotten. True fear.

Drunnyak simply stopped walking.

His eyes drifted from the monster ahead to the horror around him.

The stone floor beneath the giant's feet was slick with old blood, the air thick with the stench of rot, sweat and suffering. Scattered across the cold hall were the broken forms of two women, too still to be alive. Bones jutted from torn flesh, eyes swollen shut, lips cracked and bruised. Their pain lingered in the air like a scream no one had answered.

For a moment, the entire hall seemed to hold its breath.

Drunnyak's gaze remained locked on the women for a brief moment. His brow didn't furrow. He didn't clench his fists. He didn't roar or curse the heavens.

He only stood.

His chest rose and fell once, then again – measured. Calm, but his eyes changed.

Whatever warmth had remained within him… vanished.

Whatever restraint still lived in his heart… dissolved.

There was no fury.

No grief.

Only a quiet, chilling stillness.

The kind of stillness that frightened even the wicked.

The Fire Giant King shifted uneasily on his throne, the laughter fading from his lips.

Around him, the others – hulking brutes who moments ago had jeered and joked – went silent, their amusement bleeding into something colder. They didn't understand what they were seeing.

They didn't need to.

They could feel it.

Drunnyak's silence wasn't mercy.

It was the promise of what came next.

The hall trembled with low, rumbling laughter.

The Fire Giant King leaned back into his throne of lava-forged stone, his massive arms draped lazily over the sides as he watched the lone man walk with no fear, no weapon. "Look at this one," he growled, voice thick like rolling magma. "No blade. No armour. Just pride and a death wish. At least the elf didn't waste his time, and escaped."

His son, broad-shouldered and covered in blood, chuckled as he stepped down from the throne's platform, dragging a rusted cleaver across the stone floor. "You think he's broken already, Father?" he said, sneering. "Maybe he came to beg like those girls."

The King scoffed. "If he begs, break his jaw."

The son looked over his shoulder, grinning wide. "Why don't *you* show him his place?"

The Fire Giant King grinned, sharp teeth glinting through cracked lips. "Oh no, boy. He's yours. A gift."

The son turned to Drunnyak, spreading his arms mockingly. "You hear that, little one? You're a gift. A toy. A breath before boredom sets in again. I'll make sure to beat the elf into a pulp with your skull."

He spat blood at the ground and raised his cleaver.

The son stepped down from the throne steps, dragging a cleaver behind him.

"You think I fear you, dark one?" the Fire Giant King sneered from his throne, his voice echoing with cruel amusement.

Drunnyak didn't answer.

"Come. Let's end your fairy tale."

The young fire giant launched himself from the steps of the throne, a molten blur of arrogance and brute size. His cleaver, as long as a cart and twice as heavy, came crashing down with the full weight of a beast who had never once faced resistance.

Drunnyak slowly moved. Opening his arms as if welcoming the attack.

In a swift move he simply stepped forward, and as the blow fell, his arms came up in a blur.

Clang.

The sound was not metal against metal, but flesh halted by will.

The cleaver stopped.

Dead in the air.

Drunnyak's bare hands had caught the wrists of the giant in mid-swing. The giant's entire momentum was caught in that moment, frozen, like time itself dared not challenge him.

A tremor ran through the stone floor. The hall gasped.

The young giant stared down, disbelieving, his muscles straining – but nothing moved.

Drunnyak didn't even blink. His voice came low and cruel, like something ancient rising from the depths. "Is this what you use to break little girls?"

The young giant growled, panic rising. He tried to yank his arms free, but they didn't budge.

Drunnyak squeezed.

The giant screamed.

Snap.

The cleaver dropped from his grip, clattering against the floor with a scream of steel.

Before the boy could react, Drunnyak twisted the captured arm behind his back, contorting it so far it shattered at the elbow.

The giant dropped to his knees.

Another crack – the wrist, broken. A pop – the shoulder, dislocated.

The boy screamed louder now, not in anger, but in raw, primal fear.

Drunnyak towered over the young giant, gaze flat, unblinking. Then, without looking away from the King's eyes, Drunnyak squeezed. "You thought pain was a game. That blood was theatre. That strength came from size." He leaned down, close enough that the giant could see the black in his eyes – not empty, but bottomless. "But you never fought a god, boy. You just raped the weak."

With a roar, Drunnyak drove the giant face first into the stone, cracking the floor. Blood exploded across the rock like spilled paint.

The other giants had frozen.

One dropped his meat. Another took a step back. None of them moved to help.

On the throne, the Fire Giant King's smirk twisted. He sat straighter. No longer amused. No longer entertained.

Concern crept into his expression.

Drunnyak released the broken body of the son. It collapsed like a sack of limbs, twitching. He turned, facing the King now. His voice

247

rang like thunder in a dead world. "How can I make this even more enjoyable?" Locking his eyes on the Fire Giant King's.

For a heartbeat, the entire hall was silent.

The only sounds were the crackle of fire and the wet gasping of the broken thing that had once called itself the Fire Giant King's son.

Drunnyak turned.

His heavy boots dragged rivulets of blood across the black stone floor as he walked – slowly, purposefully – toward the collapsed body.

The giants watched. Frozen. Wide-eyed.

Fear gripped them by the spine.

One of them whimpered. Another urinated, the stench of shame wafting through the smoke. Their massive bodies trembled, not from cold or injury, but from something they had never felt.

Powerlessness.

The Fire Giant King's smirk had vanished. Replaced now with the stiff, alert silence of something cornered.

He rose from the throne, towering even over his kin, fire licking from his cracked shoulders – but he hesitated.

And that moment of hesitation? Drunnyak seized it. With one massive hand, he grabbed what remained of the son's mangled corpse, dragging him by the arm like a broken puppet. "Here," he growled, voice like an earthquake. "Let's see what kind of legacy you've made."

Drunnyak surged forward, a blur of fury, and swung the mangled body of the young giant like a war club. Thwack – bone met bone and flesh met flame as the son became the weapon that struck the father.

The sound thundered through stone and soul alike.

The body slammed into the King's face. The force of it sent embers flying, and the sound of shattering bone echoed through the hall.

The King roared – not in pain, but in shock – as blood sprayed from his lip.

Drunnyak stepped forward.

Another swing.

Crack.

The corpse hit the King again – this time across the jaw, snapping it sideways. The King stumbled back, rage rising – but before he could form a spell, summon fire, or even beg for his life...

Smash.

Another blow. Another eruption of blood.

"This is your strength?" Drunnyak snarled between strikes, his voice rising with every word. "This is your kingdom? You sat on a throne made of screams – and now you choke on your own blood."

He struck again. And again.

Blow after blow, he struck. Until the body was pulp. Until the King collapsed at the steps – broken, breathless, too humiliated to roar.

The stone giants stood, paralysed, jaws slack, souls retreating inside themselves as if to hide.

Their pride – their monstrous, cruel pride – was shattered.

Because this wasn't a man.

This was judgement.

Drunnyak dropped the remains of the son with a wet thud, then looked at the other giants. His voice lowered to a growl that cut through the silence like a blade. "Sit."

No one moved.

"Or run." His eyes burned like coals now. "Either way, your world ends tonight."

The Fire Giant King collapsed to the floor, blood cascading from his mouth, mixing with the ashes around the throne. His once-terrifying presence now reduced to a broken shadow of a tyrant.

But Drunnyak didn't look at him.

He turned – slowly – toward the others.

The stone giants, once the tormentors of man, stood frozen, eyes wide, backs pressed against the bloodstained walls of the fortress.

One of them whispered in disbelief, "He's not a man..."

Another dropped his club. The thud echoed like a heartbeat of doom.

Drunnyak took one step forward.

And then the slaughter began.

The first giant tried to run.

Bad choice.

Drunnyak lunged – faster than something his size should ever move – and his fist connected with the back of the giant's head.

The skull collapsed inward, bursting like fruit under stone. The body fell, twitching, sliding forward several feet before it stopped.

A second tried to fight, swinging a hammer the size of a boulder.

Drunnyak caught the handle in mid-swing, ripped it from his grip, and used it to obliterate the giant's ribs, the entire chest caving in with a crunch so deep it made the others retch.

He didn't stop.

Another giant roared, charging him.

Drunnyak ducked under the swing and punched – his fist tore straight through the giant's stomach, exiting with blood and organs wrapped around his forearm like a grotesque gauntlet.

The creature fell forward, screaming, only to have Drunnyak rip his jaw off in one final wrench and toss it aside like garbage.

Bones shattered. Eyes burst. Skulls cracked.

Blood painted the walls in streaks, like a violent artist had taken up crimson as his only colour.

Every scream echoed with desperation.

Every step Drunnyak took was followed by a broken body.

One giant begged, falling to his knees. "Please... mercy..."

Drunnyak grabbed him by the face – his entire hand covering the creature's skull – and slammed him down again and again and again, until nothing remained but pulp and splinters of bone.

The throne room was soaked.

There were no words.

Just the crack of sinew, the wet sound of muscle breaking, the rattle of giants dying in horror, and the unrelenting sound of a god's fury.

By the end, there was silence.

Only Drunnyak stood.

Breathing.

Covered head to toe in blood.

The Fire Giant King, still lying on the steps, had watched it all. His lips trembled. He looked upon the piles of his fallen servants – a dozen, reduced to carcasses. "Imp...os...sible..." he rasped as he spat out the last of his teeth.

Drunnyak finally turned his gaze back to him – slow, inevitable, merciless. "Not yet," he said. His voice was thunder on stone.

The Fire Giant King gathered whatever strength he had and knelt amidst the ruins of his court, his chest heaving, his eyes wild.

The blood of his kin ran in rivers around him. The mighty were now meat, strewn across stone that had once echoed with their laughter and the screams of the oppressed.

And now, only one remained.

He looked up at the god walking toward him – not fast, not eager. Just certain.

Each step that Drunnyak took echoed with the final beats of a dying reign.

"W-wait..." the King stammered, trying to rise, slipping in the blood of his son and throne-guard. "There... there is more I can give – gold, slaves, alliances!"

Drunnyak didn't slow.

"I can kneel!" the King begged, lowering his head with trembling hands. "You... you can rule! I will be yours to command!"

Still, Drunnyak walked.

The giant's voice cracked into sobs, his massive body shaking like a child, desperate, grasping at air.

The Fire Giant King, now a broken heap of flesh and pride, writhed across the blood-slick stone floor, each movement a pitiful drag of his hulking frame. His one good eye flickered with desperation as he clawed toward the rear of the cavern, toward the shadowed alcove behind his throne.

His scorched fingers fumbled at a crevice in the stone – searching, grasping – until they closed around a ring. Ancient. Etched with runes that pulsed faintly like a dying ember.

251

He jammed it onto his finger, grinding it with frantic circles, whispering something lost beneath the tremble of fear.

And then... he turned.

His gaze rose to the towering shadow above him.

Drunnyak.

The King's voice was cracked, shrill and broken. "Please!" he shrieked. "Don't—"

Thud.

Drunnyak's hand shot forward, seizing the King by the top of the head, fingers digging into his flaming scalp like iron claws.

The giant didn't even finish his scream.

With a sickening crack, Drunnyak ripped his head from his body, tearing muscle, spine and fire from its core. Blood geysered from the neck, splattering the pillars and burning coals nearby.

For a moment, Drunnyak just held the head – staring into the lifeless, wide-eyed face – and then, with a single flick, he hurled it across the room, where it thudded to the centre of the chamber, bouncing once before rolling to a stop.

Silence.

No breath.

No resistance.

Just the drip of blood, and the sound of footsteps.

Drunnyak turned away from the carnage.

Not looking back.

He passed the shattered remains of the table, the throne, the walls stained in legacy and failure. And as he crossed the threshold of the throne room, he paused only once – to reach for his sword.

Still embedded in the stone wall where he had left it.

With one hand, he pulled.

The wall cracked. The stone split, and the blade came free.

Drunnyak slung it over his shoulder, now more like a shepherd's staff than a warrior's weapon, and without a word, he walked out.

The fortress was silent now.

The kind of silence that didn't come from peace, but from the absence of cruelty.

His broad silhouette emerged through the broken threshold of the fortress, limbs caked in blood, flesh, and shattered bone. Gore painted his skin like war paint, his eyes low – not in shame, but heavy with something deeper.

The snow had started again. Soft flakes drifted down like feathers, untouched by the fury that had just passed.

He didn't notice.

He sat on a fallen pillar acting as a bench, sword resting beside him, broad shoulders hunched as if the weight of a mountain pressed against his back.

He stared into the void of the horizon, unmoving, but his eyes were glassed, rimmed red, and as the wind touched his face, a tear fell.

Not from pain.

Not from regret.

But from something deeper.

Exhaustion. Grief. The soul-tired agony of having been the sword and the storm.

Only silence left, as if the very air held its breath.

Nearby, amidst the recovering villagers, Alentar stood surrounded.

The people leaned in toward him like moths to fire, whispering his name with awe.

"Alentar."

"The Bow of the Wild Dawn."

"Did you see what he did? How he moved? Like wind... like death itself..."

Alentar said little in return. His attention was not on their praise.

It was on his brother in arms, his teacher. His friend.

Not the berserker who had torn giants apart like straw, but the man now walking with no celebration, coated in the truth of what vengeance costs.

At Alentar's feet, villagers tended to the rescued girls – two young women, cloaked in furs, their bruised bodies trembling but alive.

Annah, the granddaughter of the fallen hero, lay resting with her head gently cradled in an older woman's lap. Her face, though pale and battered, had colour returning to it. Breath in her chest.

Beside them, Drokan – the quiet stone giant – knelt on one knee, his massive frame hunched low. He worked with startling care, crushing herbs and binding leaves into poultices. His thick hands moved gently over the girl's wounds, his eyes full of guilt and something almost paternal.

Still, Alentar didn't watch them.

He watched Drunnyak.

The warrior approached slowly, the weight of his steps shaking more than the ground.

Not rage. Not triumph.

Something hollowed, and as he drew closer, Alentar's proud smile faded. His voice, low, almost mournful, barely reached the villagers beside him. "He saved us all… and still he walks as if carrying a curse."

Their eyes turned to Drunnyak now.

No longer a god in motion.

But a man covered in war.

In truth.

And Alentar, who had seen him laugh, hunt, and rise through legends… had never seen him look with so much sorrow.

He left the crowd without a word.

His steps were soft.

Drunnyak didn't look up.

Alentar stood behind him for a moment, not speaking – just watching the tremble in his massive hands. "It's over," he said gently.

Drunnyak didn't respond.

Alentar stepped closer, and his voice dropped lower, softer. "You avenged them."

Still, no reply.

Until Drunnyak's head lowered, his shoulders shaking. He spoke in a breath, barely audible. "I hate what I had to become."

The words hung in the air like broken glass.

Alentar closed his eyes. Then, he stepped forward and, without hesitation, wrapped his arms around Drunnyak's shoulders from behind.

A soldier's embrace. A brother's bond. A silent shield against the weight of the world.

"You became what they needed," Alentar said, his voice steady. "Not because you wanted to, but because no one else could."

Drunnyak's hands clenched, knuckles white, and then he broke.

Not in rage. Not in fury. But in tears.

The great warrior who had crushed monsters and torn giants limb from limb now wept like a boy who had held too much for too long.

And Alentar held him.

Tight.

Solid.

Present.

Not as a god.

Not as a legend.

But as a friend.

The snowfall continued, blanketing the crimson-streaked earth with a softness that felt almost sacred – as if the world itself wished to cover the violence, to give peace where there had been none.

Alentar still held Drunnyak, silent and steady, but from behind them, footsteps crunched through the snow – cautious at first. Then faster. Braver.

It was the villagers.

Drawn not by fear this time, but by reverence.

By concern.

By love.

They didn't speak. Not yet. But their presence surrounded the two gods like a warm circle of humanity, eyes wide with gratitude, awe... and something else.

Understanding.

Then, from among the crowd, a small figure broke through.

A little boy, no older than five winters, his cheeks red from the cold, bundled in furs far too large for his tiny body. He waddled forward on unsteady legs, undeterred by the blood or by the size of the man before him.

He didn't see a god.

He didn't see a killer.

He saw someone hurting, and so, without a word, the boy threw his small arms around Drunnyak's massive leg, clinging tightly, resting his cheek against the bloodstained leather.

"Are you hurt?" the child asked, his voice small, trembling with innocence. "I can help. Where it hurts, Mister?"

Drunnyak froze.

His breath caught in his throat.

Slowly, his head turned, tears still glistening in his eyes as he looked down at the boy – this tiny soul who stood before him without fear, without judgement, offering all he had with open arms.

Their eyes met.

And something broke inside Drunnyak – not violently, but gently.

A wall that had stood too long.

Drunnyak reached down, hands still shaking, and gently lifted the child into his arms. The boy looked at him with wide, trusting eyes.

Drunnyak smiled through his tears, resting his forehead against the child's. "You already helped me, my son," he whispered.

Around them, the villagers fell silent.

Many wept.

Some knelt.

NAMES WORTH FOLLOWING

The snow had stopped falling.

In its place came stillness.

Not silence – stillness. The kind that settles only when something has truly ended… and something else is about to begin.

Drunnyak stood at the foot of the fortress path, the boy resting quietly in the crook of his massive arm. His face was calm, but his voice carried like a slow drumbeat echoing over stone. "You've endured too much pain in this place," he said. "Too much silence. Too many names lost to fire and cruelty." He turned toward the people – a village once shattered, now gathered like embers around him. "I won't ask you to forget this place. But I will ask you to choose something more." He pointed west, toward the mountain line beyond the trench, where smoke no longer choked the sky. "There's a village – Garrents. Freed. Fed. Guarded. Where no one kneels for their bread, and no child watches the door in fear." He adjusted the boy in his arm and offered him a quiet smile before raising his voice once more. "Come with us. Build again. Laugh again. Live again. This can be the end of chains… and the beginning of something that lasts."

The villagers were still. Holding their families. Looking at one another. Weighing something heavier than mere travel.

Then, from among them, Halrek – the son of the fallen elder – stepped forward. He bore the same posture once beaten into him by giants, but now he stood differently. His chains were broken, even if his scars remained. He looked to his daughter, who hadn't let go of his hand once, and then turned toward the crowd. "We were born into survival. Not living," he said. "But I want more for her. For us." He turned to Drunnyak, then Alentar, who had joined his brother in arms and stood with quiet intensity beside him. "If what you say is true, then lead us. We will follow."

The people began to murmur.

Hope, cautious but hungry, bloomed like green through frost.

And then a voice rose. "Before we follow you, please tell us your names. We want to hear from your mouths, even though you've proven that the songs are truthful."

The villagers fell into quiet again, all eyes locked on the two figures who had shattered their chains.

Drunnyak turned slowly to Alentar. A moment passed. A shared breath. A weight. Then he looked back at the villagers. "You deserve names." His voice carried – not with arrogance, but with truth. "My name is Drunnyak. I've crushed bones in a thousand battles, broken the walls of tyrants and kings, and stood against monsters that would make your skies shatter." He turned his head slightly. "Today… I held a child who asked if I was hurt. And I cried in his arms. So know this – if you come with us, you don't follow a warlord. You follow a shield. You follow a man who has broken so no one else has to."

He stepped aside, his eyes falling on his companion.

Alentar took one breath. His tone was quieter. Sharper. But no less powerful. "I am Alentar. I've hunted things older than your nightmares, moved unseen through lands where no life grows. I've stood in silence as empires fell." He lifted his gaze, emerald eyes gleaming like frozen fire. "But today, I remembered why I learned to walk in shadows. So the rest of you could walk in light."

A pause.

Then Drunnyak raised his voice once more, his tone like a war drum shaking off the dust of ages. "We are your family – if you choose us."

The villagers stood motionless.

Then Halrek knelt, his daughter beside him.

And with that, others followed.

One by one, dozens fell to their knees in reverent silence – not from fear or worship, but from hope.

When the last had bowed their heads, Drunnyak looked out over them. "You don't need to kneel ever again in your lives."

Alentar glanced at him, a smirk pulling at his lips. "Well said, brother."

As the villagers knelt and slowly began to rise, murmuring to one another, gathering family, belongings, and what little hope they still held, Drunnyak turned to Alentar, the wind brushing gently against their cloaks.

Their eyes met.

No words were needed at first – only the quiet understanding of men who had walked battlefields too long.

Then Drunnyak spoke, low but certain. "Go to Garrents."

Alentar's brows raised, slightly curious.

Drunnyak nodded toward the distant hills, already shadowed by the coming grey. "Tell them we're bringing more. A whole village now. Mothers, children, wounded. They'll need shelter, food… safety. We can't march them fast." He exhaled, looking at the villagers beginning to prepare. Some cried. Others laughed. Most just moved in stunned silence. "I'll stay. Help them pack. Keep them calm. They trust me now." Then, a glance back at Alentar – more serious now. "Bring the others. All of them – except one. Leave someone to watch over Garrents. One is enough. We're needed here."

Alentar's smirk flickered, though there was respect in it. "You're starting to sound like a leader, old friend."

Drunnyak looked down at the boy still in his arm, now quietly dozing against his chest. "Maybe I'm starting to remember what that means."

Alentar stepped beside him, placing a firm hand on Drunnyak's shoulder. "Brother, you should go."

Drunnyak turned to meet his eyes, a question forming behind the quiet storm that still lingered.

"Let me stay," Alentar said, his voice calm but resolute. "These people need time. Supplies. Their wounded need care. Their hearts need steadiness. I'll see to all of it." He glanced over his shoulder at the looming shape of the mountain, its shadow stretching across the snow like a buried secret. "And this place..." he murmured. "This mountain holds answers. I can feel it. I'll find them. Whatever was carved into its bones – whatever the giants twisted – there might be something left for us to uncover."

Drunnyak held his gaze for a long moment.

Not with resistance.

But with understanding.

A slow nod.

A silent trust.

Alentar gave him one last look and the briefest smirk – soft and sincere. "You carry their hope now."

With that, Drunnyak turned.

Shouldering the weight without words.

And as he began to move, the villagers slowly stepped aside, parting in reverence, watching as he passed like a storm that had spared them.

The road ahead waited, and Drunnyak walked it now...

Not to destroy.

But to lead.

And behind him, Alentar remained.

Not idle, but still.

Among the wounded and the weary.

Among secrets etched in stone.

Among the beginnings of something new.

ECHOES BENEATH THE MOUNTAIN

The villagers gathered near the stone path leading to the gate, pressing together in quiet reverence. A few of them handed Drunnyak tightly bundled packs – food, furs, and even a flask of warmed honeyed brew. Their eyes held a mix of awe and gratitude as they passed him supplies with trembling hands.

Drunnyak accepted each offering with a grunt, a nod, or a quick word of thanks, his voice low but sincere. He moved with purpose, but when he reached the last figure in line, he stopped.

Drokan.

The stone giant stood awkwardly, looming above the others, clutching a sack of herbs in one massive hand. But he wasn't the towering brute they'd first feared. Not any more. He looked almost… sheepish. Maybe even proud. Until Drunnyak looked up at him – really *looked* – with those savage, smouldering eyes.

The air shifted.

Drunnyak's expression darkened, a slow curl creeping into the corner of his mouth. He stepped in close – too close – forcing Drokan to lean back instinctively. Every muscle in the giant's massive frame tensed. He swallowed hard.

Drunnyak's face turned to stone.

Silence.

Then…

"Boo."

Drokan jolted like he'd been struck by lightning. His enormous legs wobbled, and for half a breath, everyone thought he might drop like a toppled tree.

Laughter exploded.

First from Drunnyak, loud and guttural.

Then from Alentar, sharp and uncontrollable, his face buried in one hand.

Even the villagers – tense moments before – joined in with hesitant chuckles that turned into full-bodied laughter. The tension, finally, broke like a cracked dam.

Drunnyak turned to Alentar with a grin as wide as the mountains. "See that?" he barked, jabbing a thumb toward Drokan. "That's gonna be *you* one day, you smug little cunt."

Alentar only shook his head, wheezing with laughter. "Not unless you grow taller or learn how to sneak."

As the last chuckles settled into warm murmurs, Drunnyak reached out with a strong arm and offered Drokan a barbarian's handshake – forearm to forearm, strong and sincere. The giant hesitated… then clasped him back, firm and steady.

Drunnyak's voice dropped to a serious, grounded tone. "Thanks. I won't forget what you did." He nodded toward the villagers. "Keep them safe. Keep an eye on Alentar too… if anyone can."

Drokan didn't answer at first. He just stared at Drunnyak like a man would stare at a storm rolling off a cliff. Then he nodded, just once, a deep, anchoring nod – not of submission, but of respect. One warrior to another. "Aye," he said. "With my life."

Drunnyak stepped back, inhaling deeply, the cold air cutting through his lungs like knives and fire. He turned to Alentar. "Don't let them rest too easy. Keep them sharp."

Alentar gave a knowing smirk. "Don't give them a reason not to."

Then, without another word, Drunnyak turned toward the gates. He broke into a run, his broad form gathering speed – like a boulder tumbling with purpose – until he reached the threshold and, with a mighty leap, he soared.

Over the gates into the white beyond.

Gone – but not lost.

Only on the path ahead, and those left behind stood in silence, watching where he'd vanished, feeling safer simply knowing he was somewhere out there.

Alentar turned, his cloak catching the breeze as he faced the gathered villagers. His eyes swept across them – worn faces, hopeful hearts, and quiet reverence behind their silence. He spoke without raising his voice, but it carried like a wind through their bones. "Go to your homes." A pause. "Eat as you've never eaten before. Rest like it's the first night peace ever found you." His gaze softened as it found the wounded and the healers. "Tend to the girls. Be gentle. Lay Eamonn to rest with the honour he earned… and more." There was no ceremony in his tone – only truth, and that made it stronger than any oath. He stepped forward, his eyes locking with Drokan's. "Drokan," he said, nodding once. "First watch is yours, my friend. Keep the gates. Keep them safe."

The giant straightened, puffing out his broad chest – not with pride, but with purpose. He nodded, a rare solemn expression painting his craggy face.

Alentar gave a final glance toward the village – toward the life they had reclaimed with blood, fire and tears – then turned, his body already slipping into shadow. "I'll be inside," he said, almost to himself now. "There's still more to see… and more answers waiting."

And with that, he stepped toward the yawning entrance of the fortress, his form fading once more into the dark.

As Alentar crossed the threshold of the ancient dwarven hall, the warmth of the village faded behind him, replaced by a breathless hush. The stone beneath his boots, blackened and cracked from battle, seemed to hum with the echoes of violence. Blood had long since dried

263

in wide, sweeping arcs – not the panicked stains of fleeing men, but the deliberate, clean slashes of warriors who had struck with precision. He recognised Drunnyak's work like a signature carved into chaos.

He stepped further in, his stride slowing. Then… he stopped.

The silence stretched.

He closed his eyes and breathed.

The air was thick with the scent of ash and sweat, of cold iron and spilled marrow. Beneath it, fainter, he caught the echo of sulphur – a fire giant's lingering stench, heavy and unnatural. A breeze stirred faintly from deeper inside the mountain, brushing past him like a ghost, carrying hints of damp moss, stone lichen… and something older. Something buried.

He opened his eyes again, slower this time, not just looking – reading.

The walls bore deep cracks, too wide to be the scars of age. No, these were made by fists the size of shields, stone war hammers swung in fury. Bits of dark red flesh clung to the corners of the broken pillars, and there, at the far side of the room, a groove in the floor – long, wide, and smeared with blood. A body dragged. A giant, he assumed. Perhaps two.

Alentar knelt.

His fingers brushed the dusty floor, pressing into a faint imprint – a heel. Massive, heavier than any human could leave. But then, just beyond it, lighter steps. Quicker. Precise. His own, from hours ago. And others.

"They ran," he whispered to himself, almost smiling. "But not far."

He turned his gaze upward to the high vaulted ceiling. The stonework, though partially shattered, still held remnants of dwarven craftsmanship – angular runes carved into beams, now dulled and charred. He traced one with his gaze – a rune for binding. Another for silence. These halls had been forged not for beauty, but for containment.

"A place meant to hold power," he murmured. "Or to keep something hidden."

A flicker caught his eye.

Near the wall, half-buried beneath rubble and viscera, something glinted – metallic and out of place. He strode over, brushed away the debris with the back of his blade. A chain. Thick and old. Too large for a man. He followed it with his eyes, and found a shattered ring embedded in the wall... as if something had been bound here once.

He rose to his feet.

This wasn't just a place of battle.

It had been either a prison or a vault.

Something had lived here once... something the dwarves had tried to hold in check, and the giants had claimed.

He glanced toward the narrow corridor leading deeper into the mountain – a dark artery into the unknown.

Alentar's expression sharpened. His hunter's senses weren't whispering any more.

They were screaming.

"Something's still here," he said quietly, hand resting on the hilt of his blade, and he walked on.

The passage narrowed.

No longer carved for the grandeur of giants, the corridor ahead bore the intimate scale of its original builders – the dwarves. Alentar had to stoop as he walked, his shoulders brushing runes etched into the stone walls. Dust stirred at his boots with each step. The air grew colder, tighter. Not with chill, but with silence – a silence that pressed in like the mountain itself was listening.

He lit no torch. He didn't need to.

His emerald eyes had long since adapted to the dark, pulling in the faintest glow from the magma veins threading the rock like ancient arteries. Thin pulses of dim red light blinked like dying embers, guiding him deeper. Deeper still.

The chain from the outer chamber continued down the hall – or at least, remnants of it did. Links the size of manacles had been fused into the walls, but they'd snapped violently at some point. Whatever had once been bound here hadn't left gently.

And then the floor changed. From worn stone to something smoother... deliberate.

He knelt again.

Glass.

Melted. Not carved. Melted smooth by an intense heat that had scorched through dwarf-forged stone. Alentar pressed a hand to the glassy floor. Still cold – but it told him all he needed.

"Something escaped..." he whispered, rising slowly. "Or... something was released."

Ahead, the passage opened into a circular chamber.

Vaulted, domed, unlike anything above. It had the feel of a temple, not a throne room. The walls were carved with murals – some defaced, others intact – depicting gods and titans, dwarves in chains, others standing tall beside beings cloaked in fire and light. The artistry had a reverence, a warning.

In the centre of the room was a pit. Not deep – barely waist-high – but wide, rimmed with scorched runes long since cracked. It pulsed faintly, not with heat, but with *memory*. Alentar stepped closer.

The moment he crossed the pit's edge, the air changed.

A pressure built behind his eyes. A static hum crawled across his skin.

Then... a whisper.

Not in his ears.

In his *mind*.

Faint. Ancient. And not in any language he knew. Yet he understood.

Who walks with stolen time?

He froze.

Hand instinctively on his blade, but he didn't draw.

He stood still, listening.

Another voice answered. Distant. Mournful. *Not stolen... returned.*

Alentar's breath caught.

He turned slowly, but the chamber was empty and yet not.

This place, this *vault*, was not dead.

It remembered.

It *knew*.

He stepped back from the pit, heart thudding – not with fear, but with recognition.

The gods had been here.

The *first time.*

Before the fall. Before the silence.

Perhaps something still lingered. A remnant. A shadow. A guardian. Or worse – a prisoner who had not yet escaped.

He backed away slowly, the hum dimming with each step until it fell silent again.

Alentar reached the door.

Paused.

"We'll need to come back here," Alentar murmured, his voice low, reverent.

His eyes lingered on the pit, then drifted upward, scanning the broken murals that circled the domed chamber. For a moment, something caught the corner of his gaze. He stepped closer, brushing his gloved fingers across a time-worn carving half-shrouded in soot and shadow.

A symbol. Faint, almost erased.

A mountain split by a river of gold, flanked by crossed hammers, and encircled by a ring of broken chains.

Alentar exhaled slowly, his breath misting in the chilled air.

Taril's mark.

Not stylised. Not decorative.

Sacred.

Older than anything Alentar had seen above the mountain.

"Maybe he'll remember," Alentar whispered, more to himself than to anyone else. "Maybe this place will stir something in him."

He let his fingers fall away from the stone, his emerald eyes sweeping the room one final time.

A chamber of forgotten power.

A vault of truths left buried and now… found.

He turned, his cloak stirring faintly in the stale air, and with one last glance at the ancient pit of forgotten purpose, he vanished into the dark once more.

Alentar moved with quiet purpose through the scorched halls, his boots whispering over stone still warm from the blood spilled only hours before.

He entered the throne chamber, the air heavy with ash, iron, and the bitter remnants of fire. Here, the echoes still lingered. Not just of sound, but of memory.

The long feast table was overturned, crushed beneath the weight of giants now dead. The stone floor bore cracks from Drunnyak's onslaught, and the throne itself – carved from molten obsidian and fused with magma veins – stood like a wound on the world.

Alentar's eyes scanned everything.

The scattered bones.

The splintered shields.

The trail of blood smeared across the floor in wide, brutal arcs.

He stood still, narrowing his gaze. As if he could see it all again – the exact moment the beast fell. Drunnyak's silhouette, the trembling giants, the wrath of justice made flesh. Alentar smirked slightly, lips curling at the corners.

"Always the theatrical one," he murmured fondly.

But then... Something caught his eye.

Far in the corner of the chamber, nearly swallowed by shadow and debris, a faint shimmer. Barely there. A ring of etched stone, almost imperceptible beneath dust and soot.

He stepped closer, crouching, brushing the filth aside.

Runes. Ancient. Elven in shape – but twisted, repurposed. Reforged for another's hand.

The pattern curved in concentric arcs, carved with precision. This wasn't a place of worship. It was a conduit. A gate. A spell circle.

Not for summoning.

For teleportation.

Alentar's breath caught, his gloved fingers hovering just above the runes. He could feel it. The lingering hum of old magic, like a memory buried too long under snow and stone.

And then it struck him. The ring.

He remembered the Fire Giant King's hand, adorned with a single band of blackened steel, carved with runes not unlike these. At the time, it pulsed with unnatural heat and energy. Alentar had felt it. A key.

Not crafted by the brute... but gifted.

"That's how he moved," Alentar whispered, eyes narrowing as the pieces fell into place. "Why they brought her down there... and why they never climbed."

He stood slowly, scanning the room.

His eyes flicked toward the narrow stairwells, too tight for something as massive as a fire giant. Then to the freight elevator – sturdy enough for crates, barely for men, but not for monsters made of flame and ruin. The layout wasn't just inconvenient – it was impossible for them.

They didn't descend.

They bypassed.

This circle – it wasn't just a relic.

It was a gate.

Not only a way for the fire giants to move through the mountain, but a passage for the produce and spoils stolen from the villagers. A direct route, somewhere beyond.

His hand hovered once more above the ancient runes, now pulsing faintly as if sensing his nearness.

If this was truly what he thought it was, then the answers weren't buried below...

They were scattered across the world, and the key – the ring – was still here, likely clutched in the cold fingers of a tyrant now slain.

Alentar's pulse quickened.

His fingers curled around the hilt at his side – not in fear, but in readiness.

This wasn't the end of a war.

It was the first thread in a deeper web, and now... he had found it.

Suddenly, Alentar heard steps.

The steps were barely audible – so soft, so precise, that even the shifting dust did not stir.

Alentar froze.

No villager could move like that. Not even Drokan's careful tread could fall this silently on ancient stone, and still the sound came – measured, disciplined, patient.

A hunter's rhythm.

Without a thought, Alentar pressed himself into the shadows – into the very curvature of the wall, where light dared not linger. His form blended, vanished, consumed by the stillness. Only his breath remained – calm, steady, cold.

And then... It started.

The aura.

He hadn't summoned it, but it answered all the same.

From far above, he felt it – the villagers, whispering his name in reverence. Their awe, their hope, their belief in him... like wind fuelling a fire. It surged through his bones, coiling around his spine, flooding his limbs with forgotten strength.

A red aura, dark as drying blood, flickered into being around him, low and alive. It shimmered like liquid shadow, dancing along his skin, curling from his shoulders. His emerald eyes, always sharp, now burned with something else. Something ancient. Feral.

The world shifted. It lost colour.

No light, no darkness.

Just layers.

Edges.

Contours.

He could see the tremor of breath behind stone. The ripple of fabric brushing against old mortar. He could feel the heartbeat of the fortress. Hear the veins pulsing in its quiet places. The animals resting. The wind trembling through cracks.

And then... him.

Alentar's gaze narrowed, locking on a form that moved just beyond the archway.

Each step was fluid.

Measured.

Silent, but not unfamiliar.

The lean, muscular frame crept with purpose, every movement exact. His armour was pieced from deep forest hide and dark iron etched with flowing, natural symbols – runes of their ancient order. A cowl shadowed his features, but the jawline was firm, the posture proud. He moved with a grace Alentar had seen only once before.

The realisation hit like lightning through the storm of his senses.

Alanteas.

His first ranger.

The first he ever trained.

The one he had once called 'brother'.

A ghost.

Alentar didn't speak.

Not yet.

He simply watched, aura curling with tension, emerald eyes locked as his former disciple stalked forward.

A test?

A reunion?

A threat?

One heartbeat passed.

Two.

And in the blackness between them, only the hunt remained.

Alanteas stepped fully into the chamber, every muscle taut beneath his dark leathers, the flicker of torchlight catching the ancient runes etched into his chestpiece – runes Alentar himself had once carved. He stopped in the centre of the hall, heart pounding, hands open at his sides. His voice came quiet, but it cracked – raw with emotion that decades had failed to bury. "I know you're there," he said. A pause. His breath caught. "I've felt it. The wind changed. The ground breathed again. And the whispers…" He swallowed. "Your name, Alentar. They're speaking it again. Praying it like it never left their tongues." He turned in place slowly, eyes scanning the corners, the rafters, the shadows that even fire couldn't pierce. "I couldn't believe it. I told myself it was a lie. That I was chasing ghosts." His voice grew softer, trembling. "But

I always knew... if you were truly back..." he turned toward the wall where Alentar stood merged, invisible to all but gods, "you'd never let me find you first." A wet sound escaped his throat, and the hardened warrior – hunter of giants, shadow among the trees – broke. His heart uncontrolled now. His knees struck stone. He knelt, trembling, head bowed. "Please," he whispered. "If there's even a fragment of truth left in the world, let it be this. Let it be you." His eyes, brimming with tears, searched the dark. "Please... be true."

Silence.

And then, the shadows stirred.

A breeze moved where there should be none, and from the blackness, like dawn from night, Alentar stepped forward.

No words. No dramatic proclamation.

Just presence.

Emerald eyes glowing, his red aura curling like a memory brought to life.

Alanteas looked up – and wept. "Master," he breathed.

Alentar stepped closer, slowly, and at last, he knelt too.

Their forearms met in the clasp of warriors.

Of teacher and student.

Of two who had once faced the end of the world together.

"I left you too soon," Alentar whispered.

"No," Alanteas said through the tears. "You gave me everything."

They stayed like that, the two hunters in the hall of ruin, and for a moment, the fortress that had once echoed with suffering held peace.

Their reunion – raw, eternal – was shattered in a breath.

A sudden tremor pulsed through the stone beneath their feet. A deep hum followed, rippling through the chamber walls like an ancient breath drawn after centuries of silence.

The portal – once dormant, etched faintly into the wall – began to shimmer.

Light spilled from the runes in twisting streams of green, gold and violet. The ring in Alentar's hand vibrated violently, then glowed, its inscriptions burning with magic. It lifted slightly from his palm, speaking in fractured tongues – elvish, draconic, and something older still. A language that stirred the bones of the mountain itself.

Alentar narrowed his eyes, stepping between Alanteas and the circle.

The wind surged. Even the remains of the giants – bones, weapons, fragments of armour – were pulled toward the portal's awakening maw. Dust and power churned as the portal widened, its centre glowing with a violent, unnatural light.

Then… a voice.

Clear.

Calm.

Familiar.

"Alentar… my friend…"

Alentar froze.

The voice curled into his chest like a blade sliding between ribs. "Opilkhos needs you."

"Ian?" Alentar whispered, disbelief crackling in his voice.

The voice did not answer again. It didn't need to.

But someone else did.

Alanteas spun, eyes wide, stepping in front of Alentar like a child shielding a father. His voice trembled with fury and dread. "No, master! Don't go! That's Verrlov's magic!"

Alentar blinked. The name meant nothing. Not yet. "I don't—"

"It's a trap," Alanteas begged, his hands trembling as they grabbed Alentar's tunic. "Please, *please* don't leave me again."

And for a moment – just a moment – Alentar's face softened, that eternal calm flickering like candlelight. He stepped close, placed a hand against Alanteas's cheek, and kissed his forehead. A gesture older than their lifetimes. "Protect the villagers," Alentar said, his voice gentle but resolute. "Until my brothers return. I shall not be long."

Alanteas dropped to his knees, still gripping his master's cloak, eyes filled with desperate grief. But as Alentar turned, something changed in the younger elf's gaze. No longer a frightened child, but a disciple receiving his charge. He lowered his head. Nodded once. "I shall not fail you again."

Alentar turned back, pausing at the threshold of the portal. He looked over his shoulder, a rare and warm smile crossing his lips. "You never did."

And then he was gone.

Without hesitation. Without fear.

One step into the light and the portal swallowed him whole, its blinding power surging once more before vanishing entirely, leaving only silence.

And Alanteas standing alone.

Eyes full of memory and purpose.

STONE AND ROOT,
HEART AND HEARTH

The sun never truly rose in Garrents – but that morning, something brighter stirred.

The light wasn't in the sky, it was in the people.

Warmth passed between hands as fires were stoked, doors opened, and voices hummed soft greetings across stone paths dusted with new snow. The frozen wind, though sharp, no longer howled like a curse. It moved through the village like a whisper of the old world... and the start of something new.

Taril and Nashir walked beside Garric and Eldric, their footfalls slow, steady – measured as men not simply walking ground, but relearning it. Around them, life stirred in harmony with their presence. Birds nested above the rooftops, wild goats roamed close to the fences, and wolves slept curled at the foot of porches, unmoved by the nearness of children.

A village once braced for death now breathed.

Garric gestured as they moved through the streets, pointing out key homes, trade stalls, the bakery half-dug into the hillside, the forge warmed with fire that now burned brighter thanks to Nashir's blessings. Near the old watchtower, a group of young villagers practised spear throws under the guidance of seasoned guards – smiling for the first time in memory.

Taril's gaze lifted to the massive stones reinforcing the walls, nodding thoughtfully. "Who laid the foundation?"

"Tharn," Garric said. "Tharn of Ironmark."

Eldric grinned. "Grumpier than Borgrim before ale, but his hands are steadier than the mountains."

Nashir chuckled softly, crouching near a flowering vine pushing through the frozen ground – one that had bloomed from the roots he'd planted the night of the gods' return. "We must meet him," he said, brushing frost from a soft lavender bloom. "Stone and soil deserve the same reverence."

Elsewhere, laughter echoed from the tavern as Opilkhos and Niv sat near the window beside Borgrim, sharing thick slices of bread, cured meat, and stewed root vegetables, steam rising in waves from their bowls. Niv had her boots kicked up on the bench beside her, a mug of something sweet in hand, eyes gleaming as she teased Opilkhos.

"Did you really get all broody again at breakfast? You can move hearts with your grin, but sulk when someone gives you jam?"

"I just find sticky food distracting," Opilkhos replied, lifting an eyebrow, his tone dry.

Borgrim nearly choked on his ale with laughter. "Stickier than undead guts? I find that hard to believe."

Niv smirked, tilting her head as she leaned back with lazy grace. "We really need to teach you joy, ancient soul," she teased, her voice rich with mischief. "You're the youngest of us, yet you carry yourself like a grumpy old sage."

"I know joy," Opilkhos said, reaching for another piece of bread. "It just usually comes in quieter forms."

Borgrim gave him a side-eye and grinned. "Well then, time to get loud."

Outside, the village stirred with something even greater than movement – belonging. The gods didn't stand above. They walked among. They helped carry lumber. They lit torches. They tended broken fences and weary bodies. Nashir stopped to tend to a wounded hound. Taril inspected the forge, offering tips with a surprisingly artistic eye.

And in it all, Garric walked taller. He saw not just hope returning, but purpose.

A dawn not marked by sun, but by the slow rising of life.

The sun may not have pierced the clouds, but the world felt lighter as Nashir and Taril followed Garric and Eldric through the heart of Garrents.

They passed the winding main path, where frost clung to wood and stone, approaching a figure already hard at work, his silhouette hunched beneath a wide-brimmed leather cap, hammer tapping rhythmically against the foundation of a home perched on elevated stilts.

He didn't look up as they approached, not at first. His thick hands – wrapped in worn gloves – moved with the precision of a master. Each stroke of his chisel seemed more like a conversation with the stone than a carving of it.

"Tharn of Ironmark," Garric called with a faint smile. "Still arguing with the mountain, I see."

Tharn grunted, standing to his full height – short for a human, built like a boulder, with shoulders too wide for most door frames and a beard that reached the buttons of his coat. "The mountain listens," he said, wiping his brow, "if you know how to speak her tongue."

Nashir stepped forward, offering a respectful incline of his head. "And what language does she speak, master builder?"

Tharn looked the elf up and down, his grey eyes narrowing beneath bushy brows. "Mostly complaints," he muttered. "About fools who build too close to her bones."

Taril chuckled, stepping beside Nashir. "You two will get along."

Introductions passed quickly, but formality faded fast in the presence of shared purpose. Soon, the three stood over a rough sketch scrawled onto a stretched piece of hide – lines, angles, notes, all crammed between thumbprints of dust and grease.

Taril knelt beside it, tracing one of the elevation lines. "You've done well with what you had."

Tharn snorted. "I did what I had to. Didn't have gods back when I started."

Nashir crouched beside them, his fingers brushing lightly over a spot where water tables had been marked. "You've avoided tapping into the groundwater."

"I'm not about to flood half the homes for a few extra buckets," Tharn said. "The slope's too steep. You dig too far, you'll wake the rock's temper."

Taril nodded. "We've seen what that temper can do."

"But," Nashir said gently, "if we guide the water instead of taking it, use natural descent… here…" He pointed to a narrow split between two elevated homes. "We could direct a flow through living roots and stone, softened by nature rather than hammered through."

"Filtered?" Tharn raised a brow.

"And self-sustaining," Nashir said.

They spent the next hour in deep discussion. Taril spoke of reinforcing homes built against the cliff face, anchoring them with metals that would shift with the rock rather than fight it. Nashir pointed out areas where vegetation could both support and conceal structural joints, lessening the stress on outer beams during tremors.

"We don't need to tame this mountain," Nashir said quietly, "only ask it to hold us. And listen when it warns."

Tharn stood silently for a moment, then let out a low breath. "Never thought I'd see the day gods gave a damn about homes sliding off slopes."

Taril smiled faintly. "We've lived long enough to understand what's worth saving."

And as frost melted from the edges of the drawn plans, a partnership was born – one forged not in divine command, but in calloused hands, careful minds, and a shared promise not to let this place fall again.

Back in the tavern, the fire crackled lazily as Niv leaned back in her chair, stretching like a lounging cat with her plate cleaned and her fingers stained with berry jam. She glanced sideways at Opilkhos, who had been tracing runes across the wood of the table absent-mindedly, eyes distant. "Study the place, find soft spots, make it impenetrable…" she repeated mockingly, quoting the words they'd been tasked with.

Then she kicked her boots up, crossing them with a grin. "Sounds like your kind of poetry."

Opilkhos didn't look up. "It's necessary."

"Oh, I know," she said, rising to her feet, licking her thumb clean. "But it's no use staring at wood and toast crumbs, is it? Show me around your moody little empire, oh, keeper of brooding silence."

His brows lifted. "My what?"

She winked. "You're clearly the village's new favourite dish. Might as well enjoy the flavour."

Despite himself, Opilkhos chuckled softly, rising with a sigh, brushing off his robes. "Fine. Let's go see what needs protecting. And what you mean by 'my moody little empire.'"

The doors creaked open as the pair stepped into the morning air – cold but gentle, filled with birdsong and laughter. The village was alive in a way few places ever were. Children darted between legs, and animals, some furred and wild-looking, mingled with the people without fear. The homes seemed to breathe with warmth now, glowing from within with cookfires and newly repaired hearths.

As they passed the fountain in the square, some villagers looked up – some bowed their heads respectfully, others offered hesitant smiles. One older woman handed Niv a piece of warm bread stuffed with cheese and herbs, which she took with a flirtatious thank-you and a kiss to the air.

"I like it here," Niv said, biting in. "These people smile with their whole faces."

Opilkhos didn't answer. His eyes moved over every roof, every street corner, the edges of the mountain behind them. Measuring. Calculating. Protecting.

Then, with a small thump, something attached to Niv's legs.

"Where's Drunnyak?!" Caelan asked breathlessly, his arms wrapped around her knees as if he'd never let go. His wide eyes were brimming with worry and excitement.

Niv staggered a step, then looked down with a mock gasp. "Gods, you again? You never stop sneaking up on me, little lion!"

She knelt and tousled his hair, her expression softening.

279

"He's off on a mission," Opilkhos said, crouching to meet the boy's eyes. "But he'll be back. That's a promise."

Caelan looked between them, frowning. "You sure?"

"As sure as the mountains stand," Niv said, straightening. "Now, come. Walk with us. We've got work to do – and if you're going to follow Drunnyak around, you better learn how to spot danger before it spots you."

The boy grinned and fell into step between them, one hand in hers, the other occasionally pointing at things he thought were important – "That chimney's too loose! That cow escaped again! That chicken is *definitely* undead."

As Niv and Opilkhos made their way toward the trench, the path curling around frost-kissed boulders and wind-carved ridges, Caelan trailed just behind, chattering away, pointing at hawks soaring high above, or tugging Niv's sleeve to show her the twisting roots that peeked through the snow.

But as they reached the edge of the trench, where nature now bloomed like a quiet miracle under Nashir's touch, the boy's steps slowed.

He stared into the distance at the wild threshold where the gods had once fought – where the world had started to change.

Then he looked back toward the village. Toward the sound of hammering, the echo of voices, and the warm figure of his father somewhere beyond the rooftops.

"I think I'll go back," Caelan said softly, eyes still wide in wonder.

Niv gave him a playful nudge. "What, the trench too much for you, little wolf?"

He grinned sheepishly, then turned and ran – his small form bouncing back down the path, arms out like wings, as if racing the wind back home.

And so they walked – an old soul, a fire-kissed mischief, and a bright spark of youth – through the heart of Garrents, ready to protect it with all they had.

The air was crisp, the morning cold softened by the green miracle Nashir had left behind.

Opilkhos and Niv walked side by side along the edge of the trench, its once-brutal cut across the land now softened by thick vines and flowering undergrowth. Trees had begun to sprout in places no roots had dared before. What was once a battlefield – a scar of cold and death – now breathed with quiet life.

"I'll admit," Niv said, her hands tucked behind her back, eyes scanning the reborn horizon, "our leafy brother's got a dramatic flair. This place used to look like a wound."

Opilkhos offered a rare, quiet smile. "Now it looks like healing."

They paused at the edge where the trench once yawned open like the jaws of a beast. The natural wall Nashir had summoned pulsed faintly with life, its woven thorns and bark-covered spears standing like an army of green sentinels.

Niv crouched and touched a flowering vine twined along the stone. "Hard to believe we bled here. That your light shook the skies."

Opilkhos didn't answer at first. His gaze drifted across the mountain peaks. The memory hit like a slow avalanche – flashes of battle, of Lena's voice echoing through him, of Harinnil's shadow twisting through his soul. "It started here," he said at last. "When the past began chasing us again."

Niv stood, brushing off her hands. "Then maybe it's fitting we start protecting it here too. Make this place so unbreakable, no darkness dares crawl out again."

Opilkhos turned toward her, eyes glowing faintly. "We'll need more than walls."

She smirked. "We've got more than walls. We've got gods. And me."

They shared a laugh – short, warm. Not the kind of laugh one gives in joy, but in stubborn hope. In defiance of a world that had already taken too much.

As they moved again, their boots crunching softly on frost-tipped earth, the mountains loomed above them – ancient, unmoved. But Opilkhos glanced over his shoulder once more, as if expecting the past to rise from the trench like the undead they had slain.

It didn't.

Instead, a gentle wind stirred the vines, whispering through the trees. Not a warning.

A promise.

They walked on. Two gods – one cloaked in shadows, the other radiant with fire – carving a path not just through the village, but through what remained of their forgotten selves.

As they continued along the trench's edge, Niv picked a strange flower sprouting from a twisted vine and twirled it in her fingers. "Do you think this one's poisonous?" she asked, eyeing it dramatically before holding it up toward Opilkhos's face. "Wouldn't want the local kids munching on the gods' leftovers."

Opilkhos raised an unimpressed brow. "If it was, Nashir wouldn't have let it grow."

She sniffed it anyway. "Smells like regret."

"Fitting," he replied drily. "That's what you left behind at the tavern when you drank Borgrim under the table."

Niv laughed, tossing the flower over her shoulder. "I let him win. You know – boost morale, give the old dwarf something to brag about."

"You were face down in a bowl of stew."

"Details."

They crested a ridge where the trench curved back toward the village. The warm glow of early light filtered over the rooftops, and they could see villagers moving about – some beginning to reinforce outer walls, others tending to the animals Nashir had brought. It looked… hopeful.

"Do you ever think," Opilkhos said, watching the people, "we're actually… doing what we were meant to?"

Niv tilted her head. "You mean *not* obliterating armies or fighting cosmic horror-fathers?"

"Something like that."

She bumped him lightly with her shoulder. "You've always been the broodiest of us. Ever think maybe you were meant for quiet things? Protection. Hearths. Not just storms and fury."

Opilkhos looked at her, truly *looked* – his normally unreadable gaze softened. "And you?"

She grinned. "Please. I was born to be fabulous and stab things creatively. But I don't mind keeping a few villagers alive while I do it."

They stood in silence for a beat, watching the clouds curl over the distant peaks.

Then Niv squinted. "You know what would really make this place impenetrable?"

"Don't say a lava moat."

"A lava moat."

Opilkhos sighed. "You've been talking to Taril again."

"Only a little. He drew me a diagram. There were ducks."

They both burst into laughter, a sound that echoed over the trench and rolled down into the village like thunder turned warm.

For a moment, it didn't feel like gods walking old scars.

It felt like friends. Like family. Like the world might actually hold together this time.

The path along the mountain edge quieted as they reached a bend where the wind grew still. Below them, the trench now bloomed with life, a cradle of green stretching where once only death had lingered. Nashir's touch was everywhere – vines wrapped like guardians around ancient stone, and wildflowers peeked defiantly through the frost. But neither of them was looking down.

Opilkhos had stopped, eyes fixed on the horizon. His shoulders, always held with that calm poise, sagged a little. The light in his amber gaze dimmed.

Niv slowed beside him, still chewing on the edge of a fruit she'd stolen from one of the baskets they'd passed. Her smile, always just a bit too sharp, faded as she caught the look on his face. "You're thinking about her again," she said. It was not a question.

He didn't deny it. "How much do you remember?" he asked quietly, as if his voice might disturb the very mountains.

Niv exhaled, brushing a strand of silver-blonde hair behind her ear. "Not much," she admitted. "Nothing clear. But when I try to remember her, it's like a warmth starts in my chest and spreads everywhere. Like something good I lost and never found again."

Opilkhos's jaw worked as he stared into the distance. "Her eyes... they were green, weren't they? Like the heart of spring."

Niv nodded slowly, her voice soft. "Glowing. Alive."

"She had hair like midnight," Opilkhos whispered, as if the words had only just returned to him. "Black as the sky before the stars come out. But she *glowed*. Not from magic. Just... from being."

"She was carved of the same strength as Drunnyak," Niv added, her voice growing fond. "You could feel it in her steps. But she was softer somehow. Her skin was bronze, like the warmth of the earth right after rain."

Opilkhos looked down at his hands. "She smiled at everyone. Even the ones who didn't deserve it. And when she touched you, it felt like she already forgave you for something you hadn't done yet."

Niv blinked, her throat tight. "She made me laugh. I don't even remember the joke. But I remember the sound. And thinking, *Maybe I could love someone like that.*"

"She wasn't just a goddess," Opilkhos said. "She was... the *heart* of us, right? The centre."

A hush fell over them.

Then, after a long moment, Opilkhos spoke again, lower now. "I see her sometimes. In dreams. We were in a cabin. Wooden walls. The sea outside. Birds singing. I don't remember much else... But she called me Opilkhos. She named me. Not as a god, or a warrior. Just a man." He looked to Niv, his eyes rimmed with mist. "She saw the part of me that wasn't *him*. Not Harinnil. Not the brother who turned. Just... me."

Niv stepped closer, placing a hand gently over his. "I don't think she ever doubted the real you," she said. "Even when the rest of the world forgot."

Opilkhos looked at her, grateful.

"And I think she knew," Niv added, a small smile tugging at her lips, "that the good in him – *you* – would find its way back."

He let out a shaky laugh, wiping his eyes on his sleeve. "I hate that I forgot her," he said.

"She's not forgotten," Niv said. "She's in every good thing we do. Every time you keep going."

"And you?" he asked.

Niv gave him a playful shove. "Oh, I mostly remember how *annoyingly* perfect she was. Gods, Lena made *me* feel plain. Can you imagine?"

Opilkhos laughed, and the sound felt right again. Like something that belonged to the world they were building.

They stood there for a moment longer, side by side, with the wind brushing past them like a memory.

"She would've loved this place," Opilkhos said.

"She *will* love it," Niv replied. "When we bring her back."

He looked at her, startled.

Niv shrugged. "Just a feeling. But you know me – I usually listen when the universe whispers."

As they turned back toward the village, they walked slower, closer, sharing the silence, carrying Lena with them.

Opilkhos stopped.

The wind pulled gently at his cloak.

"You've been quiet," Niv said, casting a sideways glance at Opilkhos. "Brooding again?"

He smiled faintly, but didn't respond.

Niv rolled her eyes with a grin. "Fine. Be the mysterious one. But let me ask you something."

He raised a brow.

"How much do you remember of her?"

The question landed like snow – soft, but heavy.

Opilkhos stopped walking.

His lips parted, but no words came.

Niv's expression softened. "You can't keep her out of your mind, can you?"

He looked away, the wind catching the edge of his cloak.

"I don't remember much of my own past," Niv went on, voice quieter now. "But when I try to think of her – Lena – it's not like remembering a person. It's like remembering warmth. Light. The exact moment before a star bursts into life." She smiled to herself. "Gods, she was *beautiful*. Skin like twilight bronze, hair dark as the void between stars. And her eyes… green like mine, but brighter. Like spring fought through winter just to bloom in her."

Opilkhos breathed in slow. "I see her sometimes… in flashes. Like a dream I almost had."

He closed his eyes, as if the wind itself carried the memory to him.

Niv reached out, her fingers absently conjuring flame that flickered across her palm like a heartbeat. She looked at him again, smiling quietly. "You know, everyone used to think Harinnil and I were close. I guess we were. But not like that."

Opilkhos opened his eyes and glanced over.

"He was always around Ian," she continued. "Always watching, always listening. That quiet type – the one with the weight of the world behind his eyes. I think… I think I wanted to be closer to him. Not because I loved him, but because I could tell he was standing at the edge of something. Something vast."

Opilkhos glanced at her, surprised.

"But no," she said, snuffing the flame with a snap. "It wasn't him." She smiled with something between amusement and longing. "I had a thing with Ian."

Opilkhos blinked. "Ian?"

"Oh, shut it," she laughed, punching his arm. "He had that bookworm confidence! Books, scrolls, spells… and this weird charm like he knew the answers to questions no one dared ask. I liked that."

Opilkhos chuckled. "I don't remember much of him, but I'll definitely never look at him the same again." He chuckled.

"Don't you dare tell him when we finally see him," she said, mock-threatening, then grinned. "But Harinnil? He was like a little brother, in a way. Quiet. Curious. Full of questions, but too afraid to ask. I used to catch him staring at Ian, you know? Like Ian held the key to every door." She paused, letting the wind fill the silence. "I had this dream," she said. "Last night. I saw them. Ian writing, muttering to himself, and Harinnil – young, so young – just watching him. Not speaking. Just… there. Absorbing everything." Her voice cracked slightly. "I think… I think they loved each other in a way neither of them knew how to say."

Opilkhos closed his eyes for a moment. The breeze carried scents from long ago – salt and fire and ash. Things half-remembered, emotions without names. "I don't know what I feel," he said softly. "Only that it's deep. And it doesn't go away."

"She would've loved you either way," Niv whispered. "Whether you were Harinnil or Opilkhos. Or both. Or neither."

He looked at her, something ancient and fragile in his gaze.

Then Niv stepped in and wrapped her arms around him. No words. Just warmth. And when she pulled away, she socked him in the arm. "I'm *not* hitting on you, brooding storm cloud," she said with a grin. "You're *her* man. Always were. Always will be."

Opilkhos smiled – quiet and pained and grateful. "I can't describe what I feel for her," he said. "Words… fall short."

"They usually do," Niv replied. "That's why we have poetry and silence."

He gave her a look.

"Come on," she said, bumping his shoulder with hers. "Let's go make this village unbreakable. And maybe find you a haircut."

He laughed – really laughed – for the first time in what felt like centuries, and together, they walked on.

As Opilkhos and Niv turned the corner toward the heart of the village, their steps slowed, drawn in by the silent awe that had settled over the crowd.

Every villager stood still. Some with mouths slightly parted, others with hands clasped over their chests. Even the children, in mid-chase or laughter, had frozen where they stood, eyes wide as saucers.

And at the centre of it all… wonder in motion.

Nashir stood atop a platform of twisting vines and roots, his staff glowing softly, green energy pulsing through the earth beneath his feet. Beside him, Taril worked like a sculptor of the world itself, his war hammer held not as a weapon, but as a tool of creation. Each strike to the ground shaped stone as if it were wet clay. They weren't just building.

They were transforming.

From the outer homes, now partially elevated, thick stone stairwells coiled up the mountain wall like growing vines of granite, connecting with walkways held aloft by massive arches of entwined roots and rock. The bridge above the village stretched from one cliffside to the other, formed where nature met craftsmanship, suspended by thick, living branches reinforced with cut stone. Moss grew already along the edges, flowering buds blooming where Nashir's hands had passed.

Water, previously a trickle barely feeding their needs, now flowed freely. A smooth channel had been carved into the earth, lined with moss and shimmering crystals. It poured in a soft, constant current, gliding through the village like a river reborn – until it reached the fountain at the centre. Once cracked and barely flowing, it now overflowed with clear water, sparkling in the morning light. A soft hum echoed from it, as if it too were singing in relief.

Villagers had gathered with buckets in hand, but none moved to collect the water just yet. They simply watched – watched a new life forming before their eyes.

Opilkhos exhaled slowly.

Niv, beside him, whistled low, impressed. "All right… they're really showing off."

He nodded. "And yet, for once… I don't mind."

One child broke the silence, tugging at his mother's arm and whispering, "Mama, it's magic."

Taril stood proudly near one of the bridges, his massive frame dusted with bits of stone, his beard braided tighter than usual. Nashir knelt beside the newly grown roots of a thick tree, whispering thanks in the ancient tongue as the branches curved to cradle a nearby platform.

When Taril spotted them, he straightened and grinned, his voice booming as they approached. "Well, well! Look who finally stopped admiring the mountain view and came to see how the real work is done."

Niv grinned. "Please. I walked so far I nearly became one with the cliffside."

Opilkhos folded his arms, smirking. "You do know the cliff talked back, right?"

Nashir chuckled, rising smoothly. "It said she complained too much."

"Traitor," Niv muttered with mock offence.

Taril gave a hearty laugh, clapping Nashir on the back. "They've missed us."

"Clearly," Opilkhos said drily. "Though I must admit, the place is changing fast. Looks like a true home."

Taril's expression softened at that.

Opilkhos then said, "The trench – she still needs tending. That edge of the village… it's too open. If the undead come again, I'd rather not have nature alone standing between us."

Taril turned, gesturing toward the edge where the wilderness still crept along the jagged rocks. "What do you two see out there?"

Opilkhos stepped forward, folding his hands behind his back as he surveyed the distant ridge where the threshold still shimmered faintly with Nashir's gift. He squinted into the distance, thoughtful. "There needs to be a gate," he said finally. "Not just a wall – something proud. Stalwart. Stone carved into strength, etched with our names, our symbols. A statement. This is Garrents, and it will never fall."

Taril nodded slowly, his eyes alight. "A gate worthy of the gods, eh?"

"No," Opilkhos said with a small smile. "A gate worthy of the people who gave us something to protect again."

Nashir tilted his head. "I could braid roots through its base. Let the trench itself rise against any threat."

Niv crossed her arms, then glanced toward the trench and raised a brow. "As long as there's a proper arch. And none of that dwarven obsession with corners everywhere. Let's make it elegant, for once."

Taril huffed. "Blasphemy. Corners bring order!"

"Corners make stubbed toes," she shot back.

Their laughter echoed across the village – gods, kin and friends all standing shoulder to shoulder in a place that had once been nothing but cold stone and fear. Now, it grew with promise.

As night approached, the warmth of the day clung to the stones and timber. The hum of laughter and distant conversations stirred gently through the crisp mountain air as villagers returned from their tasks, already sensing that something special was coming. Fires were being stoked, benches dusted, and little ones bathed by the well. The village – still raw from pain, still reborn from ruin – stood on the edge of another night, but this time with joy instead of fear.

Garric and Eldric approached the gods near the trench's rim, where the four stood surveying the improvements. Garric's hand rested on his brother's shoulder as they walked, their expressions serious but warm.

"We're starting on preparations for tonight," Garric said, his voice firm but carrying that unspoken reverence for those who now walked among them. "A proper meal again. For everyone."

Eldric nodded, smiling. "Borgrim's already cursing at the firepit like it's a traitor, so I'd say the cooks are in full swing. We'll set the long tables outside, under the lanterns. The whole village needs this."

Taril grinned, cracking his knuckles. "Aye, nothing like roasted elk and stew to ease tired bones."

But before he could continue, Nashir raised his staff with a subtle, glowing flicker of green light, his eyes narrowing slightly. "No meat tonight," he said with calm authority. "Only the meat we already have stored. Tonight, the land shall provide."

Taril turned, arching a brow and smirking. "Meat is also from nature, lad. Last I checked, boars don't grow from stone."

Nashir gave him a flat look, unamused. "Not tonight," he said again, the power beneath his words rumbling faintly in the earth.

"All right," Niv cut in quickly, hands on her hips, trying not to laugh. "Before we get another lecture on the balance of nature, how about this?" She spun toward them, firelight catching the gleam in her eyes. "Taril, Opilkhos, you two go start working on that gate. Big, proud, very impressive. Maybe with a little flourish this time," she added, flashing Taril a mocking grin. "I'll help Garric and the others organise the tables, and Nashir can do his leafy conjuring thing and feed the masses when you're done."

Taril looked at Opilkhos and then at the distant trench. "It shouldn't take more than a few minutes."

Opilkhos gave a faint nod, eyes gleaming under the dusk sky. "Let's build something they'll remember."

"Good," Niv said, already waving villagers over to clear space and string lanterns between beams. "We'll hold the feast down here, you boys go knock rocks together."

As the gods split, Taril and Opilkhos walking side by side toward the edge of the village, a soft wind stirred the trees. Villagers looked on, smiling and whispering, some placing candles in windows and laying wildflowers along the walkways. Children began to place wooden plates along the long tables, chasing each other between barrels and stools, while elders sat nearby, basking in the warmth of this rare calm.

And in the centre of it all, Borgrim cursed at a pot of boiling water like it had insulted his lineage – though a smile curled behind his beard.

The wind hissed softly through the broken stones, brushing against Taril's beard like an old companion's whisper. He and Opilkhos moved steadily through the gloom, boots crunching snow and gravel, the vast trench stretching ahead of them like a wound in the earth.

"Right, lads," Taril said with a gruff but kind voice, turning back to a few soldiers stationed near the pass. "Go on, then. You've earned a hot bowl and a seat by the fire. No one's getting through tonight."

The soldiers exchanged glances, then nodded with relieved salutes, moving back toward the village.

Opilkhos walked beside Taril in silence for a moment, eyes tracing the edges of the trench as if measuring it with his mind.

Taril gave him a sideways glance, the corner of his mouth tugging into a grin. "You're thinking about foundations already, aren't you?"

Opilkhos smirked. "I was wondering whether it's better to anchor the outer gate into the cliff wall directly, or if we'd do better creating a staggered entrance."

"Staggered." Taril grunted in agreement. "A direct gate's easier to batter down. But if we channel the approach into a zigzag, no ram will get a proper charge. And we can put elevation above each angle. Archer nests. Kill zones."

Opilkhos nodded slowly. "Exactly. And stone – true stone – layered with living root from Nashir's craft. It won't just stand – it'll heal. And hold. I've seen barriers break before… this one won't."

Taril thumped his massive hand against his chest. "We'll layer dwarven technique with elven breath. Old-world stone and new-world life. A wall that remembers what it was made for."

They reached the trench's edge, and both stopped. Taril crouched, resting his hand on the icy ground. "We'll dig anchor pillars into the earth, flare them wide like dwarven teeth. That way, even if the enemy brings down the wall itself, the roots will hold it from collapsing in."

Opilkhos stared into the darkness. "And the gate?"

Taril rose, tapping his chin with thick fingers. "Double-hinged stone, reinforced with timber inside. A crest above it. Something that says this place belongs to more than men."

"To gods?" Opilkhos asked with a half-smile – almost with a snigger.

"To those who stood for something," Taril said. "Call it what you will."

There was a moment of silence between them. Not awkward – just full. Heavy with meaning.

Opilkhos looked at the looming silhouette of the trench and nodded. "Then let's build it right. Not just strong… but eternal."

Taril cracked his knuckles. "Aye. Let's make the world think twice before sending monsters to this doorstep again."

And with that, the two of them got to work – one chisel in hand, the other with a whisper to the stone – brothers in creation, as they had been in battle.

The trench groaned beneath their feet, ancient and vast. But where others saw emptiness and danger, Taril saw shape and form – potential hidden in shadow.

He took a deep breath and stepped forward. "Time to wake the bones of this mountain," he muttered.

Taril planted his feet wide, braced like a sculptor before a block of stubborn marble. From his belt, he withdrew a thick, rune-carved chisel – the kind only a dwarf god would carry. He traced a wide square in the air with the tip, etching invisible lines with such precision it looked like the wind itself cut through the dark.

And then… he struck.

With a roar that echoed through the trench, Taril brought down his war hammer like thunder. The ground trembled. A seam of glowing gold traced the lines he'd drawn in the air, shooting down into the earth. From the wall of the mountain, stone groaned and pulled free – block by perfect block, massive yet uniform, like teeth torn from the mountain's own mouth.

Dozens of them.

Each block landed gently, as if cradled by unseen hands, forming neat stacks along the trench edge.

Opilkhos raised a brow, his mouth tugging into a grin. "Show-off."

Taril snorted. "What's the point of being a god if you don't make your own gravel?"

They both laughed, then Opilkhos turned thoughtful. "What if Nashir helped shape the earth below? A living foundation… we could make another trench, one deeper – wider, even, and harder to cross. With vines and thorns that shift at his command. A second defence, before the wall."

Taril rubbed his chin, already envisioning it. "A trench around the trench. I like it. Give the bastards two thresholds to break."

"And a bridge," Opilkhos added. "One that can be pulled up or collapsed when needed. Something the villagers can use without relying on our strength."

"Leave that to me," Taril said. "I'll design a winch system using weighted counterbalances, pulleys, and levered stone. You pull a rope, gravity does the rest. No brute strength required."

"But what if it fails?" Opilkhos asked, frowning. "If something goes wrong and we're not here—"

Taril raised a hand. "Then they use the fallback. A secondary manual crank. I'll mark the pattern into the stone, step by step. No one forgets how to use it. The mountain will remember, even if the men don't."

Opilkhos looked over the trench as Taril conjured another wave of shaped stone, slamming his hammer once more and summoning another dozen blocks. The mountains didn't resist him – they obeyed him, groaning and stretching, reshaping as though they knew their kin had returned.

Together, they laid the first stones.

Opilkhos whispered to them, infusing the edges with ancient runes, protection woven into every grain. Taril shaped the stones like a puzzle – every block locking into the next, fortified by strength and symmetry. A fusion of will, magic and stone.

Above them, dark clouds churned in the sky – but below, in this corner of the world, something new was rising.

Not just a wall.

A promise.

Opilkhos wiped his brow, even though the chill in the air hadn't dared touch him. His hands brushed against one of the fresh-hewn blocks, still humming faintly from Taril's magic. He looked toward the village, where laughter and preparation stirred the evening into life. "Hold the hammer," he muttered, already sprinting.

In moments, he crossed the village's heart. Smoke curled from fires, tables were being dragged into neat rows, and the smell of pine-scented oils and warm bread mingled with the air. At the fountain's base, Nashir stood, his eyes closed, staff raised, and the earth singing beneath his feet.

It was beautiful.

The soil opened like a flower, unfurling in concentric circles. From within came fruits of vibrant colour – crimson apples with golden veins, deep purple figs, stalks of sweet grain, and twisting vines carrying peppers and soft herbs. Almond trees bloomed in seconds, their trunks lifting from the earth like rising breath, bearing nuts and fragrant blossoms. Edible mushrooms unfurled like velvet parasols near their roots.

Along a vine-covered table, flowers burst into bloom and became soft loaves of steaming bread, pastries filled with honey, and bowls of roasted root vegetables, all warm to the touch. Even thick-cut cheese wheels emerged from sprouting moss-covered shelves that grew right into the bark of summoned trees.

And then came the drinks. Springs bubbled through the stone, filtered through enchanted moss into wooden vessels – clear waters, fruit wines, and even sweet meads.

Villagers stood frozen, eyes wide with wonder, as the bounty of nature revealed itself. Children clapped. The elderly wept.

Opilkhos stepped carefully into the clearing, hesitant to disturb such harmony. "Nashir," he said softly, as if speaking too loudly would break the spell.

The elven god opened his eyes – green glowing brighter than the food he'd conjured. He smiled gently. "You missed the fruit bloom," Nashir said with a wink.

"I saw enough to feel jealous," Opilkhos chuckled, then leaned in, voice lower. "We're building the new wall. Trench, bridge, gate – everything. Taril's laying stone. We want your hand in the foundation… something alive."

Nashir's smile deepened. "Ah, so now the brooding mage comes running to the gardener."

Opilkhos gave him a look. "Hurry up, leaf boy."

Nashir laughed, staff in hand. "Come, let's see what our brothers are up to."

Together, they walked – Opilkhos with long, deliberate strides, Nashir graceful and light. Villagers parted as they passed, bowing their heads, offering quiet thanks.

As they reached the trench, Taril was in full swing – literally. His war hammer clanged rhythmically, sending up sparks with every strike. Enchanted blocks fell into place with unnatural precision, locking and sealing by design. A towering wall was already forming, not jagged but majestic – columns etched with dwarven symbols of protection, with space for torches and even battlements above.

Opilkhos took one look and nodded in satisfaction, then hoisted a block half his height and carried it with ease to the base. "Start the roots," he called to Nashir. "Let's give this place a second skin."

Nashir raised his staff. The ground obeyed instantly.

From the new trench's depths, vines thick as rope surged upward, weaving into an intricate net along the outer rim. Thorns and blossoms twisted together into natural barriers. With a few graceful gestures, Nashir whispered commands into the soil, ensuring the vines would retract, open, or strike as needed.

Taril watched with mild annoyance. "Bloody vines're too elegant. I'll add some spikes of my own."

"Balance, stone-blood." Nashir smirked.

"And teeth, leaf-hair," Taril answered, cracking a grin.

Opilkhos didn't even try to hide his amusement. He summoned a shimmering barrier of light above the gate itself, inscribing it with protective sigils that pulsed once, then faded into the stone as if becoming part of its essence.

In less than an hour, the old trench was no more.

What now stood was a true entrance worthy of the gods.

A massive stone arch, carved with flowing dwarven runes, entwined with living vines blooming with luminous white flowers. A wide bridge of interlocking stone, reinforced by thick roots, spanned the new chasm, with a gate carved of reinforced bark-laced stone and lined with gilded patterns – a union of strength and grace.

Taril crossed his arms, proud.

Nashir brushed dust from his robe, nodding.

Opilkhos placed a hand on the new gate, his fingers lingering over the etched wards.

Then, silently, all three looked to the horizon, proud of what they'd accomplished.

Night in Garrents never truly turned black. The sky, as always, remained a churning canvas of deep greys, with wisps of cloud shifting like restless spirits. But the village glowed from within – fires crackled in great braziers, torches danced along the edges of rooftops, and the central square was alive with warmth, laughter, and the scent of food.

As they reached the village hearth, tables had been drawn out from every corner of the village, lined with steaming dishes: roasted roots

296

and wild vegetables, sizzling mushrooms marinated in herbs, flatbreads baked over open flames, nuts and berries fresh from Nashir's enchanted stores, and fruits no one had seen in generations. Nashir had conjured it all with quiet grace, drawing from nature's bounty without depleting it. Food that smelled of spring and warmth, even in the midst of this cold land.

Borgrim stood near the centre barrel, mug in hand, overseeing the ale distribution like a king at court. His cheeks were flushed, his eyes proud. "If anyone's not drinkin', eatin' or laughin', I'll throw 'em in the goat pen with the slop!" he bellowed, causing a round of hearty laughter to rise from the villagers.

Taril leaned back on a sturdy bench he'd helped shape earlier, sipping from a mug and nodding as Nashir passed by with a woven tray of pastries. "You were right," he admitted. "Nature *can* cook."

"And you still need seasoning," Nashir muttered, placing a warm berry tart in front of him. "But we're getting there."

Nearby, Niv sat perched cross-legged atop the table itself, leaning over a plate of wild fruit and fire-roasted yam. She laughed with a few of the village children who gathered around her, watching her summon small shapes of flame into the air – little foxes and dancing sprites that bounced across their shoulders.

Opilkhos stood by the edge, more subdued, sipping tea rather than ale, quietly observing as he and Garric exchanged a rare quiet moment.

"You ever wonder what to do," Garric asked, "when your fight is suddenly... over?"

Opilkhos arched a brow. "You believe it is?"

Garric gave a dry chuckle. "No. But tonight feels different. For the first time in decades, I don't feel needed."

Just then, Niv overheard and leaned back with a scoff. "Oh, shut it, hero."

Garric blinked. "Excuse me?"

She grinned, elbowing him. "You're still needed, old man. These folks might sleep easier, but they still need to know how to fight. You've got experience. Teach the young ones. Help them get strong. Be the wall behind the walls." She glanced toward Caelan, who was laughing with other children near the fountain, chasing a vine that seemed to move of its own accord – Nashir's doing, no doubt. "And more than that," she continued softly, "you've got your son. He needs you. Not just to fight for him – but to live with him. You've earned that."

Garric didn't answer immediately. He looked toward Caelan, watching as the boy turned to wave at him with a huge, unrestrained smile. His throat tightened. "I suppose… I don't mind being a wall," he finally said. "So long as I get to be part of the home."

"Good," Niv said. "Because if you ever start brooding like Opilkhos, I'll set your beard on fire."

"I do *not* brood," Opilkhos muttered.

"Sure you don't," Niv replied with a wink, raising her mug.

The laughter grew louder as the night went on. Drokan, awkwardly seated near the edge of the festivities, found himself surprised when a group of children dragged him into a game involving tossing pine cones at bottles. He was terrible at it – and they adored him for it.

Taril started showing some of the villagers how to shape small bricks of stone into more useful tools. Nashir, with animals at his feet, shared quiet stories of plants that could grow even in the harshest snow, and in the corner, Garric sat with his son, arm wrapped around the boy's shoulders, watching the flames dance.

The celebration swelled around them like a warm tide – laughter bubbling up from every table, mugs clinking, music humming from strings and pipes, and the scents of roasted roots and honeyed bread thick in the cool air.

Children chased firefly-like lights conjured by Nashir, and Harwen, the jovial carpenter with arms the size of barrels, sat cross-legged in the square with six children climbing over him like he was the village's personal playground. He gave each of them a carved wooden token – animals, stars, small heroes – one for each story they'd told him.

But away from the centre of it all, at the edge of the fountain, Garric sat on the stone lip with Caelan nestled against his side. The boy's head rested on his father's shoulder, small arms wrapped around his own mug of warm herbal tea, steam curling upward between them.

For a while, neither spoke. The flicker of torchlight danced in their eyes.

"You warm enough?" Garric asked, voice low.

Caelan nodded. "Yeah."

Another beat passed.

"You know… when I first held you," Garric said quietly, "I'd just come back from a patrol. Bloody. Bruised. Barely able to stand. And then your mother put you in my arms, and for the first time… I was afraid."

Caelan tilted his head, puzzled. "Afraid?"

Garric gave a small, sad smile. "Not of a battle. Of failing you. Of not making it back next time."

Caelan didn't answer at first. He just leaned a little closer. "You came back."

"I did." Garric's voice caught. "Somehow, I did."

They sat in silence again, save for the sound of music drifting in the background, the laughter of friends and kin.

"Are you proud of me?" Caelan asked, not quite meeting his father's eyes.

Garric looked down at him, eyes wet with something fierce and ancient and unshakeable. "Proud doesn't begin to cover it, son. I'd face every giant, every horde of undead again, just to see you become who you are."

Caelan's eyes shimmered, and he tucked his head back under his father's arm. "Then *I'll* protect *you* next time."

"You already did," Garric whispered.

Just then, a loud snap echoed from across the square.

Taril and Harwen had just collapsed backwards, their chairs in splinters beneath them. Harwen wheezed with laughter, spilling half his ale onto the stones as Taril roared, "I *told* you this bench was too thin for my glory!"

Everyone laughed, but no one louder than Niv, standing atop a table, hair shimmering like quicksilver in the torchlight. She had just finished mimicking Opilkhos's brooding stance, arms crossed, chin down, voice low: "'Oh no, the weight of memory – the world is dark and full of responsibilities…'"

Opilkhos, stone-faced as ever, watched for a moment. Then he raised a brow. "If you're done mocking my shoulders," he said drily, "how about you let me show you how they move?"

He extended a hand.

Niv blinked. Grinned like trouble. "Finally."

And just like that, the two were dancing – not delicately, but fiercely. Niv spun like a flame, Opilkhos grounding each move with poise and intensity. They moved with unspoken rhythm, the echoes of a time long past threading through each step.

The villagers watched, stunned, then erupted into applause.

Taril sat up, brushing splinters off his back. "Now that's what I call a courtship dance!"

Harwen wheezed. "More like a *warning* dance! If I moved like that, the mountain would collapse!"

Back by the fountain, Garric chuckled as Caelan laughed into his side.

For the first time in many, many years, Garric didn't feel like a soldier.

He felt like a father. Like a man who had helped build something worth protecting.

As the night ripened under the darkened skies – clouds like ever-present guardians cloaking the heavens – laughter echoed through the heart of Garrents.

While Niv and Opilkhos twirled like fire and dusk upon the stonework square, drawing awe and delight from villagers and gods alike, another circle had gathered by the long tables where warm bread, roasted roots, and forest fruits filled every plate.

Taril, still brushing flecks of dust from his hands, reclined on an overturned crate beside Nashir and Harwen, the young carpenter. A small fire crackled between them, casting a flickering amber glow across their faces. The three shared a quiet moment of satisfaction, gazing across the village they had each helped shape with hands, magic and vision.

"This," Taril muttered with a deep breath, "is how a mountain speaks. Solid. Unyielding. But look at it now – alive."

Nashir chuckled softly, brushing a squirrel off his shoulder with a smile. "It speaks louder when softened by roots and rivers, Taril. You hammered the bones. I gave it breath."

Harwen, seated between them with a tankard the size of a bucket, roared with laughter. "Aye, and I hammered my fingers more than once putting it together!" He raised his drink. "But I'll be damned if this place doesn't feel like it's blooming from stone and sweat. Never thought I'd see the day."

A group of children ran past with slices of fruit and wild cheese, shrieking with joy. One stopped briefly to wave at Taril, and the dwarf god gave a low nod, his thick hand lifting in return – stone-sturdy, softened by pride.

Tharn, the old builder, set his drink down, voice lowering just a touch. "You know, I built this village once with hands blistered and frostbitten. Watching it rise again with you two… it's like reforging something holy."

Nashir placed a hand on the builder's shoulder. "Then we build not just homes, but hope."

The fire popped, and for a while, they simply watched. Children danced. Villagers sang old songs. Torches bathed the stonework in a warm golden hue that turned even the hardest corners of the village into something soft and sacred.

From where they sat, the three creators of Garrents looked on – not just as builders of walls and gates, but as keepers of rebirth.

The laughter still lingered like music in the air as Niv dipped into a playful bow, her hair glimmering in the soft torchlight, still wild from the spinning dance. The villagers erupted in cheers and claps, clanging tankards and stamping feet. Opilkhos, catching his breath, smirked and leaned in just enough for Niv to hear over the noise.

"Thank you," he said, quietly but sincerely.

"For the dance?" she teased, lifting an eyebrow. "Or for not setting your boots on fire this time?"

He chuckled, shaking his head, and Niv spun off with a flick of her fingers, sparks trailing faintly behind her like embers catching wind.

Nearby, Eldric and his wife stood with Garric and Caelan, their voices warm with shared stories and quick laughter. The soft glow from the surrounding lanterns cast golden halos around them. Niv, eyes bright, caught the way Garric held his son, the steady strength in his posture, the worn care in his face.

And for just a moment – just a heartbeat – he looked *so* much like Ian.

Her gaze lingered, softer now. Garric turned, sensing it, and their eyes met – two memories flickering to life behind a pair of smiles too shy to be called anything but tender. She stepped forward again, slower this time, not with performance, but with purpose.

Caelan noticed her first. "Niv!" he called, running to her, still half-dragging his blanket behind him.

"Too tired for one more spin?" she asked, kneeling to meet him.

"I think I'm done dancing forever," he said with a yawn. "But… could you come with us? I don't want to go to sleep yet."

"Hmm…" Niv tapped her chin dramatically. "How about… I come and help tuck you in? Maybe even sing something soft?"

Caelan lit up like a torch. "Could you teach me how to do magic like you do?"

She smiled gently, brushing a strand of hair from his face. "One day, perhaps. But tonight, how about a story instead? One about your forefather. About Ian."

Caelan's eyes widened, and he turned eagerly to his father. "Can she? Please?"

Garric glanced at Niv again – her face, soft and patient, lit with something warm and far away – and gave a slow nod. "Of course. I trust her with anything."

Their eyes lingered again. No words. Just heartbeats. Just silence stitched with something unspoken.

Niv extended her hand to the boy. "Shall we, little sorcerer?"

Caelan took it without hesitation, and together they walked toward the edge of the gathering, disappearing into the paths that led home.

Opilkhos, still by the fire, watched them go.

He smiled – not the cold, guarded thing he so often wore, but something full and real.

She was happy.

As they walked toward Garric's home, Niv's fingers curled gently around Caelan's smaller hand. He swung her arm playfully, skipping a bit, still energised by the excitement of the night. Niv smiled down at him, but her eyes occasionally lifted, drawn to Garric walking just ahead, his broad shoulders slightly tense, as if aware of her gaze but unsure whether to meet it.

He didn't.

Not until Eldric, laughing from behind, called out into the evening, "Try not to set the house on fire, Niv! Or the boy's imagination!"

Garric turned at that – just for a moment – and their eyes locked again, and this time he *didn't* look away.

Niv gave a half-smirk, half-smile, and squeezed Caelan's hand. "Come on, my little mage. Time for stories."

The village behind them slowly quieted. The music faded to murmurs, the clink of cups grew sparse. Only Taril's roaring laughter – deep and echoing – cut through the dark, followed by Borgrim's bark of a reply.

Niv and Caelan crossed into Garric's home, and at once, the warmth wrapped around them like a thick blanket. The scent of woodsmoke and worn leather lingered in the air, soft and lived-in. As Niv stepped further in, Garric scratched the back of his neck.

"Don't mind the mess," he said, voice a bit rougher now. "Still figuring out how to *live* in peace."

Niv let her eyes wander – over the carefully folded blankets stacked on one chair, the sword propped by the door out of habit, and a little drawing pinned near the hearth. "Looks like home to me," she said, her voice lower now, softer.

Caelan tugged at her again. "The story! Please!"

She chuckled, and with a flick of her wrist summoned a trail of shimmering red-orange light that hovered above the hearth, dancing and shifting into a vague, heroic shape. "Once," she began, lowering herself to sit cross-legged beside the fire, "there was a man not unlike your father. Strong. Proud. But clever, too — and kind, in a way that went deeper than words."

She stretched out her hands, and the flame burst into swirling visions — stars and runes, a long cloak in the wind. Caelan gasped, eyes wide.

"Ian Garrents," she whispered like a spell, "the one who stood where others fell. The one who faced storms and called them kin."

Garric quietly added a fresh log to the fire, kneeling by the hearth. The glow caught his face, outlining the faint smile he tried to hide. He sat beside them — close, but not too close — and simply watched as his son leaned closer to the dancing lights.

And Niv?

She wove the past like a tapestry, her voice strong and bright, her magic swirling around them.

In that little house, on that quiet night, peace lived and breathed.

And it sounded like a story told by firelight.

As Niv carried on with the story, her voice slowed, softened, like the final rays of a dying fire settling into embers. The flickers of magic above the hearth faded into a warm, golden haze, and without meaning to, she began to sing.

It started as a hum, low and steady — an old elvish lullaby, its tune older than the mountains outside. The melody poured from her lips like water from a still spring — pure, effortless, hauntingly beautiful. The language itself danced with grace, and though Garric didn't understand the words, the feeling behind them was undeniable.

Her voice carried through the room, brushing against the walls like a mother's touch, wrapping around Caelan like a protective charm. It wasn't loud. It didn't need to be. It shimmered with memory, with magic, with something sacred.

And as she looked down at Caelan's wide, blinking eyes – eyes slowly giving way to sleep – her own heart stirred with something unfamiliar. Fierce, gentle. Protective. As if the boy were hers. As if he'd always been.

She didn't understand where it came from, only that it filled her chest with a warmth so full it nearly cracked her open.

Caelan shifted in her arms, the corners of his mouth curled in peaceful delight, and Niv gently lifted him. Still humming, she rocked him close against her, her lips brushing the top of his head. His breathing slowed. His small hand tugged gently at her tunic.

Garric, silent by the fire, met her eyes – and for a breath, they simply stared at each other across the flickering orange glow. She gave a small nod, her face still glowing with softness. He returned it, his jaw tense but his eyes impossibly tender.

Without a word, she carried Caelan through the hall. The door creaked gently as she entered his room, the lullaby still faint on her lips. She laid him down, careful not to wake him, and tucked the blankets around his small frame with practised gentleness.

The last notes of the lullaby faded into silence.

She stood there for a long moment, just watching him.

She turned and closed the door, leaving only peace in her wake.

Niv stepped softly from Caelan's room, the door clicking shut behind her, she found Garric still near the hearth – one hand on the mantel, the other hanging idly at his side. The fire crackled between them, casting long shadows that danced like memory along the stone walls.

Their eyes met.

And held.

It was subtle at first – just a shared quiet. The kind that breathes between people who've known loss and still found themselves standing. But then the hush stretched into something else. A flicker. A breath that lingered too long. A silence filled with all the words neither dared speak.

Niv gave a small smile, brushing her silver-blonde hair back from her cheek. "I should go," she said, voice low.

Garric didn't answer with words – only a faint movement in his brow. A soft, involuntary furrow. Sadness, just for a moment. A shadow of a feeling.

Her eyes followed the line of his gaze to the wooden cabinet in the corner, worn with time, carved with gentle hands. Elise's. She recognised the craftsmanship. The care. "She made that?" she asked softly.

Garric nodded. His voice didn't come immediately. When it did, it was a low whisper. "She had a way of making things feel… permanent."

Niv moved closer – not pressing, just enough to be near. "You loved her deeply."

His eyes didn't move from the cabinet. "Still do."

"I know," she said, and the words didn't sting. They warmed. "And yet…"

This time he looked at her. Really *looked*. And in that gaze, there wasn't betrayal or conflict, but honesty. A man who had known love. A man who had lost. And a man still living.

She stepped into the glow of the fire beside him. Their hands brushed.

"And yet," he repeated, voice like gravel and silk, "I'm still here."

Her fingers found his – tentative, then sure.

He turned to her, his breath slow, deliberate. "You make it hard to forget I'm still alive," he said.

Her smile curved – soft and knowing. "And you make it hard not to care."

The fire crackled louder as if catching its breath.

His hand lifted, gently brushing a loose strand of hair from her face. His thumb lingered along her cheekbone, his skin rough from battle, hers glowing in the firelight.

They leaned in – not fast, not certain – like two survivors learning to breathe again, and when her forehead rested gently against his, her lips just inches from his own, time slowed.

A moment suspended between love remembered… and something new, just beginning to take shape.

Garric's eyes stayed on the fire, the dancing flames flickering in the blue of his gaze like ghosts he hadn't made peace with. His voice was barely a murmur, gravel-deep. "It's hard to believe life could change so much, so soon." His jaw flexed as he swallowed. "I only wish she could've seen it. Elise... she would've loved this peace."

Niv didn't speak at first. She just watched him – really watched him. The quiet strength, the burden still sitting heavy on his shoulders, and the guilt that hadn't yet loosened its grip. She stepped closer. Her breath slowed. Then quickened just slightly, just enough. "I lost someone too," she whispered, her voice soft like silk, like memory. "I believe, at least. Our memories are returning – flashes, feelings – but I can't explain how close I feel to you now. Like I've always known you. Like we're tangled in something older than this life."

He looked at her, and his eyes said more than he could. Then, he looked down, unsure, a crease forming between his brows. "I don't know if I can do this," he admitted. "It's not about you, it's just... it feels like stepping into something sacred, after living in the shadow of someone I loved so deeply."

Niv tilted her head, watching him for a heartbeat. Then a grin curled at the edges of her lips. She leaned in, whispering near his ear, her voice warm and teasing. "You know... I was worried you meant something else," she said, eyes twinkling. "You had me thinking maybe age had finally caught up to you. I was ready to conjure a spell for... ahem... circulation."

Garric blinked. Then burst into laughter, shaking his head, his cheeks flushed with colour.

"Oh, don't laugh too hard," she added, smirking. "You might pull a muscle."

He laughed harder, and for the first time in what felt like lifetimes, the sound wasn't weighed down.

She leaned back, brushing her fingertips down his arm. "I'm not asking you to forget her," she said gently. "I'm just asking you not to forget yourself."

Garric met her eyes. His hand found hers again – firm, steady. And though he said nothing, his thumb traced over her knuckles slowly, as if memorising her.

"I'm still here," she whispered.

"I know," he said. "And gods help me… I'm glad you are."

Niv tilted her head toward the buckets near the door. She wore that grin again – the kind that could melt ice and bend steel – and walked her fingers along the edge of the nearby table. "Well," she said softly, voice like velvet, "you do have a tub in the corner, don't you? After a day like this, I'd say we both earned a wash."

Garric raised a brow, still caught in the gravity of her presence. "I'd have to warm the water first," he offered, more out of habit than necessity, but she was already stepping closer, hands folding behind her back.

"Would you now?" she said, mock-pouting. Then, with a flick of her fingers, the air shimmered – the buckets began to steam, the scent of lavender rising from the water as if summoned by the gods themselves.

Garric blinked. "How…?"

She gave a slow, wicked smile. "Father's gift," she whispered. "And maybe just a little showmanship."

He opened his mouth to speak, but the words never came. With one fluid movement, Niv slid her thumbs beneath the clasp of her armour. Leather, silk, silver – all of it slipped away like a whispered secret, and then she stood before him – bare, fearless, luminous.

The flickering firelight traced every line of her, casting gold across her skin. For a long moment, Garric couldn't move. Couldn't breathe.

She looked at him – not just as a warrior or a man, but as a woman unafraid to be seen. Truly *seen*. "You going to fill the tub, soldier," she said playfully, "or just stand there gawking like a stunned ox?"

He swallowed, his voice caught somewhere between reverence and disbelief. "I think," he murmured, clearing his throat, "I'll need a moment."

She laughed, the sound full of light and mischief, already pouring the water into the tub herself, and from the look in her eyes, Garric knew this night was far from over.

ANOTHER DAY IN PARADISE

The village still slumbered under the deeper hues of the morning's first breath – soft, bluish darkness clinging to the rooftops, the ever-present clouds above just starting to lighten, casting silver fog along the narrow alleys and stone paths. The world was quiet. Not in mourning or in fear, but in peace.

Niv strolled barefoot, boots slung over her shoulder, her tunic loosely tied at the waist. Her hair was still tousled from the night before, catching the faint light like silver silk as it danced over her bare shoulders. Her lips wore a grin – soft, secretive, the kind only stolen hours and shared warmth could leave behind.

She walked with a sway in her hips and a spring in her steps, content and careless, like a woman who remembered exactly who she was.

As she passed the tavern, her sharp ears picked up a rumbling sound that made her smirk.

"Taril," she muttered under her breath, amused. "Still competing with earthquakes."

The doors were shut tight, but the mighty snore echoed against the frost-laced wood. She chuckled and waved at a sleepy raccoon climbing across a nearby window ledge. Even the animals, once wild and untamed, seemed calmer now – like they too had found something here worth staying for.

She made her way to the heart of the village, still humming a faint tune to herself, her bare feet padding against the stone. The fountain ahead shimmered softly in the low light. A crystalline trickle of water spilled into its basin, gentle and serene.

Thirst tugged at her. Niv knelt beside it, brushing her hair back with one hand as she leaned over the edge.

And then...

She froze.

A crackling sensation rippled through the air. Not from cold – but from magic. Old, heavy, dense... and familiar.

Her amber eyes narrowed.

The water glimmered unnaturally, its surface no longer just a reflection of the clouds above, but a swirling dance of deep blue light.

She leaned closer.

A sudden pulse surged from within the depths of the fountain. Not loud. Not violent. Just... present. As if the magic had been watching. Waiting.

And at the centre of it all, resting beneath the gently lapping ripples, hidden for gods know how long, was a gem.

A sapphire.

Perfectly cut.

Embedded into the stone like the heart of the fountain itself.

It glowed. No, it *breathed* – its surface alive with arcane veins of power. The jewel called to her, a silent, throbbing rhythm that danced across her skin like heat from a flame.

She reached forward – but stopped just short of touching the water.

The air had shifted.

Something ancient was stirring.

A seal broken. A truth long buried.

Her breath caught, her lips parting slightly.

"What are you?" she whispered.

And in the silence, the fountain answered with another pulse of light.

She was no longer alone. Not just in the square, but in the world.

Something had awakened.

And it had chosen *her* to see it first.

As Niv's fingers closed around the sapphire, a ripple of light burst outward – blue and bright, yet not blinding. It wasn't harsh. It was alive.

Her breath hitched.

The moment her skin touched the gem, it was as if the air had been punched from the world.

Boom.

Magic roared through her veins. Her hair lifted, weightless in the surge of power. Her aura flared around her – amber-gold swirling with deep sapphire now, spiralling around her body like ribbons caught in a storm.

And then – darkness.

Not the kind that frightened, but the kind that *remembered*.

A memory – no, a *vision* – dragged her under.

Before her, suspended in a world made only of shadow and magic, stood a staff.

Tall. Regal. Radiating power.

Carved of ancient obsidian wood, coiled with etched metal veins that pulsed in time with the jewel in her hand. Inlaid into the head of the sceptre were eight gems, each of a different colour. Faint at first. Then, one by one…

Crimson. Emerald. Sapphire. Topaz. Amethyst. Opal. Pearl. Onyx.

Each gem pulsed.

Each gem *remembered*.

Then the staff *screamed* with light.

An explosion – pure magic tearing through the void. Threads of memory, power and creation crackling into life around it.

And there – behind the storm, emerging from the blinding fusion of colour and shadow – was a silhouette.

A man. Cloaked in fire and wind. Hands raised not to command, but to protect.

Ian Garrents.

His face serene. His eyes filled with purpose. His mouth opened, calling not words, but *names*.

And Niv… remembered him.

Her breath returned.

The vision shattered.

She was back – but not alone.

The square around her was soaked now, the water of the fountain flowing outward in small, glittering streams. And standing just a few feet away…

Opilkhos.

Taril.

Nashir.

They stood frozen, caught in the same resonance. Their auras had flared the moment hers had ignited. Colours danced across them – Nashir's greens swirled with gold, Taril's deep grey shimmered with earthen fire, and Opilkhos stood cloaked in dusk and flame.

None of them spoke – until the water began to move again.

A groaning sound echoed beneath their feet. Stone ground against stone.

The fountain's base split open, parting like ancient doors forgotten by time.

Water burst forth – not wild or destructive, but cleansing. Gentle waves cascaded over the stones, flowing into alleyways and courtyards, caressing the village like a blessing. Animals stood still. Torches didn't flicker – they bowed. The villagers came to their windows, speechless, entranced.

The water didn't *flood*.

It *unfolded*.

Glowing as it moved. Stretching to every corner of Garrents. And then…

A distant shimmer up the mountain.

High above, like the sweep of a curtain pulled across the stars, a thin veil – an invisible dome none of them had seen – dissolved into nothing. Like shadow retreating from dawn.

Whatever had hidden them… was now undone.

Opilkhos stepped forward slowly, staring at the sky, then down at the jewel in Niv's hand. His voice was low, reverent, certain. "That's Ian's magic… I'd know it anywhere. He wasn't just hiding the village from the cold or the dead… He hid it from *eyes that looked down from above*."

They turned to Niv.

She stood at the centre of it all – wind stirring her silver-blonde hair, the gem cradled in her glowing hand, her amber eyes burning like twin suns.

The gods looked at each other.

None of them spoke.

Because something had begun.

And whatever it was, it was no longer hidden.

The fountain's water still glistened across the square like a river of light when Garric came crashing through the eastern alley.

Sword in hand.

Eldric was right behind him, followed by Borgrim, axe raised, his beard wet with sweat and breath like smoke. A few soldiers, wide-eyed but determined, charged forward with them, ready to face whatever had broken the earth.

Garric's eyes scanned the scene – the glowing water, the opened stones, the gathering villagers. Then he saw Niv, her body trembling slightly, held in place by the strange power of the jewel.

"Niv!" Garric barked, not just a shout – a plea.

But Opilkhos was already moving.

He crossed the flooded stone in long, certain strides, his boots cutting small waves across the silver-coated ground. His cloak shimmered faintly, and his hand reached out – not just in support, but in protection.

Niv blinked slowly, her lips parted in silent awe.

"You all right?" Opilkhos asked softly, eyes narrowing as he gently helped her steady herself. His hand touched her back as a man, a friend grounding her.

She didn't answer.

She just clutched the gem tighter.

Behind them, Taril's hammer hit the ground once – not in anger, but to anchor the moment. The clang echoed through the stone paths.

"Stand down!" he roared to the soldiers. And then more softly, to the villagers gathered behind them, frightened but holding fast, "This isn't an attack. But it *is* something we need to understand."

Nashir's glowing eyes swept over the courtyard, the water, the opened earth, the pulsing sapphire in Niv's hand. His hands moved gently, drawing symbols in the air as green wisps followed his fingers. He frowned. "I've worked every part of this land," he murmured, half to himself. "I've *listened* to it. Heard the roots and the stones. And yet..." His eyes darkened, as if failing something sacred. "I never heard a hollow this deep. This... this was hidden from me."

The revelation stung him. More than confusion – it was betrayal. A secret kept from a god of nature himself.

"It wasn't just magic," Taril said grimly. "It was *buried* under old laws. Older than even us, I think." He turned to the gathered villagers. "Don't be afraid. But listen carefully – stay clear of this place until we know more."

Then his gaze turned to his companions – Opilkhos, Nashir, and finally Niv, who still stood at the heart of the pool, breathing heavily, the gem clutched like it was part of her.

Taril's eyes were steady now.

Focused.

He gave a single nod, not to reassure the villagers, but to signal to his brothers and sister.

Let's check this out.

The gods stepped forward.

And the earth, once again, seemed to hold its breath.

Opilkhos and Taril exchanged a wordless glance – silent as the depths that awaited. Then, without hesitation, they stepped forward. Side by side, they passed the outer circle of the broken fountain and crossed the threshold where the stone had opened like a wound beneath the village.

The stairs descended sharply into shadow, winding like a forgotten memory. The deeper they went, the colder it became – not the biting chill of snow or night, but the old cold of time lost and secrets buried.

Behind them, Niv paused, her eyes still glowing faintly from the sapphire's pulse. She held it close, almost protectively. "This isn't just hidden earth," she said, her voice low but certain. "This is something else. Something folded between the cracks of our world. It's a portal… from another plane. One that merged into ours just now."

Nashir turned to her slowly, understanding dawning in his eyes like a rising sun behind storm clouds. The worry in his face melted – not completely, but enough to steady his step. "A plane that lived beside ours," he murmured, "and now breathes through this place." He nodded, almost to himself. "I feel it now. Not of the forest… but not unnatural. Just… distant."

The group moved together, deeper into the mountain. As they descended, torches began to light themselves – blue and gold flames flickering to life along the carved walls, casting their shadows in dancing patterns. The air grew heavy with memory, laced with the sharp scent of ash and time-worn magic.

And then…

They emerged into a vast chamber.

A massive hall, its ceilings impossibly high, held aloft by columns of blackened stone carved with intricate sigils. It was unmistakable, especially to Opilkhos and Niv.

It was a sanctum – a place for learning, for discovery, for power.

"Ian's…" Niv whispered, her voice catching.

They stepped forward slowly, reverently. But whatever it had once been, it was now a battlefield.

The floor bore scars of devastation.

Walls shattered. Ceilings cracked. Arcane sigils burned halfway into the stone, interrupted in mid-incantation. Furniture reduced to splinters. Alchemical tables overturned. Books turned to ash. The scent of long-extinguished fires still lingered.

But most haunting of all…

Two massive trails of magic had etched themselves into the very bones of the room. As if two titans of spellcraft had clashed here – one of righteous flame and layered, crystalline order, the other of chaotic void, tendrils like smoke tearing through the stone.

315

"This was him," Opilkhos muttered, his voice low and almost reluctant. "This was Ian's lab." And then, slowly, his eyes drifted to a jagged fracture across the centre of the hall – a fault line, where the floor had split as if from the weight of a final spell. "And this," he whispered, "was Harinnil."

Taril's jaw tightened as he surveyed the damage. "They fought here," he said. "Gods damn it, they *fought each other*."

The room had not been destroyed by decay or neglect. It had been torn apart by power – divine, personal and tragic.

Whatever had happened here, it had changed everything, and they had just opened the door to another truth in their path.

They spread out in silence, each drawn to a different corner of the ruined sanctum – like threads of fate unravelling across the hall.

Nashir stepped lightly across the fractured floor, his bare fingers brushing along stone and earth. He knelt beside a collapsed wall, placing a hand to the floor, then closing his eyes. "This place remembers," he murmured, voice barely a breath. "The roots here whisper… but they're afraid."

He reached further – not with sight, but with spirit – searching for animals, even insects, anything living. But the silence screamed louder than any voice. Nothing had lived here in a very long time… or dared to.

Across the chamber, Taril stood still for a moment, the weight of the place sinking into his bones. He muttered a low dwarvish oath, then unslung his massive war hammer and brought it crashing to the floor once, twice, the echoes like thunder in the hollow depths. His deep, gravel-thick voice followed, chanting in the ancient tongue of his people. "*Khol'dar… rek marûd… kezzan dei… kar'dun…*"

Each word sent ripples into the stone. He listened. Waited. Somewhere in the old dwarven bones of this place, he sought resonance, some hidden truth etched deeper than ruin.

Near the centre, Niv moved gently among the debris. Burnt pages crumbled in her hands as she sifted through the remains of a collapsed bookcase. Most were ash – but here and there, a glyph still burned faintly upon torn parchment. Her eyes scanned quickly, pulling together fragments of meaning, her lips parting in astonishment.

"These symbols…" she whispered. "They're from before even *my* time." A heartbeat passed. "Ian was studying something more than planes. He was preparing for a return. Or a war."

At the far side of the room, Opilkhos stood completely still.

He hadn't moved an inch since stepping into the chamber.

But his eyes… his eyes scanned the walls, the floors, the shattered runes like a god watching the stars.

To the others, it looked like he was merely observing.

But within…

The ancient language of magic revealed itself, sigil by sigil, as if etched upon his soul.

Lines of power no longer burned with colour, but cold silver and violet, flickering like frost across glass.

Then suddenly, every torchlight died.

The blue flames were snuffed out.

The magical light on Niv's fingertips sputtered.

The sanctum fell into total blackness.

And with it, a chill swept in.

A true cold. Not of snow or wind, but of something deeper, something older. A presence.

Even Nashir staggered back. "Something just… *touched* this place," he said, his breath visible in the sudden frost that clung to his lips.

Taril stopped in mid-chant, gripping his hammer tight.

Niv's arms prickled with gooseflesh. Her voice caught in her throat.

Even Opilkhos turned his head slightly – his first movement since entering. Not fear, but alertness. Readiness. He knew this feeling.

A darkness that didn't belong in the shadows.

It had sunk into their flesh.

Wrapped around their hearts.

And for the first time since awakening in the cold world of Maud…

They felt the echo of fear.

A low chuckle broke the silence.

At first, it was nothing – just Opilkhos laughing quietly to himself, head bowed, shoulders trembling.

But the laugh grew.

Deeper. Wilder. Unhinged.

His hands came up, covering his face – but the sound wouldn't stop. It clawed its way out of his chest, tearing through him like it wasn't his at all. It twisted higher, distorted, like two voices fighting for the same breath. One familiar. One ancient. One... *wrong*.

The temperature dropped further.

And then...

A surge of light erupted from him. His aura flared out like a solar storm, blindingly bright – but not alone.

It was tainted.

A second aura burned within it. Darker. Thicker. Viscous like smoke and ash. The two clashed and merged, not peacefully, but violently. They warred in the same vessel.

The laugh turned hollow.

A rasp. Bone scraping bone. A voice without flesh. Without mercy.

Taril's eyes went wide.

Niv staggered back, whispering a name she had no memory of speaking aloud.

Nashir's face drained of colour.

The laughter wasn't coming from Opilkhos any more.

It was Harinnil.

The light twisted – and now there were two forms. Not separate. Not whole. One soul wearing two faces. Their outlines danced like ghosts around each other – Opilkhos and Harinnil. But it was the latter who stepped forward now, solid, real, terrible.

His carmine eyes flared.

The earth trembled beneath him. Wind exploded outward from his chest in a spiralling gale, knocking the others back. Ancient glyphs lit beneath his feet – runic circles once carved in protection, now burning in rage.

Taril roared and flung his war hammer – a comet of divine stone.

It struck – but the weapon rebounded in mid-air, as if swatted aside by an invisible god's hand, and smashed directly into Nashir.

The impact launched the elven god backwards, sending him crashing into the stone wall behind. The granite cracked. Dust rained down. And Nashir's body – usually fluid and serene – slumped, half-buried in a crater of broken earth.

"*Nashir!*" Niv screamed, racing toward her brother, magic already gathering in her palms.

But Harinnil moved faster.

A single gesture.

A bolt of pure, blistering magic – so intense it rippled the air like fire through oil – struck her across the chest.

Her armour – scintillating, silver, divine – melted in places, singed black. Her body was hurled like a rag doll across the hall, crashing into the remains of a pillar. She collapsed in a heap, groaning, unconscious, trembling.

Taril stood alone now.

Covered in the dust of his fallen comrades.

Facing a brother returned in the shape of a nightmare.

But his grip didn't falter.

His stance didn't break.

"So you've come back wearing a dead man's face," Taril growled, eyes burning with fury and grief. "Then I'll remind you of what it means to stand against a dwarf who remembers his kin."

Harinnil turned toward him.

Eyes aflame. Mouth curled in disdain.

His very presence fractured stone. The hall shook. Shadows danced.

But Taril didn't flinch.

Because in this moment, before the storm of gods… he remembered.

He was a god too, and he would not kneel. Not to a memory. Not to a monster.

Not even to a brother.

Taril roared, lowering his stance and lifting his great shield before him as he charged through the gale. The wind slammed into him like the fists of a god, but his legs did not yield. Stone cracked beneath his boots. His muscles burned. Each step a thunderclap.

He rammed forward, divine fury blazing in his veins, shield first, aiming to crash into the being before him, to shatter the very storm with his will.

But Harinnil raised one hand.

The world stopped.

Taril froze in mid-step. The air around him compressed like a vice. His shield trembled in his grip, pushed back by a force so ancient, so vast it bent the very rules of the world.

Their faces were inches apart.

Harinnil smiled.

His carmine-red eyes blazed, the fire inside them laughing, mocking.

But then…

They changed.

The red dimmed.

A flare of blue pulsed from within.

Then gold.

A halo-like shimmer swept across his form as a new aura fought to break free.

The wind faltered.

The mocking smile… wavered.

And from deep inside that twisted frame, a voice screamed, "Nooooooooooooooooooooooooooo!"

The voice shattered the air like a comet smashing into stone.

Opilkhos.

The real one.

His soul erupted.

Golden light burst outward, searing and radiant, tearing through the darkness like the dawn itself. It wasn't just magic – it was will, clawing its way out of damnation. The foundations of the world quaked. Dust and light burst out of the cavern entrance, racing across the village like a solar wind.

Above ground, villagers screamed and stumbled, thrown from their feet as the earth howled in pain.

Below, the aura consumed the hall.

Taril and Niv were hurled against the wall, caught in the brilliance of something both divine and broken. Nashir's limp form was enveloped in gold, his wounds knitting closed, his chest rising again with breath. Eyes fluttered open, dazed, but whole.

And in the silence that followed…

A single figure stood in the centre of the cratered hall.

Opilkhos.

He lowered from the air, arms outstretched, as if born again in sorrow.

Golden radiance spilled from his hands, bathing the room in light. His body trembled – not from exhaustion, but from grief.

He fell to his knees.

Tears ran freely down his cheeks, golden like the magic still lingering in his veins.

"I… I could've killed you," he whispered, voice cracked and raw. "My hands… my soul… I…"

He couldn't finish.

He just wept.

And then…

Light bloomed behind him.

So brilliant, so pure, that the others had to shield their eyes. But the gods did not blink. They saw.

They all saw.

A figure emerged.

Not solid. Not flesh.

A shape made of light and memory, of warmth and presence.

Lena.

Her form shimmered with every step, hair like midnight, eyes like living emeralds. A glow surrounded her that was neither past nor present, but something eternal.

She stood behind Opilkhos.

Laid her hand upon his shoulder.

His body shook at the touch.

He looked up, wide-eyed. "Lena?"

Her smile – gentle, sad, infinite. She leaned forward. Pressed a kiss to his cheek. And whispered, "You found your way home."

And then, just like that…

She was gone.

Light trailing like stardust.

He reached out after her, fingers stretching toward the emptiness.

But she was already fading, melting into the air like a dream departing with dawn.

And all he could do was kneel.

His hand still outstretched.

The tears still falling.

And the gods around him – his kin, his friends, his family – stood in silence.

For they all understood…

This wasn't just a rescue.

It was a reckoning.

The golden light faded.

The hall was quiet again.

Dust hung in the air like snow suspended in time.

Niv winced, her breath shallow as she sat up, bits of her melted armour clinging to her body. With shaking hands, she peeled it off, revealing the bruises and burns beneath. Her skin steamed where the magic had seared it, but her spirit did not waver. She clutched the shredded cloth across her chest, shivering – not from cold, but from the weight of what had just passed.

Taril stumbled across the cracked stone floor, falling to his knees beside Nashir. "Brother… I didn't mean… by the forge. Please forgive me," he rasped.

But Nashir, groaning as he sat up from the crater he'd left in the wall, placed a hand over Taril's trembling fist. "You struck no friend, Taril," he said softly. "Only fate."

Taril's face crumpled, and for a moment, the unshakeable dwarf buried his forehead in Nashir's lap.

Opilkhos stood apart, chest rising and falling with unsteady breath. His hands trembled. His eyes wide and haunted. He stared at the floor, afraid to meet their gazes. "It was me," he whispered. "I felt him inside… clawing. Laughing. I couldn't stop it. I almost… I almost killed you."

He turned slowly, as if fearing what he would see.

But Niv stood, clutching the tattered remnants of her armour, tears streaking down her dirt-smudged cheeks. She limped forward.

She didn't speak.

She wrapped her arms around him.

Held him close.

Then Taril joined them, arms like hammers curling into gentleness.

Nashir stepped forward, wincing, and laid his hand over all of theirs. "You are still you," he said, voice raw. "You came back."

Opilkhos collapsed into their embrace, broken in guilt but caught in the unshakeable net of their love.

Then…

Torchlight.

A rush of heavy boots.

Garric, Eldric and Borgrim stormed into the ruins, torches held high, breath steaming in the cold. Their eyes scanned the room – the torn floor, the shattered stone, the scorched markings on the walls.

"What in all the frozen hells just happened?" Garric barked, stepping into the room, breath catching at the sight of the damage. "We felt the quake all the way in the heart of the village."

Nashir raised a calming hand. "It's… contained."

Eldric, eyes darting to Niv, then Nashir, then Opilkhos, stepped forward. "Is anyone hurt?"

Taril shook his head. "Only our pride. And perhaps a few layers of trust… but we're mending."

Borgrim's voice rumbled. "Looks like a gods-damned war just happened in here."

Niv looked up, still holding Opilkhos. Her voice was hoarse but firm. "It nearly did." Niv exhaled, rubbing her arms. "The past is clawing its

323

way back to us, and it seems we're not ready for all of it as we thought before."

Garric looked toward Opilkhos – still silent, still stone. Garric stepped forward, eyes moving from the broken remains of Niv's armour, to the bruise on her face, to the crack in the wall where Nashir had fallen. "Who attacked?" he demanded.

Opilkhos straightened, his voice shaky but clear. "I did."

The torches flickered.

Eldric narrowed his eyes. "What do you mean?"

"It wasn't just me," Opilkhos said, gesturing to the cracked floor where moments ago another presence had stood. "He… it… was inside me. I don't know how. Or why. But Harinnil – his echo – was still with me. Still trying to break through."

Borgrim stepped closer, face grim. "And he almost did, didn't he?"

Opilkhos nodded slowly. "He used me. Turned me against them."

"And yet," Nashir said, placing a hand on his shoulder, "*you* stopped him. We saw the fight. You drove him out."

Taril grunted. "Threw me like a pebble first, mind you."

"*Through me,*" Nashir muttered.

That drew a soft, broken laugh from Niv.

Borgrim looked around, eyes narrowing on the scorch marks and the cracked runes. "So this is what it means to be gods," he murmured. "To fight yourselves and win."

Garric stepped closer. His voice was quieter now. "You're not alone. None of you. And if this happens again, *we'll be here.*"

Opilkhos looked at him, tears still clinging to his lashes. "Even if it means I become him?"

Garric gave him a long, hard look… and then placed a hand over Opilkhos's heart. "Then we'll drag you back out. As many times as it takes."

The group stood there together, silent in the aftermath – gods, warriors and mortals bound not by blood, but by loyalty stronger than any curse, and though the air still hummed with the scent of burnt stone and old magic…

They were not afraid, because they were together.

Opilkhos turned without a word, making his way up the spiral path toward the village. As he stepped into the faint evening light, villagers – huddled together, frightened – watched him.

Mothers shielded children. Men lowered their eyes, and that was when the guilt tore deeper.

He couldn't bear to look at them.

They tried to call him back.

He raised a hand.

"Just… give me a moment." His voice cracked.

He walked away, deeper into the mountain's heart, toward the silent side of the village opposite the trench. The part rarely touched.

Behind him, the others emerged slowly.

"Let him go," Nashir said softly. "He needs to breathe."

"We'll handle the people," Taril added, rolling his shoulders. "Make sure no one panics more than they already are."

Niv hesitated.

She turned toward Opilkhos's retreating figure, then rushed forward, catching up just enough to place a gentle hand on his arm.

He paused.

"Hey…" she said, voice low.

He looked at her with storm-filled eyes.

"You're not alone," she said. Then, more playfully, with that signature fire, she kissed his cheek and smirked. "Try not to break the mountain this time, will you?"

And with a cheeky tap on his rear, she turned and strolled back, her long hair swaying, her grin defiant.

He didn't respond.

Just stood there until she was gone, and then he walked on. Alone. To face the silence. To face himself.

The mountain path narrowed with every step.

Rocks jutted from the sides like jagged teeth, snow crusted thick in the crevices. It wasn't a trail meant to be walked, not really. More a forgotten passage, chiselled once by dwarves long ago, now overgrown by time and neglect. Even the wind hesitated here, reduced to a whisper between the towering stone walls.

Above, the sky churned, as it always did in this cursed world – no sun, no stars, just layers of heavy clouds smothering the heavens. Darkness pressed close – not night, but that strange hush between the hours when the world paused to grieve.

Opilkhos climbed alone, the last stretch steep and unforgiving. The path became a ledge. The ledge gave way to stone. And the stone rose in a spire, overlooking the village below.

There, he stopped.

He turned his head. Just once.

The lights of Garrents glimmered below – soft, warm. Laughter floated on the wind, distant now. Faint.

He made sure he hadn't been followed.

Then he knelt.

And all the pain he had buried – all the questions he refused to ask – came roaring up.

"Why?!" His voice echoed off the stone, raw and cracking. "Why do I have to carry this? Why *me?*" His fists slammed the ground. Stone cracked beneath him. "Who am I?!" The air thickened. "Am I Harinnil? Or just a shadow they pity? A ghost in someone else's body?" His breath came ragged, violent. "Why don't I remember?!" The last word tore from his throat like a wound that wouldn't close. "Why don't I *feel* like him? If I *am* him, where is his love? His anger? His… *everything?!*" He clutched his head, fingers digging into his temples as if he could tear the truth out from his skull. "Am I even real?" he whispered, barely audible now.

His shoulders hunched. His great frame, so often poised with power and presence, now curled in on itself like a broken thing. Snow began to fall, gentle flakes landing on his back, unmelted, untouched by the fire that had once surged from within.

And still, no answer came.

Only silence.

Only wind.

Only the echo of his voice trapped between stone, but from that silence, something else stirred. Not words. Not a presence. But a feeling. A whisper deep in his bones.

You are not what you were. But neither are you nothing.

And as Opilkhos knelt there, shattered and alone, the wind carried that whisper into the void.

He didn't rise.

Not yet.

The grief had been given voice, and sometimes, maybe, that was the first step toward remembering.

The wind around Opilkhos shifted.

Not just a breeze, but a pulse. An echo of warmth, of memory.

His golden aura flared once again – not wild and violent like before, but steady, rhythmic… alive. It surged like a tide of forgotten light. The snow beneath him shimmered, evaporating in a quiet hiss as the energy coursed outward.

And then…

The world vanished.

He was young. Younger than he remembered ever being.

The halls of the Celestial Temple stretched high and wide, walls etched with runes, air thick with magic and the scent of old stone. Statues of the first gods lined the corridors – Taril, proud and chiselled; Nashir, calm and eternal; Ian, ever watchful with his staff raised high. Their eyes weren't made of stone, not in Opilkhos's memory. They burned with life.

And there, in the centre, stood Harinnil.

Small. Barely more than a boy. Shy, with robes too large for his thin frame, sleeves falling over his hands, curls of black hair hiding half his face. He held a book close to his chest – Ian's journal, stolen, borrowed, taken without asking. He didn't care. He needed to learn.

"Why do the sigils fold like this when layered?" he muttered to himself, fingers tracing invisible patterns in the air.

A sharp crack interrupted his study.

Running. Heavy footfalls. Laughter.

Then, the crash of someone eating stone.

He turned.

"Alentar!"

The elven boy lay in a crumpled heap, mud on his cheek, his tunic torn at the shoulder, a new bruise rising along his jaw. His bow clattered nearby.

Harinnil dropped the book. Rushed to his side. "Taril again?" he whispered, already lifting Alentar's arm to check the swelling.

Alentar grinned through bloodied lips. "He said I needed to *dodge* better."

Harinnil scowled. "He's trying to kill you."

Alentar chuckled. "That means he likes me."

Harinnil rolled his eyes and dug into the satchel at his hip. He had herbs. Bandages. A salve he'd made while copying Nashir's work in secret. "Stay still. I read something about mending tendons with magic while applying pressure…"

"You mean you stole another of Ian's books."

Harinnil didn't deny it. He just pressed the cloth to the wound and muttered a soft chant. The air around his hand shimmered. Light coiled from his fingers, precise and gentle.

Alentar went still. "You're getting better."

"I learn."

A beat passed.

"You *care*," Alentar added quietly.

Harinnil looked away. "Someone has to."

Another flash.

Years later now. A forest ablaze in golden light.

The gods together – children no more.

Drunnyak, bare-chested and roaring, lifting an entire fallen tree just to prove a point. Taril hammering stones into perfect angles in mid-air while grumbling about geometry. Niv chasing flames up the trees, laughing like the sky belonged to her. Nashir sitting beside a newborn fawn, his eyes closed, listening to the roots speak. Ian, far in the distance, arguing with stars.

And Harinnil?

He stood back. Not because he wasn't part of them.

But because he was always watching. Always learning.

A student of them all.

And yet, as Alentar waved him over, motioning with that ridiculous grin…

He ran.

He ran toward the firelight. Toward the laughter. Toward the family that had once saved him from his own stillness.

More moments flickered.

Ian's hand on his shoulder as he completed his first binding spell.

Taril's nod of approval when he fortified a wall on his own.

Drunnyak carrying him on his back across a canyon because he twisted his ankle and refused to ask for help.

Niv tossing a flame high into the air, shaping it into a phoenix, and yelling, "For Harinnil the bookworm!"

And Lena.

Always Lena.

Watching from the edge. Eyes that pierced him. Smiles that undid him.

He didn't see her face clearly, not yet.

But her presence sang in the memory.

And then… silence again.

Opilkhos was back.

Kneeling.

Tears streamed down his face – not from confusion this time.

But from remembrance.

He had been the last created. The youngest.

Not weak.

Just quiet.

He was the one who listened. Who watched. Who felt.

And now, the pieces were starting to return.

Not all, but enough to remember what he once was and why it had hurt so much to forget. The wind whispered through the jagged stone of the mountain pass, but Opilkhos stood in stillness.

He no longer knelt.

He rose.

The mountain – silent and immovable – seemed to shift around him, no longer pressing inward like a cage, but opening, as if recognising the soul that stood among its peaks. Light curled softly across the ridges, though no sun pierced the ever-clouded sky. It came from him. A low hum beneath his skin. A resonance in the world.

His breath drew slower. Deeper.

The confusion, the torment, the desperate ache of separation that once twisted within his chest eased.

Not erased.

But… quieted.

Balanced.

There was no longer any doubt.

He was Harinnil.

And he was not.

The memories coursed through him like streams finally reunited with their river – echoes of the young, timid god poring over Ian's scrolls; the stolen laughter shared with Alentar beneath starlit leaves; the bruised pride from Taril's gruff corrections; the fiery challenge of Niv's sparring staff; Drunnyak's roars of praise after a victory; Lena's laughter, softer than all the rest, yet ringing louder in his soul.

Harinnil had once been the youngest.

The one always learning.

Always watching.

And now… he was the one returning.

His eyes burned golden – not with rage, but with clarity. He blinked, and the mountain around him shimmered faintly with arcane threads, once invisible. He could feel them.

The veins of the world.

Magic in its purest state.

His body pulsed with new-found power, yes – but more than that, he understood. The language of the world, once a murmur, now spoke to him clearly. The balance of things. The design. Wisdom not granted, but *earned*.

And yet...

A weight still pressed on him.

Harinnil had stayed. Had decayed.

And he – *Opilkhos* – had been given something else. A fragment of soul plucked and carried away. Given peace. Given Lena. A love so perfect it made the rest of the world feel like shadow.

And still, he could feel it.

Her warmth.

Lingering.

Not just in memory, but near.

"If Ian and I remained awake," he whispered to the wind, "then perhaps..."

His heart quickened. Not with hope, but with purpose.

She was out there.

Somewhere.

Maybe still asleep.

Maybe watching.

Maybe... waiting.

He looked down at his own hands, light coursing beneath his skin like rivers of gold beneath cracked earth.

No longer broken.

No longer lost.

A god reborn, not just in name, but in will.

Opilkhos turned his eyes to the horizon.

And for the first time since waking in this cursed world...

He smiled.

He stood alone at the mountain's edge, the sky dim and brooding above, the last breath of the stormless calm long faded behind him.

Time had passed.

More than he realised.

The air was colder now, biting deep, though he barely noticed. His golden gaze – sharpened by new-found sight – had caught something etched into the stone under his feet. Subtle. Ancient. A ring of markings, so faint even time itself had nearly forgotten them.

But he hadn't.

Not now.

He stepped closer.

The symbols spiralled into each other, woven in a language that should not exist – elvish grace, draconic structure, and something older... primal. But to him, it was clear. As if Ian himself had whispered the key into his mind.

The spell glowed faintly beneath his boots, pulsing with expectant silence.

Opilkhos raised a hand, fingers trembling not with fear, but with anticipation. His voice, low and resolute, stirred the magic into life: *"Vaer'lin dara'sen... sha'vela tolorien." Whatever I will... take me there.* And he *did* will it. His heart ached, cracked open by memory and loss, hope and rage. "Lena..." he whispered, the name itself almost breaking the spell.

The glyphs flared blue, almost opening... only to falter.

A flash of light...

A violent shuttering...

And then... darkness.

The portal collapsed into itself.

Blocked.

Barred.

As if the very world denied him her.

He clenched his jaw, eyes burning now not with sorrow, but with defiance. "You hide her from me?" he growled, voice rumbling like the roots of mountains.

His shoulders squared.

His magic surged.

And again, he spoke the spell – but this time, not with longing. With purpose. *"Vaer'lin dara'sen... sha'vela Harinnil." Whatever I will... take me to Harinnil.*

The runes exploded into life.

A shock wave burst from the circle, hurling snow and ash in every direction. The sky above cracked with thunder – lightning laced across the clouds, not of storm but of raw, arcane power. Wind howled around him, tearing at his cloak, tugging his hair like a thousand unseen hands trying to stop him.

But he would not be stopped.

The ring ignited, flames of sapphire and gold rising like a vortex of colour and sound. The ground trembled as if the mountain itself were resisting the spell's demand. The sky darkened, clouds swirling into a great eye above the peak.

And then...

The centre of the ring tore open, forming a window of pure arcane light, swirling and humming with a sound like a heartbeat made of thunder.

Opilkhos stepped forward, cloak billowing behind him, eyes lit with the fury and resolve of a god no longer asleep.

He didn't hesitate.

He walked through the storm and vanished into the light.

The wind howled through the skeletal remains of the frozen forest, its mournful wail echoing through the twisted, leafless branches. A thick fog clung to the ground, swirling around Opilkhos's feet like the grasping hands of lost souls. He looked around, and as the light started to vanish around the portal, he focused his attention on what was ahead of him.

Each step he took crunched against the brittle frost coating the dead earth. Snowflakes, sharp as glass, drifted from the endless grey sky, cutting through the air in jagged patterns.

The bridge before him stretched across a chasm, its stonework ancient and cracked, dusted with ice that shimmered in the dim twilight. Below, the river had long since frozen, its jagged surface locked in time – deep, opaque and silent, as though it too feared what lay ahead. The wind carried whispers, unintelligible yet insistent, as if the very world warned him to turn back.

But he did not.

Opilkhos advanced, his divine presence like a smouldering ember in the winter's grasp, his very being resisting the lifeless cold. As he stepped through the arched entrance of Harinnil's lair, a suffocating darkness swallowed the light. The air reeked of death and sorcery, thick with the hum of necromantic energy. The walls pulsed faintly, veins of eerie green light tracing symbols of long-forgotten power.

The denizens of this cursed domain – shambling ghouls, restless spectres, and twisted monstrosities – stirred at his presence but did not dare to approach. The frost-crusted bones of the dead lay strewn about, yet not a single one dared to rise. Even the shadows recoiled, slithering away as if afraid to touch him.

With each step, the darkness parted before him – not out of welcome, but out of fear.

Opilkhos stood at the entrance of the cavern, the jagged maw of stone exhaling an unnatural chill. The air reeked of decay, thick with the cloying stench of magic long festering. From deep within, a guttural, rhythmic chanting slithered toward him – low voices murmuring in a tongue that the dead understood but the living feared.

He stepped forward. The moment his foot crossed the threshold, the cavern seemed to breathe, the temperature plummeting further. A faint, sickly glow pulsed along the jagged walls, illuminating runes carved by hands long since rotted away.

And then, he saw him.

At the heart of the lair, upon a throne of polished obsidian and frozen remains, sat the one he had come for. The Lich and archimage, once known as Harinnil, lifted his head, crimson eyes burning like twin stars in the abyss. A grin – thin, knowing, cruel – etched itself upon his skeletal face, barely remembering the man he was once.

"You should not have come," the Lich murmured, his voice slithering through the void like a serpent. "This place does not welcome the living."

Opilkhos did not falter. "I did not come for welcome."

The cold grew sharper. The darkness deepened. The dead stirred.

And so, the two halves of a once-whole soul stood face to face once more.

Their gazes locked – intense, unrelenting, each seeing in the other a distorted reflection of themselves. Though torn apart by fate, twisted by time, they both knew the truth that no force in existence could erase.

They were the same.

If a third eye – some unseen witness, a silent observer beyond time – were to gaze upon them now, it would see the undeniable resemblance. Beneath the scars of divinity and decay, beneath the weight of two millennia, they were still one.

Harinnil, cloaked in flowing black-and-crimson robes, moved like a spectre of death itself. The sacred golden armour he once wore still lay beneath, but it no longer shone with divine light. Where once it radiated the brilliance of the heavens, now it pulsed with an abyssal glow, a dark aura that swallowed the air around him.

And then there was Opilkhos – his form still wrapped in that same divine radiance, his armour gleaming gold, untouched by the corruption that had consumed his other half. A beacon of all they once were.

Light and shadow. Two beings, two paths. But one truth.

They stood in silence, the air between them thick with unspoken words.

The past could not be undone, and the future would decide what remained.

Harinnil stood at the heart of the chamber, waiting. His once-golden armour had long been stripped of its former radiance, and was now dulled and fractured, a mockery of what he had been. His skeletal face bore the faintest remnants of what had once been his divine visage, now twisted, wretched. But it was his eyes – twin pits of crimson malice – that burned the most.

Opilkhos did not falter. "Harinnil."

The Lich let out a slow, amused chuckle, the sound dry as brittle parchment. "Brother," he crooned, the word curling into the air like poison. "What an unexpected delight. To what do I owe the honour of your visit?"

Opilkhos met his gaze, divine power humming in his veins. "We need to talk."

Harinnil tilted his head, feigning curiosity. "Do we?" His grin widened. "Funny. I seem to recall our last conversation ending rather… definitively."

"You and I are not separate," Opilkhos said, his voice firm. "We are two halves of what was once whole. This path you walk – it is not yours alone."

Harinnil let out a cold, bitter laugh – sharp as shattering glass. "Ah, there it is… that insufferable righteousness." He stepped forward, slow and deliberate, the shadows curling eagerly around his feet like loyal hounds sensing blood. "Still clinging to the illusion that broken things can be mended." His eyes flared – fire and contempt woven together. "Tell me," he whispered, the edge of mockery sharpened to a blade, "did you truly believe you could step into this place and stitch the past back together? That anything I became could be undone?" He raised a hand – not in threat, but to gesture to the void around him. "I never even knew you existed, little echo. Not until you stood before me." His voice lowered, now trembling with fury. "So don't speak to me of unity. I never felt your absence – while *my* brothers slept, I was the one left behind, rotting in the dark."

"We both paid the price for that battle," Opilkhos said, his voice steady despite the weight of their history pressing down upon him. "But this? The rot you have embraced, the dead you command – this is not fate. This is surrender."

For a moment, silence hung between them.

Then, the cavern trembled.

Harinnil's grin vanished, his skeletal jaw clenching. A deep, guttural growl escaped him as an immense, vile aura exploded outward. The air grew thick, oppressive, vibrating with raw, necrotic energy. The walls of the cavern pulsed as if they were alive, reacting to his rage. "You dare say that to me?" Harinnil's voice was no longer amused – it was sharp, deep and venomous. His voice filled with echo the whole lair, sending shivers to all his undead servants. His red eyes burned brighter, searing with the weight of centuries of pain. "I am the one who paid the price!"

The darkness surged. Shadows slithered and thickened, taking monstrous forms. His minions, once mindless, shambling corpses, twisted and grew, flesh knitting itself into grotesque, towering forms.

The air crackled as his power seeped into them, warping them into something far deadlier.

Opilkhos stood firm, but the weight of Harinnil's fury was undeniable.

"I lost her." Harinnil's voice cracked, grief twisting into malice. "I lost everything. While you slumbered peacefully, I endured two millennia alone, trapped in this decaying world. And in that time, I did what none of you could." He raised a hand, and his creations roared in unison, their glowing eyes locking onto the living god. "I surpassed you all."

The creatures charged.

Opilkhos braced himself, divine energy crackling at his fingertips. He struck down the first, sending it crashing into the cavern wall. The second he cut through with a radiant burst of light. But the third – larger, faster – was already upon him.

Before he could react, a jagged, corrupted claw sliced across his cheek.

A thin line of divine blood dripped down Opilkhos's face, steaming against the frozen air.

Harinnil chuckled darkly. "Ah… how long has it been since you last bled?" His voice slithered with satisfaction. "Good. You should savour the feeling."

Opilkhos wiped the blood with the back of his hand, his expression unreadable. Then, his aura flared, brighter than before. "I am done watching you rot in your own misery, Harinnil." His stance shifted, readying for battle. "If you will not stop this, I will."

The cavern erupted into chaos.

Opilkhos struck first, divine energy surging from his hands as he blasted the nearest abomination into the cavern wall. The creature crumpled from the impact, but even before its body fully hit the ground, its bones snapped back into place, flesh reforming, sinews twisting into something even stronger.

Harinnil watched from his throne of darkness, amusement flickering behind his burning crimson eyes. "You fight so desperately," he mused. "Yet you refuse to see the truth, abomination."

Opilkhos ignored him, his focus shifting as three more horrors lunged at him. He twisted, dodging one, then another, striking down the third with a crushing divine blow. But again, they reformed – faster, stronger. Every strike made them worse.

A claw as large as a sword scraped inches past Opilkhos's throat, missing by a fraction. He countered with a radiant burst, sending his foe sprawling, but already another beast was upon him. He barely managed to bring up his arm as jagged fangs sank deep into his gauntlet, its force nearly crushing his bones. He roared in pain, ripping himself free, but the creature was unfazed, eyes burning with the same wicked light as Harinnil's.

Everywhere he looked, the same horrifying reality unfolded – nothing stayed down. The battlefield was shifting, tilting in Harinnil's favour.

He stood tall, his aura pulsing, feeding life into his wretched creations. His power oozed through the cavern, warping it, making it an extension of his will.

"You still don't understand, do you?" Harinnil stepped forward slowly, every movement measured, deliberate. "You cannot win. Not here. Not against me."

Opilkhos gritted his teeth, forcing himself to stand taller. "You may have grown stronger," he said, panting, "but you are still a broken fragment."

Harinnil's eyes flared dangerously.

The next wave struck.

A monstrous beast, its form barely resembling anything mortal, slammed into Opilkhos's back, sending him crashing onto the frozen cavern floor. Pain exploded through his ribs, the breath ripped from his lungs. He barely had time to roll before another clawed limb came down, narrowly missing his spine. He lashed out in desperation, golden energy bursting from his palm, but his strike merely slowed them.

A heavy boot slammed into his chest, sending him sprawling.

Opilkhos gasped as his back hit the ground. His entire body screamed in agony. His arms trembled as he tried to push himself up, but the weight of the overwhelming darkness was pressing down on him, suffocating.

Through hazy eyes, he saw the shadowed figure of Harinnil approaching, slow and methodical.

"Look at you," Harinnil sneered. "Crawling. Weak. A pitiful remnant of what we once were."

Opilkhos tried to move, but his limbs felt like they were trapped in ice. His breathing was ragged, sharp pain stabbing into his ribs with every inhale. His fingers clawed against the cavern floor as he struggled to drag himself forward.

From his place on the ground, Harinnil loomed above him, impossibly tall, his wicked aura curling around his form like a living entity. His skeletal face twisted into something resembling amusement, though there was no warmth – only cruel satisfaction.

"Do not misunderstand me," Harinnil murmured, his voice almost gentle. "If I wanted you dead, you would be nothing more than dust in the wind." He knelt slightly, his crimson eyes burning into Opilkhos's. "No, abomination. I have plans for you."

His gauntlet-clad fingers stretched forward, gripping Opilkhos's face, tilting it upward. The divine god flinched as Harinnil's touch burned – not with heat, but with the unbearable sensation of something rotting inside his very soul.

"You are mine now," Harinnil whispered.

Darkness shut out Opilkhos's vision, as he fainted, helpless.

Harinnil exhaled slowly, his crimson gaze lingering on Opilkhos's broken form. His fingers flexed once before he withdrew his hand, rising to his full, imposing height. He let the moment sink in, basking in the weight of his victory.

He stared down at Opilkhos, a slow, mocking smile curling at the edges of his cracked lips.

Then – with deliberate cruelty – he ground the heel of his boot against Opilkhos's face, scraping frost and filth across his mouth like a final insult.

He didn't speak.

Didn't need to.

The gesture said enough.

And then, without a glance, without a care…

Harinnil turned his back and walked away, as if Opilkhos were nothing but dust clinging to his shadow.

His skeletal grin stretched, pulling at the remnants of flesh clinging to his skull. Though his features were barely human any more, the amusement was unmistakable.

With a simple nod, his servants began to move.

The grotesque creatures lurched toward Opilkhos, their twisted forms shifting unnaturally, bone and sinew flexing as they reached for their fallen prey. Their claws curled hungrily, relishing the chance to drag the god deeper into Harinnil's domain.

But then… Thwip. Thwip. Thwip.

Arrows, black as the void, as if mimicking the surrounding area, sliced through the air in a deadly volley.

In an instant, the cavern erupted in chaos again. The first arrow struck a towering beast in the throat, its grotesque wail cut short as it crumpled. The second pierced the skull of another, silencing it before it could react. More followed, dozens of arrows finding their marks with lethal precision.

Bodies dropped. Harinnil's creations, so confident in their master's power, fell in heaps.

Harinnil's smile faded.

His crimson eyes flickered with something rare – surprise.

The air shifted.

From the depths of the cavern, beyond the flickering torchlight and curling shadows, a voice – steady, unyielding – cut through the silence. "Leave him alone."

Harinnil's head turned slowly.

From the darkness, a figure emerged.

Alentar.

His presence was a stark contrast to the twisted abominations surrounding them. Tall, broad-shouldered, his strong frame spoke of centuries of battle, of a warrior honed by hardship. His black hair, long and wild, almost covering his elvish features, framed a face weathered by time and war. His emerald eyes – sharp, unflinching – fixed on Harinnil with the certainty of a man who had already chosen his next move.

And then he stepped forward, proving something Harinnil had long believed impossible.

The shadows did not belong solely to him.

The cavern seemed to react, the darkness shifting as Alentar moved, as though it bent to his will rather than Harinnil's. Alentar's bow remained steady in his grasp, another arrow already nocked and drawn.

Harinnil tilted his head, his gaze narrowing as realisation settled over him. His glowing eyes flickered, his head tilting slightly more as he whispered the name. "Alentar."

There was no mockery in his voice. No twisted amusement. Just something deeper – an emotion buried beneath two millennia of hatred and solitude.

Alentar remained still, his sharp gaze locked onto Harinnil. His bowstring was still drawn, fingers steady, yet they both knew.

He would never release it.

Not against Harinnil. Not against his friend. Their friendship and brotherly love could never be described in words.

The cavern felt impossibly still, the echoes of battle fading into the silence between them. The creatures, sensing their master's sudden hesitation, did not move. The darkness itself seemed to wait.

Then Alentar's gaze shifted.

The arrow.

It was still there, lodged deep in Harinnil's chest, just above where his heart had once beat. Ancient, weathered, yet unchanged by time.

The very same arrow.

A breath hitched in Alentar's throat. His fingers trembled for just a moment before he slowly lowered his bow, his sharp features tightening with grief.

Harinnil's skeletal fingers traced the broken shaft protruding from his ribs. For centuries, he had ignored it. It was no more than a relic now, buried beneath his overwhelming power. Yet, as Alentar's eyes lingered on it, something stirred in him – a forgotten pain.

This arrow had been their final act before the world was shattered.

Two millennia ago, it had soared through the battlefield, aimed with unerring precision – the last desperate strike before victory. The moment it had struck, the world had shifted, the gods had fallen… and Harinnil had split.

What remained – this husk, this Lich – had been abandoned, left to fester in darkness. Alone.

Alentar took a slow step forward, his voice quiet, heavy with sorrow. "That arrow…"

Harinnil's gaze snapped up, locking onto him.

"Was the last thing we did together."

A shadow flickered across Harinnil's skeletal face. "Together?" His voice was rough, almost mocking, yet there was no strength behind it. He let out a bitter chuckle, his fingers curling around the shaft of the arrow. "No, Alentar. *You* won. You and the others… you all moved forward." His voice dropped, something raw creeping in. "And I was left behind."

Alentar's jaw clenched, his gaze never wavering. "I never wanted this."

Harinnil's hollow eyes burned. "But you left me anyway."

The silence stretched between them.

For the first time in centuries, there was no battle. No war cries. No clash of light against darkness.

Just two warriors – two brothers – staring at the wound they had both inflicted.

Harinnil let his hand fall away from the arrow, his expression unreadable. "So tell me, Alentar… why are you here now?"

Alentar took another step forward, his rough voice quiet but firm. "Because this is not how your story ends."

A sudden pull. Time unravelled.

The battlefield faded, swallowed by blinding light, and in an instant, Harinnil and Alentar were no longer standing in the cold depths of a cursed world.

They were back. Back at the end of the war.

The divine battlefield stretched before them – gods fallen, the heavens torn apart. Storms raged, the sky splitting with fury as the world itself trembled beneath the weight of their final battle.

Amidst the chaos, Harinnil stood within the Fountain of Creation, his golden armour gleaming, though battered from war. The sacred water swirled around his ankles, glowing with ancient power. He reached forward, his fingertips mere inches from the shimmering barrier that separated him from her – Lena, the goddess of life.

His unprofessed love.

She pressed against the other side, her radiant form trembling, hands outstretched. Their fingers should have met, their souls should have intertwined – but their father, the All-Father, would not allow it.

He stood above them, his body fractured, barely holding form. Yet his power – his will – remained absolute. With what little strength he had left, he held the barrier firm, an unbreakable wall of divine force.

A violent hurricane tore through the battlefield, winds howling between them. It wasn't just wind – it was his father's will, an unrelenting force meant to keep them apart. Harinnil braced himself, pushing forward using Drunnyak's broken sword, trying to cut the air that imposed upon him. Lena tried the same using her powers. Their eyes met – desperate, determined. They refused to surrender to fate.

"Lena!" Harinnil's voice was hoarse, strained against the storm.

"Harinnil!" she cried, her voice raw, her palms flattening against the barrier.

He had taken the power of every god that had fallen. He was the only one who could end this, but without her – without Lena – he wasn't strong enough. He had to reach her. He had to absorb her divinity, to become one with her light. Only then could he strike down their father.

But the barrier held.

Their father's eyes burned with divine wrath. His final strike was coming.

And then… A gasp, hoarse and broken.

Alentar.

Wounded, barely able to move, he forced himself up from the bloodstained ground. His vision swam, every breath agony, but his trembling fingers found his last arrow.

His body screamed against him. His soul shattered under the weight of the choice before him.

His love for Harinnil – his devotion, his longing, his *everything* – burned in his chest, unspoken for centuries.

The arrow felt impossibly heavy in his grasp.

His hands shook. His breath was uneven.

But he *knew*.

Harinnil needed to touch her, to be with her in order to complete the process, and there was only one way.

Tears spilled down Alentar's face, lost in the howling winds. His heart pounded, threatening to break free of his chest. His lips parted, a whisper lost to the storm. "I'm sorry, please forgive me, my friend. I love you."

A single tear fell.

It struck the arrow's shaft, and for a fleeting moment – a heartbeat – the arrow pulsed with a brilliant aura, absorbing his sorrow, his love, his very essence.

Alentar's body finally gave in.

As the arrow left his fingers, he collapsed, lifeless.

The wind did not slow it.

The storm did not stop it.

It cut through the chaos, sharp as fate itself.

The arrow struck Lena.

Her body jolted forward, a small, breathless gasp leaving her lips.

Harinnil's eyes widened, horror and disbelief flooding them as the golden fletchings protruded from her back.

Yet... something miraculous happened.

The barrier shattered.

Lena stumbled forward, her body collapsing into Harinnil's arms.

The arrow – Alentar's arrow – pierced them both, binding them together.

Her warmth flowed into Harinnil. Their hands clasped, their foreheads pressed together as golden light burst from their forms, the energy of creation itself surging between them.

Tears streamed down both their faces.

No words were needed.

She smiled through the pain.

He wept as he held her.

Their father roared, divine fury shaking the heavens, but it was too late.

Harinnil, now complete – his soul intertwined with Lena's – lifted his gaze. His armour burned with celestial power. His sorrow, his love, his rage became one, and with a final, world-shattering strike…

The All-Father was no more.

A cataclysmic explosion erupted, swallowing the battlefield in radiant light. The very fabric of existence trembled, and in the last moments before everything faded…

All that remained were two figures, their hands entwined, their tears lost in the light.

Back in the present, Harinnil and Alentar stood frozen, the memory burning in their minds.

And between them…

The arrow, broken but eternal, remained lodged in Harinnil's chest.

Only the blackened tip and splintered shaft still jutted through his robes, pulsing faintly as if echoing with the last heartbeat of the one who had loosed it.

A wound not of pain.

But of purpose.

Of sacrifice.

Alentar stood motionless, the wind brushing his cloak behind him like the last breath of a dying god. His eyes were steady, not with regret, but with the weight of memory. Of truth. "You remember," he said quietly. Not a question. A knowing. He nodded toward the arrow. "I made the shot… but you made the choice."

Harinnil's voice was like wind on old stone – cracked, deep. "I remember the storm. The barrier. Lena's hands reaching. My strength failing." He paused, the fire in his carmine eyes dimming into embers. "And I remember you. Standing, bleeding... crying as you drew that arrow."

Alentar looked down briefly. The wind caught his hair as he exhaled slowly. "I aimed with sorrow... but I shot with faith."

Harinnil gave a bitter smile. "It took all of me to reach her. I had nothing left." His hand ghosted toward the arrow. "Until *you* gave me yours."

Silence lingered between them.

Then Alentar stepped closer.

No weapons. No tension.

Only the shadow of brotherhood that still flickered in their souls.

"It wasn't betrayal," Alentar said. "It was devotion."

Harinnil didn't flinch. "I know." His voice was softer now. "She fell into my arms... glowing, radiant. And the world cracked open when we touched." His fingers clenched slowly at his side. "And then I fell with her. Into shadow. Into silence."

Alentar's jaw tightened, and a flicker of grief touched his eyes. "You bore the burden so we could live on. You... and Ian."

Harinnil's gaze lifted again. "I died that day. All that remains is the rot." He gestured vaguely to the darkness around them. "This place, this shell – it isn't me. But somehow... you still call me brother."

Alentar reached out, placing a hand gently on Harinnil's chest, above the arrow. "I always will."

For a moment, neither spoke.

A god of shadow and a god of the hunt, frozen in time.

Bound by pain.

Bound by love.

Bound by a memory that could never be undone.

Then Harinnil's voice came low. "She was worth it."

Alentar closed his eyes, a single tear tracking down his weathered face. "She always was."

Harinnil raised his hand, fingers long and skeletal, yet graceful in their motion.

The ground rumbled softly – not in threat, but in obedience.

From the walls, the darkness peeled back.

Ghouls, shadows, and bone-bound sentries parted without a sound, clearing a solemn path forward.

Alentar stepped into the space with quiet poise, his cloak brushing the frostbitten floor, eyes never leaving the figure before him. "Do you think," he asked softly, "we could talk a little?"

Harinnil's withered face twitched. His eyes – those infernal, empty pits of carmine – shimmered. If there had been tears left in him, they would've fallen. Instead, he said, voice like a cracked bell, "Red wine. Still?"

A flicker of a smirk touched Alentar's lips. He nodded.

Without a word, Harinnil gestured again.

The shadows swirled – and then simply vanished.

Revealing behind them a long-abandoned table, carved of obsidian and old oak, thick with centuries of dust and spider silk.

Two chairs stood like thrones of ruin, their forms distorted by time, but still standing.

They didn't hesitate.

The hunter god and the lost soul sat side by side – not facing each other, but looking ahead into the quiet gloom.

Servants, ethereal and silent, emerged from the dark. One placed a bottle in the centre of the table. Another brought two tarnished goblets, pouring carefully from a bottle so aged the label had turned to brittle ash.

"The finest wine left in this cursed place," Harinnil said, swirling the glass in long fingers. "No food, I'm afraid. I gave my cook a day off."

Alentar chuckled, the sound low and unexpected. "Dead men don't eat."

Harinnil cracked a dry grin. "Then let's toast to ghosts."

The glasses clinked with a soft chime, dust rising like memory between them.

They drank.

And for a long moment, they said nothing.

No explanations. No apologies.

Just silence shared by two gods who once stood side by side in the light and who now found themselves again beneath the weight of eternity.

But in the quiet, in the stillness, a smile lingered between them.

Not forgiveness.

Not healing.

But something near enough to begin again.

Harinnil suddenly stilled, his head tilting slightly, like a beast catching a scent on the wind. His carmine gaze turned inward for a moment, then narrowed sharply. "You need to leave," he said, voice colder now. More distant. "Now."

Alentar didn't move.

He studied his old friend's face, seeing the shift not just in tone, but in something deeper.

Something that did not belong.

"I'll make sure the portal takes you back," Harinnil continued. "To where you came from. But you won't be able to use it again."

Alentar's voice was calm, but edged. "Is it your servant who will open it for me? The one called... Verrlov?"

The room chilled.

Harinnil's expression twisted. Not in sadness. Not even in rage. But in something far more terrifying – pure, unfiltered hatred. He stood in a breathless silence, and then growled, "Don't ever speak that name in my presence again." His tone could shatter bone. "Or I'll forget we were ever friends." Then, without warning, the fury drained away to be replaced by a grin, crooked and malevolent. "You're in for a surprise, old friend," he whispered darkly. "Now go. And take that trash with you." He waved a hand dismissively toward Opilkhos's unconscious form, still collapsed on the floor like a broken promise. "I won't be so kind to him next time."

From the shadows behind them, a figure began to form.

A silhouette shaped from smoke and bone. Tall. Impossibly thin. Draped in robes that clung to nothing.

Eyes like hollow voids, mouth a slit of whispered secrets.

Alentar knelt and gathered Opilkhos into his arms. The moment his hand touched the god's body, he felt the heat still lingering inside – the struggle, the chaos, the guilt.

Harinnil turned away, already vanishing into the black, his voice echoing down the corridor like falling ash. "Go."

The servant said nothing. Only raised a clawed hand and traced a shape in the air.

A ring of light ignited. Howling winds tore through the chamber as a portal burst open, wild and ravenous.

"Describe the place," the servant hissed in a voice like dead leaves. "The one you seek to return to."

Alentar, standing tall with Opilkhos slung across his shoulder, said firmly, "A village beyond the southern ridge. Giants once ruled it. Men call it free now."

The veil split, and the portal pulsed into being.

With a final glance toward the empty chair across the dusty table, Alentar stepped forward.

The wind swallowed them whole, and they were gone.

The portal flared open with a rush of wind, and Alentar stepped through, Opilkhos slumped over his shoulder like a fallen banner.

He landed in the hall – the hall of reckoning. The one Drunnyak had drenched in fury and blood, where the monstrous rule of the giants had ended in bone and ash.

But the scent that filled the air now was different.

Fire. Smoke. Burnt stone and flesh.

The corpses of the stone giants lay stacked in grotesque towers, engulfed in a roaring pyre that lit the chamber in a sickly orange glow. The flames licked the ceiling, casting long shadows of the slain, their twisted silhouettes writhing in the fire as though trying to flee one final time.

It was no funeral.

It was a purge.

Alanteas had been here, Alentar thought to himself. That much was clear. The precision of the cleansing, the arrangement of the pyre – it wasn't chaos. It was intention. Judgement.

Alentar exhaled sharply and stepped away from the portal. Behind him, the ring of runes that had glowed with the power of Harinnil's magic flickered… then one by one, the symbols burned away, searing the stone before vanishing.

Only a faint scar remained – a wound on the wall, like a memory erased.

A whisper drifted through the air behind him, more felt than heard.

Harinnil's voice, like smoke curling around his spine, muttering words in the same language in which the runes were written. Some powerful spell.

Alentar didn't flinch.

Didn't look back.

The flames continued behind him, crackling as the past was consumed, and as the light of the pyre painted the ancient hall with flickering gold, he walked forward, carrying not just a brother, but a warning.

He shifted Opilkhos on his shoulder. The god's body was heavier than it had been – less from weight, and more from the magic coiled within him, still rattled, still unstable.

But then… A breath.

Barely audible.

Opilkhos stirred.

Alentar stopped.

Slowly, Opilkhos turned his head against Alentar's shoulder, his brows tightening as if waking from a long, painful dream. "Alentar…" he rasped, his voice a gravelly whisper, cracking like something ancient and brittle.

"You're back," Alentar said, calm but firm, not slowing his stride. "And still too dramatic, I see."

Opilkhos let out a dry cough that might've been a laugh, or pain. "What happened?"

"You fell. Again," Alentar muttered, ascending the first of the stone stairs cut into the cliffside, each step echoing with their combined weight. "But I carried you, as always."

Opilkhos closed his eyes again, the memory of Harinnil's presence still echoing like a thunderclap in his bones. "I saw him. I spoke with him. I—"

"I know," Alentar cut in gently. "He let us go. But that place... it's not done with us."

Wind howled from above, pulling the scent of burning stone and ash into the freezing air as they ascended. The staircase spiralled along the mountain wall, steep and narrow, carved in the old dwarven way – practical, enduring, but not made for comfort. Far below, the crackling fire still screamed its judgement.

Halfway up, Opilkhos pushed weakly against Alentar's shoulder. "I can walk," he murmured.

Alentar paused, then shifted to lower him gently onto the next step. Opilkhos wavered for a moment, but caught himself. He stood – unsteady, but proud. His eyes were darker than before, touched with something haunted... and something more aware.

Alentar watched him for a beat longer, then nodded and continued walking.

As they ascended, Opilkhos placed a steadying hand against the wall now and then, finding balance with Alentar at his side. The gods' silence said more than words could – the quiet pact of those who had once been brothers, now bonded again through pain and understanding.

And then the village revealed itself.

Smoke rose gently from the chimneys. The morning's deeper gloom gave way to a silver-toned clarity, reflecting off rooftops wet with melting frost. The mountain air carried the sound of hammers and pulleys, and the rhythmic chant of a stone giant – the one who had chosen to stay, helping rebuild what his kind once helped destroy.

Drokan stood at the trench's new gate, advising two young villagers in how to stack the stone properly. His massive arms pointed, gestured, always gentle despite his size. He wiped his forehead with a cloth that looked like it had once belonged to a tavern curtain, now tied around his head as a bandana. A strange kind of pride radiated from him.

Children ran past, carrying water buckets. One stopped and bowed awkwardly at the two gods from afar before sprinting off, cheeks red from cold or awe. Alanteas, further down the path near the old tower ruins, was standing beside a group of humans, instructing them in how to preserve the roots and extract seeds for the journey. His cloak billowed with each breath of wind, his voice firm yet warm.

"Looks like they didn't wait for us to prepare themselves for the journey," Alentar said softly, his eyes scanning the bustling village below.

"No…" Opilkhos's voice was hoarse, but held wonder. "They're thriving. What happened here?"

Nods and quiet gestures followed from the villagers. They were still wary, still uncertain – but their reverence was clear. No longer the silent fear of their captors, but something gentler. Earned trust.

Opilkhos slowed. Alentar matched his pace.

Alentar's gaze swept the bustle below. "Exactly what Garric said," he replied. "Plenty of potential, but with giants running the show it was all just survival wrapped in fear." He inhaled slowly. "Drunnyak changed that. There's no more fear here. Not from them." A pause. "Soon, they'll join Garrents. Start over. Free."

Opilkhos nodded, watching the villagers lift their faces and hands in coordinated motion. "And they believe it?"

Alentar glanced sideways at him. "They do now."

They stood in silence, just for a breath, the weight of everything unspoken still thick between them, but at least they would reunite with the others soon enough.

NO REST FOR THE GODS

Drunnyak slows his pace as he reaches the gates of Garrents, eyes widening with a grin on his face. The new walls and the gate stand tall, and he can't help but let out a laugh. "Well, well! Look at this! At least those lazy bastards finally did something right," he chuckles, shaking his head in disbelief. "I thought I'd get here and find nothing but rubble and shivering fools, but this... this is something."

His voice echoes, and just as he's admiring the sight, a loud voice booms behind him.

"If it isn't Drunnyak himself!" Taril calls out, walking into view with his war hammer slung across his back. "You've been running like a madman through the snow! Leave anything behind, or just flatten everything in your path?"

Drunnyak spins around with a wide grin. "Taril! You know me – didn't even stop to catch my breath. But hey, this wall, it's solid enough, right? I thought I'd get here and have to rebuild the whole damn thing myself."

Taril chuckles, giving him a friendly but forceful slap on the back. "Solid? You'd probably knock it over with a sneeze! But, yeah, it looks better than expected. Guess they didn't just bury themselves in snow like I thought."

Drunnyak laughs, wiping the snow from his brow. "See, this is why I love you, Taril. Always looking for the bright side."

The two share a laugh, but then Taril's expression shifts, and his voice becomes a little more serious. "All right, enough about the damn walls. Have you seen Opilkhos, lad? I haven't seen him around, and I'm starting to get worried. We found Ian's lab and something happened. He left after that, and no one's seen him since."

Drunnyak blinks, his grin fading slightly. "Ian's lab? What happened?"

Taril's face tightens, and he steps closer. "Opilkhos… he and Harinnil shared his body for a few seconds and we couldn't face him. He disappeared after that, feeling sorry for hurting us all. But I'll tell you everything inside."

Drunnyak's expression shifts, a rare seriousness in his eyes. "That's not good, Taril. Opilkhos disappearing like this… it's bad. We need to find him, and fast."

Taril nods, his face grim. "That's what I've been saying. I just don't like this – I don't believe he's the type to just vanish like that."

Drunnyak takes a deep breath and then lets out a slow sigh. "All right, we need to gather everyone – they all need to know what happened in the giants' village, but I'd rather do that in the tavern, get some food in me while we're at it. I've been running non-stop. If we're gonna deal with this, we need to do it together, with a full belly and a clear head."

Taril raises an eyebrow, a faint grin appearing. "Well, you're not wrong there. A good meal never hurt anyone. Let's get to the tavern. We'll get the others, and then we'll figure this out."

"Exactly," Drunnyak says, clapping him on the shoulder. "Let's get the group together. Whatever's coming, we face it all together. But first… food."

Taril laughs, nodding as they head toward the tavern. "You always know how to make a problem sound less like a crisis, Drunnyak. But yeah, food first, then we talk."

As Drunnyak and Taril catch up, the conversation about Opilkhos's disappearance lingers for a moment before Taril, ever the one to lighten the mood, raises his hands in mock surrender, looking around with exaggerated caution.

"So, Alentar's not behind me, is he?" he asks, his voice laced with playful suspicion, as if he expects the hunter to pop out from behind him at any moment.

Drunnyak laughs heartily, his deep chuckle echoing through the area. "Not this time, Taril," he says, shaking his head. "Alentar stayed behind to organise the villagers for their trip here. He's handling things, making sure they're ready to move. He also wanted to check the fortress. I believe the giants adapted it from a previous dwarven kingdom. You know how good he is when it comes to checking those things."

Taril smiles with his eyes. "Something I definitely want to see with my own eyes." Taril lowers his hands, feigning disappointment. "Pity. I was hoping he'd be here to take the edge off this gloomy mood. I thought I could use him as a distraction from all the... heavy talk. Instead, we're stuck with you, grumpy old warrior." He grins, clearly enjoying the banter.

Drunnyak rolls his eyes, his smile softening. "Yeah, we were hard on him, weren't we? But you know what? He did pull through. Sneaky little bastard, but he's talented. Can't deny that."

Taril nods, his grin turning more thoughtful. "No kidding. He's made himself useful, even when we thought he was just some kid with more ambition than sense. But now, he's stepping up. I never would've expected it."

They share a brief moment of quiet camaraderie, both acknowledging how far Alentar has come, despite their earlier doubts. The laughter fades, but the respect between the two warriors remains, unspoken yet understood.

"Guess we're all growing up in our own way," Drunnyak mutters, leaning back in his chair. "But don't tell him that. Let him think we're still clueless about his little schemes."

Taril laughs again, his voice booming across the tavern. "If he catches wind of that, we'll never hear the end of it!"

The two share another round of laughter, the weight of their responsibilities lightened, if only for a moment, by the bond of shared experience.

As Drunnyak walks through the village, his boots crunching in the snow, his eyes take in the changes. The air is thick with the scent of pine and wood, but there's something new, something different about the place. "So, not just a new wall and gate," Drunnyak mutters under his breath, "but a whole damn village, too…" He chuckles to himself, a low sound of surprise and admiration. "Congratulations, I guess. Looks like you finally got your act together."

The village, once a desolate, barely standing settlement, now pulses with life and energy. The sturdy, towering wall gleams under the faint light, and the gate stands as a proud testament to their survival. But it's the changes in the heart of the village that truly draw Drunnyak's gaze.

He sees that the fountain – once a symbol of the village's fragile hope – is gone. In its place, steps rise from the snow, leading downward to an area he doesn't recognise. The stones look ancient yet fresh, as if they were carved from the earth just days ago.

Drunnyak's eyes narrow as he studies the steps, his mind swirling with questions. What lies beyond them? And who decided to make this place more than just a defence against the cold? The transformation is… unsettling.

Before he can delve deeper into his thoughts, a voice calls out from the shadows of the village, breaking the quiet tension.

"Drunnyak!" Nashir's voice rings out, warm and calm, as he steps forward, his green robes flowing as he emerges from the wooded area beside the village. His presence is gentle, like a breeze that stirs the leaves in a forgotten forest. His glowing green eyes lock with Drunnyak's. "Welcome back, my friend," Nashir says, his voice rich with both relief and concern.

Before Drunnyak can respond, another voice echoes, this one sharp and full of energy. "About time you showed up!" Niv steps out from behind the newly constructed homes, her silver-blonde hair catching the dim light. Her amber eyes gleam with mischief, though there's a sharpness to them as well, a reminder of the tension hanging in the air. She strides up to Drunnyak, her confident gait unwavering. "Been waiting for you," she says, her smile playful but tinged with something darker. "Taril's already here, looking all serious and grumpy. So, tell me – any luck finding Opilkhos?"

Drunnyak's expression hardens at the mention of Opilkhos, but he forces a grin, his usual bravado slipping back into place. "Not yet. Taril and I are about to gather everyone to figure out what happened. But, you know, I'd rather do that in the tavern, where there's food, something warm, and maybe a drink to go with all the bad news."

Nashir's eyes flicker with worry, the light in them dimming just slightly. "We've searched, but he's nowhere to be found. It's as if he vanished into thin air… Something's not right. Have you heard anything?"

Niv's eyes, usually so fierce, soften for a moment. "We've looked everywhere we could think of. But this place, with all its changes… I'm not so sure this is the same village we met a few days ago."

Drunnyak's gaze hardens as he glances around the village. The changes are subtle but unmistakable. The fountain gone, the steps leading to some unknown place – there's something ominous in the air, something that doesn't sit right with him. But he hides it behind a grin. "All of us need to be together on this. And for that, we need to get everyone in one place." He looks toward the tavern, his voice low and serious now. "Then we talk. But first…" He gives a dramatic pause, his smile returning with a touch of irony. "Food."

Taril, standing a little way behind, chuckles darkly. "You always know how to lighten the mood, Drunnyak."

Drunnyak laughs, his voice echoing through the village, a sound full of strength and assurance. "Ain't no one better than me to keep things from getting too heavy." His gaze drifts back to the mysterious steps and the changes around him. "But once we've had a bite, we need to figure this out here, and we need to be ready for it."

The group, now gathered together, shares a moment of quiet understanding. The weight of what's happened, and what is to come, hangs in the air.

As Drunnyak, Nashir and Niv make their way toward the tavern, the village feels quiet around them. The new walls rise like silent sentinels, but the warmth of The Stubborn Goat tavern beckons with the scent of roasting meat and spiced wine. As they approach, they're met by two familiar faces – Garric and Eldric.

"Well, well, look who finally decided to show up," Garric says with a hearty laugh, his stern features breaking into a grin as he clasps Drunnyak's forearm in a warrior's greeting. "The soldiers have been talking about you since dawn. We knew you couldn't stay away for long."

Eldric, always a little more reserved, gives Drunnyak a nod, his tired eyes betraying the weight of his responsibilities. "It's good to have you back. Things are… tense around here."

Drunnyak gives them both a wide grin, his rough voice booming with energy. "Tense? If I had to run through this snowstorm for much longer, I'd say you've been making it *too* quiet here. Enough of the pleasantries – let's get to the important stuff. I'm starved! I need food, and I need it now."

The group laughs, though there's an edge of tension beneath the joking. The questions about Opilkhos, about the changes in the village, and the unsettling news from the lab all hang over them, but Drunnyak's need for food seems to take precedence.

They enter the tavern, and immediately the warmth hits them – flickering firelight, the crackling of a hearth, and the sound of Borgrim's booming voice welcoming them.

"Ah! The heroes return!" Borgrim shouts, his iron-coloured eyes twinkling as he greets them. "I've got food for you all! No waiting around for this lot," he says, wagging his thick, braided beard in a way that feels both gruff and affectionate.

On the long oak table, he's laid out plates piled high with hearty food – roast meats, golden-brown loaves of bread, steaming bowls of stew, and fresh cheese. The air smells of rich, savoury dishes and freshly baked bread, and the food is warm and comforting in contrast to the cold that lingers outside.

Drunnyak wastes no time. He grabs a plate, piling it high with slices of roast boar, thick wedges of bread, and a generous scoop of stew. He sits at the table, his massive hands quickly filling his mouth with food. He looks around the table as he chews, and his gaze lands on Niv and Garric, both seated across from him.

"So, what happened with the fountain?" Drunnyak asks between bites, his tone suddenly serious. "And what happened at this lab you found? What's going on around here?"

Nashir, who has been silently watching the exchange, looks uneasy as the question hangs in the air. Niv's eyes find Garric's, and for a breath, they share a private smile – unnoticed by the others, yet filled with silent understanding.

Borgrim, who's been busy pouring drinks and making sure everyone is well fed, pauses for just a moment, his gaze shifting to the others, sensing the gravity of the questions.

But it's Niv who responds first, her tone steady and calm. "The fountain's gone. It's been replaced with steps leading to what used to be Ian's lab… it wasn't what we expected, Drunnyak. There's more going on than we realised."

Garric, who's been quietly observing, leans forward, his brow furrowing. "There's no easy way to say this, Drunnyak. The lab… it's tied to something bigger. We've uncovered more than we bargained for, and it's not just about Opilkhos any more. There's something we're all going to have to face soon."

The room quiets as the weight of his words sinks in, but Drunnyak, ever the pragmatist, grabs another hunk of bread and takes a large bite. "Well, it sounds like you've all got your hands full," he says, his voice muffled by the food in his mouth, but his eyes are sharp, the glint of determination in them never wavering. "But we'll face it together. All of us. Now, enough talk. Let's get to the good part – more food, more drinks. We'll worry about all that later." Drunnyak sets his plate aside, the last of his meal barely touched, as his gaze turns serious. He leans forward, locking eyes with the group. "All right, enough of the small talk," he says, his voice low but firm. "I know we're all worried about

Opilkhos, but we've got other problems right now and he's a big boy, so he can take care of himself."

The room falls silent, and everyone's attention snaps to him.

Niv's brow furrows, her usual fire replaced by curiosity. "What do you mean, 'other problems', Drunnyak?"

Drunnyak's expression hardens as he folds his arms. "I've been in the giants' village, and it's over. We killed the giants. Their village is empty now, and the people there are free. But they've suffered too much, and they need a new home."

Nashir's eyes widen, and he leans in, clearly unsettled. "You… killed the giants? Just like that?"

Drunnyak nods grimly. "Yes. It was the only way to free the villagers. The giants weren't just a threat to us; they were tearing this village apart, forcing them to produce large amounts of supplies to somewhere else. But now… now we need to bring those people here, unite the two villages. They've been through too much to leave them to rot in the cold in that cursed place. Alentar asked to stay, to check the fortress and prepare the carts with supplies. Also to protect them against the weather. It's a long trip for humans. What took me a little over a day running might take them over a week at a slower pace."

Garric shifts, his face thoughtful. "Uniting the villages… that's not going to be simple, Drunnyak. These people have been under giant rule for so long. They won't just blend in here."

Drunnyak meets Garric's gaze, his eyes full of resolve. "I know it won't be easy. But we can't leave them to suffer. They need protection, and we need the strength that comes with uniting our people. If we work together, both villages can defend each other, even becoming a bigger village. We'll have the manpower, the resources, and the strength to face whatever's coming. Rebuild it bigger under our protection."

Niv crosses her arms, her sharp gaze flicking between Drunnyak and the others. "You're right. We can't let them stay where they are. But how do we convince the villagers here to accept them? They might see them as a threat."

Drunnyak grins, though it's more of a grim smile. "That's where we come in. We'll bring them here with force if we have to, but we'll show them that together, we're stronger. The villagers here will understand that. It'll be a hard sell, but it's the only choice we've got."

Taril slams his fist down on the table, making everyone jump slightly. "All right, Drunnyak. I'm in. But we're doing this with a plan. No running in blind. If we're going to unite these villages, we need to make sure it's done right."

"Agreed," Drunnyak says, nodding. "We'll do it smart. But we can't waste time. The giants may be gone, but there's still a lot of rebuilding to do. And there's no time to waste if we want to protect them – and ourselves."

Garric looks at Drunnyak with a serious expression, then turns to the others. "We'll make it work. We'll gather the villagers, get them settled, and prepare the defences. But we move quickly, and we stay ready for anything."

Drunnyak leans back in his chair, his hands clasped together as he looks around the table, meeting each of their eyes. "Good. Let's get to it, then. No more delays. The longer we wait, the harder this'll be. We get those villagers here, and we unite them. Together, we'll be unstoppable."

As Drunnyak speaks, the others nod, the weight of his words settling in. They know the road ahead will be tough, but they also know that together, they have the strength to face whatever challenges come their way.

As the group discusses their plans to bring the villagers from the giants' village, Nashir leans forward, his voice steady but thoughtful. "I think Taril and I should stay here for a bit. We can help build new houses, or maybe a larger shelter until everyone is settled. It'll take time for them to adjust, and we should make sure they're properly taken care of once they arrive."

Drunnyak nods, understanding the need for this. "Good idea. You two can help with the heavy lifting. It'll be a while before the villagers are ready to contribute on their own."

Nashir continues, his eyes drifting toward the window where the cold wind is howling. "Plus, Opilkhos might show up. We'll need someone here, just in case."

Taril grins, slapping his hands on the table. "Well, I was planning on seeing that fortress you mentioned. Built by dwarves, right? I'd like to get a better look at it. Might be useful for future defence." He looks at Drunnyak with a wink. "And besides, we'll need the numbers to bring all those villagers back. The more hands, the better."

Nashir nods in agreement, a quiet confidence settling over him. "I can handle the houses. I'm happy to stay here alone if need be. We'll make sure there's enough protection, just in case something unexpected happens."

Niv, who has been quiet, speaks up, her voice filled with concern. "I don't like this," she admits, glancing at Nashir, then back to the group. "I'm worried about what's been happening with Opilkhos, especially after Harinnil took possession of his body momentarily. I know we need to focus on the villagers, but... what if Opilkhos shows up in a worse state than we expect?"

Garric, who has been listening quietly, catches Niv's gaze. Their eyes meet, an unspoken understanding passing between them.

Niv steps closer to Garric, her voice soft but resolute. "I'll do whatever is needed, but we have to be prepared for anything. If Opilkhos is truly influenced by Harinnil, then I don't know what we're facing. I don't want to risk losing him... or anyone else."

Garric places a reassuring hand on her shoulder, his face sombre but steady. "We'll be ready, Niv. We'll make sure we can protect everyone, no matter what happens. Let's stick together, and we'll handle this, one step at a time."

Niv gives him a nod, taking a deep breath. She looks around the table, the weight of the decision settling on her shoulders. "All right then, let's do this. We'll bring the villagers here, make sure they're safe, and deal with whatever comes next."

The room falls quiet for a moment, the gravity of their situation hanging in the air, but there's a sense of unity in the group. They all know the road ahead will be difficult, but they're ready to face it.

Nashir rises from the table, his eyes glinting with quiet determination. "All right, everyone, get ready. Gather your supplies for the journey. You'll need everything you can carry." He pauses, his gaze sweeping over the group before focusing on the village outside. "I'll use the nature around us to wrap the village in a cloaking. It will look as if nature has taken control, hiding us from unwanted eyes. It'll reduce the chance of being spotted from a distance." He then turns to Garric and Eldric, his tone shifting to a more tactical command. "Garric, Eldric, gather the villagers. But do it after the others leave, make sure it's done quietly. We don't need a commotion before we're ready."

As Nashir finishes speaking, Borgrim, who has been quietly listening, shuffles in from the back, carrying baskets and bundles. "Heard you all talking," he grumbles with a smile. "Got your supplies ready. Even threw in a few sweet pies. I remember Niv's fondness for 'em."

At the mention of the pies, Niv's eyes light up, her excitement barely contained. She jumps up from her seat and rushes over to Borgrim, throwing her arms around him in a warm hug. "Borgrim, you are a gem!" she exclaims, her voice filled with genuine affection. She pulls away just slightly, smiling brightly before planting a quick kiss on his cheek, her lips soft but full of gratitude. "Thank you, thank you, thank you! You know the way to my heart."

Borgrim chuckles, his face turning a shade of red under his thick iron-coloured beard. "Aye, always a pleasure to see someone happy, lass. Just make sure you don't eat 'em all at once, or you'll be too full to fight the giants if they show up!"

Niv laughs, stepping back with a playful wink. "Don't worry, I'll save enough for the journey. But these..." She glances down at the sweet pies with a satisfied grin. "These might not last long."

The group chuckles, the light-hearted moment a welcome reprieve from the weight of the task ahead. With their supplies gathered and their spirits lifted, they prepare to take the next step in their mission, ready for the challenges that lie ahead.

Taril flashes a mischievous wink at Borgrim, who nods with a knowing smile before disappearing behind the counter. Moments later, he returns carrying Niv's repaired armour, gleaming and vibrant as if it has been newly forged. The damage from the earlier battle is completely gone, and the pieces now shimmer with a renewed, radiant light.

"Here you go, lass," Borgrim grunts with a smile, handing the armour to Niv. "Don't worry, I made sure to keep the elven magic intact. Just added a little something from my dwarvish heritage, to make it a bit more durable. Figured it could use a little… extra strength." His voice is gruff but warm, clearly proud of his work.

Niv's eyes widen in excitement as she takes the armour from him, immediately starting to slip into it without hesitation. "Borgrim, you're a lifesaver," she says, her voice full of appreciation. She quickly dons the pieces, and when she stands fully armoured, she can't help but smile at how much it shines – almost as if it has been reborn. "Is it my birthday?" she asks with a smirk, looking around playfully, but her gaze lingers on Garric for just a moment longer. The unspoken connection between them is clear, and Garric catches her eye, understanding exactly what she's thinking. Niv approaches him, her steps deliberate but teasing. She leans in close to his ear, her breath warm against his skin. "If only I had more time…" she whispers softly, her voice low and intimate. Before he can react, she discreetly nibbles on his earlobe, just enough to send a shiver down his spine.

The playful moment lingers between them, but both know that duty calls. Yet, for a brief instant, the world outside the tavern fades as they share a private, electric connection.

As the group steps out, the air is crisp, charged with the promise of the journey ahead. Nashir leads the way, his presence a calming force amidst the bustle. The towering figures of Borgrim, Eldric and Garric follow behind, their faces set with purpose. They move toward the centre of the village, where the gathering villagers are waiting to hear the news that will change everything.

They whisper among themselves, eager for word from the travellers. In the distance, the others begin marching, saying their farewells to the village that has been their home. Their departure, filled with solemn purpose, is a quiet one, the weight of their mission heavy in the air.

Nashir stops at the heart of the village, surrounded by the strong, steady presence of Garric, Eldric and Borgrim. He turns toward the villagers, his expression solemn yet calm, and nods to Garric. The warrior understands immediately, stepping forward and raising his voice for the crowd to hear.

"My friends," Garric calls, his voice commanding attention. "We have news – good news. Soon you will have new members joining you, people from the giants' village who have been freed. They have suffered, but they will not suffer any longer. Together, we will stand strong, united."

As Garric speaks, Nashir raises his staff high, his eyes glowing a dense emerald green, the magic within him flowing to the surface. The ground beneath his feet trembles slightly, and as if answering his call, the world around him begins to shift.

Roots and vines start to emerge from the earth, twisting and curling with ancient energy. Leaves, thick and vibrant, burst from the branches as tree trunks rise from the soil, weaving together to form a canopy above. Slowly, vines climb upwards, wrapping around branches, intertwining, and reaching toward the sky, creating a massive dome of foliage that nearly blocks out the heavens. Only enough of the sky remains visible to allow the flow of air, a natural ventilation that ensures the villagers remain calm, not fearing the change.

The beauty of the sight is breathtaking – every villager stands in awe, eyes wide as they watch the transformation unfold before them. The canopy forms a protective embrace over the village, its leaves catching the light of the lanterns as they flicker into life, casting a warm glow across the gathered crowd. The scent of fresh leaves and earth fills the air, mixing with the soft rustling of the branches in the breeze. Birds perch on the branches, their songs filling the air, and small animals – deer, rabbits and squirrels – emerge from the surrounding woods, encircling the villagers in a peaceful, magical harmony.

The scene feels timeless, a perfect moment of serenity in the midst of their tumultuous journey. The villagers, once uncertain and fearful, now stand in awe, hearts lifted by the sheer beauty of what Nashir has wrought. The canopy above them is a symbol of protection, of nature itself wrapping them in its care. For a moment, everything feels right.

As the last of the lanterns light up, casting their warm glow on the villagers below, the final pieces of the puzzle fall into place. The village is safe, for now. And as the animals watch from the edges of the crowd, their eyes filled with the same quiet reverence, Nashir lowers his staff, his work done.

Nashir pauses for a moment, his face set with a quiet resolve. He turns back toward the entrance of the lab, the place where dark secrets were once uncovered. He knows that the area beyond is too dangerous, too tainted with the unknown to let anyone – especially the villagers, with their curiosity and their children – wander too close.

Raising his staff once more, Nashir's eyes glow with that same emerald intensity. With a deep, steady breath, he extends his will into the earth, summoning the ancient forces of nature to act as a shield. Vines and roots surge from the ground, twisting and curling with supernatural speed, their dark green leaves gleaming with power. They quickly form an impenetrable barrier, thick as any wall, stretching across Ian's lab entrance. The branches interlace so tightly that not even the faintest light could pass through.

As the foliage settles into place, it's as if nature itself has decided to protect the area from prying eyes. The entrance is entirely hidden, cloaked by the living force of the land – roots so tightly wound that even the gods would think twice before attempting to breach them. A sense of calm pervades the air, a silent warning that this is not a place for anyone to venture – not now, not ever.

Nashir lowers his staff, his work done, but the feeling of responsibility still lingers in the air. No child's curiosity would tempt them beyond this point. No villager would unknowingly step into a place so steeped in danger, a place that not even the gods would dare to brave alone.

With a final glance toward the newly sealed entrance, Nashir nods to himself. The village is protected, both by nature and by the decisions they've made. As he turns to join the villagers, the weight of their next steps presses down on him, but for now, the lab remains untouched, hidden, and sealed away by the ancient power of the land.

Once more, Drunnyak sets out toward the giants' village, the familiar path stretching before him like an old memory. This time, however, he is not alone. Taril and Niv march beside him, their presence a steady strength. The journey is long, the snow thick underfoot, but with their added numbers and the knowledge Drunnyak gained from his first trip, there is a new-found sense of confidence among the group.

The cold wind bites at their faces, but the three of them press on, moving as one, with matching strides. Drunnyak's experience with the land, coupled with the unwavering determination of his companions, makes the journey feel less daunting. Where once the terrain felt foreign and fraught with danger, it now welcomes them with quiet certainty – Drunnyak knows the way, and with Taril's mighty presence and Niv's sharp eyes, they are more than ready to face what lies ahead.

As they travel through the snowy plains and dense forests, they share stories and light-hearted conversation, the camaraderie among them growing with each passing mile. There is a quiet strength in their bond, forged through their shared purpose and the understanding that, together, they are unstoppable.

With the giants' village on the horizon and their hearts set on bringing the villagers to safety, they know that soon they will return. The weight of the task ahead is not lost on them, but there is no hesitation in their stride. They are ready – for the villagers, for each other, and for whatever challenges the journey may throw their way.

THE COMING TOGETHER

Alanteas stood still for a moment, feeling the air around him shift, the familiar presence of someone drawing near. His sharp eyes narrowed as he turned, sensing rather than seeing the figure that approached. The tension in his posture relaxed for a split second, and then recognition bloomed.

There, just ahead of him, stood Alentar.

Alanteas raised a hand – not in salute, but in a gesture of greeting. A smile tugged at his lips, a rare flash of warmth, and relief coursed through him. The tension in his shoulders released as he felt the unspoken bond between them, a respect that was forged in a time long past.

But then his gaze shifted, and his smile faltered.

Standing beside Alentar was someone Alanteas hadn't expected to see – someone who shouldn't have been there. Opilkhos.

Alanteas's heart skipped a beat, and for a fraction of a second, all he could feel was a sudden, sharp chill, as though the air itself had turned cold. A gasp rose in his throat, but it was stifled by the surge of instinct that followed. His eyes widened, a mixture of fear and worry flooding his thoughts.

Alanteas had lived alongside Alentar and the other gods before their final battle with the All-Father, so he knew Harinnil well – knew him as both a brother to the gods and as a foe whilst they were away.

But this? This was not the Harinnil he had known. Seeing Opilkhos with the same features as the old Harinnil, his heart sank. The truth of the split was unknown to Alanteas, and he was unaware that Opilkhos was not the same undead monstrosity he had been hiding from for the last two millennia. In Alanteas's eyes, the figure standing beside Alentar was Harinnil, the evil creature he had fought so long to avoid. The resemblance was too great, and Alanteas's mind raced in terror, flooded with memories of the creature who had tormented him and his kin for so long.

His instincts screamed at him, the memory of Harinnil's malevolent presence pushing every thought from his mind. Without thinking, without the rationality of what should come next, Alanteas acted.

In a blur of speed, faster than the eye could track, his body coiled like a spring, muscles tensed and ready to strike. The world around him seemed to slow, his senses heightened, and before Alentar or anyone else could react, he surged forward, a warrior's reflexes guiding him as he lunged toward Opilkhos.

The sword at his side flashed as it came to life in his hand – a gleaming arc of silver aimed with deadly precision at Opilkhos, believing with every fibre of his being that the threat had come, that the attack was imminent. His heart pounded with the urgency of battle, his breath ragged as his body moved before his mind could stop it.

"Get back!" he shouted, his voice raw with command, the panic of the moment driving his every movement.

But as he closed in, Alanteas's eyes locked with Alentar's – only for a split second. Time seemed to freeze, and in that brief instant, a flash of understanding passed between them. A silent plea for calm, for clarity. Alanteas's blade faltered in mid-swing, the reality of what he was doing crashing down upon him.

His arm froze in the air, the deadly arc halting just inches from Opilkhos's chest. The tension was palpable, thick as the cold mountain air. Alanteas stood there, sword raised, his breath caught in his throat, as the fear slowly began to ebb away, replaced by an almost suffocating realisation.

Opilkhos didn't move. He didn't attack. But the danger – *that* danger, the one Alanteas had felt – had been a product of his own fear, his own misjudgement.

Alanteas lowered his head respectfully, his heart still pounding from the tension. He knew of Alentar's bond with Harinnil – he had witnessed their friendship and their battles side by side. But now, with this creature before him, he couldn't shake the fear that gripped him. "Master Alentar," Alanteas spoke quietly, his voice steady but urgent, "I know you and Harinnil were once… friends. But I must urge you, do not trust him." His gaze flicked to Opilkhos, his eyes filled with a mix of fear and hatred. The resemblance to Harinnil was too much for him to ignore, and his instincts screamed for caution. But out of respect for Alentar, he didn't act on it – he stood still, watching, waiting for his master's response.

Alentar and Opilkhos shared a silent glance, a moment of understanding passing between them. It didn't take long for the truth to dawn. Opilkhos shifted slightly, his posture relaxed as he looked back at Alanteas, recognising the confusion in his eyes.

Alanteas's mind raced, the realisation not fully forming in his head. *What's happening?* he thought. *Why is he… why is Harinnil here? What has changed?*

Alentar spoke at last, his voice calm but firm. "Alanteas, I know this is confusing for you," he began, stepping forward and addressing his old friend with patience. "But this is not Harinnil." He paused, the weight of his words settling in the air. "This is Opilkhos. He was never the undead you fought, the evil you feared."

Alanteas looked up, his confusion evident. "But… the resemblance… the features… you—"

"I know," Alentar interrupted gently. "It's not easy to understand, especially after everything that's happened. Opilkhos and Harinnil were once part of the same being, but after the battle with the All-Father, they were split into two separate entities." Alentar's eyes softened as he continued. "Opilkhos is not the monster you remember. He is not the evil that haunted us for so long."

Alanteas's brow furrowed, the flood of memories and emotions overwhelming him. "But... I've spent centuries hiding from him. Fearing that one day Harinnil would come back and finish what he started. How am I to know that this... *Opilkhos* is not just the same thing in a new form?"

Alentar placed a hand on his shoulder, a gesture of reassurance. "I understand your fear, Alanteas. I do. But Opilkhos is not what you think. He has no intentions of harming us, and he stands with us, not against us."

Opilkhos, standing quietly nearby, met Alanteas's gaze with a calm expression. "I know my counterpart's past actions can never be erased, but I am not the same as he," he said softly, the weight of his words carrying a sincerity that reached Alanteas's core.

Alanteas stood still, the internal struggle still evident in his face. He had always trusted Alentar, but this was a truth he had never expected. The years of fear, of running from the undead terror, suddenly felt distant, like a nightmare fading into the light of day. His heart still hammered with uncertainty, but Alanteas knew that if Alentar trusted Opilkhos, then so too must he – though it would take time for the trust to be fully earned. Alanteas finally nodded, though not without hesitation. "I will trust your judgement, master. But know that I am still uncertain. This is... overwhelming."

Alentar smiled, his tone gentle. "I know, old friend. But trust that we will face this together, as we always have." He gave Alanteas a firm nod, letting the reassurance sink in. "Now, let's move forward. The past is behind us, and we have a future to build."

Alanteas took a deep breath, his fear tempered by the warmth of his friend's words. Slowly, he allowed himself to relax, understanding that the path ahead would be different from the one he had imagined for so long. Feeling the weight of his actions, he humbled himself and approached Opilkhos with a new-found respect. His posture shifted, and with a deep breath, he lowered his head slightly, his voice sincere. "I... I apologise for my abrupt reaction. I was overwhelmed by the past, and it clouded my judgement. But I see now that you are not the same as Harinnil."

Opilkhos looks at him, his expression calm and gracious. "There is nothing to apologise for, Alanteas," he replies, his voice steady and warm. "Your instincts were true – your loyalty to Alentar is something I can respect. The fact that you came to defend him means that you have gained my trust and my friendship." He gives a small nod, his eyes reflecting a deep, silent understanding.

Alanteas stands a little taller, a sense of relief washing over him. He nods back, his mind slowly settling. "Thank you," he murmurs, though his voice still carries the weight of the conflict he's just resolved within himself.

Meanwhile, Alentar stands slightly to the side, observing the unfolding exchange with quiet contemplation. His gaze drifts to the villagers, who have been watching the entire scene unfold before them. There is an unspoken tension in the air, as the villagers, unsure of what to make of the confrontation, now begin to whisper among themselves. Some look at Opilkhos with lingering suspicion, while others simply appear curious, waiting to see how this new development will affect them.

Alentar, seeing the villagers' reactions, steps forward, his calm and steady presence commanding attention. He doesn't speak immediately, but his expression carries a weight of both leadership and the need for reassurance. He understands that this moment – this shift in dynamics – will take time for everyone to accept.

As the villagers begin to settle, a figure can be seen approaching from the distance, cutting through the snowy landscape.

Drokan advanced, his massive frame looming larger with every step he took.

Alentar watches him for a moment, the familiar sight of Drokan bringing a sense of reassurance. The giant, once a supposed adversary, now a valuable ally, symbolises the strength of their unity. Soon, they will be together again – united in purpose, ready to face whatever challenges lie ahead.

Drokan humbles himself, bowing his head slightly, a sign of respect despite his towering presence. His deep voice carries a quiet, respectful

372

tone. "Everything should be ready soon," he says, offering reassurance with a steady gaze. "The convoy is almost prepared for the journey." Then, turning toward Opilkhos, he lowers his head further in a more formal greeting. "I am Drokan," he says, his voice gentle for someone of his size. "And you are…?" he asks, his curiosity clear but his approach measured, seeking to learn the name of the one who stands beside Alentar.

Opilkhos walks slowly, his movements deliberate as he steadies himself, still feeling the effects of his earlier disorientation. He raises his head, meeting Drokan's gaze with a calm expression. "I am Opilkhos," he says, his voice soft yet firm. "A friend of Alentar's." His words are simple, but the sincerity behind them is unmistakable. Despite the dizziness lingering in his mind, there's a quiet strength in the way he speaks, a sense of calm that seems to resonate with the giant.

Drokan turns toward Alentar, his massive form casting a shadow over the group. His brow furrows slightly as he looks at them. "Do you know how long it will take for Drunnyak to return?" he asks, his voice steady but carrying a hint of concern.

Alentar, standing tall and calm, considers the question before answering. "It will probably take a day or so," he says, his tone reassuring yet thoughtful. "Even though Drunnyak left not long ago, they should be here soon."

Opilkhos, standing beside them, listens quietly for a moment before his eyes shift downward, his expression growing more sombre. "The others must be worried about me," he mutters under his breath, his mind racing. "I left without a word, disappeared without explanation. They're likely wondering where I've gone, what happened to me."

Alentar meets his gaze, understanding the weight of the words. He steps closer to Opilkhos, his voice low but comforting. "I know, Opilkhos. They will have questions, but we'll explain it to them. There is no need to carry that burden alone."

Opilkhos nods slowly, grateful for Alentar's words but still burdened with the thought of his disappearance. "I just… I don't want them to think I abandoned them. Especially with everything that's happened."

Alentar looks over at the others, who are standing a little farther off, waiting for the next steps. "They will understand," he assures Opilkhos, his gaze moving between the two. "Once we're all together again, they will see that you did what you had to. We'll face it together, all of us."

Opilkhos takes a deep breath, finding some comfort in Alentar's reassurance. He looks out over the group. His mind is still heavy, thinking about what happened at Ian's lab and the people he left behind.

Alanteas turns to Drokan, his expression focused as he takes in the next set of tasks. "We should finish the preparations," he says, his voice steady. "Make sure Halrek and the villagers are truly ready for the journey ahead. It's important we don't delay." With that, he begins to step away, but before leaving, he reaches into his satchel and pulls out a small flask. He hands it to Opilkhos with a quiet but deliberate gesture. "This," he says, "is a drink made from ancient herbs. It will help you recover sooner, and the effects will ease the dizziness." His voice is sincere, offering something tangible to help with the lingering weakness.

Opilkhos takes the flask with a small nod, grateful for the gesture. "Thank you, Alanteas," he says softly.

Drokan, observing the exchange, shifts his attention to Alentar and Opilkhos. "I'll speak with the villagers," he rumbles in his deep voice, the weight of his responsibility clear. "I'll ask them to prepare food and find a place for you to rest while we wait for Drunnyak's return. We'll need to be well rested before we continue."

Alanteas nods in appreciation, his gaze steady. "Thank you, Drokan. We will need the time to gather ourselves before the next step." Without turning, Alanteas speaks softly, his words carrying an edge of contemplation. "You're really like Harinnil. Almost impossible to distinguish, if not for your posture and eyes." Then, as he turns to face Opilkhos fully, his gaze lingers on the other's features, his voice carrying a deeper, more thoughtful tone. "Your blue, clear eyes, sharp as diamonds, are nothing like the dark hazel his eyes used to be. Now, they burn with a fire – crimson, like smouldering embers, vivid and fierce." With a bitter edge to his voice, Alanteas mutters, "I can't wait to close those eyes forever." His words drip with a deep, simmering hatred as he turns away, the weight of his emotions evident in his posture. Without another word, he strides over to the villagers, joining them in their preparations, the anger still burning within him, but focused now on the tasks ahead.

Opilkhos takes a deep drink from the flask Alanteas gave him, feeling the energy slowly returning to his limbs. The dizziness that plagued him begins to fade, and he feels stronger with each passing moment. He glances over at Alentar, who is already walking among the villagers, greeting them with a calm and reassuring presence.

As they move through the village, the people watch them with a mix of curiosity and gratitude. It's clear that the villagers are slowly starting to accept the changes, though the memory of past struggles still lingers in their eyes.

From the crowd, a young girl approaches – Annah, Eamonn's granddaughter. She walks with a slight hesitation, but her eyes are full of sincerity as she nears Alentar. The moment she is close enough, she stops and looks up at him, her small hands holding something tightly. "Alentar," she begins softly, her voice a little shy but full of gratitude. "Thank you... for what you did. For saving me, for saving all of us."

Alentar smiles warmly, bending slightly to her level. "It was not just me, Annah. We all did this together. But I'm glad to have been able to help."

Annah smiles shyly, then hands him a small medallion, the chain glinting slightly in the sunlight. "This," she says, her voice growing more confident, "this belonged to my grandfather. He always kept it with him. It's been with our family for generations. I want you to have it, as a token of our thanks."

Alentar takes the medallion gently, his fingers brushing against the worn edges. The weight of the small, simple object feels significant in his hand, a piece of their history and a symbol of the trust they now place in him. "You honour me, Annah," he says, his voice soft but filled with respect. "I will carry this with me always."

As the young girl smiles and steps back, Alentar looks at the medallion in his hand, its quiet importance sinking in. Opilkhos, standing beside him, watches the exchange, a flicker of understanding passing through his gaze. The villagers are beginning to see them not as outsiders, but as part of their future.

The path ahead is still uncertain, but in this moment, there is hope – a shared bond between the gods and the people they have vowed to protect.

As night falls, a quiet stillness settles over the village. The undead, though ever-present, are held at bay by the fortified gates, their restless moans and groans muffled by the towering walls. Inside, the villagers rest, a rare moment of peace washing over them. They sleep soundly, knowing that the gods now walk among them, protecting them from the horrors that roam the night.

Alentar, standing at the centre of the village, looks over to Opilkhos and Alanteas, his face serious yet calm. "Gather your strength," he says, his voice steady, carrying the weight of the responsibility ahead. "We'll need it when the others arrive. This peace is only temporary. The real test will come soon enough."

Opilkhos and Alanteas exchange a brief glance, understanding the gravity of Alentar's words, but their hesitation is clear.

"Are you sure you'll be all right here alone?" Opilkhos asks, his concern evident in his voice.

Alentar gives a reassuring nod, though his eyes remain focused on the horizon. "I will keep watch. You both need rest. I can use the silence, the quiet of the night. It will help clear my mind."

Alanteas opens his mouth to protest, but sees the look in Alentar's eyes – one that speaks of the burden he carries, of the quiet strength he draws from solitude. With a deep sigh, Alanteas nods in understanding. "Very well," he says. "But if you need us—"

"I will call for you if needed," Alentar interrupts softly, his voice firm yet kind. "Now, rest. We all have our roles to play."

The two gods exchange another glance before turning to find a quiet place to rest, their footsteps fading as they disappear into the shadows. Alentar, standing alone now, watches over the sleeping village, his gaze unwavering as he keeps his vigil through the night. The wind rustles the leaves above him, a soft reminder of the power that flows through the land, and the duty he carries – protecting the village until the others arrive.

Alentar stood at the top of the wall, his figure silhouetted against the darkened sky, his keen elven eyes sweeping over the landscape before him. The wind tugged at his cloak, carrying with it the faint scent of the wilderness that bordered the village, but his focus was elsewhere – on the undead that roamed just beyond the gates.

The undead, those wretched creatures that rose every night like clockwork, moved with unnatural jerks, their bodies twisted and broken from years of death and decay. Alentar's eyes, sharper than any human's, tracked their movements effortlessly, noting their sluggish pace and the way they seemed to cluster around the village, drawn by some invisible force. It was as if they were searching for something, though Alentar could not yet discern what that might be. Why did they return every night? What force, dark and mysterious, summoned them from their graves? The questions lingered in his mind like a distant echo, but answers eluded him.

He looked farther into the horizon, his gaze shifting upwards to where the sky, once filled with the brilliance of sunlight, now lay blanketed under an endless layer of thick, oppressive clouds. No light ever pierced through. The sky remained a constant shade of grey, a dull, colourless mass that seemed to block the warmth and clarity the sun once provided. Alentar's thoughts drifted to the old stories – the legends of the world before, when the sky had been blue, when the sun had bathed the land in warmth. But now, nothing had the warmth of the sun. The thick clouds had smothered everything beneath them, and with it, the very life that once thrived here. Why? What had caused such a change? Had this curse been brought upon them by the gods, by their own actions, or was it something far darker, something that had yet to reveal itself?

His elven eyes sharpened as they scanned the farthest reaches of the land. Beyond the walls, the terrain stretched out in a vast, frozen expanse. The once-thriving forests now stood barren, their trees twisted and gnarled like broken skeletons, their limbs reaching skyward as if pleading for the return of light. The snow, ever-present and unyielding, blanketed the land in a thick, impenetrable layer. Yet even in the stark, lifeless landscape, Alentar's sharp eyes could catch the smallest of movements – the faint trace of a shadow slipping between the trees, a flicker of something in the distance.

His gaze moved further, focusing on a distant ridge where the black silhouette of the mountains loomed like an ancient sentinel. He could see, even from this distance, the faintest signs of movement – figures moving in the shadows, their shapes indistinct but unmistakably human. These were once the survivors, the commoners who had adapted to this world of endless twilight, forced to make their homes in the cold and the dark. They now struggled, being forced to roam the nights as undead creatures. It was evident in their every movement, their huddled forms working together, searching for what they could with the meagre resources at their disposal.

With a sharp intake of breath, Alentar turned his gaze back to the undead near the gate, the dark army that never seemed to cease its march. His mind continued to churn with questions: *Why do they come? What keeps bringing them back to this place?* The answers seemed as elusive as the sun behind the clouds.

Yet Alentar's resolve remained firm. He could see the traces of hope in the village below, the signs that, despite the eternal night and the creatures that stalked the land, life continued. The villagers had adapted to this new, harsh reality, their will to survive unbroken. And though the answers to the mysteries that plagued the land remained just out of reach, Alentar knew one thing for certain: he would protect them. The undead would not breach these walls while he stood guard.

As the first light of morning broke over the horizon, a stillness hung in the air, and with it, the undead began to fade, retreating into the shadows from which they came. The gates that held strong against the night's horrors now stand silent, their presence a symbol of the protection offered throughout the darkness. Slowly, the villagers begin to stir, the quiet hum of activity growing as the dawn arrives, and they work tirelessly to ensure everything is in place – preparing for the journey ahead, readying the supplies, and making sure that nothing is left to chance.

Alanteas and Opilkhos move through the village, each of them carrying baskets filled with food and drink to bring to Alentar, who remains atop the wall, ever watchful. Their approach is quiet, but their presence is a welcome one. Opilkhos hands a flask to Alentar, and Alanteas offers a warm loaf of bread wrapped in cloth, his gaze briefly meeting Alentar's before he speaks.

"We've brought food," Alanteas says, his voice calm, but there's a flicker of something unspoken between them, a shared understanding of what lies ahead.

Alentar nods, accepting the bread with a quiet thank-you. He takes a moment to gaze out across the land, his keen eyes scanning the distance. The day is just beginning, and there is still so much to be done, but something catches his eye – a small movement in the distance, barely visible against the darkening morning sky. His heart quickens as he squints, trying to focus on what lies beyond the walls.

The figures come into focus slowly – three familiar shapes. His heart stirs with recognition as he realises who they are.

Drunnyak, the giant warrior, his imposing form making his way toward the village. Taril, the dwarven god, walking with his signature swagger, and Niv, her confidence unmistakable as she strides beside them. The reinforcements have arrived.

Alentar's expression shifts into a smile as he watches them approach, and without a word, he stands tall, his eyes trained on the newcomers.

The gates are opened wide, and the first sound of footsteps – the rhythmic pounding of boots on the earth – rings through the air as Drunnyak and his companions approach. Drunnyak's voice breaks the silence, greeting them, booming across the open space as he raises his hand in a cheerful wave.

"So, there you are, Opilkhos!" Taril calls out with a hearty laugh. "You could have told us you were taking a long walk!" His voice is filled with genuine warmth, the laughter echoing off the stone walls.

Niv grins, her sharp eyes twinkling in amusement. "You could've sent us a map or something," she adds, stepping forward with a playful jab at Opilkhos.

Drunnyak, ever the jovial one, lets out a deep chuckle, clapping Taril on the back.

Alanteas, Opilkhos and Alentar share a light-hearted moment as the trio approaches the wall. The tension that hung in the air dissipates as laughter spreads among them. The air feels warmer, and for a fleeting moment, the shadows that haunted the village seem to retreat.

As Drunnyak and his companions reach the top of the wall, the villagers begin to gather, slowly but steadily, their eyes lighting up at the sight of their heroes – Drunnyak, the mighty warrior, Taril, the god of the dwarves, and Niv, the fierce and confident warrior who has earned her place among them. The villagers cheer, a wave of relief and joy flooding through them as they greet the newcomers.

"You've come!" one villager calls out, her voice filled with awe and gratitude. "Our heroes, back to lead us!"

The gates swing open wide, and the villagers pour forward, welcoming not just Drunnyak, but his companions too, with open arms. There is no hesitation, no wariness in their reception. They know these gods – these warriors – fought to free them, stood to protect them, and now will lead them toward a future they've only begun to imagine.

With a final laugh and a clap on the back, Drunnyak waves his hand toward Alentar and the others. "Well then," he grins, his voice booming, "let's get to work!"

The villagers, now filled with hope, gather around, eager to hear their next orders, ready for whatever the gods and their heroes will guide them through. The wall is no longer just a place of defence; it's a symbol of the unity that has been forged between gods and humans, the beginning of a new chapter in this frozen world.

As Drunnyak, Taril and Niv approach the wall, the air grows thick with anticipation. The trio's steps seem to echo louder with each passing moment, their figures growing clearer in Alanteas's sight. The weight of the years, the weight of the memories, presses down on him.

Alanteas's heart pounds in his chest, his breath quickening as emotions he thought long buried rise to the surface. Without thinking, he kneels, his movement smooth and deliberate. The sound of his swords clinking gently against the stone is all that fills the space around him, before he lowers his head in reverence, his hands resting on the hilts of the blades as he places them gently on the ground.

The weight of the moment is almost too much to bear. He looks up, his face a mixture of awe and quiet sorrow as his gaze falls upon the three figures. Their faces, even though they haven't aged a single day from the last time he saw them, look harder, and yet somehow so familiar. Time has stolen much from them, including their memories, but not from Alanteas. He remembers them clearly – their stories, their battles, the endless days spent together when they were all whole, unbroken.

His eyes, normally so steady, begin to water, the emotion surging through him like a floodgate suddenly opened. The memories, so vivid, crash over him. He recalls their shared laughter around campfires, the plans they made, the fights they won together – battles where their bonds were forged in the heat of the moment, when life and death danced so closely around them. He has never forgotten them, never forgotten the comrades who once stood side by side with him, never forgotten the gods who once were so much more than just beings of power – they were his family.

But they did not remember him.

Alanteas felt that loss like a sharp blade in his chest. They had forgotten so much. They didn't know the stories he carried with him – the quiet, stolen moments when they had all shared a bond stronger than any weapon. They didn't remember the times they had spent travelling through harsh lands, the laughter shared, the quiet understanding that had passed between them when words weren't enough.

Still, he could not help himself. His heart cried out with the recognition of their presence. His voice trembled as he spoke, though it was barely a whisper. "You are back," he murmured, almost to himself, as if speaking to the gods themselves, not daring to disturb the sacred nature of the moment. "After so long, you are back."

The emotions flooded through him – sorrow, joy, relief, and an aching sense of familiarity. He could feel their power, their presence, even if they no longer remembered him. They had returned, and with them, something Alanteas had not realised he had been missing: hope.

Taril's eyes flicked to Drunnyak and Niv, but the dwarf said nothing, his gruff demeanour softening just slightly, as if sensing the depth of Alanteas's reverence. Drunnyak's large figure moved toward Alanteas, his steps heavy with concern and unspoken words, but he said nothing either, understanding that the moment was too big to be interrupted.

Niv, ever perceptive, stopped just beside them, her gaze softening as she took in the scene before her. The warrior who had stood in silence, remembering what they had forgotten.

Alanteas finally spoke again, his voice thick with emotion, as he slowly rose to his feet. "Even if you no longer remember, I remember. I remember you, my friends. I remember the stories, the battles, the bond we shared." His eyes meet Alentar's, his words meant for all three of them, though only Alentar will know the weight behind them. "I never forgot."

The others remain silent for a moment, the gravity of Alanteas's words sinking in. For a brief moment, time feels as though it has slowed. The past and the present blend, the space between them filled with unspoken understanding.

Finally, it is Alentar who speaks, his voice soft but full of strength. "You've carried that burden well, Alanteas," he says, his tone warm and reassuring. "We may not remember it all, but we are here now, and we will build something new together. We will find our way again."

And in that moment, despite the weight of lost memories and time, Alanteas feels a shift – a quiet resolve, as if the past and present have finally aligned. The gods have returned, and with them, they will find the strength to move forward, together once more.

Alanteas, standing before Niv, feels a deep connection stir within him, a connection that bridges the vast stretch of time and memories lost. His heart beats faster as he moves closer to her, reaching out with hands that tremble slightly, both from emotion and from the weight of what he is about to say. Slowly, gently, he takes her hands in his. Despite Niv's defiant spark – and the flicker of uncertainty at his sudden shift – she allows it.

For a moment, silence hangs between them, the air thick with unspoken words. Alanteas gazes deeply into her eyes, his expression softening. His voice, when it comes, carries more than just reverence – it carries a truth long buried, and with it, a revelation.

"Even though Alentar was my teacher," he says, his words almost reverent, "I could never forget you. Mother."

The words hang in the air, and Niv is struck frozen, her breath catching in her throat. The weight of what he said crashes into her, and for a moment, she doesn't know how to react. The shock in her eyes is clear, and her legs tremble as if the very foundations of the world have shifted beneath her.

Mother.

It's a word that causes a rush of memories to flood back, memories she had forgotten, lost to time. She suddenly sees it all – the distant past, now made real again. She remembers standing by the fountain, the cool, serene water flowing around her feet. Alentar and Nashir, so young, standing beside her, looking up with wide eyes as she shaped a form from her own essence. Not born from her body, but from her very being – her power, her essence, her love.

Lena's power, a soft breath of life, filling the form. And as the life took shape, Niv held it in her arms – a newborn elf, her first son, her first child. She presented the small, delicate form to Alentar and Nashir, the two young brothers who gazed at the newborn with awe. This was Alanteas, the child born of Niv's essence, a part of her very soul.

Niv's heart stutters in her chest as the truth floods back, overwhelming her with a mixture of confusion, shock, and deep, bittersweet joy. Alanteas, the child she made, had become a ranger, a protector, someone she lost in the passage of time. "Alanteas..." Niv whispers softly, her voice faltering with the weight of his revelation.

Alanteas, holding her hands firmly, looks deep into her eyes, as if trying to convey all the things words could never say. His face softens with a quiet ache, an emotion that transcends the years of separation. "Mother, I've never forgotten you," he says, his voice filled with tenderness and a quiet sorrow, as though he's trying to bridge the gap of years that have torn them apart.

Niv stands still, struggling to process the overwhelming flood of memories and emotions. For so long, she has believed those days are behind her, locked away in the distant past. But now, as Alanteas stands before her, his words and the look in his eyes stirring the ancient bond between them, she realises that the past has never truly left. It has always been a part of them, woven into their very souls. As she stands there, her heart racing, she finally allows herself to fully understand. Alanteas, her first child, her first elf, has returned. Not as the child she once held in her arms, but as a warrior, a god, a protector of the world they created together. She looks down at his hands, still clasped in hers, and for the first time in so long, she feels the overwhelming weight of love and loss and reunion all at once. "Alanteas," she whispers again, her voice filled with a quiet awe. "My son."

And as the words leave her lips, something shifts within them both, as if the universe has realigned, and the years of separation have finally come to an end. They stand together, no longer separated by time or memory, but united in this moment, ready to face whatever the future holds.

Alentar stood still, his eyes never leaving the scene unfolding before him. His posture remained as firm as the stone walls that protected the village, yet within him, a quiet storm was building. As he watched Alanteas and Niv, mother and son, reunited in a moment of profound revelation, something long buried stirred deep within him.

The villagers all around them were celebrating – cheering for the heroes who had returned to lead them, to give them hope once more. But to Alentar, the sight of his sister and his nephew standing together, their bond revealed after so many years, was far more powerful than any celebration could be. There before him was a truth he had never fully understood, one that had always been just beyond his grasp.

His first ranger – Alanteas, the child of Niv's essence, had always been something more to him than just a companion in their battles. But now, seeing the two of them together, the weight of it all became clear. Alanteas was not just another ally; he was a part of something ancient, a piece of the world that had been shaped by their shared history. Alentar had cared for him more than he had ever realised, had seen him as a protector and a warrior, but now he understood: the bond they shared was far deeper. It was woven through time, forged in the fires of their first battles, in the moments of quiet, struggle and blood. His kin.

The villagers' joy, the clamour of their cheers, faded into the background for Alentar as he allowed himself to feel this revelation, this understanding. His eyes softened, the weight of his silence shifting as a quiet emotion began to swell within him.

Alanteas, his first ranger, had come full circle. And with that realisation, Alentar understood why he had always cared so much for him, why the loss and the distance between them had always weighed on his heart. It wasn't just about battles fought, or even the wars they had endured – it was about something more profound. It was about connection, family, a shared journey that transcended time and memory.

As Alanteas embraced Niv, the warmth of their bond lighting the cold morning air, Alentar felt the stirrings of something ancient and powerful deep within him. His duty as a leader, as a god, had always been clear. But now, seeing the strength of the bond between mother and son, he realised that this was the core of it all – unity, the deep ties that bound them all together. They were no longer separate entities, no longer distant from each other. The past and present had converged, and in that moment, their fates had aligned in a way that could never be undone.

Alentar took a slow, steady breath, feeling the warmth of the connection between them all – between him, Alanteas, Niv, and even the villagers below. For all their struggles, for all the pain and loss, they had found each other again. And that was worth more than any victory.

Though the celebration around him continued, it was the quiet, intimate moment of realisation that would shape them all moving forward. This embrace, this recognition of their bond, would be the foundation of the strength they would carry into the future. Alentar's heart swelled with pride as he looked toward them, knowing that this, this understanding, was the greatest triumph of all.

A CELEBRATION INTERRUPTED

The tension in the air eases as they are reunited, the bond between them undeniable. There's a subtle shift – a deep understanding, a moment of recognition in their eyes.

Drunnyak, with his towering form, takes the first step forward. His presence is as powerful as ever, but there's a softness in his gaze as he scans the village before him. "So this is where they've been hiding," he mutters, the warmth of his voice cutting through the otherwise quiet air. "Looks like they've done well for themselves," he adds as he watches the amount of supplies they've gathered for the journey.

Behind him, Taril adjusts the weight of his armour. His face is one of quiet curiosity as he looks upon the village for the first time. "Seems peaceful enough," he remarks, though there's an edge to his voice that speaks of the harsh reality that lies beneath the surface.

"Sure. Now it is." Drunnyak smirks.

Niv, with her confident stride, steps forward with a smirk. "It's another mission accomplished," she says, casting a glance at the villagers below, who are already beginning to gather, watching the gods' return with a mixture of awe and reverence.

As they approach the gates, the villagers begin to stir. Drokan, the giant whom Alentar and Drunnyak spared, stands tall among them, his massive form casting a shadow over the gathering. His eyes are filled with warmth as he steps forward to greet them.

"Drunnyak," Drokan says, his deep voice resonating through the air, his gaze softening as he looks at him. "It's good to see you again. I trust the journey was not too taxing?"

Drunnyak's voice rumbles as he answers, a grin on his face. "I've been worse off. And it's good to see you as well, Drokan. You've done well." His eyes flick to the villagers, a silent acknowledgement of the bond forged in preparing everything.

The villagers begin to take a step forward, hesitant but clearly relieved. Annah, Eamonn's granddaughter, is one of the first to approach. Her eyes are wide, filled with gratitude as she looks up at the gods.

"Alentar, Drunnyak," she says, her voice quivering slightly. "Thank you for everything… for saving us. My family… they're all gone, but thanks to you, I can carry their legacy." She hugs Drunnyak as her eyes fill with tears.

Alentar steps forward, showing her the medallion she gave him before. "You've shown strength, Annah. We did this together," he says softly, his voice filled with respect.

Behind her, Halrek, the son of the elder who once cared for the village, steps forward. His shoulders are squared, and though his life has been hard over the last few months, his eyes burn with determination. "Drunnyak," he calls out, his voice strong. "You've kept your promise."

Drunnyak looks down at him with a smile that is both warm and proud. "I promised I'd come back," he rumbles, placing a hand on Halrek's shoulder. "And I'm here. We'll protect you all, just like we promised."

As the villagers slowly begin to gather around, the realisation of what's happening sets in. The gods have returned, but it's not just their presence that gives the villagers hope – it's the bond they've shared with each other since they were given freedom, and the promise of what they can do together moving forward.

Drunnyak turns toward his companions, his eyes sweeping over Alentar, Opilkhos and Alanteas. "It's time to rebuild," he says, his voice steady and resolute. "I'm sure Garrents will be a better place with them there."

Niv nods in agreement, her sharp gaze scanning the gathered villagers. "A lot of work ahead of us," she adds, but there's a playful glint in her eyes. "But I'm sure we'll manage."

The atmosphere shifts. The villagers, once wary and hesitant, are now filled with a sense of purpose. Their heroes have returned, and with them, the hope of a brighter future. The gates of the village swing wide open, and the villagers pour forward, ready to not only welcome their saviours, but to work alongside them in this new chapter of their lives.

As the morning over the village wears on, their faces set with determination. They have arrived, but before they can rest or prepare for the journey ahead, they agree to take one more careful sweep through the village. They will not leave anything to chance.

"We'll make sure everything is ready before tomorrow," Alentar said, his voice steady and firm. "We need to check every corner, every supply, to ensure the villagers are fully prepared. But there's more to this place than just the village." He turned his gaze towards the distant silhouette of the fortress. "We must also look to the fortress – the secrets it holds could be crucial for our next steps. We'll definitely need to return here, especially you, Taril."

Taril grinned, his eyes glinting with both curiosity and a touch of mischief. "Aye, if there's stone to be turned, you know I'll be the one to shape it," he said, his voice low and steady. "Let's see what secrets this fortress is hiding after making sure they are safe and settled at Garrents."

Drunnyak's eyes darkened slightly as memories of Garrents flashed in his mind. "We must be careful. We can't risk what happened last time. The memories we regained came at a great cost, almost destroying the village in the process. We cannot let that happen again."

They exchanged sombre glances, each of them understanding the weight of Drunnyak's words, especially Opilkhos after what happened at Ian's lab. They would tread lightly this time, ensuring they didn't repeat the mistakes of the past, but knowing that the knowledge within the fortress might hold the key to everything they needed.

Alanteas didn't understand much about it, but he knew they were treading lightly for some reason.

Each of them sets out to do their bit.

As Alentar walks through the village, he notices a farmer, an older man with weathered hands and a deep tan from years of working the land. Delm's hands are worn from tilling the earth, his eyes sharp but tired.

Alentar approaches him, sensing the weight of years carried on Delm's back.

Delm straightens when he sees the saviour approach, his body still strong despite his ageing bones. "God of the hunt," he says respectfully, his voice humble but filled with gratitude. "I never thought I'd see the day when you walked among us."

Alentar smiles softly, a flicker of kindness in his gaze. "The earth, the land – it speaks to you, doesn't it? Your name is Delm, I believe. I heard the others looking for your thoughts on how to proceed, most of all," he asks, noticing the farmer's deep connection to the soil.

Delm nods, his hands resting on the handle of his plough. "It does. It always has. The crops, the seasons – they tell me what must be done. But it's been hard, more than ever. The land, it's changing… nothing grows like it once did."

Alentar pauses, looking over the fields, where sparse crops fight to survive in the frozen ground. "The land will heal," he says, placing a hand gently on Delm's shoulder. "We will help you heal it. Together, we will restore what was lost. I'm sure you will love meeting my brother, Nashir. He stayed behind, from what I gather, to help build homes. I can definitely say that, like you, he has green fingers."

Delm looks at Alentar, his heart lifting at the god's words. "If anyone can help the land return, it is you and your companions," he says, his eyes brightening for the first time in years. "Thank you. You give us hope once more."

Alentar nods, giving him a reassuring smile before moving on, knowing that his presence can help the villagers see the future with renewed strength.

The clang of metal against metal rings through the village, and as Taril moves past, he spots Garrk, the village's blacksmith. His face is grimy from sweat and soot, and his brawny arms are covered in muscle, evidence of years spent at the forge. He's hammering away at an iron rod, the rhythmic strike filling the air with power.

Taril, ever the dwarf, steps forward, the sound of his heavy steps interrupting Garrk's work. Garrk looks up, startled for a moment, then sees the mighty dwarf standing before him. His expression shifts to one of awe, his brow furrowing as he tries to contain his disbelief.

"God of the dwarves," Garrk says, his voice still hoarse from the work. "I never thought I'd see a god at my forge."

Taril chuckles softly, his thick beard shifting with the movement. "We dwarves like to keep the fire alive," he says, eyeing the forge with curiosity. "Your work here is impressive, Garrk. The forge is the heart of any settlement."

Garrk grins, wiping his brow. "It is. But even the best tools are only as good as the hands that wield them. I've seen the state of our weapons – dull, weak. We need more than just iron. We need better forges, better weapons to protect the village."

Taril's eyes glint, and he steps forward, reaching for the forge tools, inspecting them with an expert eye. "You need better tools? Then I'll show you how to make them. We dwarves know the secrets of the forge. Let me help you. Together, we'll create the finest weapons this village has ever seen."

Garrk stares at him, a mix of disbelief and gratitude in his eyes. "I never expected to see a dwarf, even though the fortress was built by your kind and I learned a lot from what your people left as instructions, but a god of the forge helping *me?*" His voice cracks slightly. "If you're offering, then I'll take it! It'd be my honour to learn from you, sir."

Taril slaps him on the back with a hearty laugh, sending Garrk stumbling forward. "Then it's settled. Help prepare whatever the horses need to pull the carts, but make sure you rest before the journey. When we get to Garrents, we'll build a forge like no other."

In a small corner of the village, the healer Maela, an elderly woman with a gentle face, tends to the sick and wounded. Her hands are soft but steady as she mixes herbs and remedies. Her small hut is filled with the sweet smell of flowers and medicinal plants.

Niv approaches quietly, her movements graceful, though her usual irreverent energy is subdued in the presence of the healer. She watches Maela work with reverence, and the older woman looks up, her soft, wise eyes meeting Niv's.

"You're Aneeve, aren't you? Some people used to call you Niv," Maela asks, her voice kind but knowing. "The goddess of battle and a sorceress. The mother of all elven kind. My mother used to tell me a lot about your people. How a gracious elf maiden were the perfect mix of sorcery and combat. I'm Maela."

Niv nods, crossing her arms with a quiet smirk. "That's me. Though I'm more accustomed to making a mess of things than to fixing them."

Maela smiles, continuing her work as she carefully grinds herbs into a fine powder. "Even strength needs healing. No one can fight without a place to rest, to heal. You've fought long, haven't you?"

Niv looks away for a moment, the weight of Maela's words sinking in. "I suppose I have. But I never thought I'd be standing here, letting others heal while I... Well, I've always had to be the one on the front lines."

Maela looks up at her with knowing eyes. "Strength is not always in battle, child. It's in knowing when to fight and when to heal. And sometimes, we heal others in ways we can't understand."

Niv's lips quirk in a small, reflective smile. "I guess you're right."

Maela holds out a small vial of herb-infused oil. "Here. This will help you sleep. The body needs rest too, after all."

Niv takes the vial, nodding gratefully. "Thank you, Maela. Maybe I can learn a thing or two from you." With a playful grin, Niv can't help but tease, "And thanks for calling me 'child'. You just made me feel like I've travelled back a few millennia."

The healer's smile softens, a quiet warmth in her eyes.

In the village, a small group of children plays in the snow, their laughter filling the air. Lena, a young girl of around eight, is at the forefront, leading the others in a game of pretend battle. Her wild energy makes her stand out from the others, her face bright with excitement as she swings a wooden sword around.

As Opilkhos walks past, his towering form drawing the children's attention, he stops when he hears the name of the child, and watches them. Lena stops in mid-swing and stares up at him, wide-eyed. Her friends follow suit, their innocent faces full of curiosity.

"You... you're a god, aren't you?" Lena asks, her voice filled with awe. "The god who walks with the earth?"

Opilkhos bends down to meet her gaze, his eyes soft despite the weight of the years he's carried. "I am Opilkhos, and yes. Or at least, that's what they say," he says quietly with a gentle smile. "But you need not be afraid. I stand with you, just as I stand with this land."

Lena grins, her excitement bubbling over. "Do you think you could teach me to be as strong as you?" she asks eagerly, her grip on her wooden sword tightening.

Opilkhos chuckles softly, his deep voice full of warmth. "Strength comes from more than just the sword, little one," he says. "It comes from within. From the heart. Be kind, and you will be stronger than any sword could make you."

Lena nods seriously, her eyes shining with the weight of the god's words. She picks up her wooden sword and swings it high, her imagination turning the game into something much bigger.

Opilkhos watches the young Lena for a moment, his gaze softening with a rare, knowing smile. "You know," he says gently, "you share the name of a goddess – Lena, my beloved. She too was strong, with a heart full of light and power that could shake the heavens."

The little girl's eyes widen in awe, her excitement bubbling over as the weight of the revelation settles in. A playful glint sparkles in her eyes, and she stands taller, her voice filled with dramatic flair. "You shall bow before me," she announces, her hands on her hips. "I have the name of a goddess!"

The other children burst into laughter, the playful spirit spreading like wildfire as they surround her. She grins, basking in the new-found power of her name, fully immersed in the role she's taken on. In that moment, the two worlds of gods and mortals feel closer than ever, woven together by the strength and joy of the young.

As the day passed, the gods moved through the village, connecting with the villagers. A sense of security settled over the settlement as preparations for the journey continued. The villagers were busy, some ensuring their belongings were packed, while others made final checks to the supplies. The gods, too, focused on their tasks, carefully avoiding the fortress for the time being, choosing instead to help the villagers prepare for the long trip ahead.

Niv and Taril, working together, crafted a cart that stood out from the rest. It was more than just a cart – it was a small house on wheels. Fully enclosed and equipped with magical heating stones, the cart was designed to keep the villagers warm through the journey. The enchanted stones provided a steady, comforting heat, ensuring that the cold would not become a burden. The cart could hold at least twenty villagers comfortably, and it was designed to connect to the other carts in the convoy. Drunnyak, ever the strong and willing beast of burden, would pull the carts as if he were an ox, ensuring that most of the villagers would not have to endure the long, gruelling walk to Garrents.

The day was calm, the village bustling with the final preparations for the journey ahead. Hope and purpose filled the air as villagers and their protectors moved about, ensuring the carts were packed, supplies were in order, and everyone was ready for a new life. The gods mingled with the people, helping where needed, yet always aware that the calm might be fleeting.

Then, as the night started showing in the sky and they were preparing for their last night at this cursed place, a low rumble broke the peaceful air. At first, the villagers thought it was just the wind, but soon it became clear that it was something more.

From beyond the gates, where Alanteas had buried the remains of the fire giants – their limbs and broken bodies cast aside in the earth

– there came a heavy presence. The ground beneath their feet seemed to tremble as two towering figures appeared in the distance, stepping from the mist. The fire giants had returned. The King and his son were now undead, massive creatures. The very giants Drunnyak had slain only days before now rose once more, reformed in the very place where Alanteas had left them.

The villagers froze, their hearts gripped by the same fear they had known for so long, as they heard the undead giants attacking the gate. Panic spread like wildfire, and the people began to scatter, retreating from the gates and gathering at the centre of the village. The massive forms of the fire giants, dull flames flickering along their skin, slowly advanced, a terrifying reminder that no death was permanent in this forsaken land.

But Alanteas knew. He had buried them, after all. He understood the pattern of the dead – they always returned to where their bodies had been laid to rest. He stood still, a dark understanding settling in his chest, even as the fire giants made their slow, deliberate approach. He watched as they moved toward the village, their flaming eyes filled with wrath.

As the giants drew nearer, a deep, guttural growl echoed from within the walls of the fortress. The stone giants, the others whose bodies Alanteas had gathered and hidden in the fortress, began to stir. One by one, their massive forms started emerging from the dark recesses of the fortress, their stone-grey skin shimmering in the dim light. These towering behemoths, slow to rise but inevitable in their return, lumbered toward the village, as if summoned by the earth itself.

The villagers' terror reached its peak. They had barely survived when these monsters could think and act on their own, and now they were mindless creatures with only one goal – to feed on living flesh. The same threat had returned, only worse.

Alanteas stepped forward, his eyes cold but resolute, warning the others as he noticed Alentar resting on a hammock. His expression was calm, and there was no sign of fear as he didn't even bother opening his eyes to speak.

"They will keep coming," Alentar said, his voice steady. "I'm sure you guys can take care of them tonight, and don't bother me again until the dawn." And he shifted his body on the hammock to get more comfortable.

The others turned toward him, understanding immediately what he meant. Alanteas had witnessed this cycle before, and now the villagers would have to face it once more.

Drunnyak was the first to react, his imposing form stepping forward with measured determination. "Here we go again," he muttered under his breath, his hands tightening around the hilt of his sword. His massive presence radiated power as he strode forward, his steps purposeful.

Niv, her fiery eyes flickering with the same intensity, reached out, flames curling around her fingertips as she prepared to take action. "You've fought them before," she said, her voice almost casual, but the fire in her eyes revealed her true readiness. "We'll fight them again. Together."

Taril grinned, his axe glinting in the light as he raised it high. "Then let's get to it," he said with a laugh, though there was no mistaking the grim determination in his voice.

The fire giants towering above them moved with unnatural slowness, but their power was undeniable. Opilkhos's eyes remained fixed on them, knowing that they would not rest until they had destroyed everything in their path.

And yet, the gods were ready. In perfect unison, they moved as one. Niv summoned a wave of flames that danced with ferocity, her fiery hands sending a blast of heat toward the nearest fire giant. Drunnyak, with his immense strength, hurled himself toward the King, his sword cutting through the air in a deadly arc, cleaving the creature in half before it could even react. The ground shook with the force of the strike.

The stone giants, still emerging from the fortress, made their move. But Opilkhos was already on them, sword and shield at hand, faster than their massive bodies could respond. Each swing striking the giants' weak points with precision, bringing them to their knees.

Taril, ever the warrior of the forge, was in the thick of it, his hammer crushing through stone and bone alike. "You'll find that we don't break so easily," he muttered, his voice filled with dark humour as he took down another stone giant.

The battle raged, but it was clear that the villagers were no longer alone in their fight. The warriors acted swiftly, their power overwhelming the undead giants one by one. The villagers, frozen in fear at first, slowly began to realise that the gods were not just here to protect them – they were the very force that would drive the darkness back.

As the final giant fell, its massive body crumbling to the ground, the village once again fell silent. The undead giants were gone. For now.

Alanteas stood amidst the rubble, his expression unreadable. He had seen this before, and he would see it again. The dead never truly stayed down. But for today, the villagers were safe, and that was enough.

They gathered together, their presence unwavering. The villagers slowly began to emerge from their hiding places, their eyes filled with awe and gratitude, realising that, as long as the gods stood with them, they would not fall.

Alentar turned to the others, his voice quiet but resolute. "Alanteas, you should continue to watch. Keep an eye on the other undead that should appear, but don't waste arrows if not needed." He looked toward the villagers, who were now gathering around them, their fear replaced by a quiet hope.

And with that, they cleaned their weapons and gathered again with the villagers for a proper meal before the morning, and to the villagers' surprise, it looked like nothing had happened.

The chaos of the battle seemed to vanish as quickly as it had come. The gods standing among them bore no signs of the fierce fight they had just endured – no exhaustion, no mark of struggle.

It was as if the battle had been nothing to them. To the villagers, it seemed a miracle. Had the gods not been there, it was clear the village would have been overrun. Yet they were more than mere warriors – they were protectors, the embodiment of strength and resilience, and in their presence, the impossible had been made easy.

As the evening settled over the village, the warriors sat among the villagers, their presence a calm reassurance after the earlier chaos. The warmth of the hearth crackled in the background, casting a soft glow over the gathered group. The air was filled with laughter, the sounds of villagers sharing stories, enjoying food, and revelling in the safety that now enveloped them.

Halrek sat across from Alentar, his eyes filled with respect and gratitude. "I never thought I'd see the day," he said, a quiet smile on his lips. "My father used to tell stories about gods walking among us, but I always thought they were just that – stories."

Alentar nodded, his gaze kind but firm. "The world has a way of proving us wrong, doesn't it?" he said softly, his voice carrying the weight of centuries of knowledge.

Nearby, Annah, her young face lit with excitement, leaned over to Drunnyak as she admired her saviours.

Niv gave her a playful smile, brushing a lock of hair behind her ear. "We don't let anyone get left behind. Not while we're still standing."

Laughter rippled through the group as Drunnyak, his voice booming with amusement, joined in. "And don't forget, lass," he added, his grin wide, "we're *always* standing, even if it takes a bit of effort."

The villagers chuckled at Drunnyak's boisterous nature, the fear that had once gripped their hearts now replaced by warmth and camaraderie. The sound of a flute played in the distance, a song carried by the wind, and a few children – Annah among them – began to dance, their steps light and carefree.

As the night deepened, Halrek stood, raising a mug of ale. "To our protectors," he said, his voice steady with emotion. "To the gods who walked with us, who saved us. You've given us more than safety. You've given us hope, the will to live. To *thrive*."

The villagers raised their glasses in unison, their faces shining with gratitude and new-found strength. The gods seated amongst them shared a quiet moment of understanding, knowing that their mission was more than just protection – it was the restoration of a way of life, the rekindling of a light that had once flickered dim, but now burned brightly again.

In that moment, as the fire crackled and the village came alive with laughter and joy, it was clear that this was not just survival. It was life.

But then, just as the lightness of the evening reached its peak, a sudden shift in the atmosphere caused the conversation to die down. A figure emerged from the shadows near the trees where the villagers had once farmed. His tall silhouette cast a long shadow as he stepped into the firelight, his presence demanding attention.

"Well, I see that nobody invited me to the party." A smooth, commanding voice echoed across the gathering, pulling everyone's gaze toward the newcomer.

The villagers froze, their hearts skipping a beat, unsure of who had appeared before them. There was something ethereal about him, something familiar in the way he moved, but also distinctly different from the others. His figure stepped fully into the glow of the firelight, revealing Nashir, whose presence seemed to cause the very trees to sway around him. His dark hair and glowing green eyes were unmistakable, yet his appearance seemed to catch everyone by surprise.

His friends, too, reacted instantly. Taril, still holding his mug of ale, sputtered and then spat it far, the liquid flying through the air in shock. "What in the name of the earth...?" he muttered, wiping his mouth, his voice full of disbelief. His hand fell from his mug, forgotten, as he stared at Nashir.

Alentar, always composed, widened his eyes in surprise, his brows knitting together for a brief moment. "Nashir?" he asked, the name leaving his lips in a low murmur of recognition. His voice carried a note of confusion as the daze began to lift. "You were supposed to be at Garrents. We expected to meet you there."

The villagers, still unsure of what was happening, exchanged confused looks. Nashir's sudden appearance was startling, and the shock spread across the crowd.

Nashir, seeming to sense the tension, raised an eyebrow with a wry smile. "Surprised?" he asked casually, though his eyes were filled with a warmth that instantly put the villagers at ease. His voice, though full of power, carried an undertone of amusement, as if this was all an unexpected twist. "I've been waiting for the right moment. I stayed behind to protect Garrents, kept watch over the village as we planned, and waited for Opilkhos to return. I see you've all been keeping busy."

Drunnyak was the first to recover, a broad grin spreading across his face as he shook his head in disbelief. "You really know how to keep us on our toes, Nashir," he said, a laugh escaping him. "But it's good to see you, brother. Why didn't you wait for us? A lot could have happened to Garrents while you travelled."

Niv, still somewhat stunned, couldn't suppress the playful smirk that tugged at her lips. "So, you were lurking around all this time while we were out here saving the day, huh?" she teased, her eyes sparkling with a mix of admiration and amusement.

Nashir chuckled softly, his gaze sweeping across the villagers, who were still absorbing his presence. "I couldn't leave Garrents vulnerable, but there was always the chance you would need me here, so I remembered something."

The villagers, hearing Nashir's calm words and seeing the confidence he exuded, began to relax. Though they didn't yet fully understand, they felt safer, nevertheless.

Nashir stepped forward into the gathering, his voice filled with quiet authority. "Now, let's not waste any more time with formalities," he said, his eyes glinting with a touch of humour. "The work isn't done yet, so let me explain how I got…" As he looked over the group, his gaze suddenly locked onto Alanteas. His expression shifted, recognition dawning in his eyes. "Alanteas? Is that you?" Nashir said, his voice softer now, filled with a warmth that took the others by surprise. "My nephew!"

The group fell silent. The gods exchanged puzzled glances, and the villagers stood still, watching the unexpected moment unfold.

Alanteas, equally surprised, took a small step forward, unsure if he had heard correctly. "Do you remember me?"

Nashir's smile deepened, and he nodded, his voice filled with quiet understanding. "I knew you before. Long before the world was forgotten. Somehow, I… remember now." As he moved to put his hand on Alanteas's shoulder, his gaze flickered with the weight of something ancient, something powerful, as though his memories were returning piece by piece. "As our power grows, I think our memories return. They are coming back to me now. All of us are starting to remember, I believe – isn't that right?"

Taril, still processing the revelation, raised an eyebrow. "None of us remembered him. Not even Niv, who created him."

"That's what I was trying to explain before," Nashir said, his voice filled with quiet certainty. "I think it's because of my deep connection to nature and its nurturing essence that I'm starting to remember more of our past. I've even remembered something… something that allowed me to get here in a heartbeat." He motioned towards the nearby trees, the leaves shimmering slightly in the evening light. "Come with me," he said, his tone inviting yet purposeful.

As the gods and villagers followed Nashir, he caught Alanteas by the arm and, in a rare moment of joy, kissed him lightly on the forehead.

"I'm so happy to see you again," he murmured, his voice soft and warm.

Alanteas smiled, feeling the genuine affection in Nashir's gesture, his heart lightening in the face of the reunion.

They walked together to the edge of the trees, where Nashir raised his staff high. With a fluid motion, the air around them seemed to hum with energy, and suddenly, before their eyes, a portal began to form between the trunks of the ancient trees. Unlike the portals that Alentar and Opilkhos had used, this one was not born from their kind of magic. It was something different – something ancient and tied directly to the essence of nature itself. The air shimmered as if the trees themselves were alive with power, the roots twisting and connecting to the very soul of Maud.

"This is not like the portals Ian used to conjure," Nashir explained, his eyes focused on the swirling energies. "This is the power of nature – its purest form. A place where all life is intertwined, a realm that connects us through the very land we tread upon." The portal opened wider, revealing a glimpse of Garrents – a distant, peaceful place that seemed to pulse with nature's own heartbeat. Nashir turned to the others, his expression one of quiet pride. "I've focused on all of you, on what we've shared, and through that connection, I've received this gift once more. It's how I could reach here so quickly."

The group gathered around, their awe palpable as they stared at the portal. The air hummed with an ancient, life-filled energy, the very force of Maud itself wrapped in the movement of the trees and the flow of the earth.

As the portal shimmered before them, a stunned silence fell over the group. The villagers, wide-eyed, couldn't believe what they were seeing. Before them stood a doorway to another part of this world. A way opened not through any traditional magic, but through the raw, unyielding power of nature itself. It was a moment of pure wonder, as though Maud itself had been bent to Nashir's will.

Niv, her usual sharp smile now gleaming brightly, clapped her hands in delight. "Well, well, well, look at you," she said, her voice laced with affection and mischief. "I knew you were full of surprises, little brother." She threw a playful wink at Nashir, her voice ringing with pride. "I'm so proud of you."

Drunnyak, his deep laughter filling the air, threw his head back in amusement. "Ha! And here I thought I'd be the one hauling all the weight," he chuckled, his gaze turning to the villagers with a grin. "No offence, of course," he added, his voice booming with humour.

The villagers, still awestruck, couldn't help but laugh along, the tension that had gripped them all momentarily forgotten in the wake of this new development.

Even Opilkhos, whose usual seriousness had never cracked in the face of the world's dangers, allowed a rare grin to stretch across his face. It wasn't wide, nor boisterous, but it was there – faint but genuine, an acknowledgement of the extraordinary moment unfolding. The gods, usually burdened by their purpose and the weight of their missions, now shared in a moment of pure magic.

Nashir turned to them, his expression softening with quiet pride.

Alentar, looking toward the villagers, nodded slowly. "What Nashir said makes sense. It seems the memories are coming back to us now, with our strength." His gaze turned to Nashir, who stood firm, unwavering. "And no one has had more power since we returned than you."

Nashir's eyes gleamed as he turned to the gathered crowd, the weight of their journey ahead settled in his expression, but there was also something more – a spark of excitement, of promise. The villagers were ready, the gods stood firm, and the portal was before them, glowing with the pulse of nature's energy. "Who's ready to meet our friends at Garrents?" Nashir called, his voice carrying over the crowd, filled with a quiet authority and warmth.

At the sound of his words, the villagers erupted in loud cheers, their voices ringing with hope and joy. The gods shared smiles and knowing glances as they watched the anticipation ripple through the crowd. The weight of their mission, the challenges ahead, all seemed to be momentarily forgotten in the face of this momentous step forward.

Nashir raised a hand, his voice steady but commanding as he brought the village's excitement back to focus. "I can keep the portal open," he said, his tone laced with quiet concentration. "But only a few at a time should go through. I'll need to focus the energies carefully."

Before he could say more, Taril's booming voice filled the air, louder than the wind itself. "Everyone! Let's make a line – women and children first!" he shouted, his words rolling out like a command that could not be ignored.

Laughter and cheers followed in his wake as the villagers began to form an orderly line, their movements full of energy and hope. There was something almost ceremonial about it – their journey was no longer a grim march, but a step toward something new, something better. Even the gods, always so dignified, found themselves caught up in the moment, watching the villagers' excitement unfold.

Nashir stepped to the side as the first few villagers approached the portal. With a soft wave of his staff, the air shimmered and crackled with energy, and the gateway pulsed with a vibrant, radiant light. One by one, the villagers stepped through, disappearing into the other side.

Taril, ever the one to keep spirits high, clapped his hands. "Move it along, people! We've got new friends to meet and new homes to build!"

His booming voice was met with more laughter as the line continued to move, the villagers eager to be on their way.

As the last of the villagers crossed through, followed by the carts laden with supplies, seeds, timber and provisions, the gods exchanged a quiet glance, nodding in silent agreement.

This was a moment they had all fought for, and now they were closer to their new home – the future waiting for them on the other side.

When the last person had crossed, Nashir stepped forward, his eyes glowing with the power of nature. "It's time," he said quietly, his voice filled with certainty.

With a final wave of his staff, the portal expanded, and the gods walked through one by one, following their people. The air shifted as they crossed, and the world on the other side revealed itself in breathtaking beauty. The first thing they saw was the landscape of Garrents – a place lush with vibrant greenery, the towering trees reaching into the sky, and the rolling hills of fertile land stretching out before them. It was a world of untapped promise, a land that seemed to echo with the potential of what could be built.

The villagers stepped forward, their gazes filled with awe as they took in their new surroundings, their hearts swelling with the sight of their new home. The air was fresh, and the sun – though hidden behind the ever-present clouds – gave the sky a gentle, welcoming glow. In the distance, figures moved: the people of Garrents – new companions who had been waiting for this day to arrive.

"We've made it," Niv said, her voice soft with disbelief as she looked around at the green expanse before them.

Drunnyak clapped his hands together, laughing heartily. "Not just made it – we're here to stay," he said, his voice booming across the land. "And we're going to build something great."

Alentar's eyes scanned the horizon, his hand resting on his sword. "We have much work ahead," he said, his voice steady and filled with purpose.

Nashir, watching the villagers settle in, felt a deep sense of pride. "Yes," he said, his voice full of quiet resolve. "But this – this is the beginning of a new chapter. Together, we will create something that will endure."

As the villagers and the gods stood together in the fertile land of Garrents, they realised that this moment wasn't just about crossing a threshold – it was about stepping into a new future. One filled with hope, unity, and the promise of a home built with both their strength and the gifts of nature. The portal closed behind them, but in its place, the open world of Garrents stretched out, ready to be claimed by those who would shape it into a new beginning.

The transformation of this place was striking – what had once been a simple, cold village had now blossomed into a verdant oasis. Towering trees, thick with leaves and life, surrounded them. The land, once barren and untended, was now rich with new growth – vines climbing the walls of houses, flowers blooming in patches near the fields, and the unmistakable hum of life echoing through the air.

Before they could take it all in, they were greeted by the familiar faces of Garric and Eldric, who were waiting near the entrance to the village. They stood, arms crossed, with smiles that couldn't be contained. The sight of their returning friends and the new arrivals stirred something in them – pride, relief, and perhaps even a sense of awe.

"Welcome home," Garric called, his voice booming as he stepped forward to greet them. His broad chest rose and fell with a deep breath, the grizzled blacksmith now bearing a look of satisfaction as he took in the sight of the gods and villagers. His eyes were full of pride for what they had accomplished, and as he clapped Drunnyak on the shoulder, he said, "I never thought I'd see the day when the village would be brimming with life again."

Eldric stood beside him, his expression serious but softened by the relief of seeing their new home thriving. He stepped forward to embrace the gods, a hand resting on Alentar's shoulder. "We thought we'd have to face the unknown on our own," he said, his voice deep with gratitude. "But you've done more than protect us. You've given us hope."

The gods smiled, their faces a mixture of quiet pride and a touch of disbelief – after all they had been through, the sight before them was something they had longed for.

Suddenly, a small figure darted toward them, his feet light on the earth. Caelan, his bright blue eyes filled with excitement, ran straight to Drunnyak. The giant's towering presence didn't faze him. With a burst of energy, the boy leaped into Drunnyak's arms, wrapping his own arms around the warrior's thick neck.

Drunnyak's deep laugh echoed as he caught the boy, holding him high. "You've grown," Drunnyak said, his voice full of affection, the warmth in his tone betraying his usual tough exterior.

Caelan, smiling wide, clung to Drunnyak's neck, his little hands gripping tightly. "I knew you'd come back! I knew you wouldn't leave us!" he exclaimed, his voice full of joy.

Drunnyak's gaze softened, and for a moment, the fierceness of the battle-hardened warrior faded, replaced by a rare tenderness. "We never leave those we care about, little one," he said quietly, lifting Caelan up so that they were eye to eye. "You've been strong. And you'll be even stronger now."

The boy beamed, his face glowing with pride as he rested his head against Drunnyak's shoulder, knowing that in this moment, the gods' promises had been kept.

But there was no time for too much reflection yet. The villagers began to move forward, eager to set foot on the new soil, but there was one more matter to attend to – the supplies. As the last of the villagers crossed the portal, Drokan, the giant who had helped them before, moved into view. His massive frame loomed over the group, his powerful arms working effortlessly as he began to help move the crates of food, equipment and other essentials through the gateway.

Drokan's deep, rumbling voice carried across the field as he effortlessly lifted another heavy crate, his massive hands working with the ease of someone accustomed to strength. "Get the food across quickly. We don't want to waste any more time!" he called, his words steady and commanding as he reached for yet another load.

The villagers, those who had crossed first, moved quickly to assist, passing along smaller crates and supplies like a living chain. Thanks to Drokan's might, the task was completed swiftly, and soon a neat pile of essentials was stacked by the village entrance, ready for the new life that awaited them.

As Drokan set the crate down, his towering form cast a long shadow over Drunnyak and Garric. The two warriors exchanged a look, both of them moving toward the giant.

Drunnyak's voice was calm but firm as he spoke, the weight of his words clear. "This is Drokan," he said, nodding toward the giant. "He helped us at the giants' village. We owe him everything."

Garric's eyes narrowed in recognition, his hand instinctively resting on the hilt of his sword as he looked up at the giant. "I thought you seemed familiar," he said, his voice filled with both awe and curiosity. "You showed me kindness when I was there. You could've left me to my fate, but you didn't – and I believe that's why they didn't kill me, even as they tortured me."

Drokan, for the first time, shifted uneasily, his usual confidence faltering just slightly. He didn't speak at first, but after a moment, his deep voice rumbled again. "I'm glad you made it out," he said, his words low but filled with something unspoken. "I know what it's like, being trapped... feeling like you'll never see freedom again."

As the realisation hit, Garric's eyes widened, and a flash of memory struck him. A faint but powerful recollection from that dark time when he had been imprisoned. He had been chained, bound by the giants, his strength sapped and his will nearly broken. But there was something he hadn't fully understood at the time. Something that had shifted, something that had allowed him to escape. The chains had shattered – hadn't they? Garric blinked, his mind racing. "Wait..." he murmured, a sudden clarity filling his thoughts. His gaze snapped to Drokan, realisation blooming in his chest. "It was you, wasn't it? You're the one who broke the chains. You... helped me escape."

Drokan's eyes, usually so distant and unreadable, flickered with a mix of modesty and quiet pride. He nodded slowly, his face softening. "I knew you had to be free," he said, his voice tinged with a quiet humility. "I couldn't leave you there. No one should suffer like that."

Garric's heart skipped a beat. He had been so focused on escaping, so wrapped in the pain of his own captivity, that he hadn't thought about the person who had made his freedom possible. And now, here was Drokan, standing before him as a friend, an ally – one who had been a silent force in his escape. His eyes widened in disbelief as the weight of the truth settled in. "Without you," Garric whispered, his voice thick with gratitude, "none of this would have happened. You helped me… and because of that, we're all free now."

Drokan gave a shy nod, his expression almost unrecognisable in its warmth. "And now, we are all free," he said quietly, his words more meaningful than anything that had been said before.

A silence hung between them, deep and burdened by the gravity of all they had endured together. The giant, once an imposing figure, now stood before them with a quiet dignity that spoke volumes. For Garric, it was a moment of realisation – of understanding that the path to freedom had not been a single journey, but a shared effort, where even the smallest act of kindness could change everything.

Drunnyak, standing beside them, gave a small, knowing smile. "We're stronger together," he said, the words simple but filled with truth. "Drokan's actions prove that."

Garric placed a hand on Drokan's massive shoulder, his voice filled with gratitude and respect. "And for that, we owe you more than words can say."

The giant merely nodded, looking from one to the other, his pride in their new-found freedom evident in his gaze. "The past is behind us," Drokan said softly, "and the future is ahead. We walk it together, all of us."

The three of them stood in silent acknowledgement, the weight of their shared experience lingering in the air. The villagers, moving around them, felt the significance of the moment. It was more than just the transport of supplies – it was a moment of unity, a moment where past struggles were forgiven, and a new chapter was ready to be written.

Nashir, taking in the bustling activity, couldn't help but smile. "Well done, everyone," he said, his eyes softening as he watched the scene unfold. "We've brought not only ourselves here, but everything we need to thrive."

Eldric nodded, his voice filled with pride. "This is the beginning," he said. "The beginning of something better."

The villagers began to spread out, the excitement of their new home palpable in the air. They gazed at the fields that stretched wide in every direction, the lush greenery that had been absent for so long. The sounds of nature – the rustling of leaves, the chirping of distant birds, the hum of insects – were a welcome symphony to their ears. The once-cold and barren village of Garrents had transformed into a thriving sanctuary full of life.

Nashir turned to the gathered group. "This place will grow with us," he said, his voice filled with the power of nature itself. "The land listens to us, and it will flourish as we do."

Taril, ever the one to bring lightness to the moment, slapped Drunnyak on the back with a hearty laugh. "Nashir saved us from having to carry everything after all," he said, his eyes twinkling with mischief. "Though you certainly make it look easy, Drunnyak. I might start calling you the ox of the village."

Drunnyak grinned widely, the deep rumble of his laugh echoing through the group. "Well, I'd prefer to be called something a bit more impressive, but I'll take it," he said, glancing over at the villagers, who were now beginning to set up their new homes. With the help of the people from Garrents, they were working swiftly, bringing life and purpose to the village that had once felt like a distant hope.

Garric and Eldric, shoulder to shoulder, moved around with the villagers, guiding them as they arranged supplies and secured their new homes. The homes themselves were already standing tall, sturdy and warm, built by Nashir's design. The structures were seamlessly integrated into the land, carved into the vast mountainsides that now felt like a natural extension of the village. Borgrim, always at the heart of any practical task, was already moving to ensure the hearths were properly stocked and the firewood was ready for the coming cold nights. His broad hands worked with efficiency, despite his gruff demeanour, as he exchanged grins with the other villagers.

Further down, Tharn was helping a group of villagers settle into their new homes, the elderly man guiding the children toward their new rooms, his weathered face softening with every step. Even though he was always grumpy whilst working and talking to others, his voice carried gently as he reassured the young ones. "This is your home now. Let the mountain cradle you as it cradles us."

The homes, nestled into the mountain itself, were warm and inviting, filled with the soft glow of lantern light. Nashir had used his connection to nature to ensure that each home blended perfectly with the surroundings. The mountain's great rock faces, once daunting and cold, now had purpose and warmth. Bridges built from the wood of ancient trees connected the homes, and steps carved into the stone led up the mountainside, weaving like a natural path that merged with the land. Vines, thick and verdant, wound around the buildings, keeping the warmth of the hearths inside, while the cool mountain breeze gently filtered through the windows, fresh with the scent of pine and earth.

It was a place of peace, a haven forged by the gods and the hands of those who had come together, and the villagers were already making it their own. They laughed as they worked, sharing stories with the people of Garrents, helping one another with the tasks that would build their new lives.

The laughter carried through the village, mingling with the crackling of fires and the occasional burst of cheer from the children running through the pathways, their faces glowing with excitement. The village, once cold and uninviting, was now a home filled with life. The warmth of their hearths seemed to stretch out to the mountains themselves, as if the land had accepted them, its embrace strong and enduring.

Drunnyak took it all in, his heart light as he looked at the peaceful scene before him. "Well," he said, looking at Nashir, who stood nearby with a quiet smile of his own, "you've outdone yourself this time. This place is everything we've fought for, and more."

Nashir gave a small, contented nod, watching the villagers settle into their new homes. "We've all outdone ourselves," he said, his voice full of satisfaction. "It's not just the land. It's the people. Together, we've created something lasting."

With the evening beginning and the stars remaining hidden behind the thick clouds, the village was alive with the warmth of new beginnings. The sounds of laughter, the soft murmurs of contentment, and the flickering of firelight were all that could be heard. The gods stood together, proud of what they had created.

As the evening sky darkened, villagers and gods alike gathered in the village centre. The warmth of the fires spread through the air, and the scent of food cooking filled the space. The sounds of laughter, conversation, and even the soft melodies of a flute played by one of the villagers filled the air, marking the beginning of a new chapter.

Alanteas, his gaze shifting from the bustling activity around him to the distant horizon, let out a soft sigh, his lips curling into a bittersweet grin. "It's been so long since I've seen a place like this," he said, his voice tinged with a hint of sorrow. "The memory feels like it belongs to another lifetime, one I can hardly grasp any more." His eyes glinted with a quiet joy, though, as he watched the village come to life, the beauty of it all unfolding before him. "But now, seeing this with my own eyes, it feels like something from the past, something worth remembering."

The others nodded in agreement, each feeling the weight of the moment – the weight of what had been accomplished and what lay ahead. It wasn't just the supplies that had made the journey, nor the land they had crossed; it was the sense of purpose that had brought them all here, that had pushed them forward when all seemed lost.

Nashir stood near the edge of the village, looking out at the fields. "This place is ours now. We will protect it, nurture it, and watch it grow," he said quietly, a gentle smile tugging at his lips.

As they gazed out across Garrents, their eyes moved over the villagers from both the new and old settlements, now merging seamlessly in their daily tasks. They saw the blacksmiths at their anvils, the clanging of hammers ringing through the air as they forged tools and weapons. Carpenters worked alongside builders, shaping the timber that would form the next homes, while farmers, their hands stained with the earth, carefully tended to the crops that would feed the growing community.

The gods' eyes lingered on the faces of the villagers – some familiar, some new, but all united by the same sense of purpose. The energy was different now, lighter and more hopeful. There was a rhythm to their movements, a quiet harmony in how they worked together, as if the land itself had forged them into a single, thriving people.

A peaceful stillness settled over the gods as they took it all in. The journey had been long, the road ahead still uncertain, but in this moment, they could feel that they had built a home. The village, once a place of struggle and survival, had been transformed – now it was alive with hope, with laughter, with the sense of belonging that had been absent for so long, and in the midst of it all, the villagers finally had the peace they had been fighting for. For the first time in what felt like forever, they could simply breathe.

The gods shared a quiet look, their hearts swelling with a deep satisfaction. Though the work was far from over, they knew this was the foundation of something lasting, something true.

They stood there, watching this outpouring of emotion. The sight of the villagers' joy, the raw relief and gratitude in their eyes, stirred something deep within them. And in that moment, something else shifted – inside them, within the very land itself. They felt a surge of power – not the violent, raw energy of when they first came to the village, but something far more immersive, far more meaningful. It was as though their connection to Maud had deepened, resonating with the energy of the land itself. They could feel the warmth of the earth beneath their feet, the pulse of life all around them. It was the kind of energy that made them feel alive, whole, and more connected than ever before.

Niv, standing near the centre of it all, felt it first. The sapphire she had carried since opening Ian's lab pulsed in her hand, a soft glow emanating from within. She had felt the magic surge before, but this was different – more powerful, more potent. It seemed as though the very energy of ancient magic itself pulsed within the gemstone, and now it flowed directly into her. Her body hummed with the power she held, and before she could stop it, she felt herself rising off the ground.

The villagers gasped as they saw Niv levitating, her figure glowing in the warmth of the energy around her. Her amber eyes gleamed brighter, and her silver-blonde hair shimmered with a light that seemed to come from within. She held the sapphire in her hand as though it were the very heart of the world. Slowly, she spread her arms wide, feeling the power course through her.

The energy from her hands expanded outward, a wave of glowing light that wrapped around the village like a protective blanket. The canopy above them, which had once been a simple shelter, now pulsed with the energy she had released. The light spread outward, enveloping the village in a shield of magic – a protective barrier woven from ancient magic itself, a barrier that would keep them safe from the dangers lurking beyond. The air around them hummed with an energy so pure, so powerful, that even the gods felt it.

Niv, Taril, Nashir and Opilkhos felt a surge of recognition as the energy around them pulsed. It was the same force that had stirred before – the same presence they had felt when the fountain revealed the sapphire and when Ian's lab had come to life.

Drunnyak, always the one to make light of any situation, let out a low whistle. "Well, that's a neat trick," he said, his voice carrying a hint of amusement and awe as he watched Niv's power flow through the land.

Taril grinned, his usual gruff tone softened by the awe in his voice. "Aye, lass. You've outdone yourself."

Even Opilkhos, whose seriousness had always been a defining trait, allowed the smallest of grins to creep across his face. He looked at Niv, then back to the villagers, and for once, the hardness in his eyes softened. "Impressive," he said, his voice low but filled with respect.

But as the energy expanded, something else stirred. The vines that had once blocked the steps to Ian's lab, thick and dense, began to twitch, as if awakening to the presence of the gods. Slowly, they began to part, gently retracting as if guided by some unseen force. As the vines moved aside, a new sight appeared – a vision, a memory.

A spectral hologram began to form before them. At first, it was faint, like a cloud of mist, but soon it solidified into a figure – Ian

Garrents. He stood before them, not in body, but in spectral form. His features were faint, as though seen through a veil, but the warmth and wisdom of his presence were unmistakable.

"Welcome back, brothers." Ian's voice rang out, clear and strong despite the ghostly nature of his form. His eyes, though ghostly, locked with theirs, filled with recognition, understanding, and a deep sense of peace.

The gods stood frozen, a heavy silence falling over them as they took in the sight of the elder who had guided them through the darkest days of their journey. The villagers too watched in awe. Ian's presence, even in this ethereal form, was a testament to the sacrifices that had been made, to the bonds that had been forged, and to the journey they had all shared.

Nashir stepped forward, his voice quiet but filled with emotion. "Ian..." he whispered, almost reverently. "I remember he used to leave these memories for us, or send them through the veil as messages."

Ian's image smiled faintly, the spectral figure nodding as though he had heard their thoughts, as if the very essence of the land itself had whispered to him. His form shimmered with a quiet power, his presence undeniable even in this ethereal state. His eyes, though ghostly, shone with a deep understanding, the weight of years lost, and memories forgotten pressing against his ancient soul. "You've done it." Ian's voice came softly, but with a weight that resonated deeply in their hearts. "You've brought life back to this land, and only through that could my essence be revealed through the gem I left inside this fountain. For that, I am proud." His words seemed to hang in the air, heavy with meaning, but there was something more in his gaze. He stopped, looking at them as if weighing his next words, the silence stretching between them. "I always expected you would awaken," Ian continued, his voice steady but tinged with sorrow. "I knew the time would come when you would return, though I wasn't certain when or how. I spent centuries, countless hours studying the possibilities. I pinpointed places throughout the land – places where our old home, our hall of creation, might return. Where the rift could shift from our plane back into this world. But I couldn't know for sure, since after the battle with our father, and without you around, my power became very limited. There was no certainty. Only hope."

There was a pause, as if the weight of what he was about to reveal carried a great burden. "When you vanished, so much changed." Ian's voice grew darker, his expression shifting with the gravity of his words. "I couldn't keep up with the chaos that followed. So much happened… things I could never have foreseen." Ian's spectral form flickered for a moment, as if he were gathering himself before speaking again. His gaze shifted, distant and pained, before returning to his friends before him. The sadness in his eyes was palpable, a deep, old sorrow that seemed to radiate from him. His voice, though soft, carried the weight of years of regret. "And Harinnil, our young brother…" Ian's voice trembled slightly as he spoke the name, a quiet sadness lingering in the air. "What became of him after the battle with the All-Father? I watched as he was consumed, twisted into something else – something unrecognisable. A monster, a soulless thing, drifting further away with every passing day. His heart… his heart is lost to shadow now."

He drew quiet, his gaze far off, as though the pain of those memories was too much to bear. "If I'm not here now, speaking to you in person, it is because something has happened to me too." Ian's voice broke with sorrow, the weight of unspoken years pressing down on him. "I tried to reason with him. For years, I tried to reach him, to help him find peace, but the burden of his pain… it was too much to overcome. He couldn't understand how, after everything he had done, he still couldn't find peace. The loss of Lena, the gnawing feeling of worms eating his flesh… it drove him further into the shadows. His mind, his heart shattered, and I… I couldn't fix it." There was a moment of silence, thick with the weight of Ian's words, as the sorrow deepened in his eyes. His form seemed to flicker, as though the emotions were too much for his spectral presence to bear. "I wanted so badly to give him peace," he whispered, his voice barely audible. "I wanted him to find rest, to heal. But I failed him. I couldn't save him from the torment he felt inside. I couldn't give him the solace he craved."

Ian's shoulders seemed to slump under the immense weight of his grief. "I fear the world has changed in ways we can't even begin to comprehend. What happened to him... it's beyond anything I could have imagined. But still, part of me clings to a flicker of hope." His gaze lifted then, looking directly at them. "Perhaps there is still a chance for him, though it's a path I cannot walk. Perhaps... perhaps he can be restored, but that will be for you to decide. I cannot guide you there, not now." His form grew quieter, more distant, as if he were slowly fading into the memories he had kept locked away for so long. "I only ask that you remember him – not for what he became, but for who he was before the darkness consumed him. Remember him as the brother who once fought by your side, who believed in a better world, before all of this." His voice faltered, filled with deep sorrow, before he finally spoke his last words. "I only hope that somehow, you can find him. And if not, then I pray you bring him peace – the peace I could not."

With that, Ian's figure seemed to dissolve into the air, his sadness lingering long after his image faded. The gods stood silent, each of them feeling the weight of his words, the sorrow that had followed Harinnil's descent into darkness. The memory of Ian's grief, his loss, settled over them like a shadow – one they would have to face as they continued on their journey.

"I have always believed in you all." Ian's voice resonated with quiet strength, though it trembled with the weight of time and loss. "You've done what I could not. Now, let this place thrive as it was always meant to. The world you've reclaimed is yours to shape. The path ahead, though fraught with uncertainty, is yours to walk. And you will walk it together." As Ian's words faded, his image flickered, slowly beginning to dissolve into the ether. Yet his voice lingered, a haunting echo on the wind. "But there is more to be done. You cannot rest, for there are others to save – others who still need you. Only by doing so, by restoring the lost essence of this world, will your powers be renewed. Each of you carries within you a divine essence, a gem lost over time, just like the sapphire you now hold. You must find your own, and only then, after saving the people of Maud, will you ascend to your true divinity. Only then will you become what you were meant to be."

The voice seemed to grow fainter, but the weight of his words hung in the air long after his spectral form had vanished. The gods stood in solemn silence, feeling the call to action reverberate deep within them. The world they had entered was not just one of new beginnings – it was one that required their sacrifice, their strength, and their rediscovery of what had been lost.

The promise of the future lay before them, heavy with the responsibility of what must come. But as they turned toward the work ahead, they knew this was only the beginning of the journey that would shape their fate and the fate of Maud itself.

The words hung in the air, a gentle weight that settled on all of them. The villagers, seeing the truth of Ian's words, began to cheer once again, but this time it was not just for the gods who had saved them – it was for Ian, for everything he had done, for the legacy he had left behind.

And as the villagers cheered and the gods felt the weight of the moment, the land around them seemed to come alive. The warmth of their bond, the power of their unity, resonated through the air. The village, now fully protected, was more than just a place – it was a living, breathing testament to their strength and their shared purpose.

The gods stood tall, their eyes scanning the gathered villagers, whose once-fearful hearts had now transformed into unwavering unity. The village, now one, had already begun to thrive, but in this moment, as the energy of the gods surged through the land, a deeper understanding settled within them all. The villagers, once from two separate places, now stood as one people, bound by a shared hope, strengthened by the divine presence of their protectors.

As they gazed across the village, the sound of soft murmurs and quiet laughter filled the air. Each individual, whether man or beast, had a place now, each contributing to the unity of this new world. The gods could feel the pulse of life as it surged stronger with every passing moment, the bond between them and the villagers deepening.

And then, amidst the stillness, a figure stepped forward – Caelan, his young eyes glistening with tears. He moved through the crowd, his feet light but purposeful, walking toward the gods with the quiet strength of one who had already made a vow, though none had spoken it aloud. He stopped before them, his heart full, his gaze steady as he looked up to meet the eyes of each god. Without a word, the boy dropped to his knees, his small form bowed with reverence. His voice, though soft, carried the weight of a promise, of an oath made with the purest sincerity. "I swear to protect this world, as you have protected us," he said, his voice trembling with emotion. "I will carry your strength in my heart always."

Garric and Eldric looked at young Caelan proudly. This child, at such a young age, not only felt responsibility, but also shared pain and endured. The gods stood, silent but deeply moved by the sincerity of his words.

In the stillness that followed, something extraordinary happened. One by one, the villagers – those who had once been hesitant, uncertain – moved forward. They knelt without being told, their actions born not of fear or obligation, but of deep, unwavering respect and admiration for the gods who had given them this chance at life. From the oldest to the youngest, from the animals of the land to the creatures of the forest, all of them seemed to sense the weight of the moment.

Without a single word, they surrounded the gods, not out of worship, but out of gratitude. The gods felt the energy surge in the air, the love, the trust – they were no longer just protectors, but a part of the very life force that pulsed through the land. The villagers, though no longer in awe of them in fear, now understood the full extent of what had been done for them.

In the quiet, there was no need for grand speeches or proclamations. The gods and their people shared a wordless understanding, a bond that went beyond anything spoken or seen. It was in the way the villagers gazed at the gods, the way the animals stood by their sides, the way nature itself seemed to breathe in harmony with the people and the gods.

And then, in that silence, Nashir stepped forward, his voice a steady echo of truth. "We are more than protectors," he said, his words carrying the weight of their collective purpose. "We are your guides, your guardians, and we will stand by you for as long as you need us."

Drunnyak's deep voice followed, full of warmth. "This land is as much ours as it is yours. We will give everything we have to see it thrive."

Taril raised his head, his stern gaze softened by the weight of what they had all shared. "Together, we will see this place grow. And we will guard it, always."

Opilkhos, though still composed as ever, allowed a rare smile to touch his lips, the burden of his past lightened by the unity he felt with those around him. "We won't stop," he said simply, his words filled with quiet certainty. "Not until this world is whole again."

And as the villagers rose to their feet, a sense of peace settled over them – one that they had never known before, not in all the years of their struggle. Their protectors were here. And they were not alone any more.

As the gods stood in front of them, they could feel the weight of the vow they had made: a vow not just to protect, but to restore. This was not just about survival – it was about rebirth.

Caelan, still standing before them, looked at the gods once more. His tears had dried, but his heart swelled with the knowledge that they were safe. That they were home.

The gods shared a moment of quiet, their hearts full, knowing that this was only the beginning. The villagers had already begun to build their lives, but there was much work yet to be done. They had saved Maud, but to truly heal it, to make it whole once more, they would have to dig deeper. They would need to find the lost pieces of themselves – their divine essence – and only then would they ascend to the full power they'd once wielded.

But for now, they were ready.

The gods turned toward the horizon, where the village stretched out before them – united, thriving, and stronger than ever. And in that moment, they knew their purpose was clear. They were bound to this world, to these people. Together, they would face whatever came next.

The future was theirs to shape.

As the night stretched on, the air cool and still, only a few stood watch over the wall and gate near the trench, guarding the only remaining entry to the village. This section of the village, once a symbol of the constant threat of undead invaders, now stood secure, thanks to Nashir and the other gods. Their powerful connection to nature had woven a living defence that kept the dead at bay, the vibrant plants and trees growing with purpose, sealing off the area. The land itself had become a shield, a testament to the gods' strength.

The hologram of Ian had vanished, leaving only the warmth of his final words lingering in the air, but the weight of his message remained. Garrents, though now more secure than ever, still had much work ahead.

The village needed more than just protection – it needed to be a home, a thriving sanctuary where people could not only survive, but flourish. Alanteas knew this, and as the night deepened, he felt the stirring of a greater purpose. He turned toward the gods, seeking guidance.

As the others made their way to their respective places, Alanteas stood near the fire, waiting for them to approach. With the quiet humility that came with his reverence for the gods, he spoke. "I believe we must look beyond Garrents now," Alanteas said, his voice steady, yet filled with determination. "The villagers are strong, but there are others out there – other villages still in need of protection or an opportunity for a better life like these people. I want to scout those places, find those who need saving, so we can bring them under our protection."

The gods exchanged looks, their eyes gleaming in the firelight.

It was Nashir who spoke first, his voice calm and filled with the wisdom of the earth. "You speak of the path ahead, Alanteas, but Garrents is still in its early days. It needs more than just protection – it needs to be solidified. The villagers need to be trained, to understand their place in this world. We cannot abandon them now."

Alanteas nodded, understanding the weight of Nashir's words. "Of course, Uncle," he said, a calm resolve in his voice. "But while you all focus on helping the villagers grow stronger, once they are secure and ready to stand on their own, I will probably be back after scouting new villages. I'll return with a map to guide us in our next steps."

Nashir's gaze softened as he looked upon Alanteas, sensing the determination in his voice. "You're wise to want to plan ahead, Alanteas. But remember, the village is a living thing. It needs time to establish itself, to strengthen its roots. It's your task now to explore beyond, but don't rush it. Take the time you need, and when you return, you'll bring us the knowledge we need."

Alanteas's eyes brightened as he spoke, a thought crossing his mind. "Perhaps... perhaps I could learn your magic, in some smaller form. Something less powerful, more suited to my needs. If I could do that, I could mark trees as I travel – specific ones – and return here much faster. I could create a connection between the villages and us. It might take longer for me to master, but it could be a valuable tool for our work in the future."

Nashir considered this for a moment, his eyes narrowing thoughtfully. "You've always been attuned to the land, Alanteas. It's possible you could learn the magic. It wouldn't be as powerful as mine, but with practice, you could certainly make it work in your favour. It would take time, but the bond between you and the trees would allow you to connect with them, return quickly, and guide us to where we need to go."

"Which tree would you use?" Opilkhos asked, intrigued by the idea.

Alanteas thought for a moment. "An elder oak, I think," he said, his voice calm as he gazed into the distance. "They're strong, their roots run deep into the earth. I would carve a mark on each one, leaving a symbol that would serve as a beacon for me to return to, no matter how far I travel."

Nashir nodded approvingly. "The elder oak is a perfect choice. It's ancient, deeply connected to the land. Its power comes from its endurance, its ability to withstand through the ages. If you mark it properly, you'll have a connection with the land that will allow you to return to these spots. You'll be able to travel across the land with a deeper understanding of it – and when you return, we can use that knowledge to move faster and more efficiently."

The gods stood in silent agreement, each of them sensing the potential in Alanteas's plan. Opilkhos stepped forward, his serious demeanour softening with a slight smile. "This is a brilliant idea. You can act as our scout and guide, not just finding villages, but marking them for us, allowing us to move between them without delay."

Nashir smiled. "The journey ahead is long, but with this connection, Alanteas, you will shorten the path for us. When you return, we will be ready to act. You will not only bring back the villages' information, but also the wisdom of the land itself."

Alanteas bowed his head, humbled by the trust they placed in him. "Thank you. I will learn quickly, and when I return, I'll be ready to bring you all the information we need."

The gods shared a quiet moment, knowing that this plan would set their mission on a different, faster course. With Alanteas as their scout, marked by the trees and guided by the land, they would not just wait for things to unfold – they would move faster than they had ever expected.

As the night deepened, Alanteas felt a profound certainty settle within him. His path, once shrouded in uncertainty, was now clear – a journey filled with purpose and the weight of responsibility. He was no longer just a scout or a wanderer; he was the bearer of knowledge, the one who would connect the scattered villages and lead them toward a brighter future. With the gods' blessing, his return would mark the next chapter in their shared destiny.

Without hesitation, Alanteas gathered the supplies he needed for his journey – simple provisions, paper to draw his map, a few tools for marking the land – and prepared himself to leave. Every movement was decisive. The time for doubt was gone; there was only the road ahead.

As he approached the edge of the village, Alentar was waiting for him, standing quietly in the shadow of the outer walls. Their eyes met – no words were exchanged, for none were needed. Alentar's gaze spoke volumes, his approval clear, his concern evident in the way his eyes softened. There was no grand farewell, no lengthy speech. Instead, Alanteas felt the silent weight of his master's support. The bond between them, forged through shared battles and unspoken understanding, was all the reassurance Alanteas needed.

Without another word, Alanteas stepped forward, and the two embraced – strong, brief, but full of meaning. The embrace was one of trust and love, the last moment of warmth before Alanteas stepped into the unknown.

While the villagers gathered around hearths, sharing laughter and warmth, their new lives taking root, Alanteas silently slipped into the night. The sounds of celebration echoed behind him, but his mind was already ahead – on the villages he would discover, the knowledge he would uncover, and the promise of his return. As the darkness of the night swallowed him whole, he felt the land beneath his feet, the promise of the trees and the earth guiding him forward, as the distant village of Garrents became nothing but a memory, for now.

Meanwhile, the rest of the villagers gathered around the gods, their laughter and cheer filling the air. Food and drink flowed in abundance – more than they had ever imagined. Even those who had once been sceptical, doubtful that they would ever truly be safe, now laughed without reservation. They had seen the gods' magic and the land's protection, and they believed – deeply and fully – that they had found a place where they could thrive.

As the firelight danced in the centre of the village, the gods gathered closely, their voices low but steady. They spoke to each other, exchanging thoughts of the future. The work was far from over, but for now, they would take this moment to reflect. They spoke of what should come when the morning arrived – when they would need to gather the knowledge of the entire village. The experience of every villager would be crucial in understanding how to proceed, how to ensure their continued survival and growth.

"We need to learn everything." Drunnyak's voice carried through the murmurs, his tone thoughtful but grounded. "Every skill, every lesson. We can't make decisions without their wisdom."

Taril nodded, his hand resting on his war hammer as he glanced at the villagers. "Tomorrow, we'll speak of the future. But tonight… tonight we share this moment."

And so they did. The gods, the protectors, joined the villagers in their celebration. Their voices joined in song, their hearts lifted by the bond between them. Yet amidst the revelry, Niv stood back slightly, her eyes tracing the glowing figure of Ian's sapphire, the gemstone that had once held his divine essence, now floating serenely above the canopy. The sapphire pulsed with soft light, casting a protective glow over the village. It stood as a beacon, guarding them from outside eyes, from any threat that might dare approach.

Niv's lips curved into a grin as she watched it, but her gaze soon shifted, finding Garric. Their eyes met, and for a brief moment, the noise of the celebration faded. A quiet understanding passed between them, something unspoken but deeply felt.

A blush crept up Niv's cheeks as she caught the look in his eyes – one that mirrored her own. Without a word, they exchanged their silent thoughts, their connection unmistakable.

Garric's lips curved into a smile, the corners of his eyes crinkling. "Later?" he mouthed, the word a gentle promise.

Niv smiled softly, her heart racing with the familiarity of the moment. "Yes," she whispered, her voice carrying only enough for him to hear. "Soon."

Their exchange was tender, a shared secret amidst the joy of the night, and both of them felt the warmth of it in the depths of their souls.

As the night carried on, the villagers celebrated their new-found safety, their laughter echoing into the cool air. But for a brief moment, amid the merriment, Niv and Garric shared a quiet, intimate bond. No words were needed. The future was full of possibilities, and for now, their hearts beat as one, bound by the warmth of their connection and the promise of moments yet to come.

A RENEWED PURPOSE

As the days passed, Garrents continued to flourish, each day bringing a new rhythm to the village's life. The villagers, now more unified than ever, worked together in perfect harmony, their tasks flowing with the grace of a well-rehearsed dance. The land itself seemed to thrive beneath their hands, nourished by the gods' gifts and the villagers' unyielding determination. People who had once known only the hardships of survival now revelled in the promise of a brighter future.

The gods, no longer distant figures, were now fully immersed in the village's daily life.

Garric, the general, was now solely focused on organising the village infantry, ensuring they remained vigilant, prepared for any threat, though none had come in some time. Eldric, his brother and the captain, his right hand in maintaining the soldiers' readiness, worked tirelessly to keep them at their peak performance. Together, they led the soldiers with calm strength and unwavering resolve, knowing the importance of keeping the peace while being prepared for any challenge.

But while the warriors kept the village safe, it was Stephen, affectionately known as 'King Steve', who had become the steady heart of the village. A wise man with over sixty winters, Stephen had a sharp mind for organisation and a deep understanding of people. His leadership was one of patience, empathy and quiet strength, and in the past weeks he had earned the respect of all, even that of Garric, the former leader of the village. Despite his title of 'King Steve' being more a token of affection than an official role, Stephen had proven himself to be an invaluable adviser. Garric now trusted this new leader, often seeking his counsel, and the two had become great friends.

Stephen's vision for the village was clear and thoughtful. "The elders," he had said one evening, "should now enjoy their rest, their retirement from the burden of hard labour. They've earned it." It was Stephen who had suggested that the children learn a trade that they felt drawn to, to develop their own skills and passions. But he also emphasised the importance of survival skills. "Each must learn to defend themselves," he had said, his voice steady. "We cannot be entirely reliant on the gods. They have given us the tools to survive, but we must never forget how to protect ourselves, should the need arise."

Delm, the elderly man from the village of the giants, had taken responsibility for the crops and plantations. His hands, weathered with age but steady and sure, oversaw the growth of the village's food. Delm had once been a man of hardship, forced to labour under the watchful eyes of the giants, but now, with the help of Nashir, ever in tune with the land, he continued to work closely with the farmers, teaching them to connect with the earth in ways they had never thought possible. He showed them how to feel the pulse of the ground beneath their feet, how to listen to the whispers of the trees and the plants, to understand the natural rhythms of life. His guidance was more than just practical – he helped them unlock the hidden magic of nature that flowed through every living thing.

With his help, some of the farmers discovered that they could call upon nature's magic to nurture their crops. They could coax the earth to yield fruits so vibrant, so full of life, that they could hardly believe their eyes. The apples were sweeter than anything they had ever tasted, the grains richer and more abundant, the vegetables flourishing like never before. Even the simplest of meals tasted like a feast, full of the life and vitality of the land itself. Nashir's presence had not only brought peace to the village, but had rekindled a deeper bond with nature, turning their crops into something extraordinary.

Garrk, the blacksmith from the giants' village, had proven himself indispensable. With the guidance of Borgrim and Taril, he crafted pristine armour for the soldiers, building designs that combined the practicality of dwarven craftsmanship with the durability required for battle. Each piece of armour was a work of art – strong, resilient, and designed for mobility, ensuring the soldiers were equipped for whatever challenges lay ahead.

"Look at this," Borgrim had said one day, inspecting the armour with his sharp eyes. "This will save lives. Not just a shield, but a fortress. And with Taril's expertise… I'll be proud to wear it myself if the time comes."

They were also working on tools and equipment to improve the lives of the villagers – everything from improved farming implements to sturdy carts for transporting goods. The village was no longer just surviving; it was building, growing and advancing.

And so, the village moved forward – prosperous, united, and filled with the kind of hope that had once seemed impossible.

Meanwhile, Niv and Opilkhos, despite their roles as warriors, had also embraced the more mystical aspects of their power. Niv, with her keen perception and connection to magic, spent her days identifying those in the village who could wield magic, but not through books or the written word. She called them 'natural sorcerers'. These individuals had an innate connection to magic, a gift that surged through them without the need for study. She had quickly noticed that Caelan, the young boy, was one of the most advanced among them. After only a few days of shadowing Niv, Caelan had shown an unparalleled connection to the flow of magic, his powers far beyond what one would expect from someone so young. Niv had a proud glint in her eye as she watched him, knowing that his potential would be limitless with the right guidance – after all, he was a direct descendant of Ian.

Opilkhos too had his own form of magic. Unlike Niv's natural affinity, Opilkhos wielded two distinct types of power – one that flowed from his very essence, a pure gift tied to his kind heart and spirit, and the other, more learned and structured, was magic born from deep study and spells he had begun to write. Opilkhos, like Ian and Harinnil before him, knew that magic could be both an instinct and a science. He started writing spells, codifying his teachings so that those with the potential for magic could study and harness its power in a controlled, disciplined way.

Alentar took on the task of training a new generation of scouts and rangers. With the keen focus and precision that had made him the greatest hunter in Maud, he shared his skills with those eager to learn. His lessons were about more than just tracking or surviving in the wild – he taught them the art of becoming invisible, of blending into the surroundings so perfectly that even the sharpest eyes could not catch their presence.

With each lesson, Alentar demonstrated how to move without a sound, how to vanish into the shadows, how to read the subtle signs of the land. The soldiers, intrigued by his abilities, joined in, eager to improve their own skills. They marvelled at Alentar's precision with a bow – his arrows always finding their mark, as if guided by an unseen hand. No matter the distance, no matter the target, Alentar's aim never faltered. "The key," he would say, "is patience. Every shot is an extension of your will. You must not only aim at the target, but become one with it." The soldiers watched in awe, their skills improving under his watchful eye.

And then one day, a new challenge awaited.

Annah, Eamonn's granddaughter, had trained tirelessly under Alentar's tutelage, absorbing every lesson with determination and a fierce desire to prove herself. She was small, but her spirit burned brightly – she had shown no hesitation, no fear in the face of the harshest training, and now, after weeks of rigorous practice, she was about to take her final test.

The village gathered silently as Alentar stood at the front of the clearing, a proud but quiet figure. In the distance, Annah moved swiftly, her steps light and measured, her form a perfect blend with the surroundings. She disappeared into the trees as if she were part of them, her movements as fluid as the wind. The onlookers held their breath, watching as she navigated the terrain with an expert's ease, her senses heightened, her eyes scanning for the slightest signs of danger. With each movement, she seemed to become one with the forest itself, as if she belonged to the land.

When she finally emerged from the shadows, her task completed with flawless precision, the entire group stood in stunned silence. Alentar's eyes, though usually reserved, showed a glimmer of pride. He approached her and, without a word, placed the ranger's cloak around her shoulders – simple, but symbolic of her accomplishments. Then, he handed her a set of bracers, finely crafted and decorated with intricate elvish runes. The words etched upon them read, 'A Proud Granddaughter'.

The villagers, who had been watching in reverence, erupted into a silent, respectful applause. It was a rare display, for in this moment, no words were necessary. The achievement spoke for itself. Annah stood there, her chest swelling with pride, the weight of her ancestors behind her, her lineage now part of the village's strength.

Alentar placed a hand on her shoulder, his voice soft but filled with the gravity of the moment. "You've done well, Annah. Your grandfather would be proud."

Annah's face flushed, her eyes bright with unshed tears, but she held her ground. She had earned her place, not just as Eamonn's granddaughter, but as a new member of the rangers – a protector of the village, just as those before her had been.

The gods, standing quietly on the outskirts, felt the significance of the moment. This was not just the training of a new ranger – it was the passing of a torch, the continuation of a legacy. Annah, though young, had already shown the strength and resolve of her forebears.

As the villagers clapped, the sound was not just of appreciation – it was a shared acknowledgement of their future, of the strength that now lay in their hands, the hands of the next generation. And for Alentar, the moment was a quiet triumph of his own. He had not only trained a ranger; he had helped shape a future.

Drunnyak and Taril, both masters in their own right, trained the villagers and soldiers with a fierce yet nurturing intensity, each focusing on different aspects of combat and defence. Their methods were a blend of ancient wisdom, raw power, and practical experience.

Drunnyak was a towering figure – 2.2 metres of raw muscle and battle-hardened experience. His training sessions were demanding, not just because of the physical strength required, but because of the mental focus that came with them. As a god of strength and war, Drunnyak was keen to teach the villagers and soldiers the importance of power in combat, but with a deep understanding of its limits.

When he trained, it was always hands-on. Drunnyak would often engage in sparring sessions, demonstrating each technique with brutal effectiveness. His philosophy was simple: strength is nothing if you can't control it.

He taught the soldiers how to properly wield their weapons – especially axes and swords, for he was a master with both. But he also emphasised the importance of being adaptable. "The weapon should feel like an extension of your arm," Drunnyak would say, his voice booming over the clang of metal against metal. "Know your blade like you know your own skin. If it feels like a part of you, you'll never miss your strike."

But it wasn't just about weaponry. Drunnyak, with his immense strength, made sure every soldier learned hand-to-hand combat. His movements were fluid yet powerful – every strike calculated with devastating precision. He would often fight with his students in close quarters, teaching them how to use their body weight, leverage, and brute force to take down an opponent, even without a weapon.

"Sometimes, the enemy is closer than you think," Drunnyak would grunt as he tossed a soldier to the ground with a practised swipe of his arm. "You must be able to fight without hesitation, without a weapon if necessary."

His training was gruelling, but for those who survived his methods, it built an unshakeable confidence in their physical abilities. Every soldier that passed through Drunnyak's training felt stronger – ready to face any foe, with the raw power to match it.

Taril, the god of the dwarves, was more reserved in his approach to combat, but no less effective. His focus was on defence and technique, as well as the understanding of the battlefield itself. A tactician and a warrior, Taril knew that raw strength wasn't always enough in the heat of battle. What truly protected a soldier, what truly made them resilient, was their ability to defend, to endure.

Taril's students often saw him first as a master of the war hammer, but his true brilliance lay in the way he taught them to read the flow of combat. His lessons focused on footwork, on positioning, and on how to protect themselves while being an unyielding force in their own right.

He often spoke of defence as a weapon, and he demonstrated it first-hand. "If you know where your enemy will strike, you've already won half the battle," Taril would say, his voice a deep rumble as he swung his hammer in practised arcs. "Your shield is your first line of defence, but your body is the second. Know your stance, keep your balance, and when the strike comes, meet it, don't dodge it. Let it crash into you, and use it to power your own strike."

Taril also emphasised the importance of understanding one's surroundings. He would lead his students into the mountains, where they would practise combat in difficult terrain – where they learned how to adapt and move effectively in tight spaces, up rocky slopes, and through the treacherous woods.

The villagers were taught how to craft and maintain their armour, learning from Borgrim and Taril alike. They didn't just wear armour; they understood the craft behind it. The dwarven god taught them how to fortify themselves, ensuring every piece of armour was more than just protective: it was designed for maximum efficiency in defence. The blacksmiths, led by Garrk, worked closely with the soldiers to produce the finest armour, using techniques learned from Taril's ancient ways.

"Armour should never restrict," Taril often told them, demonstrating how a soldier should move freely while still being completely protected. "It should be a second skin – strong, but flexible. It will keep you alive, but it will not make you slow."

Where Drunnyak excelled in creating warriors who could unleash devastating power, Taril taught those same warriors how to control and use that power in a more methodical and defensive way. Together, they formed the perfect balance between offence and defence.

They often worked in tandem, Drunnyak showing the raw force, and Taril guiding the people to refine and focus that power. Together, they'd set up combat simulations, wherein soldiers and villagers alike would be tested on both their physical strength and their tactical defence. These training scenarios – set up in the rugged terrain surrounding the village – would pit them not just against each other, but against simulated enemies, using shields, armour and weapons as if in a real battle.

"Know when to strike and when to stand your ground," Taril would advise. "Sometimes, your strength is in holding your ground, in waiting for the right moment. When that moment comes, then you unleash."

Drunnyak, watching a group of soldiers in action, would laugh and clap them on the back. "Good, but don't just stand there like statues! You're warriors, not stones. Learn how to strike first, and strike hard!"

Their teachings weren't just about combat; they were about building confidence, understanding the value of discipline, and learning to work as a cohesive force. The soldiers who passed through their training were not just stronger – they were smarter, more adaptable, and more connected to each other as a unit.

Through their combined efforts, Drunnyak and Taril had built an army that wasn't just an instrument of war, but a symbol of unity, strength and resilience. Together, they had given the villagers the tools to defend themselves and face whatever the future might bring.

And so, under the guidance of the gods and the leadership of the village council, Garrents was growing, evolving. Each person, each skill, each contribution mattered, creating a web of purpose that connected them all. The gods were not only protectors, but teachers, guides and friends. They had come together with the villagers, not as distant figures of legend, but as a family united by a shared goal – to ensure that this new world, one born from the ashes of the old, would thrive.

But despite all they had achieved, the gods knew their journey was far from over. They had given the village hope, they had offered them the tools to build, but the true test was yet to come. They had to find their divine essence – each god carrying a gemstone, a fragment of their former power, waiting to be reclaimed. Only then would they ascend to their true divinity, fulfilling their purpose. But for now, they watched the village flourish, knowing they had taken the first step toward a new and powerful future.

TRIAL BY FIRE

After many weeks of tireless training and preparation, the village of Garrents had transformed into something far more than just a place of refuge. The gods had guided the villagers in strengthening not only their skills, but also their connection to one another, ensuring that every individual – whether soldier, farmer or craftsman – had their part in protecting the village. Now it was time to solidify their defences and test the strength of what had been built.

The trench that once lay outside the inner walls was no more. It had been filled in, and in its place, a new set of defences had been constructed – a massive outer wall now stretched around the extended village. Made of thick stone, reinforced with sturdy wooden beams, and standing over fifteen feet high, this wall was designed to protect the expanded village and its growing population. The stone, rough and weathered, had been carefully chosen to withstand time and assault, its surface a testament to the labour and power of the gods and the villagers alike. The wall's base was wide and solid, creating a foundation strong enough to endure the passage of years and the force of any would-be invaders.

Beyond the new wall, the land had undergone a remarkable transformation. Nashir and Taril, using their divine abilities, had shaped the land itself. The area was no longer a barren wasteland, but a living landscape, thriving with purpose. A new trench, nearly a chasm, had been carved into the earth just outside the outer walls. The chasm was a natural yet formidable barrier, its edges steep and jagged, making it impossible for anyone to approach the village unnoticed. The trench had been deepened and widened, stretching for miles in an arc around the new defences. It served as both a physical and a psychological deterrent, a gaping wound in the earth that made any attempt at crossing dangerous and uncertain.

The chasm's edges were reinforced with sharp stakes and metal spikes, adding to the threat for anyone foolish enough to try and cross it. The earth itself seemed to shudder with magic as Nashir's influence caused subtle tremors at irregular intervals. The shifting ground made passage even more perilous, adding an unpredictable element to anyone who might attempt to navigate the chasm.

A bridge made of sturdy stone spanned the gap, providing access between the inner and outer walls. The bridge was reinforced with guard rails and carefully monitored by soldiers stationed in the nearby watchtowers. These towering sentinels, made of thick wood and stone, rose at least thirty feet high, offering an unobstructed view of the land beyond. The watchtowers were spaced along the outer walls, ensuring there were no blind spots in the village's defences. Soldiers trained by Garric and Eldric kept a constant watch, scanning the horizon for any signs of danger. The towers were interconnected by a network of wooden platforms, allowing the soldiers to move quickly between them and maintain their vigilance.

Outside the outer walls, the landscape had been transformed into a lush, living tapestry — vibrant with wild growth, roaming creatures, and the quiet hum of nature restored. Thanks to Nashir's magic, the soil, once starved and silent, was rich and fertile, producing an abundance of food. Vines and apple trees twisted their branches in the breeze, while peach trees stood tall, their fruits ripening under the protection of the walls. The fields of crops, neatly planted and cared for by the farmers, were now overflowing with a bounty that had been unimaginable in the past.

The wild animals, once a distant threat, now roamed freely near the edges of the walls. Deer, elk, and smaller creatures like foxes and hares darted through the underbrush, all thriving in the natural harmony that Nashir had nurtured. The balance of nature was maintained, ensuring that the land provided not only protection, but sustenance. The air was thick with the rich aromas of wildflowers and ripening fruit, filling the lungs of every villager who worked the land.

Inside the new defences, the farmers, guided by Delm, worked with renewed vigour. They tended to the crops with a sense of pride and purpose, knowing that their labour was vital to the village's survival. Their hands were calloused from hard work, but their spirits were high as they saw the fruits of their labour grow more abundant each day.

The new defences – the walls, the chasm, the watchtowers, and the flourishing crops – had turned Garrents into a fortress of life and strength. The land beyond the walls had been reshaped and protected, providing the village with both food and security. The soldiers, scouts and farmers had all trained relentlessly, learning how to protect what they had built. The gods had gifted them a haven, but it was the people of Garrents who had truly made it their own.

The village was no longer confined to its original borders. It had expanded in every direction – more homes had been built, new fields had been planted, and the once-barren land outside the walls had become an extension of the village itself. It was a place of peace, but also one of strength, a place where the people could not only survive, but thrive. The defences were now strong enough to withstand any threat, and the land was fertile enough to provide for all.

Throughout the weeks, the leaders of the village gathered daily in what had come to be known as the Hall of Garrents. This hall, the heart of the village's decision-making and strategy, was situated at the centre of the newly extended area, just beyond the inner gates. It stood as a testament to both the village's resilience and its new-found unity, its structure a blend of practicality and symbolic strength.

The Hall of Garrents was an impressive sight – a long, rectangular building constructed with strong timber sourced from the surrounding forests, reinforced by stone foundations to ensure its stability. The walls were lined with thick, weathered wood, each panel carefully fitted together to create a sense of solace and sturdiness. The large stone hearth at the far end of the hall crackled with a welcoming fire, its warmth filling the room with a comforting glow during the colder nights. The interior of the hall was simple yet grand, with rough-hewn wooden beams supporting the roof, which arched high above them, creating a sense of space and openness.

The walls were adorned with banners and symbols representing the village – emblems of unity, strength and protection. Hand-carved wooden shields hung along the walls, each one symbolising a different aspect of the village's defence or culture. There were also intricate carvings of the gods' forms – Nashir, Taril and Alentar – as well as symbols of the earth, nature and battle. These carvings, though humble, were crafted with great reverence, honouring the deities who had aided the people in rebuilding their world.

In the centre of the hall was a large, oval wooden table, polished smooth from constant use, with seats for each council member. Garric, as the general, took his place at the head of the table, his commanding presence a natural fit for leadership. Eldric, the captain, sat beside him, his focus sharp and unwavering, ever the strategist. King Steve sat across from Garric, offering wisdom and calm counsel, his age and experience lending authority to his words. Alongside them, Delm, Garrk and Halrek, the trusted members of the council, made their marks as the village's advisers in agriculture, forging, and the care of the people.

When the gods joined the council meetings, they would often stand at the back of the hall, a silent presence, but always watching over the discussions. Their magic was always felt in the air, a quiet hum of power that provided a sense of security, yet their involvement in the meetings was measured. They would often listen carefully, offering their wisdom when necessary, but the focus was always on the village's leaders and their decisions for the future.

The Hall of Garrents, though a simple structure, had become a place of strength and reflection. The stone floors were worn smooth by the countless footsteps of villagers and leaders, and the wooden beams above held the echoes of decisions, debates, and dreams for the future. It was here that plans for the village's defence were devised, the distribution of resources was discussed, and the future of Garrents was shaped.

Every day, the council meetings took place, where the leaders would discuss everything from defensive strategies and food supplies to education and trade. They were often joined by various other members of the community, who were called upon to offer their input on matters affecting their respective areas. Garric and Eldric would discuss the latest tactics for the soldiers, while Delm reported on the progress of the crops. Garrk would speak of the village's need for proper tools, weapons and armour, while Stephen guided the flow of the meeting with his calm wisdom, ensuring everyone's voice was heard.

Though the work was serious, there was also a sense of camaraderie in the room. The village was no longer just a place to survive; it had become a home. And in the Hall of Garrents, each person – whether soldier, farmer, blacksmith or god – had a voice in shaping its future.

As the days went by, the gods continued to watch over the village, their presence always felt. The meetings in the hall grew from formal discussions to places of fellowship, where ideas flowed freely, and everyone was united by their shared purpose. Niv would occasionally stand up and share insights from her work with the magical abilities of the villagers, while Taril would offer guidance on building strength through the careful crafting of defences and weaponry. Opilkhos too would share his understanding of magic, helping those who had the potential to wield it, ensuring that the village was strong not only in body, but also in spirit.

Through the Hall of Garrents, a new era for the village had begun – a place where the future was built, step by step, by those who believed in each other, in the gods, and in the power of unity.

The gods stood at the heart of it all, their eyes scanning the thriving village, knowing that this was only the beginning. There were still challenges ahead, but for now they could feel the weight of their accomplishment. Garrents had grown, had become a sanctuary – one that would stand firm against whatever might come in the future – and as the day drew to a close, with the air filled with the sounds of life and laughter, the gods knew the villagers were ready for the trials still to come.

As the night dipped beneath the horizon, a heavy silence descended upon the village of Garrents. The air was thick with tension as the gates – north, south and west – were opened wide, signalling the beginning of the test. This had been agreed upon by the gods and the council: the villagers, having trained tirelessly over the weeks, would face a controlled confrontation against the undead. The outcome would determine their readiness to protect their new home.

The first of the undead began to emerge from the darkness, their bodies broken and disjointed, shuffling slowly toward the walls. The air grew heavy with the stench of decay as they approached, and the distant growl of the creatures echoed through the night. At first there were only a few, but soon the undead began to pour in, their numbers swelling, casting long shadows on the land.

The villagers stood at the ready, their resolve hardening with every passing second. Drokan, the towering giant, was at the forefront of the defence. Trained by Drunnyak, he had been elevated to the rank of sergeant, his massive form clad in heavy armour forged by Taril. He raised his war hammer, calling his troops into formation. His deep voice boomed across the battlefield, a calm command amidst the growing tension.

"Hold the line!" Drokan shouted, his voice carrying over the walls.

The soldiers, standing behind him, braced themselves, shields locked and spears raised. The years of training were evident in their precision, their coordination. The soldiers tightened their ranks, preparing for the oncoming assault.

At the rear, the magicians and sorcerers stood, their hands weaving spells in preparation for the battle ahead. Their faces were focused, and their energy crackled in the air. As the first undead approached, the sorcerers unleashed blasts of magic, fire and lightning arcing through the air, striking down the undead before they could reach the line.

The rangers, positioned in the watchtowers, had the perfect vantage point. With sharp eyes and taut bows, they kept a steady watch over the battlefield. Arrows flew from their bows in rapid succession, each one finding its mark. The rangers were the eyes of the defence, ensuring no enemy could approach without being noticed.

Above, on the balcony surrounding the top of the Hall of Garrents, the gods and council stood in silence. They did not intervene in the battle, content to observe from above. Nashir, Opilkhos, Taril and the others watched the villagers fight with quiet pride. Their presence was a silent assurance to the defenders below, but they remained passive, trusting that the villagers could handle this challenge themselves.

As the undead surged forward, their numbers growing with every passing moment, Drokan shouted orders, pushing his soldiers forward. The soldiers stepped into action, their spears thrusting forward, shields raised to block the incoming assault. The first wave of undead crashed against their defences, but the soldiers held strong, their line unbroken.

With each swing of Drokan's war hammer, several undead were crushed into the earth, their bodies crumbling upon impact. His strength was a force of nature, and the soldiers around him drew inspiration from his example, standing taller and stronger as they fought. The front line was a wall of steel and resolve, and nothing could break it.

The magicians continued to provide support, casting spells of fire and ice that rained down on the undead, turning them to ash before they could even reach the front lines.

Despite the initial success, the undead kept coming. Wave after wave poured through the gates, their numbers never ceasing. The air filled with the sound of battle – the clash of metal, the thud of undead bodies hitting the earth, and the occasional scream of a soldier engaged in the fight. Yet the villagers never wavered. They fought as one, their unity in the face of danger undeniable.

Atop the watchtowers, the rangers continued their deadly work, picking off the undead that breached the front lines.

As the battle raged, the first signs of victory began to show. The undead, though countless in number, were being destroyed without any loss on the village's part. The soldiers held their ground, the rangers continued their precision strikes, and the sorcerers kept up their relentless barrage of magic. The tide began to turn in favour of the villagers.

Hours passed, but the villagers never faltered. Drokan, with a final mighty swing of his war hammer, sent the last of the undead flying through the gates. The battlefield fell silent.

The villagers, exhausted but triumphant, stood amidst the carnage. Their shields were battered, their swords slick with the remnants of the fight, but they had held their ground. The test had been passed, and the village had proven its worth.

From above, the gods and council exchanged approving glances. They had remained passive observers, but the battle had shown them all they needed to know. The villagers were ready. Their strength, their unity, and their training had been enough.

The villagers cheered, their voices rising in triumph as the last of the undead were driven back. The gods watched from the balcony, proud of the people they had helped forge into warriors. They had not needed to intervene. The villagers had defended their home on their own, and they had done so with honour.

As the final undead fell, King Steve raised his hand, signalling the closing of the outer gates. His voice, calm yet filled with authority, echoed across the field. "Close the outer gates!" he commanded, and the soldiers moved swiftly, their spears poised to eliminate the last of the undead, ensuring none of them could crawl away.

"Make sure they're all dead!" Garric barked, his voice carrying over the battlefield. His hand gripped his sword tightly, still fresh from battle, as he watched his soldiers systematically finish off the final stragglers. Their movements were precise and deliberate – there was no room for mistakes.

Nashir, standing at a distance, raised his arms high, his expression serene but focused. The air around him seemed to shift, alive with a pulse of energy. He called upon the power of the land itself. Vines, thick and ancient, sprouted from the earth, twisting and writing like serpents. With a subtle motion of his hands, the vines wrapped around the undead bodies, lifting them from the ground as if they were mere leaves caught in a breeze. The trees, their branches stretching far and wide, reached down with gnarled limbs to grab hold of the corpses, throwing them effortlessly over the walls and into the chasm beyond. The once-empty space now served as a burial ground for the fallen.

As the final undead bodies were discarded, Taril stepped forward, raising his war hammer high, his deep voice booming across the field. "Break the cask!" he roared, his grin wide with pride. "Let's drink, eat and celebrate! For tonight, you've defended your homes!"

The gods exchanged knowing glances, their faces lit by the flickering torchlight.

Opilkhos nodded with a smile, his normally sombre demeanour softened by the victory. "They've done it," he murmured. "They've proven their worth."

Nashir, his connection to nature still crackling with energy, glanced toward the inner walls where the villagers were beginning to celebrate. His voice, when it came, was calm yet filled with satisfaction. "They've not only protected this land, but they've also learned how to shape it, how to use it as part of their strength. This place... it's their home now, in every sense."

Taril's deep laugh echoed as he clapped a hand on Nashir's back. "We've trained them well, my friend," he said, his eyes scanning the battlefield where the last of the undead had been cleared away. "But this... this was their moment. They have found their strength."

Opilkhos tilted his head slightly, observing the villagers' growing cheer. "The land itself has made them strong," he said thoughtfully. "This will be a place of power."

The council members, including Stephen, nodded in agreement, their faces showing respect and admiration for the villagers who had fought bravely.

"They've earned their place here," Stephen said quietly, "and now they will continue to grow."

As the final barrier fell and the outer gates were shut tight, Taril turned toward the inner gates, where the villagers were already gathering, eager to honour the heroes of the night. "Open the gates!" he shouted, his voice carrying through the air. The great gates creaked open, revealing a sea of villagers already gathering food and drink to celebrate their victory.

The sounds of laughter and cheer filled the air, and Garric stepped forward, raising his hand to silence the crowd. "Tonight, you've proven not only your strength, but your unity," he said, his voice filled with pride. "You fought for your homes, for your families. And you stood firm, as one. We are all the defenders of Garrents."

The villagers cheered once more, their voices rising in a loud, jubilant chorus as they brought out large platters of roasted meats, loaves of warm bread, and pitchers of wine and ale. The heroes – Drokan, Garric, Eldric, Taril, and the soldiers – were greeted with waves of gratitude. The sorcerers and rangers were not forgotten either, as the villagers offered them food and drink as well.

The mood was celebratory, and Borgrim, ever the gracious host, had already begun distributing pies and stews, his face shining with warmth and pride. "To the defenders of Garrents!" he cried, lifting a mug high in the air. "To our soldiers, to our rangers, and to our sorcerers!"

The villagers erupted into cheers as they joined him in the toast.

The gods, still standing high on the balcony above, watched in silence.

Nashir glanced over at Opilkhos, a smile tugging at the corners of his lips. "They've come so far," he said, his voice soft. "I knew this land would give them strength, but this – this is more than I imagined."

Opilkhos nodded. "Their courage was always there, waiting to be unlocked."

Taril, the ever-jovial giant, raised his war hammer once more, his booming voice cutting through the cheers. "Let's drink! Let's eat!" he shouted. "For tonight, you've defended your home, your families, and your future!"

The village roared in response, the atmosphere thick with triumph and joy. Drokan, his massive frame standing tall in the centre of the celebration, joined in the cheers, his war hammer slung across his shoulder. His face was proud, his eyes filled with the joy of seeing the people he had fought for embrace their victory.

Garric, standing alongside him, looked over at Drokan, his face tired but filled with respect. "We've done it," Garric said quietly. "But it's just the beginning."

As some of them still stood watch, silently observing the triumph below, they knew Garrents had truly become a place of strength, unity and hope. The road ahead would be hard, but for the first time in a long while, the villagers could rest, knowing they had earned their place in this land.

As the cheers and laughter filled the air, the villagers of Garrents revelled in the glory of their victory. Soldiers, rangers and sorcerers alike gathered around the fires, toasting one another, their faces flushed with pride. Drunnyak, the giant warrior, stood as one of them – proud, humble, and still larger than life. His booming laughter echoed in the night, joining with the voices of the people he had helped protect.

The gods joined the crowd from the higher balcony of the Hall of Garrents, their eyes scanning the celebrations. Nashir smiled softly, watching the villagers savouring their hard-earned peace. Opilkhos, ever the stoical presence, watched quietly, his mind clearly elsewhere. Taril, the jovial dwarf, chuckled alongside Borgrim the tavern keeper, who filled mugs with ale for anyone nearby. King Steve stood at the heart of the crowd, his gaze filled with both pride and a quiet concern.

But amidst the celebration, something was wrong. The air, despite the cheer, felt heavy, as if a shadow was lurking just beyond the light of their triumph. It was then that they all noticed Alentar standing watch at the top of the Hall of Garrents, his silhouette sharp against the night sky, his eyes scanning the horizon like a hawk.

The gods and the council exchanged silent glances, each of them acutely aware of the reason for his vigilance. The reason they all shared but had never spoken aloud.

Alanteas hadn't returned.

It had been a couple of months since he'd left to scout the other villages and draw up the map that would guide their next steps. Not a word, not a sign. His absence weighed heavily on them all, a quiet unease gnawing at the edges of their celebrations.

Nashir was the first to speak, though his voice was low, as if speaking too loudly might shatter the fragile peace they'd fought so hard to achieve. "He should have returned by now." His eyes lingered on Alentar, who remained perfectly still at the highest point, his eyes unblinking as they scanned the world beyond.

Drunnyak nodded solemnly, his usual composure masking a hint of worry. "It's not like him to be gone so long without word. He was supposed to be back already and guiding us forward."

Taril, ever the voice of blunt honesty, scratched his beard, his eyes narrowing. "Something's wrong. If he were close, we'd have felt it. But... he's still out there." His voice trailed off, his usual warmth replaced by a rare sombreness. "This... is not like him."

The gods fell silent, all eyes returning to Alentar, whose figure stood rigid and unyielding atop the hall, his silhouette cutting through the thickening darkness. The wind, cold and biting, whipped around him, but he didn't flinch. It was clear – he wasn't just standing guard. He was waiting. Waiting for something they all feared.

The thoughts that haunted them all remained unspoken. They had waited too long. Alanteas had gone to scout the villages nearby, and even though they'd probably be a few weeks' distance away, there was no reason for him not to have returned. He was supposed to map out the terrain, to guide them in their journey to find new allies and new places to protect. But now, weeks had passed, and no sign had come from him.

Garric's face was tight, his jaw set in determination, but even he couldn't mask the worry in his eyes. His grip on Niv's hand tightened slightly, a silent reassurance, but there was no hiding the shadow of concern that darkened his features. Niv, standing beside him, had her other hand resting on Caelan's head, but she was clearly distracted. Her gaze was fixed on the distance, her brow furrowed with a mixture of worry and exhaustion. She leaned into Garric's side, her fingers intertwined with his, her worry palpable in the way her eyes darted nervously back to Alentar, still standing vigilant atop the hall.

Caelan, normally the energetic child, had latched on to her leg, his small hands gripping her with an innocent yet protective sense of closeness. He looked up at her, sensing her anxiety, and squeezed her tightly. Despite his young age, he seemed to know that something was missing, something was wrong.

Garric let out a long breath, a heavy exhale that seemed to release the tension in his shoulders, but not in his heart. He understood why Alentar stood there, unmoving, why he hadn't left his post. They were all waiting for the same thing: Alanteas's return. The truth of his fate, whatever it might be, hung over them like a heavy anchor, dragging them down, drowning them in uncertainty. His absence, his silence, felt like a void that none of them knew how to fill.

"The village is ready." Garric finally spoke, his voice thick with quiet sadness. "We've defended it. We've fought for it. But we won't be whole until we know what happened to him." His words were simple, but the weight behind them was clear. They had done everything they could, but now it was time to know the truth.

As the villagers began to disperse, making their way back to their homes with smiles still on their faces, the gods and the members of the council remained standing by the balcony. Their eyes followed the people, a sense of pride and relief filling the air. The warm light from the hearths flickered across their faces, but beneath it, a quiet tension lingered. There was more to do, more to prepare for. Still, they stood together, waving to the villagers, silently sharing in the peace they had fought so hard to protect.

Garric turned to his sister-in-law, Marianne, who was nearby, walking towards Eldric. His voice was low. "Take him to Eldric's. Make sure he's settled for the night," he said, his words carrying an unspoken weight. "We need to talk before I go home tonight, so I might stay in the hall." There was much still unknown, and despite the moment of victory, they couldn't afford to rest just yet.

Marianne nodded, her hand brushing through Caelan's hair as she leaned down to kiss his forehead. "Come on, Caelan. Let's go get you ready for bed," she said softly, though her voice held a note of concern.

Caelan, sensing his aunt's unease, looked up at her with innocent eyes before nodding obediently.

Garric and Niv walked to Eldric, who was holding his two daughters in his arms, his strong arms cradling them as they rested against his chest.

"Settle them down for the night, Eldric," Garric added, his tone firm but warm. "Stay at home tonight, since it's closer to the hall. We'll be gathering there shortly."

With a nod of understanding, Eldric smiled down at his daughters, his gaze softening. "We'll be there, don't worry," he said, his voice low and reassuring.

As they walked away, Garric turned back to the others. Drunnyak, ever the playful spirit, let out a loud whistle. The sound sliced through the evening air, and within moments, Alentar – who had been standing watch, a silent figure on top of the hall – nodded down at them. Without a word, he pushed off from the ledge, leaping into the air. His movements were a perfect display of agility, his body twisting in mid-flight to use the walls of the hall to break his fall. He landed gracefully beside Drunnyak and the others, his footsteps soft as he straightened up, a small, knowing smile on his face.

"Nice entrance, Alentar." Drunnyak chuckled, his deep voice rumbling with amusement.

"Couldn't make it easy, could I?" Alentar replied with a wink, his eyes flicking to the group before them. His feet remained light as he joined them, his gaze shifting to the hall.

Together, they made their way inside, entering the Hall of Garrents, the central meeting place that had become the heart of their efforts. The air inside was thick with the scent of wood and stone, the faint flicker of lantern light casting shadows against the stone walls. As they walked further inside, the sound of a hearty whistle broke the silence.

Borgrim, the ever-gruff but loving tavern keeper, came into view. His large hands carried a barrel of ale, and he set it down with a thud on the long wooden table. Without waiting, he grabbed a number of mugs and set them out for each of them, his eyes gleaming with the same stubborn cheer that had made The Stubborn Goat a refuge for many. "You'll need this," Borgrim said with a grin, his thick beard twitching in delight. "For the warriors, the rangers, and the gods. Drinks are on me tonight, as always."

With a knowing smile, he began to pour the ale, the deep amber liquid filling each mug to the brim. The air in the hall shifted, filled now with warmth and camaraderie. Though the night had been long and the events of the day heavy, the simple act of gathering together gave a sense of relief. A moment of peace amidst the chaos that would soon follow.

As the gods and council members gathered in the hall, they exchanged looks, their expressions heavy with the weight of unspoken concerns. The atmosphere was sombre, even after the victory they had just achieved. They all knew why they were meeting here tonight.

Niv was the first to speak, her voice softer than usual, weighed down by the quiet worry she had been carrying. She crossed her arms, looking at the others with a furrowed brow. "It's been too long," she said, her words filled with a mixture of frustration and fear. "We've done everything we can for this village, but Alanteas… he's still out there and we're no closer to knowing what happened to him."

Her gaze shifted to Alentar, who had been silent, his usual stoical demeanour giving way to something deeper – a shared understanding of the pain that lingered in the air.

Alentar's voice was calm yet determined. "I'll track him down. I'll go where I need to go, cross whatever path lies ahead, and bring him back. If he's still out there, I'll find him."

There was a quiet moment as everyone looked to Alentar, knowing the responsibility that came with his offer. The same fierce determination that had made him the best of hunters now burned in his eyes.

Nashir stepped forward, his gaze steady as he watched Alentar. "We will help you," he said, his tone firm but understanding. "But we must be careful. We can't let our emotions cloud our judgement. We've all felt the loss, but we must approach this with clarity."

Opilkhos, standing next to Nashir, nodded in agreement. "Alanteas is important to us all," he said quietly. "But the path ahead is uncertain. We cannot let his absence distract us from the village we've built. It must be protected."

The silence that followed was heavy, and for a moment, no one spoke. They all knew that Alanteas's fate hung over them, but their duty to protect the village – and to move forward – was something they couldn't ignore.

Finally, Taril clapped Alentar on the back with a boisterous laugh, lightening the mood ever so slightly. "I don't doubt you, my friend," he said with a wink. "Go and find him. Bring him back. We'll keep the home fires burning for you."

With that, the gods and the council exchanged looks, agreeing silently on the task that lay ahead.

As the conversation unfolded, Niv's concerns echoed through the room, and Alentar's determination to find Alanteas hung heavily in the air. The decision to act, to search for their missing comrade, was clear – but Nashir, ever the one to seek the balance of both strength and caution, spoke up, his voice calm but resolute.

"Wait," Nashir said, lifting his hand to still the room.

The others turned to him, their attention sharp as he continued.

"I believe I can connect with the land. The magic that flows through it, that ties everything together – it's strong, and it can guide us." He paused, his gaze distant for a moment as he gathered his thoughts, his voice filled with a quiet certainty. "If Alanteas marked the trees as he mentioned before he left, I may be able to find his last location. The land remembers. His markings should still be there, and through them, I can trace his path and create a link to the land here and there, like I did at the giants' village."

The room fell silent as the weight of Nashir's words sank in. There was a sense of hope that flickered in the air. He had been the one to bring balance to nature, to bind the land to their will in ways the others could not. If anyone could do it, it would be Nashir.

"But I will need a few hours," Nashir continued, his voice steady. "I will need time to find the right connection, to follow the path he left behind. If the marks are still there, I can lead us to him."

Opilkhos nodded, his expression softening. "I think that's the best approach. We should give Nashir what he wants and wait."

Garric, standing beside Niv, gave a solemn nod, understanding the gravity of the task ahead. "We'll wait. We can't afford to rush this, not when finding Alanteas is so critical."

Alentar, though eager to leave immediately, understood the necessity of Nashir's plan. "We wait for you, Nashir. Do what you must."

Niv's eyes met Alentar's, a silent reassurance passing between them. The tension that had been building slowly began to dissipate. They had a plan, a way forward.

Nashir gave a small, quiet smile of appreciation. "Thank you. I will return when I've found something. Rest for now. We will know more soon."

With that, Nashir turned toward the open space, his thoughts already focused on the land, on the magic that connected them all. The gods and the council members settled into their positions, agreeing to wait in silence, knowing that the next few hours could hold the answers they sought.

The room fell into a heavy silence, the weight of the night's uncertainty hanging in the air, but Drunnyak broke it with his booming laughter. His wide grin spread across his face as he slapped Taril's back so hard that the chair beneath him slid forward with a loud screech. The gods and council members burst into laughter, their tension momentarily lifted by the joyful noise. Even the weight of the situation seemed to lighten for a moment.

"Don't worry, lads!" Drunnyak boomed, his voice rich with humour, his chest still heaving with laughter. "We'll find Alanteas. He's out there, just waiting for a proper welcome when he returns!"

They all raised their mugs high, the golden ale glinting in the firelight. "To Alanteas!" they all cheered in unison, their voices echoing through the hall.

After a moment of quiet reflection, they clinked their mugs together, their spirits lightened, if only for a brief time. They shared their farewells, their eyes full of understanding and resolve. Each knowing that Alanteas's absence weighed on them all, but for now, they had to hold on to hope.

Alentar gave a brief, quiet nod as he turned to leave. His gaze, ever watchful, turned to the top of the hall. Without a word, he began the climb again, his form slipping silently into the shadows as he took his place on the high ledge, keeping vigilant. He wouldn't rest until he knew the truth of Alanteas's fate.

As Nashir walked out of the hall, he took a deep breath, sensing the land beneath his feet. His staff in hand, he began to whisper low words in an ancient tongue. The world seemed to pause for a moment, the air thick with power. Slowly, Nashir raised his staff high, and the land around him responded. Vines and roots began to creep up, wrapping gently around his legs, and the ground trembled as if acknowledging his connection. Engulfed by the very nature he controlled, he sank into a deep meditative state, his mind connecting to the earth beneath and beyond, seeking the path that would lead him to Alanteas.

The others slowly began to disperse, each of them returning to their homes. Niv, her face still clouded with worry, found comfort in Garric's presence. As they walked away, she embraced him, kissing him softly on the lips. The tenderness in her touch spoke volumes, her concerns momentarily eased by his solid, comforting presence. They walked side by side, their hands intertwined, their connection undeniable.

Meanwhile, Drunnyak and Taril walked together, their shoulders bumping in friendly camaraderie, both laughing as they moved. The ever-present warmth of Taril made him burst into his usual hearty chuckles, but this time, Drunnyak matched him, full of joy. As they made their way down the path, Drokan the giant joined them. He raised a hand in greeting, then – without warning – pulled Drunnyak and Taril into a playful embrace.

In a sudden burst of energy, all three of them leaped into the air, their laughter ringing out like thunder as they collided in mid-jump, heads knocking together with a loud thunk.

Drokan, holding his head in mock pain, groaned. "By the gods! I should learn not to do that again."

Laughing and joking as they made their way to The Stubborn Goat tavern, mugs of ale sloshing in their hands, the night air was filled with their hearty voices, the weight of the day's victory lifting their spirits. But as they rounded a corner near the inner gate, they spotted Annah, now a proud ranger, standing near the edge of the village. Her posture was strong, her eyes scanning the horizon with the focused attention of a seasoned scout.

Drunnyak, ever the one to find humour in everything, leaned over to Taril with a smirk. "She's so gorgeous," he said, his voice loud enough for everyone to hear.

Taril, never one to let a comment slide, grinned. "She's too young for you, you old goat. Nonetheless, she only has eyes for Alentar."

Drunnyak sputtered, nearly choking on his drink as he laughed. "I don't think she knows that he's not into..." He stopped in mid-sentence, looking around to see if anyone had overheard, his eyes flicking to Taril. "You know, Alentar doesn't exactly show interest in... well..." he said, a little too loudly.

Taril, who had been walking with a proud grin, suddenly gave Drunnyak a sharp look, his eyes narrowing with a warning. "Keep your mouth shut, Drunnyak."

Drokan, who had been laughing along with them, raised an eyebrow. "What don't you think he's into?"

Drunnyak erupted into laughter again, slapping Drokan on the shoulder. "Well, he's not really the type to be interested in..." But then he saw Taril's menacing glare, and his laughter died down. He cleared his throat, suddenly aware that he might have gone too far. "I mean... Alentar's... uh... focused on his training," Drunnyak stammered, quickly covering his slip. "Yeah, training. That's what I meant." Drunnyak's grin returned, but this time it was a little more sheepish.

"Well, I wouldn't say he's blind to the eyes… but I can honestly say that he's just not looking in the right direction, that's all."

The three of them stumbled back, laughing so hard they nearly lost their balance. With mugs still in hand, they shared a hearty toast and began walking toward The Stubborn Goat tavern, singing loudly, their voices echoing in the cool night air. It wasn't just the victory they celebrated now – it was the bond they shared, the strength of their unity, and the hope that tomorrow would bring them the answers they sought.

INTO UNCHARTED LANDS

Nashir stood at the centre of the village, his staff raised high, and the ground beneath him began to pulse with life. Slowly, the air around him thickened, and vines, roots and branches erupted from the earth, twisting around him in an intricate, living cocoon. The plants caressed his body, pulling him close, as if the land itself was embracing him. Nashir closed his eyes, his breathing slowing, entering a deep meditative trance. The world around him darkened, and his consciousness began to drift into a realm beyond time and space.

He felt the earth shift beneath him. The ground hummed with life, its heartbeat slow and steady, echoing in his mind. Nashir could hear the pulse of every living thing that touched the earth: the scurrying of insects, the steady march of the animals moving through the underbrush, the breath of creatures large and small. It was as though the entire land was alive, a vast, interconnected network of life that stretched across the world.

His senses, heightened beyond comprehension, surged. He felt the subtle rustle of leaves as the wind passed through them, the faintest stirrings of the earth itself as if it were alive with whispers. The rhythm of life enveloped him, and in return, he poured himself into it, sinking deeper, expanding farther.

He felt Drunnyak's laughter, distant yet clear in his mind, the booming sound reaching him like a wave crashing on a distant shore. He felt Taril and Drokan laughing beside him as they made their way back to the village. The joy of their camaraderie was as tangible to him as the feel of the wind on his skin.

But then Nashir's awareness expanded further still. He could feel the steady beat of the earth in places far beyond the village – the wilds of Maud, where the undead marched in their endless hunger. He felt their cold, relentless footsteps echoing in his mind, as though they were already upon the village. But his mind didn't stop there. He felt Alanteas's steps, left behind in the snow. The trail was faint, but it was there, his presence still lingering in the cold air, frozen in time.

Through the threads of nature, Nashir felt the past. He could taste the air of long-forgotten places, smell the salt of the sea and the mossy scent of ancient trees. He saw shadows of the past – a memory of a distant land where Alanteas had wandered. He saw the marks of the trees, carved with symbols long forgotten by time, leading him forward through the wilds. Each mark, a piece of Alanteas's journey, a step closer to the truth.

Then, after what felt like an eternity, Nashir found the last mark. It was faint but undeniable. A tree stood at the edge of an ancient forest, near a range of towering mountains – the Fanged Peaks – looming like sentinels in the distance. In the shadow of the mountains, a small cluster of huts stood abandoned. No people were in sight. The land here was still, but the undead walked, circling around the huts, moving toward the sea before turning back, as though the water was a barrier they feared.

Alanteas had been here, marking the ancient tree before leaving. This was his last stop. Nashir's heart raced. His connection to the land had brought him here, but it wasn't the end of the journey. This was only a waypoint – a signpost in the wilderness. The undead still roamed, and Alanteas's fate was still uncertain.

Suddenly, the world around Nashir began to retract. The magic that had cocooned him started to unwind, the vines pulling back into the earth. The earth groaned as he was pulled from the depths of his connection to nature. His senses snapped back from the timeless hush of the wild to the mortal din of breath, burden and choice, and the cocoon burst open, throwing him violently into the air.

He landed on the cold, hard ground, gasping for breath, his body slick with moisture. He felt as though he had been inside a womb, then reborn through the land's energy. The world was different now – more alive, more vibrant – but the truth still lingered like a dark cloud. Nashir struggled to his feet, water dripping from him as though he had just emerged from a river. His eyes glowed faintly, still attuned to the land, but the weight of the vision remained heavy on him.

He stood there for a moment, breathing deeply, his heart still racing. The journey had taken him further than he had ever gone before, but now he had the truth he needed. Alanteas had left a mark, a breadcrumb leading him through the wilderness. The path was clear now, and soon they would know more.

With a final glance toward the earth, Nashir knew that the next phase of their journey was about to begin. He had found the answers they had sought – but now they had to move quickly.

As Nashir staggered to his feet, the world around him still felt blurry, a haze clouding his vision. He was dizzy from the overwhelming connection with nature, the vastness of it all still lingering in his senses. But through the fog, two figures came into focus – Alentar and Niv stood nearby, their faces etched with concern.

Alentar, his posture as ever, remained vigilant, though the slight dip of his head signified the relief he felt upon seeing Nashir return. Niv, on the other hand, couldn't help the playful smile that tugged at the corners of her lips as she observed Nashir's disorientation.

"You're back." Alentar spoke simply, his voice low but filled with gratitude. His eyes flickered to the horizon, where the last remnants of the undead had begun to fall, their bodies returning to the earth. The sentinels, posted high in the watchtowers, had already sounded the horn, signalling the end of the danger for now, but as they saw

Nashir returning, they sounded a different horn, a specific one to call the attention of the gods.

For Nashir, it felt like no time had passed at all. What had been a journey stretching through the depths of the land felt like only a moment for him. However, outside, nearly three days had passed, and the village had been holding its breath the entire time.

"Are you all right?" Niv asked, something unguarded flashing across her eyes – swift, protective – as she stepped in to steady him.

Nashir nodded, still trying to shake off the dizziness that clung to him like a fog. He leaned against Alentar, his brother's firm support grounding him. "I'm fine, just… a little overwhelmed," he said, rubbing his temples as his senses slowly returned to normal.

As Niv watched him, her lips curled into a playful grin. She leaned in slightly, teasing as she licked him. "You taste like honey, Nashir." Her voice was laced with mischief.

Nashir, not expecting the comment, let out a startled laugh, but before he could stop himself, he spat out a thick, sticky liquid, much like the nectar of a thousand flowers, which had been pumped into his body during the ritual. He wiped his mouth in surprise, chuckling despite the strange taste. "I feel like I've just been reborn," he muttered, wiping his face, his laughter still light. "But I don't remember tasting *this* sweet."

The sound of heavy footsteps and laughter broke the moment, and soon the others arrived.

Taril came bounding forward, a napkin hastily wrapped around his neck, and in one hand he clutched a massive turkey leg, still steaming, and a mug of ale in the other. He waved the turkey leg toward Nashir, as if presenting a grand feast. "Did you miss me, brother?" he bellowed, his voice warm with the familiarity of years spent in close quarters. "I got you a *delicacy* for your return. Hope you're hungry." With a sad brow, as he pretended to eat that delicacy.

At the same time, Drunnyak appeared, his pants half-pulled up, clearly having been in a rush. His expression was one of mild embarrassment, but that didn't stop him from giving a hearty laugh. "I was *busy*, you know," he said with a wink, before adding with a shrug, "but there's always time to greet a friend – especially if that..." he sniffed Nashir, "if that friend smells like honey!" His grin was wide, and the playful glint in his eyes matched the teasing tone of his voice.

The group gathered around Nashir, each of them offering a gesture of welcome, their smiles sincere and their spirits high. Even after the heavy moments of the past few days, it was clear that the bond between them was unshaken.

Nashir, still wiping the last remnants of the nectar from his lips, felt the warmth of his companions surround him. "Thank you, all of you," he said with a grateful smile. "It seems I was gone longer than I thought."

Alentar, ever watchful, gave a small nod. "We've been waiting, but now we know. You found him, didn't you?"

Nashir met his gaze and nodded. "I did. Alanteas... He left a mark. We have a place to go. He's still out there, near the mountains... near the ocean."

The others gathered around, their expressions serious as they listened. The light-hearted moment had faded, replaced by the weight of the task ahead. But for now, they would savour the fact that Nashir had returned, and their bonds were stronger than ever.

Taril raised his mug, the ale sloshing slightly as he grinned at Nashir. "To our nephew's return," he said. "And to the next adventure – wherever it leads us."

A sense of unity filled the air, even as they knew the road ahead would be filled with unknowns.

The air was thick with anticipation. After a few moments of tense silence, King Steve arrived, his horse's hooves clattering against the cobblestones as he made his way to the group. His weathered face was marked by years of leadership, his steady gaze unwavering as he dismounted and greeted Nashir and the others with a respectful nod. Behind him came Garric and Eldric, their serious expressions giving way to brief smiles as they approached.

The gathering of the gods, along with the leaders of the village, stood together, as if united by some invisible thread. Nashir watched them all, taking in the familiar faces of his companions. They were all battle-worn but resolute. It was in their unity that they found strength.

Garric walked up to Niv, and without hesitation, he leaned in to kiss her. The gesture, though tender, was met with a cheeky surprise. Niv grinned and, in a playful movement, gave him a light clap on the rear, her eyes twinkling with excitement.

"Ready for the next adventure?" she teased, her voice low but filled with enthusiasm. "Looking forward to finding Alanteas and the answers we need?"

Garric chuckled, squeezing her hand, his voice a quiet, reassuring murmur. "You know I am." But the unease behind his smile didn't go unnoticed, as the weight of Alanteas's absence was still heavy on their hearts.

Opilkhos, who had been silently observing, turned to Nashir, his eyes narrowed in thought. "How long will it take to establish the connection to this far land?" His voice carried a quiet urgency, but his calm demeanour belied the tension everyone was feeling.

Nashir, standing tall and focused, his connection to the earth still lingering, sighed deeply. He felt the pull of the land beneath him, still slightly disoriented from his earlier journey. "I'll need to rest for a couple of hours," he said, his voice steady but tinged with the weariness of his earlier exertion. "But by nightfall, I will be ready. We can establish the link to the far land, to where Alanteas left his mark."

The gods exchanged a glance, but before the conversation could continue, Alentar stepped forward, taking charge of the situation. His voice was steady, firm, as he addressed the group.

"We all need to go." His eyes locked with Garric, Eldric and the others. "While we are together, we are stronger, and more importantly, each of us may find something more – some deeper connection to our past. Perhaps even the source of our individual divine essence."

The air seemed to shift with his words, the weight of the decision heavy but undeniable.

Alentar's gaze moved across the group, sensing their worry about leaving the village unprotected. He spoke again, this time softening his tone. "I know we are all concerned about leaving the village. But this is bigger than any one of us. We must trust that the villagers, strengthened by everything we've trained them for, can defend themselves."

A pause settled over the group as they all exchanged glances, unsure but resolute. The village needed them, but their mission was too urgent.

The stillness was broken by Alentar's sudden, sharp cry – an animalistic sound, low and resonant, that echoed through the village like a summons from the wild. The nearby trees seemed to retract, their leaves rustling as if in answer to his signal. From the shadows, Annah emerged swiftly, appearing at Alentar's side within moments.

Alentar gave her a brief, encouraging nod, his expression softening as he spoke to her. "Annah, I need you to stick with Nashir. While he establishes the connection for us, I want you to learn. You have a natural connection to nature's power. Learn how to call upon it when necessary. If the need arises, you'll be able to come and get us."

Annah met his gaze, her determination evident in her sharp eyes. She nodded, the weight of the task ahead settling into her. "I will," she said, her voice steady. "I won't let you down."

The others stood silently for a moment, the weight of their plan settling in.

Drunnyak, ever the optimist, broke the silence with a boisterous laugh. "Let's get this show on the road, then!" he boomed, slapping Taril's back with a grin. "We'll find Alanteas, and we'll bring him back with stories to tell! And maybe a little more ale, eh?"

The laughter was contagious, lightening the atmosphere once again. But beneath it all, the resolve to succeed remained. They knew their mission was clear, and they had no time to waste.

With that, they all prepared to part ways. Nashir began walking toward a small, secluded area, the ground underfoot shifting to accommodate and help him rest. As the others retreated to gather their supplies, Alentar took a final, lingering look at the village before turning away to prepare himself.

Mid-morning, after Nashir had rested enough, his eyes gazed at the land with a quiet intensity. Nashir and Annah stood alone in a secluded area just outside the village, but still inside the fortified walls, surrounded by towering trees and the earth that seemed to breathe beneath their feet. The sky above, though dim with clouds, held a stillness, as though the world itself were holding its breath. The air was crisp with anticipation.

Nashir stood with his staff planted firmly in the earth, the tip glowing faintly as it absorbed the life force of the land. Annah was beside him, her face set in determination, her posture straight as she focused intently on his every movement. The land felt alive, and her senses were heightened, attuned to the rhythm of the world. This was her first true test of magic, and she could feel the power within her, waiting to be unlocked.

"Are you ready?" Nashir asked, his voice calm, but carrying the weight of the ancient knowledge he was about to share.

Annah nodded, her breath steady. She had practised the words, felt the pull of the earth beneath her, but this was something new. Something deep.

"This magic is not just about speaking the words," Nashir continued, his voice low. "It is about surrendering yourself to the earth. You must become part of it. Only then will the land open to you." The incantation he was about to teach her was ancient, older than time itself. It was a spell that connected the caster to the very heart of nature, allowing them to create a bond so strong that even the farthest reaches of the land could be touched. Nashir raised his staff, and the air hummed with power. He turned to Annah, meeting her eyes. "Remember the words. Feel the earth in your chest, in your veins. Allow it to flow through you." He nodded to her, giving the signal to begin.

Annah closed her eyes for a moment, focusing, gathering her thoughts. She could feel the pulse of the land beneath her feet, a subtle hum that she now understood was the heartbeat of nature itself.

"*Elvannos'lan vaeleth, ilva tuhnar. Jarn esthirn dothaal, vaen marenth,*" Nashir intoned, the words flowing from his mouth with the deep, reverent cadence of an ancient ritual.

Annah repeated the words after him, her voice at first unsure, but as the syllables fell from her lips, something deep within her stirred.

Nashir nodded, encouraging her. "Again."

She repeated the words again, this time with more confidence, and as she did, the air around them shifted. The ground beneath their feet trembled, but it was a warm, welcoming sensation rather than a threatening one. The earth seemed to respond to her, welcoming her to the fold. "*Elvannos'lan vaeleth, ilva tuhnar. Jarn esthirn dothaal, vaen marenth.*" *I surrender myself to the earth, to the roots and life beneath. The earth will guide me, the soil will remember my steps, and the winds will carry my path.*

The earth responded, vines beginning to emerge from the ground at their feet, twining around Nashir's staff. Annah felt the connection deepen. She could hear the earth's heartbeat, its rhythm pulsing beneath her skin. It was a sensation like no other. It was as though she could feel everything around her, from the smallest insect in the soil to the farthest tree at the edge of the forest.

As the day passed, Nashir continued guiding her, ensuring she maintained her focus and connection with the land. The sun sank lower in the sky, but the power surrounding them only intensified. Nashir's voice was steady and strong, constantly reminding her to surrender herself completely. "The land will hear you, it will guide you, but you must be open to it. Trust it."

Hours passed, but Annah never wavered. She felt the land around her, now as much a part of her as the air she breathed. Nashir stood at her side, his voice a steady presence, encouraging her to speak the words with more conviction each time.

"*Elvannos'lan vaeleth, ilva tuhnar. Jarn esthirn dothaal, vaen marenth.*" She said the words again, her voice stronger now, more confident. The words flowed from her like a chant, the magic building within her with every syllable.

As Annah spoke, the vines around them grew stronger, wrapping around the staff as if calling forth growth from the ground – as though the land itself had taken a breath. She could feel the land reaching back, stretching far into the distance. In her mind's eye, she saw trees – ancient trees, with roots so deep they seemed to touch the core of the earth. She could feel Alanteas's steps, though he had passed through weeks ago, his path still marked in the land.

The final piece of the spell came as Nashir instructed her. "Feel it, taste it, let the earth pull you into its memory. The land holds all things, even the past. This is where the connection begins."

The moment the last syllables of the incantation left Annah's lips, the world around them shimmered. The air crackled with energy. The ground shook briefly, and then everything went still.

Nashir watched as Annah stood in silence, her breath coming in soft, steady intervals. He could feel it too – the earth was alive with energy, her connection to it now a permanent link. "You've done it," he said, his voice filled with pride. "You've connected to the land, to its very heartbeat. Now you can travel through it, connect to its distant parts when you need to. You will bring us to where we need to go, whenever it's time."

The day had passed in a blur of concentration and magic. The night was beginning its descent, casting long shadows over the land. Nashir and Annah stood together, the air still and charged with energy. The earth hummed beneath them, resonating with the connection she had just forged. Annah felt as though she could taste the very essence of the land, the soil beneath her feet, the wind that brushed past her skin.

Nashir turned to her, his expression softening as he noticed the deep well of emotion in her eyes. The connection they had just created was powerful, and it was dangerous. He placed his hand on her shoulder, his grip firm but gentle. "Annah," he said, his voice calm but carrying a weight of caution. "This magic… it is not something to wield lightly. The land is vast, and its power can be overwhelming. Do not travel through it with another, not yet. It is beyond your current capabilities. You must only use it when necessary, to return to us when there is no other option."

His gaze was steady, and Annah could feel the gravity of his words settling deep within her. The power she had tapped into was vast, but it was still fragile. She nodded, the seriousness of his warning not lost on her.

"I understand," she replied quietly, her eyes filled with respect and gratitude. "I won't misuse it, I promise, Master Nashir."

Nashir nodded, but then he softened slightly, his expression warming. "Good. You have a strong heart, and that will carry you far." He paused for a moment, letting the silence stretch between them. Then, with a small smile, he continued, "But you don't have to call me 'Master', Annah. You're part of my family now, as much as anyone else here."

At those words, Annah's heart swelled. She had come so far, learned so much, and now the gods saw her as part of their family. There was no mistaking the bond that had formed between them. She couldn't help it – her emotions, her gratitude, and her respect all boiled over in a rush. Without thinking, she stepped forward and wrapped her arms around Nashir, holding him in a tight hug.

Nashir stood frozen for a moment, surprised by the sudden warmth of her embrace. But then he gently placed his hands on her shoulders, returning her gesture with a kind smile. "You're welcome, Annah."

For a moment, neither of them spoke. The world seemed to stand still around them, the connection between them as strong as the earth beneath their feet. Then, pulling back slightly, Annah looked up at him, her eyes filled with a mixture of gratitude and new-found strength.

"Thank you, Nashir. I won't forget this." Her voice was steady now, as though the weight of her journey had lifted, even if just for a moment.

Nashir smiled softly. "I know you won't. Now, go – be with the others. We have much to do, but remember, your path is your own, and it is for you to walk."

As the night began to settle in, casting long, deep shadows across the village, Nashir knew it was time. He had prepared himself and the land, his senses attuned to the subtle shifts of energy that told him the moment had arrived. His eyes briefly closed, feeling the wind brush past him, the earth beneath his feet steady and welcoming.

With a soft gesture, he summoned a small bird, no bigger than the palm of his hand, its wings a flurry of movement as it landed gently on his outstretched finger. The bird's eyes gleamed with an understanding, the creature attuned to the deep magic of Nashir's will. The moment was quiet, but the tension was palpable, like the calm before a storm.

"Go," Nashir whispered. "Find Jorik so he can let the others know."

The bird took flight, its wings cutting through the air with purpose. As it soared toward the watchtower in the distance, Nashir stood tall, watching it disappear into the dimming sky.

Atop the watchtower, Jorik stood vigil, as he had many times before. His eyes were sharp, scanning the horizon for any signs of trouble. He had learned to read the signs of nature, to understand the language of the animals, and as the bird approached, he knew immediately what it was there to tell him.

The bird fluttered in front of him, its call a soft melody, the same one he had come to understand as a summons. As it sang, the message became clear – Nashir was ready, and the call was to alert the village. Jorik's mind quickly processed the command.

Without hesitation, he stepped to the horn station, lifting the large horn to his lips. The first blast rang out across the village, a low and powerful sound. It was a signal for the soldiers – *Prepare the outer walls and guard the village well; the night is upon us.* The second blast followed swiftly, higher and sharper. The call for the gods.

Below, scattered across the village, the movement began.

First to arrive was Stephen, the ever-present leader of the village, his horse's hooves clopping steadily against the cobblestones as he approached Nashir. His face was calm, but his eyes held a hint of urgency. "I'm here. The night approaches," he said, nodding to Nashir with respect. His voice was quiet but strong, a pillar of stability in these uncertain times.

Next came Drunnyak, his imposing figure appearing at the edge of the gathering. His lion-hide clothing, now fitting snugly around him, caught the fading light of the day. He was the first to strap his weapon to his back, his massive broken sword gleaming with readiness. His broad shoulders and stern face were etched with determination, though there was a subtle air of excitement behind his eyes. "Ready to face whatever comes," Drunnyak muttered to himself, adjusting his clothing.

Shortly after, Taril emerged, the sound of his boots crunching on the gravel as he moved swiftly toward the gathering. He had just finished fitting his last piece of armour – a thick, ornate pauldron that gleamed in the fading light. His war hammer rested at his side, heavy and dependable as always. He grabbed his shield from the nearby table, the metal polished and strong. Taril's gaze met Nashir's for a brief moment, a silent acknowledgement passing between them. "Let's hope we find him, Nashir." His voice was steady, his eyes fierce, but there was a flicker of something deeper – worry, perhaps, for the unknown.

Niv was next to arrive, her feet barely touching the ground as she sprinted toward the gathering. She was full of energy, twisting and turning in acrobatic flourishes, stretching her muscles as she ran. Her swords flashed in the light, catching the torchlight like a spell being cast. Her laughter rang out, echoing through the evening air, as she seemed to float toward them, her movements graceful and fluid.

"You're looking excited," Nashir commented, watching her.

"Of course." She grinned, playful as ever. "Can't let you all have all the fun, now, can I?"

As she joined the group, Alentar appeared from the shadows. He had been resting most of the day, his presence as silent as ever. He stood slightly apart from the group, his bow slung across his back. His eyes met Nashir's briefly, a simple nod acknowledging his readiness. He had been watching, as always, calculating and waiting for the right moment. "I've been watching the sky. The winds are steady." His voice was quiet, his gaze faraway as though already on the journey ahead.

Finally, Garric and Eldric walked toward them, their footsteps echoing in the quiet evening.

Garric, the stoical leader, offered a firm handshake to Nashir, his expression serious but filled with respect. "We're ready for this," he said, his eyes flicking over to Alentar and Niv. "Find him and bring him back. We're holding down the fort here."

Eldric, his second in command, was a mirror of Garric in many ways, his expression calm but firm. "We'll be waiting."

The group gathered, readying themselves for the journey ahead. They were warriors, rangers, sorcerers – each with their own talents and strengths. But it was not just their skills that would carry them. It was the bond between them, the trust, the understanding that no matter what lay ahead, they would face it together.

Nashir nodded, a quiet signal for them to prepare. "Rest easy, my friends. The land will guide us."

He stood before his companions, his gaze sweeping across the group. His eyes met each of theirs, and in that silent moment, an unspoken understanding passed between them – a shared burden, a shared resolve. The journey that lay before them was not merely one of distance, but one of fate itself. Their hearts, bound by an ancient purpose, knew well the weight of what they sought.

The air seemed to still, as if the land itself held its breath. There was no doubt in their eyes, no hesitation in their hearts. The search for Alanteas was no mere mission. It was the call of destiny, the echo of a forgotten bond. With a single nod, they acknowledged their unity, their shared path.

Nashir, the keeper of nature's will, turned his gaze upward, his face solemn, his purpose unyielding. His fingers, like roots reaching deep into the earth, pressed against the ground. The very air around them seemed to tremble with the weight of his command. "By the land and by the winds, by the earth that cradles us, I call upon thee." His voice rang out, resonant and ancient, as if the very words were forged in the bones of the world.

The earth beneath him groaned in answer, a low hum reverberating through the air. The wind stirred, rustling the leaves and sweeping across the land like a thousand whispered voices. The sky above, heavy with the weight of the coming moment, darkened, as though nature itself responded to Nashir's summons.

From his outstretched hands, the power of the land unfurled like a great and terrible tapestry. Vines, twisted and ancient, began to wind their way up from the ground, their leaves glowing with the faintest light. Trees bent their boughs, their trunks groaning as though waking from a long slumber. The earth itself seemed to crack and open, as a portal of swirling green energy began to manifest before them.

It was different from any portal they had seen before: stronger, deeper, more alive. The ground shuddered beneath them, and a vast chasm of verdant light opened wide. The scent of earth, of moss, of life and death filled the air. It was as if the very fabric of the land itself was bending, reaching across vast distances to unveil a hidden path, one that had long been shrouded in silence.

The members of the council of Garrents, soldiers, and villagers who had gathered to witness the event stood in awe, their eyes wide with wonder. The power that Nashir summoned was unlike anything they had ever seen. The portal before them was a living thing, thrumming with energy, more potent than the one Nashir had cast when bringing the villagers from the giants' village.

Their breath caught in their throats as they saw the green light pulse and shimmer, as if it too were breathing. The magic that filled the air was a tangible force, an unearthly power that seemed to stretch beyond the stars themselves, carrying with it the weight of ages long past.

Even the land itself seemed to watch, its heart pounding, as the portal stabilised, crackling with energy. And there, at the heart of the chasm, the last marked location of Alanteas glowed faintly, etched into the fabric of the world by his footsteps.

The air was thick with anticipation, the villagers stilling in reverence, the warriors bracing for what was to come. Once more, Nashir's power had reached far beyond their expectations. It was not just the magic of nature. It was the power of the world itself, opening a path where none had been before.

Nashir's voice, quiet but filled with resolve, broke through the awe-stricken silence. "The way is open. We must step forward, for our journey has just begun." His words hung in the air like an ancient prophecy, a promise made to the land, to their people, and to Alanteas.

With that, Nashir stepped forward, the portal now flickering with a life of its own, awaiting them. It was not just a passage, but a bridge to the past, to the unknown, to the future they must face together.

And as Alentar, Taril, Drunnyak and the others gathered around the portal, the weight of their purpose settled on them. The world seemed to breathe with them, as if the land itself had called them to this moment, a moment where their past and future intertwined.

The portal shimmered one final time, its energy crackling through the air, ready to guide them on the path to Alanteas. Their journey would begin here. And the land, vast and wild, awaited their footsteps.

THE CALL OF THE LOST

As the gods stepped through the portal, they were met with a world unlike any they had yet seen. The air, thick with salt and the weight of the sea, tasted of brine and ancient winds. The land stretched before them in an expanse that felt both foreign and familiar – vast, untamed, and filled with the untold stories of time long past.

Before them lay a rugged, windswept shore, where the land kissed the sea in a jagged embrace. The towering mountains – massive, ancient sentinels – rose in the distance, their jagged peaks lost in a shroud of fog. These mountains stretched endlessly to the horizon, their snow-capped ridges catching what little light filtered through the dense, thick clouds. Their presence loomed large, casting long shadows over the land, as though they were watching over the world, silent and eternal.

The night sky was heavy with darkness, the stars hidden behind an ever-thickening veil of mist. The horizon, once a faint line of possibility, was now swallowed by an impenetrable fog, stretching as far as the eye could see. The ocean, a vast expanse of deep black, crashed relentlessly against the shore, its waves fierce and far-reaching, echoing in the distance like a wounded beast, each wave breaking with a mournful roar.

The land at their feet was a stark contrast to the natural beauty around them. The beach, once pristine, now lay scattered with the remnants of time – dry, coarse sand that blew with the wind, occasionally shifting like the secrets of forgotten lives. A few huts, crude and weather-worn, stood eerily on the shore. Their rotting wooden frames and thatched roofs seemed as though they had long been abandoned, their presence a ghostly reminder of a time before.

From the edge of the shore, a few undead emerged from the ground, their hollow eyes glowing faintly in the moonlight. They rose slowly, their limbs jerking with unnatural stiffness, as though the earth itself resisted their return. Others shuffled aimlessly near the huts, their presence adding to the oppressive, haunted feel of the place.

The sound of their movements was drowned by the thunderous crashes of the waves, but their unnatural groans still pierced the air, sending a chill through the group.

Out in the open water, the flicker of torchlight from boats drifted across the sea, their flames dancing precariously against the winds. The boats rocked gently with the tide, their silhouettes barely visible in the thick fog that surrounded them.

The sea itself was alive – its waves strong and violent, crashing against the shore with the fury of something ancient and unsettled. The deep rhythm of the ocean echoed far into the distance, each wave a reminder of a power that could not be tamed. The air smelled of salt and decay, as though the very water had been tainted by the land's dark secret.

Nashir stepped forward, his eyes scanning the horizon, the weight of the moment pressing against him. "This is not just a place of the dead… this is a land of lost memories." His voice was quiet, but filled with reverence for the place's darkness.

Alentar moved to his side, his sharp gaze taking in the scene. "There is something strange here. The land… the sea… they're both full of sorrow."

Taril's hand gripped his war hammer tightly as he surveyed the shore. "Let us not waste time pondering. We must find Alanteas, and we must do it quickly."

The land stretched out before them – an open expanse of mystery, danger, and haunting beauty. The eerie quiet of the night was broken only by the constant crash of waves against the shore and the occasional rustle of movement in the distance. But the group knew one thing: they had come to the right place, and now they must face what lay hidden beneath the fog.

As Alentar scanned the horizon, his powerful eyes pierced through the dense fog that obscured much of the coastline. He stood still for a moment, his elven senses stretched to their limits, and then his gaze narrowed. From a distance, nearly a mile away, he could just make out the faintest movements within the boats. His heart skipped a beat. "There's movement in the boats," he said quietly, his voice steady but firm. He turned to Nashir, whose connection to the land was undeniable.

Nashir stood next to him, his hands resting lightly on the staff he carried. His deep green eyes closed as he tuned in to the subtle rhythms of the earth. The sound of the crashing waves, the wind rustling through the trees, and the thrum of life that pulsed beneath their feet all blended together into a single awareness. He spoke in a low, contemplative tone, almost as if speaking to the earth itself. "There's a river to the east. Not far. It merges with the ocean." His brow furrowed slightly as he continued, his senses reaching farther. "The land itself seems... restless."

Opilkhos, standing silently beside Nashir, raised his head slightly, as if listening to the land as well. His piercing eyes scanned the same expanse, but his expression was unreadable. His lips barely parted as he spoke. "What do you make of it, Nashir?" His voice was quiet, yet it carried the weight of curiosity and wariness.

As the wind howled around them, they all felt it – the air was heavy with something beyond just the temperature. The cold had nothing to do with the biting winds or the lack of warmth from the distant sun. It was a coldness that permeated the very earth beneath their feet, as if the land itself had been frozen in time, awaiting something. The unease rooted itself deep in their bones.

Nashir looked toward the east, a pensive frown pulling at his lips. "The land... it has been tainted, touched by something unnatural. This cold is not of nature." His gaze moved back toward the group. "We must be cautious. There is more here than meets the eye."

Alentar's lips tightened in determination. He turned to the group, his gaze moving over each of them, his expression calm but resolute. "We'll investigate. The boats are too suspicious to ignore." He met Drunnyak's eyes for a brief moment before turning to face the others. "I'll go ahead. Stay ready, and stay close." He paused, his gaze drifting for just a moment as if deep in thought, before a subtle grin tugged at the corners of his mouth. "I've discovered something… something new. I can move unseen through shadows. Watch."

Niv, who had been silently observing the exchange, stepped forward, her amber eyes alight with both curiosity and determination. "How will you…?" she began, but before she could finish her question, Alentar was already moving.

With a fluid motion, he stepped behind Drunnyak, his massive frame blocking his path. The others could feel a shift in the air as Alentar's body seemed to vanish into the shadows that clung to the edges of the camp, melding seamlessly into the night. It was as though the darkness itself embraced him, as if he had become one with it.

Nashir and the others stood still for a moment, watching in awe, though they had known Alentar's skill with stealth. They had seen him perform feats of agility, but this was different – this was a mastery over the shadows themselves.

Drunnyak turned his massive head, blinking in surprise as he watched Alentar disappear. A low chuckle rumbled from his throat. "That's a trick I wouldn't mind learning." His voice was light, but there was a tinge of admiration in it.

Opilkhos's gaze remained fixed on the spot where Alentar had disappeared. He said nothing, but there was a flash of understanding in his eyes. His hand subtly rested on the hilt of his blade, an unspoken readiness as they all waited for the next move.

Nashir glanced toward Niv, whose expression was a mixture of curiosity and apprehension. Her hand too, almost instinctively, moved to her sword, fingers brushing the hilt as she watched the shadows with anticipation.

"Be careful," she said quietly, though her words were aimed more at herself than at Alentar. There was an underlying worry in her voice – something in the air had shifted, and she could feel it. She had seen Alentar fight before, but this – this felt different.

The group stood in the cold, with the shore stretching before them, the waves crashing faintly against the sand. The moonlight, dim and diffused through the thick fog, illuminated the scene with an eerie glow. The undead, their twisted forms shambling aimlessly along the shore, seemed to have an unnatural aversion to the water. They stopped just at the water's edge, as if some invisible boundary held them at bay. The air felt heavy, and the silence was deafening.

Nashir, standing tall, his staff in hand, felt the pull of the land beneath him. He could feel the weight of the mystery pressing on them, but it was the land that spoke the loudest in the stillness. He had honed his connection, but even now, the stillness rang louder than any scream.

Taril, beside him, glanced at the undead and shook his head, his war hammer resting comfortably in his grip. "They're not moving toward the water, as if they know something we don't," he mused, squinting at the thrashing sea. "They are drawn to the land – perhaps to something deeper, perhaps to some*one*."

Nashir nodded, understanding Taril's unspoken concern. "They won't approach the water. There's something unnatural here, something that keeps them at bay." His voice was low, filled with the same unease that hung heavy in the air.

The undead on the shore didn't appear to pose any immediate threat to them, yet the unease lingered. Nashir's connection to the earth confirmed that these were no mere wandering undead – they had purpose.

"We split up." Taril finally spoke, his voice cutting through the silence with quiet authority. "We need to find out what draws them here."

The gods exchanged brief glances, all understanding that the task at hand was critical.

Taril's eyes, sharp with experience, darted toward the faint silhouettes of the boats. "We will avoid the undead. They don't pose a threat if we keep our distance. We will go around them. Let's stay vigilant."

Nashir, his senses alive with the pulse of the land, stepped forward with a nod. "I will move east and see if there's any source to their attraction."

Opilkhos stepped to the left, his posture calm, yet the weight of his unspoken words hung heavily in the air. "I will move west. The sea's edge might hold secrets we cannot yet fathom."

Without further discussion, the gods began to move, splitting into different directions as they ventured into the unknown. The undead continued their aimless shuffle along the shore, indifferent to the gods' presence, their eerie movements part of an endless routine. As the group made their way further from the shoreline, the fog thickened, draping the land in an oppressive quiet. The cold, however, wasn't from the sea – it was something far older, a chill that seemed to seep from the very earth itself. It clung to the land, as if the land was remembering something long forgotten.

Nashir felt it first – a pull rising from the very heart of the earth beneath him, a restless stirring of the land's pulse. It was as though the very soil was alive, its ancient rhythms whispering to him, guiding him forward. He could feel the rocks shifting beneath him, the roots of the trees that ran deep in the ground stretching out as though waking from a long slumber. There was something here, something the land was eager to reveal.

Drunnyak moved towards the mountains to the north, his massive form cutting a path through the thick fog. His footsteps were measured and heavy, his eyes scanning the rocky terrain for any sign of disturbance. He didn't climb the mountains themselves, but instead stayed at their base, carefully inspecting the area. As he moved, he noticed a cluster of old homes perched high on the slopes. The homes showed signs of recent use – there were footprints leading up to the structures, tracks still fresh, no more than a day old. The homes appeared to have been built for defence, their elevated position offering protection from the undead. It was clear that someone had lived here recently, though the land felt abandoned now.

Niv, her eyes sharp and focused, walked in step with Opilkhos, her hand glowing softly as she used her powers to light their path. Her movements were cautious, the light a subtle whisper, just enough to see ahead without drawing attention. They moved with purpose, the sea crashing in the distance, and she silently assessed the area around them, ready to strike if necessary.

"We must be careful," Niv said softly, her voice cutting through the silence. "We don't want to attract too much attention." She stepped lightly, her senses alive with the pulse of the land, the grim weight of the undead nearby, still lingering.

Meanwhile, Taril had moved closer to the huts near the shore. His heavy war hammer was at the ready, but his focus was on the huts themselves, his keen eyes scanning every shadow. He pushed open one of the decaying doors, peering inside. The interior was cold and deserted, but the faint scent of something recently used lingered. As he moved further in, an undead shuffled toward him, its groans piercing the silence. With a swift strike, Taril dispatched it, sending the creature's body crashing to the ground. He grunted as he wiped his war hammer clean. "Ain't no peace here for them," he muttered, moving on to the next hut, keeping a sharp watch for any more undead that might emerge.

Nashir turned his attention to the east, where the river's faint outline could just be made out through the fog. He walked toward it, feeling the land's call grow stronger with each step. As he reached the river's edge, he knelt, running his fingers over the cool, clear water. His eyes narrowed as he noticed barrels and buckets sitting near the water's edge, filled with fresh water, slick with moisture. The water was untouched by time, gathered only recently. There was a strange sense of calm about the place, as if someone had been here, taking care of things just before they disappeared.

The scene before him spoke of life, but one that had quickly faltered, now abandoned. It was as though the land itself was holding its breath, waiting for something to happen.

Nashir straightened, his face set with quiet resolve. "It is still fresh… someone has been here, not long ago." He stood and began walking upstream, moving deeper into the wilderness.

Alentar moved with the shadows, his steps silent on the boat's creaking wooden planks. The night enveloped him like a second skin, his powers masking his presence from the eyes of the fishermen working just ahead. He watched them from the darkness, their figures barely visible in the dim light of lanterns swaying from the boat's mast. The large vessel groaned under the weight of its cargo, and Alentar could feel the vibrations of the waves beneath him, the boat rocking with the tide. There were several areas he had to navigate through, each section of the boat humming with its own activity.

At the bow, a handful of fishermen were busy untangling nets. The faint sound of the ocean slapping the hull was the only thing louder than their voices. Ralf, a broad-shouldered man with weathered skin, was barking orders to Theo, a lanky young fisherman who was still learning the ropes.

"Theo, get that net cleared! The storm's coming in fast!" Ralf's voice was rough, deep, carrying the weight of experience.

"Aye aye, Ralf," Theo muttered, pulling at the tangled net with a grunt. His hands were calloused and rough, stained with the salt of the sea, his face covered in a layer of stubble that seemed to speak of long, sleepless nights spent on the water.

As Alentar moved toward the stern, he could hear Gerard and Lina, a married couple who seemed to be in charge of preparing the evening meal. Gerard, the older of the two, was scrubbing large wooden bowls, while Lina, shorter and wiry, arranged what looked like dried fish in the baskets.

"The wind's picking up, Gerard. We should be inside before the storm hits." Her voice was quick and worried.

Gerard didn't look up, but grunted in response. "Supper's near ready, Lina. We'll bring it in soon enough. Storm won't stop the cooking, eh?" He smiled grimly, knowing the storm would soon be upon them.

Alentar crept further along the boat, towards the deck where a small group of men were standing. They were scanning the horizon, their faces grim.

Kade, the youngest among them, leaned against the railing, his eyes searching the foggy distance. "You think the storm's gonna hit us hard?" he asked, his accent thick with the salt and weariness of years spent at sea.

Marcus, an older man with salt-and-pepper hair, gripped the edge of the ship's railing tightly, his knuckles white. "Aye, the storm's coming. The wind's shifting, and that's not a good sign. We'll be ready to batten down before it hits."

The men shifted, gathering their things as Ralf shouted from the bow, "Get inside, all of you! Supper's ready, and we need to secure the ship!"

As Alentar listened to the men and women of the boat, their voices filled with the rhythms of their hard lives – tired, but steady with the strength of experience. He could feel their unease as the storm approached. The boat was no longer a simple vessel; it was a place of refuge, a place where these people had found purpose in their struggle against nature's wrath. And yet, there was something else in the air – the tension of something unknown. The undead's presence had already cast its shadow over them, but they were oblivious to the figure watching them from the darkness.

As Alentar stood at the edge of the boat, he caught a glimpse of the captain – Alden, a tall, broad man who stood at the wheel, staring intently at the mist ahead. His hands, like the others', were weathered by years of hard work.

"Everyone, get inside! We're taking shelter before this storm hits!" His voice was strong, but even Alentar could hear the undercurrent of nervousness. Alden had the look of a man who had lived through more than his share of storms, but the sea had its own way of terrifying even the strongest of men.

For a brief moment, Alentar stood in the shadows, unseen, hidden within the fog and the shifting shadows of the ship. He could hear their lives, their conversations, the steady rhythm of their hard labour – and yet, there was no sense of malice in their voices. These were not the monsters that lurked in the night. No, these were simple men and women, working tirelessly to survive in a world that had become far darker than it ever should have been.

As the men began to gather their things and move below deck, Alentar's heart grew heavier. He had found them – these living, breathing survivors – but there was still the darkness of the undead lurking at the edges of their world.

As the storm rolled in, the undead continued to shuffle along the shore, a quiet, relentless presence. Alentar remained hidden in the shadows, watching the fishermen as they spoke of their plans for the coming day. They had spent their nights on the boats, fishing what they could and making the best of a world turned cold and uncertain. As dawn approached, they talked about venturing to the shore to gather fresh drinking water from the river to the east, planning to return to their inland homes near the mountains once it was safe.

The humans were used to this rhythm – working through the nights and resting by day, careful not to venture too far when the undead roamed. They knew the dangers of their world, but the gods' presence remained unknown to them.

Alentar, silent and still in the shadows, allowed the fishermen to continue their preparations without interruption. He didn't want to alarm them – his task now was simply to observe. As his gaze shifted, he could just make out the figures of his companions on the shore, moving carefully through the fog. Though the humans couldn't see them, Alentar could sense the others' every movement, their silhouettes barely visible to his sharp eyes. He understood that it would be best to let the group come together first before revealing themselves. No need to cause confusion until they had gathered all the information they could.

With one final glance at the fishermen, Alentar slipped away, retreating silently into the darkness. He knew it would be best to regroup with the others and share his observations. There was no need to meet with the fishermen just yet. For now, he would stay hidden and watch, waiting for the right moment to join the others and discuss the next steps. The plan was clear – gather as much information as possible and wait until it was safe to approach the humans. Only then would they reveal themselves, when the undead were no longer a threat to the village.

As he vanished back into the mist, his mind focused on the next step, Alentar felt a renewed sense of purpose. They would find a way to help these people, to lead them to safety. But first they had to gather the right knowledge, and Alentar knew that, together with his companions, he would make his move at the right moment.

Alentar emerged from the shadows, his presence barely a whisper in the thick mist that clung to the shore. He moved swiftly, his steps sure and calculated as he approached Nashir, who stood with his staff planted firmly in the sand, eyes focused on the chaos of the storm and the relentless crash of waves against the shore. The winds howled around them, and the dark sky seemed to swell with fury. The sea, now a tumult of roiling waves, swallowed the undead as they struggled in the shallows. The bodies were dragged under, pulled by the violent tide, disappearing into the deep.

Nashir turned at the sound of Alentar's approach; though his features remained unreadable, a quiet understanding lingered in his gaze.

Without a word, Alentar nodded towards the storm. "We need to gather the others. I have news." His voice, though soft, carried with it the weight of urgency. The time to act was coming – Alanteas's path was clearer now, and the next steps were critical.

Nashir, ever the composed force of nature, gave a single nod. "Let us move swiftly." He gestured for Alentar to lead the way, and together they moved quickly, the wind lashing against them, the salty air biting their skin. The storm raged louder, the sound of thunder vibrating the earth beneath their feet, but it was not the storm that caught Alentar's attention now – it was something else. A faint trace of something familiar.

The waves crashed harder as they passed the remains of the undead, their broken bodies now nothing more than debris torn apart by the sea's might. Yet, despite the storm's fury, the brothers moved with a quiet grace, their senses tuned to the land, the wind, the sea. The air was thick with tension, the roar of the storm and the crashing waves blending with the distant echoes of their own hearts pounding with the rhythm of their resolve.

As they walked, Nashir suddenly paused. He felt the familiar pulse of the earth beneath his feet, yet as his senses reached toward the water's edge, they faltered, cut off at the shore. The ocean, though part of the land, stood beyond his reach. It was as if his connection to the land ended at the beginning of the sea, leaving him with only a sense of wonder and mystery, an inexplicable void where his powers could not reach.

Alentar, however, didn't miss the signs. His sharp eyes caught a glimpse of something. Just at the edge of the shore, hidden in the sand, were faint tracks – footprints barely visible, but unmistakable to his trained gaze. He knelt for a moment, touching the ground gently, feeling the earth beneath his fingertips. He could smell the faint trace of something familiar. Something that he had taught Alanteas long ago – black cumin seeds, left behind by their passage. These weren't ordinary marks. They were Alanteas's steps, left in the sand, a subtle trail showing where he had gone.

Alentar rose, his eyes scanning the distance, and his heart quickened as the pieces fell into place. Alanteas had been here. These were his tracks – his breadcrumb path. They had been hidden carefully, perhaps with intent to confuse, but not enough to escape Alentar's keen eye.

Nashir, sensing Alentar's change in demeanour, looked at him questioningly, his brow furrowing. "What do you see?"

Alentar didn't speak at first; instead, he looked toward the mountains in the distance. The jagged peaks loomed like sentinels against the darkened sky, the village nestled among them, safe – for now. He looked back at Nashir. "He was here. Alanteas left these marks. We are close."

Without hesitation, Nashir nodded. They knew what had to be done now. They weren't just searching for Alanteas any more – they were following the thread he had left behind. The stakes were higher now, and the path forward was clearer. "Then we must follow," Nashir said, his voice firm, filled with quiet determination.

The storm raged harder around them, but their focus was unwavering. Together, they would press on. The earth beneath them was alive with power, the storm not just a force of nature, but a sign – a challenge to be met.

As the gods moved forward, they passed through the remaining undead, each one now washed back into the sea by the violent waves. The shore was becoming quieter now, as if the very earth itself was reclaiming its dominion. The wind howled around them, but their purpose remained clear – Alanteas had left them a path, and they would follow it, no matter where it led.

They moved swiftly, the mountains growing closer with each step, the fog thickening as they neared the homes among the peaks. It was here, at the foot of the mountains, that they would find the next piece of the puzzle – the final thread of their journey.

And in the distance, the faintest glimmer of hope began to flicker – a signal that, perhaps, their search was nearly at an end.

They continued their swift journey, the air grew colder, and the thickening fog began to bite at their skin. The once-turbulent waves and stormy winds seemed to recede, but the atmosphere was still heavy with the unease of the unknown. They moved steadily, their purpose unwavering. The distant mountains loomed ever closer, the jagged peaks cutting through the fog like the spires of an ancient castle.

The homes nestled in the mountain pass came into view. They were small but sturdy, built into the side of the mountain, as though they had grown from the very rock itself. The buildings were spaced just far enough apart to offer privacy, yet close enough to form a small community, all embedded within the harsh terrain. The homes were crafted with stone and timber, their roofs sloping sharply to ward off the snow that must fall often here. A few faint lights flickered inside, and smoke rose from the chimneys, carrying with it the scent of burning wood and salt air.

At the head of the group, Alentar's eyes never wavered from the path. His mind raced with the possibilities of what they might find. Behind him, Taril walked steadily, his war hammer resting on his shoulder, eyes scanning the terrain with the same careful precision he used in battle. He had learned the value of patience during their time together – patience not only in watching, but in understanding the land and its people. His thick, fur-lined tunic kept the chill at bay, but the thought of what lay ahead kept his mind sharp, every step attuned with the gods' purpose.

Opilkhos, ever the silent observer, walked with quiet determination. His amber eyes flickered with an inner fire, a quiet intensity that only those closest to him could understand. The storm had no effect on him, for his powers and strength were linked to something much older, deeper. He felt the land like an old companion, his connection to it as natural as the air he breathed.

Niv, quick on her feet and always observant, walked close beside Taril. Her movements were fluid and calculated, the same grace she carried in battle now applied to this silent march toward the unknown. Her sharp eyes picked out the details others might have missed – the way the wind stirred the grass, the faint crunch of earth beneath their feet. Though the tension in the air was palpable, her presence was calm, a reassuring sense of control that grounded those around her.

Drunnyak, the towering figure of strength, walked with a broad grin plastered on his face despite the gravity of their task. His lion-hide armour clung to his broad chest, and his boots crunched in rhythm with the others'. Though his size and physicality would suggest otherwise, Drunnyak had learned the value of quiet observation. His ears caught the slightest sounds – the creak of a distant door, the whisper of movement in the trees – all while his large hand idly gripped the hilt of his massive sword.

Their connection was palpable, even in the silent march. Despite the quiet urgency of their task, there was a bond between them all, unspoken yet undeniable. They had fought together, learned together, and now they were united once more in their shared goal – finding Alanteas and unravelling the mystery of the undead and themselves.

As they approached the first of the homes, Taril spoke in a low voice, his words carrying across the faint hum of the mountain breeze. "We're close," he murmured. "I can feel it – the land is speaking. The pulse of the earth is alive with something more than just the undead."

Opilkhos nodded slightly, his amber eyes scanning the homes ahead. "The undead stay near the shore. But this…" He paused. "This feels different. It's not just death walking here. There's something guiding them."

Niv, with her usual clarity, voiced what they all felt. "There's a presence here – something larger than the undead, something controlling them. I can feel it."

Drunnyak, who had remained silent up until now, broke his grin into a more sombre expression. "Then let's find it," he said, his voice booming but resolute. "We've come this far. We're not stopping now."

Alentar, still leading the way, turned back to meet their eyes. "I've seen the marks," he said quietly. "Alanteas's path is clear. We are near. Stay sharp."

The group moved onward, each of them feeling the weight of what lay ahead – the unknown, the danger, but most importantly, the truth that needed to be uncovered. And as they neared the first cluster of huts, the gods felt the air grow thicker, as if the very land itself was holding its breath.

Alentar's voice was steady but urgent. "We'll find him soon. Stay close. Whatever happens next, we face it together."

The homes ahead stood like sentinels, silent and waiting. The tension in the air could be felt by all, but there was a sense of purpose in their steps. The gods were not just moving forward – they were closing in on the truth, on Alanteas, and on whatever darkness lay ahead.

Together, they entered the first home in the row, the door creaking open, and the mystery of this new area slowly began to unfold before them.

The air was thick with the scent of salt water and the weight of the storm, which had only grown fiercer with each passing minute. The gods, having traversed the rugged terrain of this land, now found themselves entering a small, humble dwelling nestled at the foot of the towering mountains. The house, though sparse, exuded the warmth of a home that had witnessed countless quiet moments – moments filled with lives lived in the shadow of the ocean and the ever-present threat of the undead.

They entered with careful steps, the storm raging outside as the sound of waves crashing against the rocks echoed in the distance. The low, rhythmic crackle of thunder rumbled overhead, shaking the very foundations of the house, yet the walls offered them shelter – a brief reprieve from the chaos.

As they gathered around a worn wooden table, the flickering light from a small hearth cast long shadows across the room. Alentar moved to the centre of the space, his figure a beacon in the otherwise dim room. He stood for a moment, gazing at each of them as the storm howled outside, the sound growing louder with each passing second.

"Sit," Alentar said quietly, his voice steady but carrying the weight of urgency. "We are not in a place to take chances. There are things we need to discuss, things we must understand. What I've seen here – the humans, their way of life – it is different from what we know. We must not underestimate them." He paused, his gaze flickering to the windows, where the storm's fury seemed to press in on them. The shadows in the room seemed to grow longer, deeper. Alentar continued, his voice low. "They dwell on boats at night, moving freely across the water, but during the day, they retreat to these homes, as they take shelter from the waves and the storm." He could feel the others' eyes on him, waiting for more. "I observed them. I listened. They mentioned their names – names I now carry with me." His eyes briefly wandered to the doorway, as if the storm beyond carried with it the ghosts of the past, the names of those he'd overheard while watching the fishermen on their boats. "Theo, they called one of them. The other, the captain, Alden. I heard others too, names of women and children, but I could not grasp them all. These fishermen live between the shore and the mountains. Though they are aware of the undead, they do not seem to fear them, having found a way to stay safely out of their reach during the night." Alentar sighed softly, the tension of the journey pressing on his chest. "They live here, in a fragile truce with the sea, but their lives are not without struggle. It is a life of survival, not unlike the others in Garrents." He glanced back at the gods, their expressions grave. "We must tread carefully and not frighten them. These people may hold knowledge of the land that we have yet to uncover. They are closely tied to the sea and the mountains. I'm certain Alanteas was here, and they may know what became of him."

The room was silent, the weight of his words hanging heavy in the air. The gods understood the gravity of the situation. This was not just a search for Alanteas any more. This was something more – something connected to the very forces they had come to terms with. The undead, the land, the sea and the humans – they were all interwoven in a way that now seemed more urgent, more dangerous.

"Now we must make our next move," Alentar concluded, his tone firm. "But we must first understand what these people know, as the sea and this storm are not the only things that hide the truth here."

As Alentar spoke, detailing his observations of the fishermen and their connection to the land, Nashir's gaze drifted to the horizon through a window, his mind still attuned to the earth beneath his feet. His voice, thoughtful and laced with a hint of unease, broke the silence.

"The river meets the ocean to the east," Nashir said, his words measured, his brow furrowing in contemplation. "But as I stood there, reaching out with my connection to the land, something… blocked me. The sea – it refused to open to me, as if it were beyond my power. All the earth, all nature, had welcomed my touch. But the sea… the fog, the depths – there is something lingering there. A presence, a power – something ancient. Maybe even older than us." He paused, his eyes narrowing as he watched the waves crash against the shore in the distance. "It is as if the sea guards something – something it will not reveal."

The group fell silent, the weight of Nashir's words settling heavily over them. The sea, normally a part of the land's natural rhythm, now felt foreign, a boundary that even Nashir's immense power couldn't cross.

The gods exchanged a look, their resolve hardening. They were no strangers to danger, but this was a different kind of threat – a threat that could change everything they had worked for.

"We must wait for the storm to subside," Alentar added, "and then we will find the answers we seek."

The fire in the hearth crackled, a small but steady light in the otherwise dark room, as the storm outside continued to rage. The gods settled in, knowing that what they had learned so far was just the beginning of a much larger journey – one that would lead them deeper into the heart of this land, and perhaps closer to the truth they had been seeking.

And so, in the quiet of the house, surrounded by the hum of the storm, they prepared themselves for what was to come. They had no choice but to wait, to listen, and to learn. The next steps would not be easy, but they knew they were ready.

TIDES OF DAWN

As the storm subsided and the eerie stillness of the morning settled over the land, the air felt heavy with the remnants of the tempest. The mist hung low, swirling lazily across the shore, the sea's angry waves now reduced to a rhythmic ebb and flow. The undead had vanished, either swallowed by the depths or dragged back into the earth, their presence now only a lingering memory in the air.

The humans, no more than thirty in number, began to stir. The larger boats that had remained anchored just offshore slowly began to untie, the fishermen lowering their smaller boats into the water with practised ease. They moved with quiet purpose, rowing steadily towards the river's edge, their heads bent against the wind. A few others disembarked, walking along the shore in the direction of the homes nestled in the mountains.

Alentar, standing at the forefront of the group of gods, nodded slowly. "We need to approach carefully," he said, his voice low and steady, though his gaze remained sharp, scanning the scene before them. "We can't afford to scare them. Their connection to this place is deep, and we need to tread lightly."

Drunnyak, who had been eyeing the fishermen with an almost playful curiosity, let out a low chuckle. "Maybe Opilkhos or Niv should

do the talking," he suggested with a grin. "Both have a way with words…
or, at least, a way of making an impression." He winked, his towering
frame standing like a mountain against the backdrop of the mist.

Opilkhos raised an eyebrow, his lips curling into a subtle smile. "I
don't think they'll be intimidated by either of us," he said drily. "But Niv,
well, her charm can disarm even the most wary of hearts." He turned to
Niv, giving her a knowing look.

Niv smirked, crossing her arms over her chest. "Charm? You mean
my 'forceful persuasion,'" she teased, a twinkle in her amber eyes. "I'll
make sure we're all on our best behaviour," she added, stepping forward
with a wink.

The air was filled with the hum of quiet laughter as the group exchanged
playful glances. There was a lightness to their banter, a camaraderie that
hadn't been there before, built through the trials they had faced together.
For a moment, the weight of their mission seemed lighter, the uncertainty
of their task softened by the warmth of their friendship.

Alentar chuckled quietly, shaking his head at the back-and-forth.
"Focus," he said, though the smile tugging at the corners of his lips
betrayed the seriousness of his words. "We have a job to do. But for
now, let's keep it steady."

Drunnyak's booming laugh echoed across the shore, and even
Opilkhos couldn't help but smile, the tension easing between them.

"All right, all right, we'll keep it steady," Drunnyak agreed, still
chuckling. "But if they're anything like you, Alentar, I might just stay
behind to let Niv handle the talking. I have a feeling she might be the
best one for the job."

With that, the group gathered themselves, their mood light but
their purpose clear. Together, they began their approach, moving
toward the fishermen, as they approached the shore, ready for whatever
they would find. The air was thick with anticipation, but with each
step, they knew they were one step closer to unlocking the secrets of
this place – and the fate of Alanteas.

The larger fishing boats remained anchored offshore, but these
smaller vessels, no more than skiffs, carried the handful of fishermen

who had managed to survive the night. They moved with practised ease, rowing towards the land with baskets slung over their shoulders and small buckets of water in hand.

Some of the humans disembarked and made their way to the homes nestled in the mountain pass, their bodies bent with the weight of both the day's labour and the night's watch. Others paused at the water's edge, unloading their cargo and preparing to collect more supplies.

Alentar stood, eyes sharp as he watched their every movement. He nodded to the others, signalling that it was time to move. The gods approached the shore cautiously, their feet sinking softly into the wet sand, as if the land itself was reluctant to welcome them.

Niv, ever the confident presence in moments like these, stepped forward. Her voice rang out, calm yet assertive, with the clarity that only centuries of experience could provide. "Fear not. We bid you a good morning," she said, her tone warm, but carrying an undercurrent of purpose. "We are seeking a friend of ours. Someone who disappeared several weeks ago. His name is Alanteas."

The small group of fishermen, initially startled by the sudden appearance of the gods, took a step back. But Marcus, the eldest among them, recognised something in their presence. His weathered eyes studied them closely, and after a moment, his gaze softened with recognition.

"You must be the ones he spoke of," Marcus said slowly, his voice gruff but not unkind. "Alanteas mentioned you in passing, though not by name. He said if anything happened to him, you would come looking."

Niv's eyes brightened, a flicker of hope igniting within her. "You've seen him?"

Marcus nodded slowly, his face thoughtful as he recalled the encounter. "Aye, we met him. Alanteas came through our village a few weeks ago, looking to help us, or at least to offer us a new life. He spoke of a place called Garrents, a village that had risen from nothing, that had saved another village from giants. They were building something bigger, a community that could bring other villages together, make them stronger." Marcus hesitated, his gaze moving to the distant sea before continuing. "He invited us to join them. He thought we might find a better life there, one away from the threat of the undead. But our captain, Alden, he didn't see it that way. We've found peace here. Our life at sea, though hard, is one we've come to balance with. Alden told Alanteas we were content here. We live part in the sea, part inland, and it's kept us safe." Marcus looked down, a trace of nostalgia in his eyes. "Alden mentioned to Alanteas that we used to trade with people from an island a couple of days up the coast, heading west. But that path... it's a dangerous one. To reach the island, you have to go through a stony shore, the rocks rising out of the water, and deeper into the sea. The fog hides much of it. No one dares go there any more, not since we were told to stay away. It's a risky way to navigate, and Alden said we don't need to take the chance, especially now." He paused, his voice heavy with the weight of time. "The islanders used to be our trading partners. When Alden was a child, and I was captain, we would make the journey and trade with them, mostly for goods, food that we can't grow here, tools, and the like. But that was decades ago. We haven't heard from them in years. Not since the last storm took their lighthouse, and the island sank deeper into isolation. We haven't traded with them since." Marcus's gaze met Alentar's, a quiet understanding between them. "A few weeks ago, Alanteas left us. He went out on a small boat, hoping to find the islanders, hoping they were still out there. We haven't seen him since."

The group stood in silence, each absorbing the weight of Marcus's words. Their eyes met, unspoken understanding passing between them like a current. There was more to the story than what they had been told, more questions to ask, more mysteries to unravel. The tension in the air was palpable, but the gods, ever vigilant, nodded amongst themselves, their resolve firm.

Drunnyak broke the silence with a low chuckle, turning to Taril. The two shared a silent nod, an unspoken agreement passing between them. Without a word, they moved toward the fishermen, their broad forms casting long shadows on the sand. Drunnyak, his towering presence softened by a genuine smile, called out to Marcus and his companions.

"Perhaps we can lend a hand," he said in a deep, booming voice. "We'd be happy to help carry the goods. A bit of warmth from our side, eh? Might even join you for a quiet night in your homes or at your boat. The journey's been long, and we could all use a bit of rest."

His grin widened, and Taril, ever the tactician, followed suit with a playful wink, adding, "We know a thing or two about hospitality and we have much to discuss."

The fishermen, initially surprised by the offer, exchanged hesitant looks. But there was something in Drunnyak's manner, his warmth and easy charm, that put them at ease. One by one, they began to nod, acknowledging the gods' offer to help. As Drunnyak and Taril approached the boats, they began unloading the fish and the baskets of supplies, their movements quick and efficient, as though they had done this many times before.

Meanwhile Alentar, ever perceptive, kept his gaze on the horizon. His sharp eyes caught the movement of other boats approaching the shore. The captain, Alden, was at the helm of one, with Ralf by his side. They were moving quickly, their faces a mixture of curiosity and caution, clearly eager to see what was happening. Alentar observed their fast pace, noting their determination to meet the group before the situation could escalate. The fishermen were not accustomed to visitors, and the presence of the gods had no doubt raised their concerns.

Alentar exchanged a look with Nashir, who stood by his side, his expression unreadable but focused. The gods knew that the conversation with the captain would be pivotal. They would need to tread carefully, gaining the trust of these people without raising suspicion or fear. The undead had driven them to isolation, and the gods could not afford to alienate them now.

"Stay close," Alentar murmured, his voice low but urgent. "The captain will want to know what's going on. We can't afford to push too hard, too fast."

As Alden and Ralf neared, the gods stood tall, prepared to face whatever questions or suspicions they might have. The air around them hummed with quiet anticipation, the storm having passed but the tension still lingering. The gods had come to seek answers, and they would have to tread carefully to ensure their mission could be fulfilled.

As Alden and Ralf approached the group, the air thickened with anticipation.

Niv, ever the one to ease the weight of a moment, stepped forward first. Her smile was warm, but her eyes betrayed the urgency of their quest. "I'm Niv," she said, her voice calm but edged with purpose. "And this is Opilkhos." She motioned to him beside her. "We're searching for a friend – his name is Alanteas. We've learned from Marcus that he passed through here not long ago, and we're hoping you might help us find him."

Alden's eyes remained cautious, as if weighing each word before speaking. "Alanteas, you say?" He nodded slightly, the lines on his face deepening as he recalled their brief encounter. "Aye, we met him. A few weeks back. He told us of a place called Garrents, where he'd helped save another village from giants. He was looking for villages and people that might be interested in joining them, even talked about a village where giants had enslaved the people, and they managed to free them." Alden hesitated for a moment, his brow furrowing as he thought. "I told him there weren't many villages left, but there's an island west of here. We used to trade with the people there, before things got too dangerous."

Marcus, standing quietly behind Alden, spoke up. "The island is a place none venture to these days. It was once a safe trade hub, where we exchanged goods. But the path there is perilous. The fog, the rocks, and the undead that lurk in the shadows of the sea. The risks are too great, even for us. We lost contact with them years ago, after the storms and the tides grew more unpredictable."

Alden nodded, his expression solemn. "Walking around the mountains would take months. The path is too long, and with dark things stirring in every hollow, no one dares to make the journey. The sea… it's treacherous. That's why we've stayed here, on the boats. We can fish, we can gather, but staying away from land keeps us safer. The undead don't seem to bother us while we're at sea."

Niv listened intently, her heart heavy with the new information. This was a crucial lead, but it also came with its own set of dangers. "So, Alanteas set out for this island, hoping to uncover the truth of what happened and whether anyone still lives there?"

Marcus nodded again, his face hardening as he continued. "Aye, he hoped the islanders might have needs that Garrents could fulfil, and perhaps they would offer him something that could lead him to the answers he was searching for. But we never heard from him after he left. Took a small boat, he did. Went toward the island. I… I warned him about the fog and the rocks, but he seemed determined."

Alden looked out toward the horizon, his hand resting on the hilt of his sword. "He left with little more than a prayer and a dream. That was weeks ago."

Niv's gaze softened, but her resolve didn't waver. "Thank you. That helps more than you know." She looked to the gods, a quiet determination settling into her heart. "We'll find him, wherever he is."

The air grew heavier with the weight of unspoken truths as Taril's eyes met Drunnyak's, and the silent understanding passed between them. They both turned to Nashir, whose gaze was already locked with theirs, a shared thought lingering in the space between them. After a few tense moments, Taril broke the silence.

"You keep speaking of the dangers of the fog, yet we've noticed you keep your boats just before the fog line," he said, his voice measured, though a quiet tension crept in. "Why is that?"

The villagers exchanged quick, uneasy glances, their expressions shifting.

It was Ralf who spoke first, though his voice faltered slightly. "The fog… It's not just fog," he said, the words coming slowly, as though he weighed them carefully before letting them leave his lips. "It's a part of the sea. You don't understand it unless you've lived with it."

Marcus, standing beside him, looked sharply at Ralf, a look of warning in his eyes. But it was Alden who seemed the most affected, his gaze lowering as if he knew the conversation was veering dangerously close to something forbidden.

Alentar's voice broke the uncomfortable silence. "I spent the night watching the fog," he said, his tone steady yet probing. "It doesn't move. Only a thin mist drifts out from it, but the fog itself... it doesn't shift. Why is that?"

The fishermen froze for a moment, the tension thick in the air. Ralf's brow furrowed, and Marcus shifted uneasily, avoiding Alentar's direct gaze. Alden, however, stood silent for a long moment, his hand tightening around the hilt of his weapon as though it was the only thing grounding him.

"We... we don't know," Ralf finally said, his voice low. "Not exactly. The fog's been like this for as long as any of us can remember. We've learned to live with it." His words trailed off, and his eyes met Alden's. There was a quiet panic there, an unspoken agreement that what was being discussed should not go any further.

Alden took a step forward, his posture defensive, though he tried to remain calm. "It's just... the way things are," he muttered. "The sea has its moods, and the fog's a part of that. We don't ask questions about it. We just stay clear. We don't go near it, and it doesn't seem to bother us. That's how it's always been."

Marcus, his face pale, glanced nervously at the others. "But..." He hesitated, his voice wavering slightly. "But don't you see? It's the only way for us to live. The sea keeps the undead away. We stay just outside the fog, on the edge of the water. If we went any further, we'd risk getting caught in it. We... we can't explain why, we just know that's the way it is." His eyes seemed to look far away, as if remembering something long buried. "When I was a child, I remember my father speaking to those who came from the sea. They'd warn us – warn us never to go beyond the fog. They said it belonged to them. The sea, the mist... it was theirs. We were allowed to fish, but only within half a league from the shore. Anyone who tried to venture further... they disappeared. Boats sank without a trace. My father used to say it was the sea's way of keeping us in line." He paused, shaking his head slightly as though trying to shake off the weight of the old memories. "It's not just the undead. There's something else... something we don't understand. But we've learned, over time, that we live best when we respect the boundaries the sea has set for us."

Marcus's eyes seemed to lose focus, as if the weight of the past was slowly creeping back into his mind. He trembled slightly, clearly shaken by the truth he had just revealed. As the silence thickened, Opilkhos stepped forward, his presence steady and calm. He moved with purpose, his stride unwavering as he approached the fisherman.

With a serene expression, Opilkhos placed his hands gently on Marcus's shoulders, offering not just a comforting touch, but a quiet strength. As his fingers made contact, a golden aura began to emanate from his body, subtle at first, but soon growing brighter, bathing the surrounding air in an ethereal glow. The fishermen, caught off guard, looked at one another in stunned silence, their eyes widening as they witnessed something they had never seen before.

The air seemed to thrum with power. The light around Opilkhos intensified, a radiant gold mixed with white, like the glow of a diamond, and his eyes met Marcus's with an unspoken invitation. It was a gaze that softened the edges of fear, offering not just reassurance, but a sense of protection.

The other gods, observing this interaction, exchanged silent glances. Niv gave a small nod of approval, while Taril and Drunnyak, though ever so stoical, seemed to sense the impact Opilkhos was having. Their auras too began to subtly swell, filling the space with their power. Nashir's presence, like the deep breath of the earth itself, added a quiet steadiness to the growing connection.

The fishermen, once tense and wary, felt the warmth and weight of the divine presence settle upon them. The oppressive fear that had clung to them began to lift, replaced by an undeniable sense of ease. They looked at one another, and then at the gods, feeling the shift in the air – a palpable, shared understanding that the gods were here to help. The gods' auras now pulsed openly, filling the space around them, and the fishermen could feel it.

Niv, ever graceful in her own way, stepped forward with a gentle smile, further easing the tension. The gods had revealed themselves, their presence unmistakable. It was no longer just a distant hope for the villagers – it was real.

Marcus, now visibly more at ease, turned to Opilkhos, his gaze filled with awe and quiet reverence. His voice, though steady, still carried the weight of the past. "Thank you," he said, his words almost a whisper, as if he could hardly believe the reality unfolding before him. "I… I didn't expect this. You've shown us what we needed most."

The fishermen, still in stunned silence, looked on, their eyes wide as they took in the divine presence before them. The atmosphere seemed to shimmer with the gods' auras, and Marcus could hardly tear his gaze away from Opilkhos, the golden light surrounding him like something out of a dream.

Finally, his voice came, hesitant but filled with awe. "Are you the gods from the legends?"

Opilkhos, his expression calm yet full of quiet strength, nodded once, his eyes meeting Marcus's with the weight of unspoken history. "We are the ones of legend, yes," he said, his voice rich with authority, but also with warmth. "We've returned to offer our protection. And we'll stand with you in this fight, as we've done before."

At that moment, Drunnyak, who had been setting down the baskets of food and supplies, straightened, his imposing figure casting a long shadow. His deep voice rang out, clear and firm, as he stepped forward. He looked at Marcus, Alden and the others, and in the powerful silence that followed, he spoke the truth they had been waiting to hear. "We are the gods you've heard of in the stories," Drunnyak said, his words echoing with strength. "We didn't come here by chance. We sent Alanteas to gather those who could not protect themselves and offer them a better life. Garrents is more than a village now – it is the heart of a movement to protect and unite, to shield others from the darkness. We've fought against the undead since our awakening a few months ago, and we know what's at stake. Alanteas was the first step, and now we will help you grow stronger."

Alden, still reeling from the revelation, finally spoke, his voice soft yet filled with a quiet urgency. "You… you mean to protect us? From the undead? But… why now? Why return after so long?"

Nashir stepped forward, his voice calm but filled with deep resonance. "The world has changed, and so must we. Our power comes from the land and from the people. We are here because you need us, but you will need to rise as well. We will teach you, we will protect you, but the road ahead is long."

Taril, ever the one to add levity, spoke next with a deep laugh, his voice booming. "And we won't let any undead stand in the way of that." He looked to the others, raising his massive war hammer high in a playful show of strength. "We're here, and we're staying. Together, we will build something stronger than any of us alone."

Opilkhos gave a slight nod to the group, his eyes taking in the reactions of the fishermen. "This is why we are here. To help you grow, to build strength together. We protect, but we also empower. We've come to restore balance, and you will be part of that. The others you've lost – those who did not join us – will be found, and they will be brought into the fold."

As the fishermen exchanged glances, a deep sense of reverence began to take root in their hearts. What had seemed impossible was now real. The gods had returned, and they were not just saviours – they were offering the promise of unity, protection and hope.

Drunnyak finished with a smile, his voice warm with pride. "Garrents isn't just a place – it's the future of this world. We've started, but it's up to all of us to make it thrive."

The silence that followed was thick with the weight of their words. The gods had spoken, and the fishermen's village was forever changed.

Opilkhos gave a small nod, his eyes still locked with Marcus's, his presence as calm as ever. "It is not just your burden to bear. The land and the sea have their ways, but we will help you find your path through them."

As the gods stood together, their auras now openly shining, the fishermen's worries seemed to melt away. The harshness of their lives, the weight of their fears, felt lighter.

As the weight of the gods' presence hung heavily in the air, the fishermen stood in awe, their minds struggling to grasp the reality of what they had just witnessed. The world had shifted, and with it, a new and profound understanding began to settle in their hearts. The gods had revealed themselves, their purpose clear – but it was Nashir, the god of nature, who would now show them the full extent of his power.

Nashir stood still for a moment, taking in the land before him, his hand resting gently on his staff. The storm had passed, but the air still hummed with a strange energy. The waves of the sea crashed in the distance, but Nashir's attention was fixed on the ground beneath him. Slowly, he raised his staff, and a deep silence fell over the land as if nature itself paused to listen. The ground trembled faintly beneath their feet as Nashir's voice rang out, low and resonant, filled with ancient power. "Let nature regain its balance," he murmured, his words carrying the weight of aeons. "Let life return where death once lingered. Protect these lands."

With that single command, the air shifted. The earth responded to Nashir's call, as if the very soil and roots recognised the voice of their ancient master. The trees around them, some twisted and barren from the harsh conditions, began to stir, their leaves rustling as new life awakened within them. Thick vines snaked out from the ground, rising to form a natural barrier between the mountain to the north and the river to the east.

The fishermen, their mouths agape, watched as the forest itself seemed to come alive. The trees, once grey and lifeless, now bloomed with vibrant green leaves, their trunks thickening with strength as if freshly imbued with purpose. Wildflowers began to blossom across the forest floor, filling the air with the scent of sweet nectar. The river, once cold and stagnant, began to flow more freely, as if invigorated by the touch of nature's hand.

Nashir's power deepened, and the very ground beneath the fishermen's feet seemed to pulse with life. Suddenly, the sound of animals stirred in the forest – the distant call of birds, the rustling of small creatures in the underbrush. Deer, elk and foxes emerged from the trees, their coats glistening with vitality. It was as if nature itself had opened its arms, embracing the land and bringing balance to the nature.

The fishermen could hardly believe their eyes. They had lived so long without seeing such abundance, with the land barren and the seas far less bountiful. But now nature had returned in full force.

Nashir, his face serene and his eyes closed in concentration, summoned the final part of his power. With a sweeping gesture of his staff, he commanded the land to protect the village from the undead. Thick vines wound themselves around trees, weaving into an impenetrable barrier, while the earth rose to form a natural wall that would deter any creature, living or undead, from passing through. It was as if the land itself had become a shield, alive with the power of the gods.

Beyond the forest and in the distance, the undead, who had once prowled the area, now would find themselves thwarted by this living barrier. They could not cross it. The river and the mountains, now protected by nature, formed an unyielding boundary. The undead, once free to roam, would be halted at the edge of the natural defence, as if the very earth had rejected them.

As the power of Nashir's spell settled into place, the fishermen began to stir from their stunned silence. They looked at one another, their eyes wide with disbelief. For the first time in years, they could see the abundance around them – the fruit trees that now bore apples, pears and peaches. The baskets they had once filled with meagre catches from the sea were now overflowing with food: fresh fish, plump and vibrant, alongside fruits they hadn't dared dream of in a long time.

Nashir, his presence still calm but filled with a quiet authority, lowered his staff. His aura of power seemed to fade, but the living barrier he had created remained, a testament to his control over nature. The land was safe – for now. "This," Nashir said softly, turning to face the fishermen, his voice full of quiet pride, "is your new reality. You are safe now. The land will provide, and the undead will no longer threaten you. The forest will guard you. The river will nourish you."

The fishermen, still reeling from the sheer scale of what had just happened, began to cheer softly. Their eyes turned to the vibrant food now abundant in their baskets, the fresh fish, the fruit hanging from the newly blooming trees. They had not seen such abundance in years – perhaps decades. Their laughter, once faint and uncertain, filled the air as they began to realise what had just been granted to them.

For the first time in what seemed like forever, the village felt alive again. The gods had returned, and nature had been restored. The threat of the undead was no more.

And Nashir, his mission complete, turned back to the gods, his eyes meeting theirs with the same quiet resolve. "This place is safe for now," he said, his voice calm but powerful. "We've done what we came to do. The land is alive again. But there is still more to be done."

Nashir stood in the centre of the clearing, his eyes glowing softly as he focused on the land around him. With a graceful motion of his hand, the earth seemed to respond to his will. The trees groaned as they shifted, their trunks twisting and growing, shaping into the foundations of a large structure. Slowly, a hut began to form, its walls woven from the sturdy trunks of the surrounding forest, branches intertwining to create a natural barrier against the wind.

The roof, crafted from thick leaves and woven vines, rose high above, arching to allow the breeze to flow through, yet offering shelter on the sides. As Nashir moved his hands, the finishing touches fell into place. A long, sturdy wooden table, large enough to seat the whole village, emerged from the earth, accompanied by solid wooden chairs crafted from the very trees around them. The table was set with smooth, polished surfaces, and as the structure solidified, a faint, soothing hum filled the air and a peaceful aura settled over the space, as if the land itself had created a home for the fishermen.

The hut stood strong, a welcoming refuge nestled just off the shore, perfectly positioned between the forest's edge and the sea. It was a place of comfort, a sanctuary from the storm, and a new foundation for the village to gather in.

As the last of the structure took shape, Taril, ever the playful spirit, made his way to the mountainside. With a grin, he gestured to the towering stones that jutted out from the landscape. "That rock!" he called, pointing to a massive slab of stone sitting near the base of the mountains. "Now, *that's* what we need to make this truly impressive!" In a moment, he moved toward the stone with his effortless strength. His war hammer, still slung across his back, was temporarily forgotten as he grasped the stone with both hands. The earth trembled slightly beneath his feet as the stone, as if understanding its purpose, detached from the mountainside. Taril carried it, with a surprising ease for its size, and placed it beside the table Nashir had created. The stone settled into place with a loud, resounding thud, becoming a massive, flat surface perfect for an additional table. "There we go!" Taril said, stepping back to admire his work, his face lit with a grin of satisfaction. "Now, that's a proper table for feasting!"

The fishermen watched in awe as the gods continued to transform the area around them. The powerful presence of Nashir, the ever-joyful Taril, and the other gods had turned what was once a barren, exposed area into something extraordinary – a home, a shelter, a place of unity and strength.

Meanwhile, Nashir, having crafted the home, turned his attention to the water supply. His staff raised high, he summoned a well from the earth, its edges shaped by the land itself. Water began to flow from the stone, clear and pure, filling the well with the kind of water the fishermen had not tasted in years. The sound of water flowing was like music to their ears, a gift from the gods.

"The purest water," Nashir said, his voice calm but filled with authority. "For you and your people. May it sustain you as the land sustains us all."

As the well filled, the fishermen – still in awe – began to unload the baskets and barrels of fish, water and food they had brought with them. They carefully set everything down near the table, some still shaking their heads in disbelief. The gods' generosity, their transformation of the land, was overwhelming, and the reality of the shift was settling into the people's bones.

"Thank you," Marcus said, his voice filled with gratitude. "This… this is more than we could've ever dreamed of."

Drunnyak, always the large presence, chuckled and clapped him on the shoulder. "We've only just begun, Marcus. This village will grow, your people will thrive, and it's all thanks to you standing strong. You've earned this."

The gods exchanged a glance, their mission still clear, but for now, they allowed the fishermen a moment of peace, of joy, of gratitude. They had made a home here, and it would be a place for the fishermen to find rest and unity.

As the evening drew closer, the gods and the fishermen gathered around the table, the massive stone surface glistening under the light of the fire as it was covered with food. They sat together, their voices a mix of laughter and conversation, with the sound of the waves crashing against the shore providing a gentle backdrop.

The storm may have passed, but this was just the beginning. With Nashir's protection and the gods' guidance, this land – this new home – would be a place of peace, strength and unity for the fishermen of the sea.

As the gods gathered around the table, the firelight flickering in their eyes and the sounds of laughter and conversation rising around them, Niv leaned back on the table, her posture as casual as ever but her expression thoughtful. Her golden hair caught the light of the flame, and her amber eyes sparkled with both mischief and determination.

The fishermen, though still overwhelmed by the gods' presence, had settled into a comfortable silence, waiting for Niv to speak. She looked at the group, her gaze meeting Alden's, and her voice was calm but carried a weight of purpose.

"We'll stay the night," she began, her voice smooth as always, but with an undeniable edge of command. "But before you all get too comfortable, we need to discuss what comes next."

She glanced around the room, her eyes briefly meeting those of Opilkhos, Taril and the others, a silent acknowledgement passing between them. They all knew what had to be done. Niv's tone shifted slightly, growing more serious. The playful, teasing smile vanished as she spoke.

"We've learned that the undead rise each night in the last place they were, and we've seen how close they are to your village," she said, her voice filled with quiet determination. "We can't afford to let them be a constant threat."

Alden and Marcus exchanged glances, the weight of her words sinking in. The room, which had been filled with the soft hum of voices and the clinking of mugs, grew quiet, all eyes turning toward Niv.

"We'll make sure that every undead is destroyed tonight. Everybody will be moved over the new natural barrier that Nashir created," she continued. "The undead will rise in places that are safe, far from your homes, where they won't pose any danger to your people."

There was a pause. The fishermen, though resilient, looked uneasy, the fear of the night's threat still fresh in their minds. Alden's lips parted as if to speak, but Niv raised a hand, silencing him.

"I know it's a lot to ask," she said, her eyes softening, "but we're here to help. We're not leaving you to fight this alone. We'll clear the undead from your shores, but in return, we'll need your cooperation. While we fight the undead, the rest of you should rest. You've all been through enough."

The room was still, as the weight of her words settled over them. The fishermen had already lost so much, living on edge, constantly fleeing to the sea to avoid the dangers lurking in the shadows of the land. But Niv's voice rang with a quiet assurance – a promise that they wouldn't face the dangers alone any more.

"As Taril and Nashir work on strengthening your homes and protecting your village," Niv continued, "we'll make sure your homes are stronger, more fortified, with natural protections. A wall, perhaps a gate – so you don't have to keep returning to the sea each night. You'll be able to sleep in your beds, at peace, and not have to fear the undead rising."

Marcus, his weathered face creased with concern, spoke, his voice low but filled with gratitude. "You would do that for us? You'll make our homes safer?"

Niv nodded. "It's the least we can do. You've helped us, and we won't forget that." Her voice was steady, but her eyes showed the depth of her compassion. "Rest tonight. Tomorrow, when you wake up, you will have to make your village a home – one that's safe and strong now."

For a moment, the only sound was the crackle of the fire, the flames flickering higher as if to echo her words. The fishermen sat in stunned silence, overwhelmed by the offer, by the weight of what had been promised to them.

And then Alden, his face softened by the heavy weight of years spent in struggle, gave a slow, respectful nod. "We'll rest. We'll follow your lead." His voice, deep and tired, held a trace of something else – a quiet gratitude that had yet to be fully acknowledged.

Niv smiled, her usual boldness returning with a glint in her eyes. "Good. We'll need all the strength you can muster for what comes next. But for now, enjoy this moment. We'll protect you."

At her words, the fishermen began to relax, their shoulders unwinding slightly as the gods' assurances settled over them. They had endured so much, but now the possibility of peace was within reach.

As the evening wore on, Niv turned to the others. Taril and Nashir had already begun to organise the work that would be done. The two of them had always been at the forefront of such tasks, their strength and wisdom guiding the gods' actions.

The fishermen, still in awe of the gods, began to move around the fire, murmuring amongst themselves. Some had begun preparing food, their movements more relaxed, no longer burdened with the heavy worry that had dominated their lives for so long.

Nashir, standing outside, raised his staff once more, and the earth seemed to hum with his power. The trees around the village creaked, their branches swaying as if in response to his will. The night air, once thick with unease, seemed to lighten. Nature was at peace, and for the first time in a long while, the fishermen felt a sense of hope rising within them.

"We'll protect them," Niv said softly to her companions, a quiet promise in her voice as she looked toward the fire. "We'll make sure they're safe."

The gods stood united, watching over the villagers, knowing that tonight was just the beginning. They had much work to do, but with the trust of the fishermen, they would see it through. The village would be safe. The land would be protected, and the bond between them would grow ever stronger.

As the night deepened, the air thick with tension, the undead began to rise – shambling figures creeping from the earth, their rotten forms emerging with grotesque slowness. But there was no fear among the gods. There was only purpose.

Opilkhos, his expression unwavering, led the charge. His golden aura blazed like a beacon in the darkness, illuminating the battlefield before him. With each step, he moved swiftly and decisively, his weapon cleaving through the air, dispatching the undead with brutal efficiency. His strikes were precise, the force of his power never faltering as the creatures crumbled before him. Niv, her amber eyes flashing with determination, was beside him, dancing through the air like a force of nature herself. With each twirl, her swords slashed through the undead, a fluid grace guiding her every movement, her power unmatched. Lightning crackled in the air, her magic flashing like a divine wrath, burning the creatures to ash before they could even advance.

Drunnyak, towering and fierce, was a force to be reckoned with. His roar echoed across the battlefield, shaking the very ground beneath him as his massive sword swung through the ranks of the undead. His laughter, deep and powerful, filled the air as he sent the monstrosities crashing to the ground, their bodies shattered by the sheer force of his blows. He moved with a ferocity that matched the storm itself, his war cries like thunder, echoing across the shore.

But it wasn't just the fighting that held the villagers' attention. As the undead fell, Drunnyak, ever the meticulous one, began to gather their remains – bones, torn pieces of flesh, even the smallest fragments – all collected in the large sacks that Nashir had crafted with his magic. The sacks grew heavy with each passing moment as Drunnyak worked swiftly, his muscles bulging with the effort, the bones of the fallen clattering into the sacks like a grim harvest.

With each sack full, he lifted them, his massive arms moving with purpose, and flung them high into the air. The sacks sailed over the forest canopy, falling far beyond the newly formed barriers that Nashir had created, scattering the remnants of the undead away from the village, where they would not rise again.

The fishermen, who had watched in stunned silence, were now shaking with awe. Their eyes were wide with disbelief, as the power of the gods unfolded before them. What they had seen as a curse, a never-ending nightmare, was being eradicated before their eyes. They could hardly process what they were witnessing. These gods – these beings of unimaginable power – were making their world safer, and they had done so without hesitation. The fear that had once gripped the people's hearts, that had kept them on the edge of the sea, was melting away.

Tears welled up in the fishermen's eyes, but they were not tears of fear – they were tears of joy, of gratitude, of a hope that had never before been allowed to take root in their hearts. They looked at each other, silently sharing the profound relief that washed over them. A cry escaped the lips of the oldest fisherman, a sound that rose in the night air like a prayer of thanks – a cry that echoed across the land, reverberating through the mountains and the sea.

The table, once a mere vision of promise, now lay before them, heaped with fruits, honey, and an abundance of food they had never known to exist. The scent of fresh apples, ripe peaches, and fragrant bread wafted through the air, making their mouths water in disbelief. Some had never tasted these luxuries before; some had never even imagined they could. It was a feast of abundance, of life – of a future they had never dared to dream of.

And then, as the last of the undead fell and the air grew still, the fishermen's eyes turned towards Nashir and Taril. They were creating more than homes – they were reshaping the very world around them. The land itself groaned and shifted as Nashir stood tall, his staff raised high. The earth beneath them seemed to breathe, to pulse with life as the mountains themselves responded to his will. Taril, with his ever-present grin, joined in, his war hammer striking the earth with a force that made the ground tremble. Together they commanded the land, and the mountains began to grow. Stone walls rose from the very ground, shaping themselves with an ease that defied belief. The village was taking form before their eyes – strong, solid and protected. A wall of pure stone, reinforced with the strength of nature itself, encircled their homes, creating a stronghold like none they had ever seen.

The other gods stood, watching in silence, the weight of their power and their purpose heavy in the air. They felt the gratitude of the fishermen in their bones, the love and reverence that the humans felt for them. It was a humbling experience. The connection between the gods and the people they had sworn to protect had grown deeper in these moments. They had come as saviours, but now they were part of something greater.

Niv, standing beside Opilkhos, looked out across the scene. The villagers, their homes now protected, their spirits lifted, were moving toward the table, their eyes filled with awe. They were taking their first steps into a new life, one where the horrors of the past could be kept at bay. But they were not the only ones who felt the shift.

The gods stood together, knowing that this – this moment – was a beginning. They had given these people the gift of safety, but they also knew that this peace would not last forever. The storm had passed, but the world beyond the shores of this village was still fraught with danger.

And yet, in this moment, the gods allowed themselves to feel the love and respect they had earned. They had done what they came to do. They had given these people a chance – a new chance – to live.

The fishermen gathered around the table, their voices a soft murmur of gratitude, their hands full with food they had never dreamed they would have. For the first time in a long while, there was no fear in their hearts, only hope.

And the gods, standing watch over them, felt the weight of their responsibility and the satisfaction of their work. The land was alive, the village was safe, and for now, that was enough.

As the night unfolded, the laughter and warmth filled the newly created shelter. Drunnyak, Niv and Opilkhos joined the villagers at the table, their presence adding to the sense of security and unity that now gripped the room. The meal was a feast – a feast not only for the body, but for the soul. The fisherwomen, Lara, Lannah and Rhianna, moved with quiet grace, bringing food and drink freshly prepared from the fires, their faces soft with the peace they had not known for so long. Their laughter filled the space, even though the children, once noisy and playful, had been asleep for some time in their hammocks, exhausted from the day's excitement.

The gods sat among them, feeling their presence as more than protectors: as a part of this new-found life. There was no distance between the gods and these people any more. They had given the villagers the gift of safety, and in return, the villagers had given them something just as valuable – their trust.

Taril and Nashir stood, their attention still fixed on the now-quiet village, as they watched the children sleep, the rhythmic sounds of their breath calming the night. As the gods conversed amongst themselves, discussing their plans and the road ahead, their eyes could not help but wander toward the children in their hammocks, where the promise of a future, peaceful and free of the dangers that had once defined their lives, lay in the stillness of the night.

As the hours stretched on and the village slept soundly, the gods remained alert. The night passed peacefully – much like the villagers, the gods too found themselves in a moment of respite, if only for a short while.

The sunless morning arrived, its muted light bathing the village in an eerie stillness. The storm from the night before had passed, leaving only the memory of its fury behind. As the first of the villagers began to stir, they awoke to a sight that could not have been imagined the night before – what had once been a simple gathering place was now transformed. Their new homes, nestled securely in the base of the mountains, stood like sentinels, their stone walls towering around the village. The sturdy wooden gate that framed the entrance was unlike anything they had ever seen – fortified, tall and unyielding.

The homes, each one carefully crafted with the skill and magic of the gods, sat along the mountainside, protected by the high stone wall Nashir had conjured overnight. The watchtowers that rose from the ground added to the sense of security, their platforms giving the villagers a view over the land and the sea. The land was safe now – no longer haunted by the threat of the undead.

In the distance, Nashir's magic had also conjured a large, sheltered area – a food storage facility unlike any the villagers had ever seen. The area, aptly named the Larder of Garanos, was massive. Wooden beams reinforced by nature's own design stretched across its ceiling, ensuring that the stored food would be preserved for years to come. Inside, Nashir had summoned animals – cows, chickens and pigs – creating a small farm where meat, eggs and milk would be plentiful. It was a new dawn for the villagers, one where they no longer had to rely solely on the sea.

At the shore, Nashir had conjured a massive boat, crafted with a sturdy metal foundation and reinforced with metal strips to ensure it could brave the sea's tempests. The boat was built for one purpose: to search for Alanteas, to find the island and the people who might have information on what had happened to him. It was a grand vessel, with large, strong oars that would carry the gods and the villagers across the waters.

As the gods looked over their creation, Marcus – who had awoken to the sight of his new, fortified home – stepped forward. His eyes were wide with disbelief, his heart heavy with a mixture of gratitude and awe. He saw the vision come to life before him, and yet he knew that this peace was only the beginning.

Nashir, with a sly grin on his face, turned to Drunnyak and Opilkhos, making sure they could see the boat. "Well, since Taril and I built the boat, you two should be the ones rowing to the island," he said, his voice carrying a note of humour, but also a challenge.

Drunnyak, always quick to find humour in the toughest situations, let out a hearty laugh. "So, you're telling me we're the ones to row this great beast of a boat? Sounds like you've got us pulling the cart now, huh?" His grin stretched from ear to ear, his eyes glimmering with mischief.

Opilkhos raised an eyebrow, his lips curling into a knowing smirk. "Aye, seems like we're the bulls now. You've got us working the oars while the real heavy lifters rest." He chuckled, looking at Taril and Nashir with mock reproach. "I didn't think I'd be doing cart-pulling in my divine years, but here we are."

The gods shared a laugh, the tension of the journey ahead easing for a brief moment. Despite the weight of their task, there was camaraderie in the air, and even the most daunting of challenges seemed a little lighter with humour shared among them.

Nashir's voice softened, his tone becoming more serious. "The path ahead is fraught with danger, but it is one we must face. We cannot stop until we find Alanteas."

As they gathered around the boat, preparing for the journey ahead, Marcus stepped forward, his expression resolute. "I'll go with you," he said, his voice steady. "I know the waters better than any of you. If you're heading into those dangerous seas, I'll make sure you get there safely."

The gods exchanged glances, impressed by Marcus's courage. His willingness to help them, despite the risks, spoke volumes about his character and the bond he now shared with them.

Niv gave him a grateful nod, a smile touching her lips. "We could use someone who knows these waters. We'll be in good hands, Marcus."

Marcus returned her smile, though there was a hint of uncertainty in his eyes. "Let's get this done. For Alanteas."

With the boat prepared, the villagers gathered, their expressions a mix of awe and hope. The journey was about to begin, and with each passing moment, the gods knew they were one step closer to finding their missing friend and uncovering the truth of what had happened to him.

As they moved toward the boat, the weight of their task ahead settled over them, but there was a sense of unity in the air. Together, they would face the dangers that lay beyond the horizon. Together, they would find Alanteas and uncover the mysteries of the island.

The gods, their hearts heavy with the promise of the journey ahead, exchanged one final look. It was time. The gods and Marcus stood at the side of the boat, the weight of the journey ahead pressing down upon them. The villagers gathered around, their faces a mixture of hope and sorrow, their eyes following the gods with reverence.

Alden, his once-stoical demeanour now softened by the enormity of what lay before them, took a step forward. The others followed, each one lowering their head in silent respect. Without words, they kneeled before the gods, the sound of the sea crashing against the shore and the wind whispering in the distance the only noise in the thickening silence.

Alden's voice broke the stillness, low and unwavering, as he looked up at the gods, the flame of determination flickering in his eyes. "We wish you a safe journey. May the winds guide you and bring you back with our brother, Alanteas. We will be waiting."

Behind him, the other villagers, though quiet, nodded in solemn agreement. There were no more words to say, for they knew that these were their saviours, and they now set out to bring back the one who had first sparked their hope – Alanteas, whose visit to the fishermen had unknowingly led the gods to them.

Niv, standing tall as ever, smiled gently, her eyes filled with gratitude and resolve. "We'll return," she promised, her voice steady. "And when we do, we'll bring back more than just answers."

Opilkhos gave a solemn nod, his usually impassive face softened by a flicker of emotion. "We will return, and the land will remember what we've done. You have our word."

Drunnyak, with his ever-present grin, leaned forward, his voice booming. "We'll be back before you can say, 'sea serpents,'" he said with a wink, his words cutting through the solemnity like a sharp blade, reminding everyone that even in the face of uncertainty, they could still find humour in the darkness.

Taril, standing next to Nashir, placed a hand on the side of the boat. "When we return, make sure you read my instructions and make me some ale."

They all laughed at that moment.

Nashir, ever the silent force, gave a simple nod. His gaze turned toward the ocean, the vastness of it stretching before him, an unknown and yet undeniable challenge. As his connection to the earth pulsed beneath his feet, he felt the pull of the journey, the promise of discovery, and the necessity of what they must do.

With one final glance at the village – at the homes now fortified, the people they'd sworn to protect – the gods turned and stepped onto the boat. The wind seemed to whisper its approval, as if nature itself was guiding them toward their destination. The waves lapped gently at the hull as they pushed off from the shore, the boat creaking in protest, but steady under their feet.

Alden, standing with the villagers, gave them a final wave as the boat began to drift, his voice carrying over the wind. "Find him. And bring him back to us."

As the boat slid into the fog, the villagers stayed at the shore, watching, knowing that the gods were not only their protectors, but now the keepers of their fate. The journey had begun, and with it, the hope of a reunion that seemed more possible than ever.

The gods, with hearts heavy and yet resolute, sailed toward the unknown with the help of Marcus, their thoughts set on the island that lay ahead. The darkness of the sea was vast, but they would face it together – undeterred, unyielding.

And so their voyage began, the quiet hum of the sea beneath them carrying the weight of their mission: to bring back Alanteas and uncover the mysteries that the island held.

THE CONVENING OF
NIGHTMARES

The boat glided steadily through the dark waters, the thick fog rolling in like a living entity, slowly swallowing the world around them. Opilkhos and Drunnyak, powerful in their movements, rowed in unison, their arms swinging with practised ease. Niv and Nashir sat at the boat's stern, their hands raised, manipulating the wind to guide them, the breeze shifting with their command. The air was thick, charged with magic, their destination beyond the mist, shrouded in an eerie quiet.

Taril sat on the edge of the boat, his eyes scanning the horizon as he glanced from the quiet sea to the fog that separated them from the unknown island ahead. Next to him, Marcus, the fisherman and former captain, sat quietly. His face, usually rugged and sure, was now etched with the weight of the past, his mind wandering back to times long buried.

Taril, noticing the shift in his demeanour, broke the silence with a low voice. "Tell me, Marcus, what do you remember about those people... the ones you mentioned before? The ones from the sea?"

Marcus stiffened at the question, his gaze lost in the sea as memories came flooding back. He didn't speak immediately, as if choosing his words carefully, unwilling to dredge up the ghosts of his youth. The fog seemed to hang around him as thickly as the memories, and for a moment, the soft sound of the waves seemed to carry him back to that distant time. "They weren't like us," Marcus finally said, his voice low and steady. "I remember my father talking about them… but never directly. More like warnings. When I was younger, we didn't know much about them, except that they lived on the island north of here, in the fog. They were beautiful… unsettling, but beautiful."

He paused, eyes distant as the boat rocked gently with the waves. Taril waited, sensing the weight of Marcus's words before he continued.

"They looked like us, but different. They were elves, but their skin had the faintest sheen, almost as if it were covered in scales, subtle like the glint of sunlight on water. Their long hair, flowing and dark, shimmered like the ocean depths. Their eyes… they had eyes that seemed too knowing, too old for their youthful faces." Marcus's voice softened as his memory deepened. "They were graceful in their movements, but there was an air of power about them. The way they held themselves, like they belonged to the sea. The weapons they carried were crafted from sea glass, sharp as any blade I've ever seen. Their spears, their knives… they were made of coral, driftwood and obsidian, their edges glistening with an otherworldly beauty. I remember seeing one with a spear, its head shaped from a huge shark's tooth, its surface smooth and deadly." Marcus shuddered slightly, not from the cold, but from the way the memories still made him uneasy. "They came to our village when I was a child," Marcus continued, his gaze drifting to the sea, as though the waves might bring him the answers he still sought. "They came atop of sea animals, almost riding them, unlike anything we had seen before. With banners that shimmered like the scales of fish. They stood on the shores, watching us – always at the edge of the fog that followed them, never fully stepping into the light. It wasn't so much that they threatened us, but there was a fear that settled into everyone's bones. A natural fear. It was their presence, the way they stood so still, as if they were watching us for a reason. They didn't speak much. But I could see it in their eyes – they weren't here to harm us. They were here to warn us." He fell silent for a long moment, his gaze distant, as if recalling the way his father had reacted back then. The fog around the boat grew thicker, swallowing the space between them and the island. "My father... after that, he wouldn't talk about them. Not to me. Not to anyone. Whenever I asked him about the sea elves, he'd change the subject or just leave the room. I remember him telling me once, when I was older, that the sea belonged to them. They didn't let us in their waters. He warned me not to get too close. The more I asked, the more he pulled away." Marcus's hands clenched around the side of the boat, the wood creaking under his grip.

"Why wouldn't he let you learn more?" Taril asked, his voice calm, yet full of understanding.

Marcus exhaled sharply. "I think... he was afraid. Afraid that if we knew too much, we'd have to leave. Our people didn't want to leave. We had our lives here. They had their lives on the water. But I saw something that day, something that my father never spoke of again. The elves, the way they looked at us, it was as if they knew our future. Knew that our time here would run out."

Taril leaned back slightly, the gravity of Marcus's words sinking in. "So you think they knew something that explains what happened to this world after our disappearance?"

Marcus nodded, the weight of his memories pressing down on him. "They knew. And maybe Alanteas was right to try and rescue the people from the island. Maybe something involving these sea elves caused the disruption in our trade. That's why he went to them. To see if they could help him understand. Maybe they're the key to understanding all of this." He looked back at the gods, his eyes meeting Opilkhos and Niv's steady gaze.

Taril turned his attention to the fog ahead, the mystery of the sea elves growing larger with every word. The island loomed ahead, and with it, the possibility of answers. "Well," Taril said after a moment, breaking the silence, "let's hope that Alanteas finds what he's looking for. But it seems that the island may hold more than we expected."

The boat continued its steady course, heading toward the island shrouded in mist, and the gods remained silent for a moment, each lost in their thoughts as the sea stretched out before them.

The fog thickened further, yet they pressed on, the journey far from over, and with every word that Marcus spoke, the path ahead grew clearer as they remained resolute.

The boat rocked slightly as the weight of the water-filled drum beneath Alentar shifted with the waves. Sitting perched atop the barrel, the elven ranger was a picture of poised concentration. His form, sleek and graceful, moved with the ebb and flow of the boat, every motion executed with the precision of a dancer. His sharp emerald eyes scanned the waters, his ears tuned to every ripple of sound, every shift beneath the surface. He could feel the creatures below – the sharks that followed them, drawn to the movements of the boat, but always careful to stay just beyond the reach of the fog.

From his vantage above the others, Nashir turned to his companions, his brow furrowed in thought. The wind had shifted, and with it came an odd sensation. He spoke, his voice filled with the weight of his thoughts. "It is strange, isn't it?" he mused, his gaze lost in the expanse of the ocean. "I can control the wind, shape the air around us, but there is something… different here. The sea refuses to open itself to me, the land beneath is closed off." He paused, letting his words settle, feeling the absence of connection to the world around him. "Since we awakened, this is the first time I've felt disconnected when we came to these shores, as if there's something beyond our reach. We must keep our eyes sharp. A storm is coming."

Nashir removed his cloak, woven from the natural fibres of the land, a garment that shimmered like the leaves in a sunlit forest, now darkened by the storm clouds. He draped it over the group, using the energy of his connection to nature to expand its protective canopy, a shimmering shield against the rain.

Meanwhile, Niv, ever the one to lend her energy with a smile, controlled the wind with practised ease, keeping the boat steady as the first drops of rain fell. She summoned a gust to keep the rain at bay, while Nashir's magic worked to strengthen the canopy he had made. Opilkhos, his presence ever calm, glanced at Marcus, who was shivering against the cold, his weathered hands gripping the side of the boat.

Without hesitation, Opilkhos kept rowing with one hand and lifting the other towards Marcus, his aura glowing softly. He reached out, the intensity of his light surrounding Marcus, and the old fisherman felt a surge of warmth, his trembling subsiding.

"You're special," Niv teased, her voice light, though her eyes sparkled with admiration. She glanced at Opilkhos, who gave her a faint smile, an understanding passing between them. Their connection – something deeper than magic – was a constant, even in moments like this.

At the mention of Marcus's shivering, Drunnyak let out a booming laugh that echoed across the boat. "Well, look at you, Opilkhos – glowing like a damn beacon while the poor lad's shaking to pieces!" He gave a broad, toothy grin, jabbing his thumb toward Marcus for emphasis. "If you shine any brighter, we'll have no need for torches – just don't forget to keep rowing, firefly, or we'll be spinning in circles 'til dawn!"

They all laughed, the tension breaking slightly, but Alentar remained focused. His sharp eyes narrowed as he studied the waves. The movement of the water around them had changed, and with it, his senses heightened. His heartbeat quickened as he felt it – a massive heartbeat under the water. It was closer than he'd like, and it wasn't just any shark. This one was different – larger, more powerful, and as it swam closer, Alentar knew they had to be cautious.

"There's a huge shark following us," Alentar said, his voice quiet but carrying the weight of urgency. "It's much bigger than anything we've seen before. If it decides to strike, it could easily tip the boat."

Taril raised his war hammer with a grin, his voice booming with bravado. "Well, if it comes for us, we'll have fish for a feast for a while!" His laughter filled the air, but Alentar quickly shot him a serious look.

"Sharks aren't like regular fish," Alentar corrected, his tone firm. "They're cartilaginous, meaning they don't have bones like other creatures. Their structure is different – they can bend and shift, and are far more agile. They don't attack recklessly. This one... it's not hungry. It's assessing. We need to be cautious."

Nashir and Opilkhos exchanged a look, their expressions mirroring Alentar's seriousness. The sea had always been unpredictable, and now, with the presence of this enormous shark, the air grew heavy with the threat of the unknown. But the gods had faced dangers before, and they wouldn't falter now.

As the boat continued on, the storm's fury began to rise in earnest, but so did the determination in their hearts. They had faced the undead, weathered the storm, and now they would face what lay ahead with unwavering resolve.

The boat cut through the waves, undeterred by the storm that howled above. Niv's fingers were still at the ready, guiding the wind to their will. Her expression was focused, the power flowing through her like an extension of herself, keeping the boat steady against the swell of the sea. Nashir stood beside her, his staff raised high, commanding the wind in tandem with her own power. The storm, though relentless, seemed to bend to their command, the waves stabilising beneath the boat's hull as they passed.

As the boat carved through the waters, Taril, ever the one to offer support, turned to Opilkhos. "You've been at it long enough," he said, a mischievous grin tugging at the edges of his lips. "If you need to rest, I'll take the wheel. I'm still young enough to row this beast of a ship."

Opilkhos arched an eyebrow, his lips curving into a small, knowing smile. "Young enough, you say? Perhaps it's Grandpa that needs a break, Taril." His teasing tone was warm yet sharp, a glint of playful energy in his eyes.

The gods shared a laugh, the tension in the air breaking for a moment. Even Alentar, who had been silent for most of the journey, allowed a brief smile to tug at his lips. The storm raged around them, but for a moment there was warmth in their shared camaraderie.

Alentar's focus quickly returned to the water. His sharp eyes never wavered from the sea. His senses, heightened by the storm, could still feel the presence of the sharks, circling below them. He didn't speak, but his sharp gaze betrayed his concern. He could feel the animals' predatory focus, waiting, watching – almost as if they were timing the moment to strike.

As the night deepened, the storm grew stronger. The thunder cracked overhead, a deep and rolling sound that reverberated across the water. The waves were becoming taller, crashing against the boat's sides, but Niv and Nashir's control kept it steady. The fog, which had been an ever-present mist on the horizon, now began to take on a more distinct shape. It lingered in the distance, a thick wall of fog that seemed to draw an invisible line between the boat and the land beyond.

The fog didn't move – it simply stood there, unyielding, as if a meticulous design had been drawn to keep them in a space between the known and the unknown. From the inland side, the mist seemed to spill out, swirling around them, covering everything from sight. They were trapped between two forces: a deep fog that refused to let them pass, and a darkened mist that surrounded them like a continuous shroud.

They rowed on, the fog pressing in on them, but it was Alentar who noticed the subtle shift in the air, the ominous sensation that they were moving closer to something unknown. The waters, while calm, now felt colder, as if something deep beneath was pulling at the boat. The sharks too seemed to be closing in, their predatory nature only increasing the tension.

The gods held their positions, silently watching the horizon, waiting for the moment when they would break through the mist. The boat was their vessel, and the storm their test. Yet, even as they moved further into the fog, there was a shared understanding between them that this was only the beginning.

The storm howled, the boat cutting through the crashing waves with relentless speed. Alentar, ever watchful, felt the shift beneath them. The sharks that had trailed them for so long began to disappear, fading slowly as the fog ahead of them seemed to turn. The thick, soupy mist parted just enough for them to glimpse the island in the distance – a land of towering mountains, jagged cliffs, and a volcano that loomed high, its molten veins spilling streams of lava into the dark night sky.

The sight was awe-inspiring, yet ominous. The distant volcano cracked, a deep rumbling sound echoing across the sea, as though the earth itself was warning them. A foul stench of sulphur and acrid gases permeated the air, burning the back of their throats. The smell was thick and pungent, like the breath of some ancient creature stirring from its slumber. The wind carried the warmth of the lava's glow even this far, adding an eerie heat to the storm's chilling bite.

Despite the danger, the island felt closer, and yet further away as the fog rolled thickly between them and their destination. Alentar's sharp eyes took in every detail. The island was vast and imposing, but the fog that stood between them and their goal refused to part.

They slowed the boat, each of them feeling the strange stillness in the air. They were so close now, but the path ahead was unclear.

Marcus stirred awake, rubbing his eyes and scanning the waters. "We're not far now," he said, his voice still heavy with sleep. "But we must be cautious. The fog… it's not to be trusted. It clouds the shore, hides everything beneath."

As he spoke, the boat slid forward with an unexpected bump. The sound of the hull scraping something beneath the water echoed out in the tense silence. Alentar's senses immediately sharpened, his instincts flaring. He could feel the heartbeats of the creatures below, their movements more coordinated, more intentional. It wasn't the sharks any more. They were something else, something deeper.

"They're here," Alentar murmured. "Not the sharks. I see them through the water. Many eyes, moving with us."

A quiet ripple of tension spread across the group. The sea elves Marcus had spoken of.

As if answering his call, the water rippled violently beneath the boat. Without hesitation, Alentar leapt from the boat, his body disappearing into the cold, dark waters. His sudden plunge surprised everyone, even the sea elves, who hadn't expected an approach so bold. Alentar dove deep, holding his breath, feeling the weight of the water pressing in on him, yet he didn't panic. As he descended into the depths, he began speaking in a language that came to him instinctively – fluid, ancient, and strange, yet comforting.

He felt the words come without thinking, as if a deep well of knowledge had been opened within him, a memory he didn't know he had.

The water shifted as one of the sea elves emerged before him, a tall and imposing figure, its body shimmering with scales, delicate but radiant in the deep water's gloom. The creature's eyes, glowing like twin moons, locked onto Alentar's with a quiet understanding. And then, before Alentar could even speak with the creature, a huge shark came barrelling through the water, its teeth bared and its body thrashing violently toward him.

Alentar didn't flinch.

The sea elf raised a hand, and the shark froze in mid-lunge, its body stilling like a statue. With another wave of the creature's hand, the shark vanished into the deep, its presence eradicated as easily as a breath exhaled.

Alentar, unfazed, offered a solemn nod to the sea elf. "I'm here with my companions." He spoke again in the strange language. "We seek passage through the fog. Please allow us to go through. We must reach the island."

The sea elf regarded him for a moment, its expression unreadable, then gave a slow nod. "You will be allowed to go through," it said in a deep, echoing voice. "I will guide you through the fog."

Alentar, feeling the weight of this exchange, asked the creature's name.

But the elf only answered with a wordless gesture, and its voice rumbled softly. "You must hurry."

The urgency in the elf's voice was unmistakable. Alentar nodded in acknowledgement, then swam back toward the boat, breaking the surface of the water in a smooth, practised motion. As he climbed back aboard, dripping with seawater, the group gathered around him. Taril was the first to speak, his voice filled with a mix of awe and concern.

"You're mad." He grinned, though there was admiration in his eyes. "But I suppose if anyone can swim with the sharks and not come back as dinner, it's you."

Alentar shook off the water, his gaze fixed on the horizon where the fog still loomed. "The sea elves will guide us," he said quietly. "They've granted us passage. We must row slowly now. We've crossed into their domain, and they will help us."

Marcus, his eyes wide with amazement, looked at Alentar with a mixture of disbelief and awe. "You spoke to them? To the sea elves? I… I've heard the stories, but to see them…"

"Be calm," Alentar said, his voice steady and reassuring. "They are not enemies. They will guide us. We must trust them."

The others exchanged looks, each processing the weight of what had just occurred. Taril, shaking his head in disbelief, took his seat again, his hand on his weapon, ready for whatever came next.

Niv, ever perceptive, studied Alentar for a moment before speaking softly. "We're closer now. I can feel it."

The group nodded, their resolve strengthening. The island lay ahead, and with it, the answers they sought. The sea elves had opened the way, and now they would follow it – together.

As the boat glided forward, the fog closing in around them once again, they moved cautiously, knowing the sea and its mysteries still held secrets they had yet to uncover. But the gods, united and unwavering, knew that this journey was far from over. The island awaited.

The boat glided gently through the mist, the air thick with tension. Nashir and Niv, their hands steady but their minds racing, felt the strange pull of the sea around them. The sea elves, their figures faint but luminous, glided alongside, their eerie glow lighting the way like guiding stars, illuminating the rocks below. The gods could see the jagged stones beneath the waves – sharp, unforgiving, and littered with the wreckage of many boats. They were all silent, the only sound being the soft lapping of the water against the hull as they neared the shore.

The fog thickened around them, the air growing heavy with the scent of salt and brine. Then, just beyond the mist, Alentar caught sight of something – the silhouette of a lighthouse, standing like a broken sentinel against the ocean's fury. The structure was no longer whole. Obsidian-like streaks of blackened rock covered its surface, as though the molten lava of a long-forgotten eruption had spilled across it, cooled, and hardened in time. The storm had long since passed, but its impact remained, leaving the lighthouse scarred and twisted by the forces of nature.

Alentar's heart thudded in his chest, his eyes narrowing as he examined the wreckage. This was not just a marker of time; it was a reminder of something darker. He glanced at the elves, their serene faces unreadable. They had led them here, but why? And what lay ahead?

As if answering his unspoken question, one of the elves met his gaze, nodding once in acknowledgement. Without another word, it vanished beneath the waves, leaving only the faintest ripple behind.

Alentar stood at the edge of the boat, feeling the weight of the moment. They had arrived.

The boat scraped against the shoreline, and the gods disembarked, the sand beneath their feet soft but thick with the remnants of what had once been a vibrant harbour. Just ahead, a pathway wound its way into the heart of the island, flanked by thick vegetation that whispered in the wind. The trees, twisted and ancient, reached toward the sky as if trying to grasp at something just beyond their reach.

The air here was different – cooler, but with an undercurrent of something unsettling. It felt ancient, charged with a latent energy that left a strange taste in the back of their throats.

Then, ahead, they saw it – the boat.

Alanteas's boat, tethered to a large, weathered post. It sat in stark contrast to their own, the wood darkened by time and the elements, but still sturdy. Alentar's heart raced. They were so close now, the final piece of the puzzle just within reach.

Before anyone could speak, Alentar held up his hand, silencing them. He stepped forward, eyes scanning the surroundings, his senses on high alert. The familiar sensation of Alanteas's trail called to him like a whisper. He moved quickly, following the subtle clues left behind. His feet moved with purpose as his sharp eyes tracked the faintest traces of movement in the earth – small, almost imperceptible marks, like the crumbs of a long-forgotten path.

It didn't take long for him to find them – the same black cumin seeds scattered in the dirt, marking the trail. Alanteas had been here, and he hadn't been gone long. But there was something else, something deeper. The wind shifted, and a cold dread swept over them all, seeping into their bones. It wasn't the usual chill of the sea – it was something darker, more profound. The very air seemed to tremble, as if the island itself were holding its breath.

Nashir, standing beside Alentar, felt it too, his connection to the land tingling with unease. He stepped forward, eyes scanning the horizon as if the very ground beneath them had shifted.

"We need to proceed carefully." Alentar's voice was low but firm. "I can feel him, but something isn't right. We don't know what awaits us."

The gods traded tense glances, the weight of unspoken fears pressing in. They had come this far, but what lay ahead was unknown. The island was a mystery, and Alanteas's absence felt like a dark omen. With each step they took, the air grew heavier, the silence more oppressive.

As they made their way deeper into the island, the wind howled around them, but the trees stood still, as if watching. The mountains loomed overhead, jagged and unforgiving, their peaks hidden in the mist. It felt as though the very landscape was closing in on them, pressing them forward into the heart of the island, where answers – and danger – awaited.

Alentar led them up the path, following the trail left by Alanteas, every sense heightened. The journey ahead would not be easy, but it was the only path to the truth. They were closer than ever, but Alanteas had left them with a trail that hinted at something far more dangerous than any of them could have anticipated.

The fog still hung thick around them, but it no longer felt like a simple veil of mist. It felt alive, swirling with an unnatural presence. Something was waiting. And as they moved forward, the weight of their mission pressed down upon them, heavy and suffocating.

They would find Alanteas, but at what cost? The island was ancient, and the secrets it held were darker than they had imagined. The next chapter of their journey had begun, and it was one they could not turn away from, no matter how unsettling the path ahead appeared.

Alentar led the group with silent determination, his sharp eyes scanning the terrain before them, ever watchful for any signs of danger.

The air was thick with tension, and every footstep echoed in the stillness of the mountain pass. As they moved deeper into the heart of the island, the ground beneath their feet began to tremble. The subtle vibrations, at first imperceptible, gradually grew stronger, a low hum resonating in the air. It was as though the island itself was alive, stirring with the power of the volcano that loomed not far off. Every now and then, the tremors would ripple through the earth, reminding them of the volatile forces at work beneath the surface.

They continued upwards, weapons in hand, their eyes sharp for any movement. The path was narrow, winding between jagged cliffs that seemed to close in on them, the darkness of the mountain threatening to swallow them whole. As they ascended, small groups of undead began to appear in their path – shambling figures, their hollow eyes glowing with an eerie light. Alentar moved swiftly, his body an extension of the shadows, silently dispatching the first wave of enemies with deadly precision. The rest of the group followed suit, each of them moving with practised ease. Niv's swords flashed in the dim light, cutting down the undead with grace and speed, while Opilkhos's sword sang through the air, its tip finding its mark every time.

They made their way through the mountain pass, a natural path between the peaks that seemed to guide them deeper into the island. As they continued to follow Alanteas's trail, they kept Marcus protected in the centre, his eyes wide with both awe and fear as he took in the harsh beauty of the island. The undead, though numerous, were no match for the gods. With every step they took, they cleared the way, ensuring that the path was safe for Marcus and themselves.

The sound of the volcano became more pronounced as they climbed higher. The rumble of the earth beneath their feet was now accompanied by the occasional hiss of steam, the distant roar of molten rock shifting and grinding within the mountain's belly. Taril, ever in tune with the land, spoke to the stone beneath them, trying to commune with it as he had done before. But as he opened his senses to the mountain, he was abruptly cut off by a sharp, unearthly voice – a warning, not from the earth, but from something far older. The stone, cold and unyielding, had not answered him. Instead, the air itself seemed to vibrate with the words of a being not of this world.

Nashir too felt the absence of life. His connection to nature, which had always been strong, was now eerily silent. There was no pulse of life around them, no whisper of wind through the trees, no presence of animals. It was as if the land itself was holding its breath. He shared his findings with the others, his voice tinged with a quiet concern. "There's nothing. No animals, no plants – no life. It's as if we are walking through an empty world."

They exchanged uneasy glances, the weight of their mission growing heavier with each passing moment. As they reached a small clearing, the ground trembled again, this time with more force. They all paused, instinctively looking upward as the air around them shifted. A colossal shadow passed overhead, so large it blotted out the stars above. The gods instinctively reached for their weapons, eyes scanning the sky for any sign of what had passed.

It was a creature unlike anything they had seen since their awakening – a massive form, winged and serpentine, soaring high above them. Its size was incomprehensible, its shape shrouded in the darkness of the night, but the sheer power of its presence was undeniable. The wind shifted as it passed, a faint screech echoing through the air as it disappeared into the distance.

The group stood in stunned silence for a moment, processing what they had just witnessed.

"What in the gods' name was that?" Drunnyak muttered, his grip tightening around his weapon.

Alentar, his gaze still fixed on the sky, was the first to speak. "Whatever it was, it wasn't here to help us. We must remain vigilant."

Nashir nodded, his mind racing. "The volcano, the undead, this creature – something's wrong here. The land itself is twisted. We have to be careful."

Opilkhos, ever calm and calculating, stepped forward, his eyes scanning the darkness ahead. "We've come too far to turn back now. But we must be prepared. There's more here than we understand."

The tension was palpable as the group pressed on, the path ahead uncertain but their resolve unbroken. The island held many secrets, and the more they discovered, the deeper the mysteries seemed to go. But with each step, they knew they were one step closer to the answers they sought – answers that would lead them to Alanteas and whatever darkness lay at the heart of this cursed place.

The ruins of the village stretched before them, a desolate wasteland with shattered walls and collapsed roofs that whispered of a once-thriving community. The air was thick with decay, the stench of rot clinging to every corner. The undead moved freely among the ruins, their hollow eyes vacant, their limbs jerking with unnatural movements. The sounds of their moaning reached the group even from a distance, mingling with the putrid smell that seemed to seep into the very earth beneath their feet.

Marcus felt his breath quicken, his body trembling despite the power of the gods that surrounded him. His eyes flicked nervously between the figures moving through the ruins, the terror of what was to come bubbling up in his chest. Despite witnessing the gods' strength, his fear was overwhelming. Even with the gods beside him, the fear was a tangible weight on his soul.

Alentar stopped abruptly, holding up a hand in a silent command. The group paused, every eye turning to him. His gaze was fixed on the ground ahead, his sharp eyes scanning for any signs of their missing friend. Then, to their horror, Alanteas's tracks, the breadcrumb path that had guided them for so long, suddenly vanished.

"They're gone," Alentar said, his voice low but firm. "Alanteas's trail... it disappears here."

The group exchanged uneasy glances, confusion rippling through them.

"What do you mean, it disappears?" Drunnyak asked, his voice tight with suspicion. "Where could he have gone?"

Alentar shook his head, his eyes never leaving the ground. "It's as if the land itself swallowed his steps."

As if on cue, a group of undead began to shuffle toward them from the ruins, drawn to the movement of the living. Without hesitation,

Alentar sprang into action, his arrows flying with deadly precision, each shot finding its mark. The undead fell with sickening thuds, but Alentar's attention never wavered. His eyes remained focused, searching for the answer, the missing piece of the puzzle that had led them here.

In the distance, past the ruins, Alentar spotted something – something that pulled at him. A fountain. The water had long since dried up, and the stone was cracked and covered in moss, but the eerie sight of it caught his attention. The trees surrounding it were dead, their branches gnarled and twisted, as if drained of life itself.

"We move," Alentar commanded. "Stay alert."

Niv, always ready for action, took her place at the back, her swords flashing in the dim light as she cut down the undead that surged from the mountain pass. They fell quickly, each blow precise and deadly, but her mind, like Alentar's, remained focused on the fountain ahead. She moved swiftly, covering their rear as the group pressed forward, their steps deliberate but cautious.

The group spread out slightly as they continued toward the fountain, keeping close enough to support each other, but widening their formation to cover more ground. The silence between them was oppressive, each footstep heavy with the weight of what lay ahead. The undead, though numerous, didn't pose much of a threat as long as the gods stayed in formation and struck swiftly, but there was a sense of something more – a dark presence in the air, a growing tension that none of them could shake.

And then, without warning, it happened.

Niv, who had been moving swiftly at the back of the group, suddenly vanished from sight. One moment she was there, slashing through the undead with ease, and the next she was gone. The space she occupied seemed to warp and twist, her figure disappearing into thin air, as though swallowed by some foul magic.

The gods froze, their eyes wide with shock.

"Niv!" Opilkhos shouted, his voice tight with panic.

Alentar's gaze shot to the spot where Niv had vanished. His mind raced, the hairs on the back of his neck standing on end. "It's magic," he muttered, his voice grim. "Dark magic."

529

They rushed to where she had been, but there was no sign of her. The air was heavy with an unnatural silence, the undead momentarily still as if the world itself had paused in anticipation.

"It wasn't a normal spell," Taril said, his voice low, his eyes scanning the area around them. "It felt… different. Something ancient."

Suddenly, a soft, haunting melody drifted through the air. It was distant at first, faint, but it grew louder, growing clearer with each passing moment. The music echoed through the ruins, and though it sounded beautiful, there was something sinister about it. It was a song they didn't recognise, but it felt wrong – like a siren's call, beckoning them to something they weren't prepared for.

Alentar looked toward the fountain, his eyes narrowing as he spotted a figure standing by the fountain's edge, partially obscured by the dead trees. The figure didn't move, but its presence was unmistakable. It was as if it was waiting for them to make their next move.

Drunnyak, his eyes narrowed in suspicion, gripped his weapon tightly. "Should we approach?" he asked, his voice low.

"We'll need to be careful," Alentar replied, his mind working quickly. "Whatever magic took Niv, it's tied to this place. We can't rush in blindly."

Taril, ever the tactician, stepped forward, his war hammer resting on his shoulder. "We need a plan. But first, we have to figure out what's going on here."

Opilkhos's eyes scanned the surroundings, his focus unbroken. "The undead aren't attacking. It's like they're being controlled."

Suddenly, the figure at the fountain moved. Slowly, deliberately, it turned its head, and for the first time, they saw its face – a face that was both human and monstrous, a twisted mockery of life.

The figure before them was a rotund man, his presence both unnerving and strangely dignified. He was sat comfortably at the edge of the huge fountain, his legs swinging idly, as if enjoying a private amusement. His posture was relaxed, yet his gaze – sharp and calculating – remained fixed on the group before him. Short, greying brown hair framed a clean-shaven face with a strong jawline, though his features, smooth and round, seemed almost too placid for someone of his clear malice. His eyes, dark and direct, held a mixture of authority and a mocking gleam, as though he found amusement in the tension around him.

Adorned in rich purple-and-gold robes, intricate patterns glistening in the faint light, he wore a necklace of gold set with large, colourful gemstones – symbols of a wealth and power that felt as oppressive as it was grand. A cane, studded with jewels and held in one hand, rested against the fountain's stone lip, the ornate handle gleaming in the dimness. His other hand casually traced where the water would be, playing with the surface as if unbothered by the stakes of the moment full of magic surrounding his hands.

Behind him, the dark mountains loomed, casting long shadows across the scene, and the ominous setting only served to amplify his insidious calm. He moved with an unsettling playfulness, a contrast to the cold, dangerous air that surrounded him.

When he spoke, his voice was almost a whisper, yet it carried in the air, each word drawn out with deliberate slowness, as though savouring the moment. His stutter was not an accident, but a weapon – each hesitation prolonging the tension. "You… are… too… late," he said, his voice thick with venom and mockery, every syllable like a slow, measured taunt.

Despite his appearance – so polished and unthreatening – there was no mistaking the chill in his words. He was no mere noble, and his soft, mocking manner only served to mask the deadly intent lurking beneath. He may not have moved to strike, but his presence alone was a promise of danger, and the gods, for all their strength, knew that this was a villain unlike any they had faced.

The gods stood frozen, their eyes widening in a mix of disbelief and fury as the villain's words dripped with a sickening, mocking pleasure. The air seemed to freeze around them, the weight of his sinister amusement pressing down like an invisible force. The vile figure in front of them twirled his cane with exaggerated elegance, savouring the moment as if he were watching a slow, inevitable catastrophe unfold.

"I was wondering how long it would take you to get here," he said, his voice laced with mockery. His tone was slow, dragging out each word to stretch the tension. "It took so long that I had to try this new plantation all alone. All by myself…" His words dripped with condescension.

The undead, standing motionless, gave no response. Their empty eyes flickered in the faint light of their surroundings.

With a casual gesture, the man pointed to a nearby tree. As his finger swept through the air, the thick, enveloping darkness began to recede, unveiling a horrifying sight.

The scene before them – Alanteas, mutilated and hanging, his body severed into pieces, animated by the undead curse – was enough to steal their breath away. Each of his limbs twisted unnaturally on gnarled, rotting branches that bent with the weight of his tortured form. The branches shook as they moved, like the twisted limbs of a grotesque puppet, now part of the sickening forest the man in robes had created. Alanteas's eyes, once full of purpose and determination, were empty, devoid of the spark they had once held.

Alentar's expression, usually calm and sharp, twisted into one of barely contained rage. His hands clenched at his sides, his powerful gaze fixed on the twisted scene. The very land around them seemed to tremble, the ground beneath their feet echoing his turmoil. His heart ached, the pain of seeing their comrade reduced to this mockery of life sharp in his chest. "You bastard…" His words were barely a whisper, but they held the weight of an ancient fury.

Nashir's face, usually a mask of tranquillity, now flickered with the power of his connection to the earth. His eyes burned with the intensity of an anger so deep it felt as though the land itself might rise up in defiance. But even he, the god of nature, was momentarily stunned by the grotesque spectacle. The very essence of life had been twisted here, mocked and desecrated. And it was clear: this abomination before them had done it.

Opilkhos stood still, his usual calm shattered, replaced with a silent, deep fury that spoke volumes. The elegant lines of his face – often serene – now carried the weight of grief and vengeful determination.

His voice, when it came, was thick with restrained power. "You... will regret this."

Taril, his massive frame taut with anger, his war hammer clenched in both hands, stepped forward, his eyes never leaving the mocking figure before them. "You dare turn Alanteas into this... this... monstrosity?" His voice was a thunderclap, deep and full of rage. "You will not escape this. Not while we draw breath."

Alentar's eyes burned with tears held back by sheer force of will. He knew Alanteas as a brother, and this desecration of his being had drawn a wound that would never heal. But there was no room for weakness now. Only vengeance. "You'll pay for this," he said through gritted teeth, the energy around him crackling, ready to lash out. "You will pay!"

Drunnyak's eyes widened in a mix of horror and rage, his hand gripping the hilt of his sword so tightly that his knuckles turned white. His usually boisterous demeanour fell silent, replaced by a quiet fury that vibrated in the air. He stepped forward, the muscles in his jaw tightening as his voice rumbled low, barely contained. "Wretched creature..." he muttered, his words thick with disgust, the weight of sorrow for Alanteas cutting through his tone.

He took a step back, the full weight of the horror sinking in. His eyes flickered with the violence of his thoughts, but he forced himself to stay still, awaiting the gods' next move. He was ready to unleash his rage, but he knew the battle was far from over.

As the scene unfolded, the villain only laughed – a soft, almost musical sound filled with malice. His gaze lingered on each of them, enjoying the suffering he had inflicted. "Ah, so much emotion. So much... passion. It's what makes this so much more enjoyable. So much... sweeter."

The gods stood united, their fury coalescing into a singular, powerful force. They would not be swayed by his words, nor by his mockery. There would be no mercy here. The creature who stood before them – this agent of pure evil – would know their wrath.

And then, in the depths of their beings, the gods made a promise: there would be no peace for this man until this wrong was righted, until Alanteas was freed from his monstrous fate.

Alentar's eyes narrowed, his body moving with a practised fluidity as his fingers nocked arrows onto his bow. The draw was so fast, so precise, that the arrows shot out in less than a heartbeat. Each arrow seemed to hum with deadly purpose, flying straight toward the grotesque figure seated in front of them. The fat man, his smile wide and unsettling, didn't flinch. Instead, his eyes darkened – pitch black, as if no light could ever touch them again.

With a flick of his hand, the arrows halted in mid-air, as if time itself had been frozen, and then they reversed. The projectiles tore through the air, returning with the same terrifying speed, piercing Marcus at several vital points before he even had time to gasp in shock. The life drained from his face as the arrows embedded themselves, his body slumping lifelessly to the ground. The gods stood frozen, their eyes wide with disbelief as the horror unfolded. Even Alentar, normally unshaken, felt a tremor of unease ripple through him.

The fat man, still smiling, let out a low chuckle – a sound like a snake's hiss, thick with satisfaction. His voice was insidious, dripping with venom. "You're really out of your depth," he sneered, his words mocking, yet filled with a terrifying certainty. His laugh grew louder, almost manic, before he choked on his own amusement, as if savouring the death he had just caused. "Bear in mind, if anything happens to me," he continued, his voice turning colder, "your precious Niv will pay the price. Not that you could do anything about me anyway..."

The air seemed to grow colder, the weight of his words settling over the gods like a suffocating cloak. The fat man slowly rose to his feet, propped up by his ornate cane. He turned his back on them, his form radiating arrogance, and snapped his fingers with a casual flick of his wrist.

A massive portal cracked open behind him, an abyssal tear in the fabric of reality. From the portal, a flood of undead poured out like a swarm of locusts, their hollow eyes locked onto the gods as they surged forth. The gods' gazes shifted between one another, realisation dawning – this was no longer a battle for survival; it was a battle for everything they had fought for.

Before they could react, a deafening roar split the air. Drunnyak, never one to back down from a fight, leaped into action, charging toward the fat man with reckless fury. But before he could even reach his target, a colossal figure descended from the heavens like a comet – a monstrous creature faster than anything they had ever witnessed. With a blur of motion, the creature grabbed Drunnyak in mid-air, its massive claws digging into his armoured form with a force that sent a shock wave through the ground. Drunnyak's roar of defiance was cut short as the creature squeezed with enough strength to crush a boulder.

The gods watched in astonishment, horror creeping into their hearts as the creature – its form massive, shadowed, and nearly too large to comprehend – carried Drunnyak through the air. The titan's speed defied all logic, making even Drunnyak, the formidable warrior, appear helpless.

Meanwhile, the fat man, still with that sickening smile, looked over his shoulder. His eyes gleamed with malicious joy. "I hope you enjoy the show," he purred. "After all, this is the price you pay for meddling in matters beyond your understanding."

With another snap of his fingers, the undead poured out of the portal like a rising tide, an unrelenting wave of death and decay. They spilled forth in numbers too vast to count – first dozens, then hundreds, then thousands. The air was thick with their presence, a rancid, suffocating aura filling the space around them. The undead surged toward the gods, their movements jerky and unnatural, driven by an insatiable hunger for life.

Nashir and Taril stepped forward in unison, their faces set with determination. Taril raised his massive war hammer, his grip firm and resolute, while Nashir's hands crackled with the energy of the earth. A low rumble echoed through the ground as the earth beneath them began to tremble, the very land responding to Nashir's call. Vines erupted from the soil, thick and gnarled, lashing at the approaching undead, but they were only a temporary barrier against the overwhelming tide.

Opilkhos stood at the front, his stance strong, his aura glowing brighter than ever before. He raised one hand, his fingers curled as if manipulating the very air around him, and waves of destructive energy shot out, reducing the undead to dust with each strike. His eyes glinted with an intense fire, the power of his aura rippling around him like a shield, but even he could feel the weight of the undead pressing in from all sides.

"We need to break through!" Alentar's voice rang out, sharp and commanding, as he fired arrows into the mass of undead. His shots were true, his arrows finding their marks with deadly accuracy. Each shot brought down one more enemy, but the sheer number of them was staggering. The gods were strong, but this... this was a battle unlike any they had fought before.

The gods, undeterred, continued to fight. They fought for their fallen comrades, for the lives of those who still had hope. But the undead were endless. The fat man's cruel laughter echoed through the chaos, a constant reminder that this was just the beginning. The gods fought back with all their might, but the darkness seemed endless, stretching farther than they could see.

And still, the undead came. With every step they took, the gods felt the weight of their own power, the cost of what they had to sacrifice to protect those they loved.

They were not just fighting for their lives – they were fighting for the survival of everything they had built, everything they had come to care for.

As the battle raged on, the gods exchanged no words. They didn't need to. Their bond was unbreakable, and together, they would endure.

The sky itself trembled as Drunnyak, his body pinned and crushed in the massive claws of the ancient dragon, found a primal, almost savage fury rising within him. The dragon, a creature older than time itself, soared higher and higher, the cold, thin air pressing against Drunnyak's lungs. His vision blurred from the lack of oxygen, but it only stoked the fire within him. The dragon, far too sure of its strength, assumed it had the upper hand – too powerful, too ancient, too invincible to be stopped by mere mortal hands. But what it had underestimated was the fury of a god.

Drunnyak's muscles, already straining under the crushing pressure, surged with untapped power, and a violent, uncontrollable rage coursed through his veins. His hands, huge and scarred from years of battle, became pikes, his fingers digging into the dragon's claws like claws into wood, each movement laced with a sheer force of will, enough to break the dragon's iron grip. The creature roared, throwing itself into wild spirals, trying to shake him off. But the rage, that primal, godly rage, didn't let Drunnyak fall.

His face a twisted mask of fury, Drunnyak's eyes never once left the dragon's back, his entire body acting as a weapon in this fight. The beast had done its best to cage him in its claws, but now, in this battle of wills, the dragon was the one being caged. With a ferocity few could ever understand, Drunnyak clawed his way upward, using the strength of his thick arms to pull himself, fist over fist, until he reached the dragon's back.

And then, with a roar of his own – a god's roar, a deafening battle cry that seemed to shake the heavens themselves – Drunnyak struck. His fist collided with the thick, scale-covered hide of the dragon. The force of the blow sent shock waves through the beast's spine, and even the thick hide – stronger than iron, tough as mountains – buckled under the impact. The dragon let out a screech that echoed across the skies, a terrible cry of agony, its wings faltering for a brief moment. It spun in mid-air, circling and trying to dislodge the god on its back, but it couldn't break his grip. Every time it tried, Drunnyak's grip only tightened.

With another furious roar, Drunnyak's fist came down again. He punched through the dragon's scales, denting them with such force that they caved inward, like an ancient wall shattering from a blow too strong to withstand. Each punch rang with divine might, and the dragon's cries grew weaker. The beast's thick hide, once so impenetrable, began to buckle and warp under the sheer power of Drunnyak's fury. Blood – black as the night itself – spilled from the beast's wounds, staining the sky. The dragon's once-proud roars turned to howls of pain, and it struggled to stay aloft as Drunnyak's relentless fists continued their assault.

The dragon, sensing its weakness, tried to reassert control, using its enormous wings to fight against the blows, attempting to dive and roll, but Drunnyak, the god of battle, refused to yield. His fury was not just that of a mortal warrior, but that of a force of nature. Every punch was a manifestation of rage born from millennia of existence, an unstoppable force, an ancient power that even the dragon could not comprehend.

And then, with one final, earth-shattering punch, Drunnyak drove his fist into the dragon's spine. The sound of the beast's bones breaking echoed across the battlefield, and the dragon, finally overpowered, let out one last scream of agony before plummeting toward the earth below.

The dragon, now weakened by Drunnyak's unforgiving assault, gathered its remaining strength in a final, desperate act of defiance. With a screech of fury, the beast's massive claws shot forward, grabbing Drunnyak in a grip so powerful it threatened to snap every bone in his body. The pressure was suffocating, the weight of the dragon's immense form pressing down on him as the earth seemed to tremble beneath them.

But Drunnyak, though trapped, was far from defeated. With a growl of fury, he pushed against the dragon's strength, the very essence of his being resisting the pull of gravity and the beast's crushing force. His muscles, already strained, burned with effort, but he refused to give in. He knew what had to be done.

With a primal roar, Drunnyak freed his arms from the dragon's grasp, forcing himself upright despite the weight and the earth-shattering force pulling them downward. His sword, still gripped tightly in his hand, gleamed with a cold, deadly purpose. With one final surge of will, Drunnyak thrust the blade deep into the heart of the dragon, driving it in to the hilt. The creature's scream of pain shook the heavens, its wings faltering as it felt the life drain from its massive form.

In its final, desperate breath, the dragon thought only one thing: *If I die, I will take you with me.* With a savage twist of its body, the dragon spun, and they both plummeted through the air, faster than

Drunnyak could process. The wind howled around them as they spiralled downward, the sheer force of their fall ripping through the air. Drunnyak, still holding on to the sword embedded in the dragon's heart, was pulled along, unable to do anything but brace for the inevitable impact.

With a deafening crash, the two collided with the earth, sending shock waves through the ground. The dragon's massive body slammed into Drunnyak with terrifying force, and the world around them seemed to explode in a cloud of dust and debris. The sound of the impact was thunderous, shaking the very foundation of the mountains as if the earth itself had been struck by the force of a god's wrath.

The dust lingered in the air, a thick cloud that obscured the battlefield. The gods, still engaged in the ferocious battle with the undead horde, could only hear the distant roar of the storm and the screeching of the creatures surrounding them. Their eyes widened in concern, each of them momentarily distracted by the deafening silence that followed the crash. They shouted Drunnyak's name in unison, their voices filled with worry and panic. But the smoke, the dust, and the chaos of the battle made it impossible to see what had happened.

The ground where Drunnyak had fallen lay still, the silence oppressive, the air heavy with uncertainty. Had he survived the impact? Had the dragon's final blow taken him with it? The gods could not tell, and they were forced to focus on the battle at hand. Yet in the pit of their hearts, a deep, gnawing fear grew — had they lost one of their own?

But as the fight raged on, they could do nothing but press forward, slaying undead and holding the line. Time seemed to stretch into eternity, each moment growing more desperate than the last. The weight of their worry for Drunnyak hung in the air, but they were trapped, bound by duty and the need to protect themselves from the threat at hand.

Drunnyak's fate was sealed in that moment, lost beneath the crushing weight of the dragon's body, but the gods' resolve was not. They fought on, knowing that, even in the face of this monumental loss, they could not afford to falter. The horde would not stop, and so they too could not stop until every last undead was eradicated. And so they continued, hearts heavy but spirits unbroken, as they carved through the ranks of their enemies, each blow a testament to their strength and their will to survive.

For Drunnyak, for Maud, for each other, they would press on.

The gods stood, their weapons gleaming in the shifting light of the battle, as the undead pressed in on all sides. The air was thick with the acrid smell of decay, and the sound of cracking bones and roaring death filled the earth. The ground trembled beneath their feet, the dead rising faster than they could fall. Yet, amidst the chaos, the gods moved with purpose, each one a force unto themselves, their power shaking the very fabric of the battlefield.

Alentar's body was a blur of motion as he leapt into the air. With his acrobatic precision, he soared over the advancing undead, his twin daggers flashing like lightning as they found their marks, cutting through bone and flesh in a fluid motion. His eyes, sharp as ever, darted from enemy to enemy, always one step ahead. He spun through the air, dodging strikes and using the momentum of his flips to launch himself into the next group, his daggers finding soft, rotten flesh with deadly accuracy. With each movement, Alentar danced around the undead, turning their own attacks against them, his speed unmatched, his grace unchallenged.

Meanwhile, Opilkhos stood like a fortress, his massive sword sweeping through the horde with unstoppable force. His shield, a shimmering golden tower, absorbed blows from all directions, each strike sparking with a divine energy that sent the undead flying. His golden aura pulsed with power, radiating outward in waves of light, disintegrating the undead that came too close. With each swing of his sword, Opilkhos cleaved through skulls and ribs, the force of his blows sending the dead reeling. He was a master of control, his shield a barrier that protected him as much as it struck down those who dared come too near. The glow of his aura bathed the battlefield in a brilliant light, illuminating the chaos in the darkness, turning it into an inferno of divine fury.

Nashir, ever the orchestrator, stood at the heart of the battle, his staff raised high. The earth beneath him seemed to come alive as he summoned the forces of nature to his aid. The ground cracked open, massive tendrils of roots and vines shooting from the earth, grabbing hold of the undead and pulling them into the dirt. The very land obeyed his command, entombing the dead in the earth as they were swallowed whole by nature's fury. Lightning struck from the sky at Nashir's command, crackling through the air and striking the undead with precision. The sky roared as his power surged, the storm above him echoing his wrath. Every motion was accompanied by the sounds of nature – the howling winds, the groaning of trees, and the rumbling of the earth as it shifted under his power. With each strike of his staff, the dead were undone, nature itself rising up to strike them down.

Taril, standing on the front lines, was a sight of brutal strength. His war hammer swung with terrifying force, smashing through the undead with bone-crushing blows. His shield, forged in the fires of ancient dwarven craftsmanship, was an extension of himself, blocking strikes and breaking the dead with each swing. Every time he struck, the war hammer sang through the air, its roar reverberating across the battlefield, as if it were a weapon of judgement itself. With each blow, undead bones shattered and crumbled, their bodies falling to the ground in broken heaps. His movements were rhythmic, powerful and deliberate, each strike reinforcing his indomitable will.

The gods fought as one, their movements coordinated and fluid. They were not separate entities but a unified force, each one amplifying the others' power. Their tactics were precise, their timing impeccable. Alentar's speed opened gaps in the undead's ranks, allowing Opilkhos to strike with devastating force, while Nashir's control of nature created openings for Taril to move in and deliver crushing blows. The undead fell, their numbers dwindling, but their relentless rise seemed to mock the gods' efforts.

And then, from the depths of the earth, from the shadows of the night, more undead emerged – endless, relentless. They rose from the soil, crawled from the cracks, and staggered from the darkness, as though the land itself had rejected them and sent them back to fight. The gods, weary but undeterred, continued their assault, but it became clear: the undead would never cease. With each undead they felled, another rose to take its place, like an endless tide.

Alentar, breathing heavily, landed with a roll as he dodged a swing from a massive undead. "We can't keep up with this," he shouted, his voice strained from the exertion.

Opilkhos nodded, his eyes glowing with determination. "We will hold," he said firmly. "We must."

Nashir raised his staff once more, summoning the elements to his aid. "Nature fights for us," he said, his voice filled with the confidence of the earth itself. "But the tide of this battle is unyielding."

Taril swung his war hammer, smashing through another undead, his movements as fluid as a well-practised dancer's. "We won't stop," he said, his voice filled with the strength of a thousand battles. "By the breath of the Deep Forge and the first fire of creation," he bellowed, voice ringing like a sacred oath, "we hold the line – so long as flame stirs in our chests, not one shall pass."

And yet, despite the gods' strength, the tide of undead did not cease. For every one they struck down, another rose, their ranks never thinning, their presence a constant threat. The storm raged on above them, the wind howling like a beast in agony as the gods fought on. The undead came in waves, their numbers multiplying faster than the gods could keep up with.

The battle raged for what felt like an eternity, and though the gods were victorious, the sheer numbers of the undead kept them at bay. They fought together, each one complementing the other, their combined strength an unstoppable force, but it became clear that the true test was yet to come. They fought on, their strength unbroken, but the undead would not stop, and the storm would not ease.

The gods' once-unshakeable resolve had begun to falter. Their movements, though still powerful, grew slower with each passing moment. Their bones ached, their powers waning as the sheer tide of the undead threatened to overwhelm them.

Alentar, once the swiftest and most precise of them all, found himself swallowed by the horde. His body was bitten and torn at, his focus and agility no longer enough to keep the undead at bay. Pain surged through him as he was dragged to the ground, the weight of the creatures pressing down on him, biting, tearing. He struggled to free himself, but the undead pulled him deeper into their ranks. He could feel the blood flow from his wounds, his strength weakening with every passing second.

Nashir, his connection to the land flickering, tried to reach his brother. He moved with the precision of a seasoned warrior, his staff crackling with energy as he tried to tear through the mass of undead that had overtaken Alentar. But as he reached for him, a clawed hand struck from behind, its strength sending Nashir crashing to the ground. The impact knocked the wind from his lungs, and his vision blurred as the undead closed in. His once-unbreakable connection to the earth was now fractured, the ground beneath him cold and unyielding. For the first time in his eternal existence, Nashir felt helpless.

Taril, ever the steadfast protector, found himself surrounded. His war hammer swung with deadly precision, his shield raised to block blow after blow, but the sheer number of undead that swarmed him was unlike anything he had ever faced. His arms were held fast by the dead, his strength slowly being sapped as they pulled and tore at him. His shield was no longer a defence; it was a weight that dragged him down. He fought with all his might, but even the strength of a god could not hold back an endless tide.

Opilkhos, bloodied and exhausted, could feel his aura flicker. He had been using his golden light to decimate the undead, but the more he struck, the more they seemed to come. Sweat poured down his face and mixed with his blood, his breathing heavy and laboured. His shield, once a symbol of his invincibility, now felt like a burden. His sword, gleaming with divine light, faltered in his hand. He could feel the weight of his friends' pain pressing on him, and in that moment, something inside him began to crack. His movements grew slower, more desperate.

He looked to the others, his heart sinking as he saw the truth in their eyes. They were failing. They were being overwhelmed. The undead were countless, their numbers growing faster than they could defeat them. He could see the exhaustion on their faces, the frustration, the fear that mirrored his own.

In slow motion, he turned his gaze to Nashir, who lay on the ground, struggling to rise. Then to Alentar, his body writhing under the weight of the undead. And finally to Taril, his war hammer slowing, his shield useless against the tide. They were all struggling, each of them giving everything they had, but it wasn't enough.

And then, as if time itself had stopped, Opilkhos's eyes locked with theirs. The pain, the fear, the exhaustion – all of it was in their gazes. It was a silent understanding. They had given their all, but the weight of the world was too much.

Opilkhos's golden aura flickered, its light dimming as if it were no longer enough to hold back the darkness. His shoulders slumped, the weight of failure pressing on him, on all of them. They had fought with everything they had, and yet here they were – on the edge of defeat. The undead were closing in, their numbers growing by the second, and the gods could do nothing but watch as the battle they had fought so hard to win slipped through their fingers.

They felt the crushing weight of failure. They had failed to protect the world they had sworn to guard. And with that realisation, they felt their strength waver, their resolve shatter, and for a brief moment, they all knew the cold, crushing feeling of being helpless.

And then, in the midst of their despair, a single thought flickered in Opilkhos's mind: *What happened to Drunnyak and Niv?* They hadn't noticed any movement from Drunnyak since his fateful fall, and the silence surrounding his absence gnawed at them like a festering wound. The question of what had become of Niv, who had vanished without a trace, weighed even heavier. The thought of losing them both – of failing not just the world they fought to protect, but the very family they had forged through their shared purpose – was a burden too heavy to bear.

But before they could dwell on it any longer, the sound of the undead grew louder, and they knew their time had run out. The gods, once invincible, were now nothing more than shadows in the storm.

The darkness closed in on them.

The battle raged on around Opilkhos, each blow he struck, each movement he made a desperate attempt to fend off the relentless tide of undead. But it was in the midst of this chaos, as the very essence of his body began to fail him, that something deep within stirred. A moment of clarity.

His mind, already on the edge of exhaustion, was suddenly flooded with a memory, distant yet vivid – a memory not his own, but that of his counterpart, Harinnil. The image of their past battle against their father, the desperation they had felt, and the brutal power Harinnil had stolen from their friends surged through Opilkhos like a shock wave. He remembered how, in the final moments of that battle, Harinnil had absorbed the essence of their companions, their strength, their very life force, to strike down their foe.

For a fleeting second, Opilkhos felt it – the power of those who had fought beside him, now a part of him. It washed over him like a surge of fire, but not just the heat of anger – this was warmth, a strength born of unity. The strength of his brothers, of his friends.

Opilkhos closed his eyes for a moment, not sure if the wetness on his face was blood or sweat. But as he breathed deeply, he felt it – the essence of their auras, their very souls pouring into him, filling the emptiness that had been growing in his heart. His body trembled as the surge of power swept through him, his muscles swelling, his aura pulsing with new-found energy. His grip tightened on his sword, his shield dropping from his hand as the power within him burned through his body.

He opened his eyes, and the world around him seemed to slow. The undead, relentless and monstrous, became little more than shadows in his vision, their movements sluggish and weak in the face of his new-found strength. He stood, his chest heaving, his breaths sharp as he gathered the full force of the essence that had been shared with him.

A battle cry erupted from his throat – raw, primal, the sound of a god's fury. His voice shook the very earth beneath him, and with it, an explosion of energy erupted from his core. A shock wave so powerful that it sent the undead flying through the air like rag dolls, their forms disintegrating or crumbling into dust as they were torn from existence. Some disappeared instantly, others flew into the air, their bodies scattering across the battlefield.

The gods, who had been fighting tirelessly for so long beside him, paused in their struggle, their eyes wide in awe at the sheer force of the explosion. Opilkhos, breathing heavily, collapsed to his knees, his muscles burning with the effort, his heart racing with the intensity of the battle. His vision blurred, but he knew – he knew they had won. He had released something, something beyond just the undead.

He looked up, and in the haze of his fading strength, he saw them – each of the fallen undead, their bodies dissolving into the air, their souls finally liberated from the curse that had bound them. The souls, shimmering and ethereal, began to rise from their remains, swirling around him like a gentle breeze. His breath caught in his throat as he felt them, their presence thankful, peaceful. Their eyes, in their final moments, conveyed a silent apology for the lives they had taken, but also a quiet relief as they finally found rest. Alanteas's soul walked slowly towards Alentar, kneeling and thanking him for everything he'd done for him. Then, he shifted his gaze towards Opilkhos, nodding with a grin before looking up to the sky and closing his eyes, as if he was ready for the next steps.

The wind picked up, swirling around the battlefield like a living thing, carrying the whispers of those Opilkhos had freed. The storm, which had raged relentlessly for so long, began to subside, its thunder replaced by a rising wind, its lightning flashing across the sky in great arcs of power. The very air seemed charged with the force of the moment, as if the heavens themselves were acknowledging the weight of what had just transpired.

Opilkhos, exhausted beyond measure, barely had the strength to stand, but his heart swelled with the love and gratitude of those he had freed. He watched, his eyes misted with tears, as the souls of the undead rose higher, swirling into the storm above. And then, for the first time in two millennia, the first rays of sunlight broke through the clouds.

It was not a warm, golden sunlight – but it was light, pure and strong, cutting through the storm, touching the land below with a glow that stirred hope from the soil itself. It bathed the battlefield in a soft, ethereal glow, a sign that, after centuries of darkness, something had changed. The curse that had gripped the world for so long was beginning to break. The first dawn of a new age was upon them.

Opilkhos fell to his knees, his body weak, but his heart full. He had done it. They had done it. The world had changed, and the first rays of a new future had broken through the darkened skies. He could feel the warmth of the sun, even if only for a moment. It was their victory – and it was the beginning of something far greater.

The winds had calmed, the storm now a distant echo in the depths of the night. Our heroes, weary and broken, found solace in the embrace of sleep. Their bodies lay scattered across the newly formed land, bloodied and battered from the battles fought. Yet their souls – undeterred by the torment – felt the weight of the moment, even as their eyes were closed to the world.

The final echoes of war faded into the frozen silence.

Above, the sky – at last cleansed of fury – stretched wide and still, its black expanse strewn with bruised clouds torn apart by the battle's rage. A silence fell, deeper than before. Reverent. Heavy with the memory of what had just unfolded.

Then – a flicker. A breath of wind.

A jagged bolt of lightning split the heavens with a deafening roar, and for a single, searing heartbeat, the world saw him. Harinnil. Cloaked in shadow, he stood atop the jagged crown of a distant mountain – his silhouette framed in ghostly silver. His long robes whispered in the wind, untouched by time, his eyes like burning coals in the night.

He stood unmoving, an ancient revenant gazing down at the battlefield below. He had watched it all – every strike, every death, every divine blow that sent his monstrous kin crumbling into the dirt.

But he had not moved.

Not interfered. Not mourned.

As quickly as he was revealed, the light died. Darkness swallowed the peak once more, and with it, Harinnil vanished – like a memory not yet ready to be remembered. Yet in that single flash, one truth was carved into the hearts of the gods: he was watching.

He had always been watching, and he would not remain in the shadows forever.

The battlefield, where so many had fallen, was silent now, the only sounds the soft whispers of the wind and the distant murmur of the shifting earth. The night stretched out, serene, as if the world itself had taken a breath after the chaos. The sky, now clear of the storm, revealed only the stillness of the heavens. The dawn of a new age had come – not in light, but in the quiet understanding of what had been won. The darkness was lifting, but not all questions were answered. Not yet.

Who was the villain they had faced? What was his connection to Harinnil, the dark brother that had once walked alongside them? And where had Niv gone? Her disappearance hung in the air, as unanswered as the darkening sky above them. The gods could feel it – an unease still stirred in their hearts, a gnawing question they could not yet answer.

And then, far beyond the heroes' resting bodies, where the land stretched into the unknown, the world whispered. Above the frozen mountains and the desolate villages, through the thick mist that still clung to the cursed earth, a shadow stirred. The winds shifted again, carrying with them the faintest scent of something unknown.

We flew across the cursed land, our vision painting the rugged mountains, the ice-covered peaks, the twisted villages yet to be revealed. In the distance, we saw the broken remnants of what once was – and what would soon be again, for there was much left to be discovered. It was a land full of secrets, full of wonder, and full of those who would soon cross paths with our heroes.

Then, as we descended into a dark corner, so deep that it seemed to be born from the very heart of the land, a pair of eyes – eyes blind to the turning of ages, now stirred awake. They were not the eyes of man, nor a simple goddess. They were older – carved from time itself, forged in the silence between stars. And in them burnt a power the world no longer dared name.

The shadows kept her hidden, swirling around her like a cloak. But in that moment, we could feel the weight of her presence – the same weight that had been building, waiting. Waiting for the moment of her awakening.

Who was she? What was she? And why had she been kept in the darkness for so long?

The questions hung in the air, unanswered. The shadows, heavy with the knowledge of the past and the future, swirled like an eternal dance, refusing to reveal her face. But we knew she was not just another foe. She was something more. And her awakening, her coming into this broken world, would mark the beginning of something much greater than the gods had imagined.

The wind picked up again, and as it blew, it carried the promise of a journey that was only beginning. The heroes may have won this battle, but the war was far from over. Their journey was still unfolding, and the road ahead was fraught with dangers they had not yet faced. But in the distance, beyond the shadows, there was hope. A flicker of it, shining against the darkness.

In that moment, the world seemed to pause, waiting. Waiting for what would come next.

The end of this chapter, yes. But the beginning of something far greater.

And so, we fade away, leaving behind only the sound of the wind and the faint echoes of a world still waiting to be saved.

PRONUNCIATION GUIDE
The Gods of MAUD

Alentar — AH-len-tahr — **God of the Hunt**, master archer and relentless tracker.

Nashir — NAH-sheer — **God of Nature**, bringer of life, guardian of the wild and twin brother of Alentar.

Aneeve ("Niv") — ah-NEEV (nickname: Niv — neev) — **Elven Goddess of Light and Renewal**, fierce warrior and graceful leader.

Drunnyak — DRUN-yak — **God of Strength and Beasts**, towering warrior clad in lion hides.

Taril — TAH-ril — **God of the Dwarves and Craftsmanship**, unyielding guardian with warhammer and colossal shield.

Opilkhos — OH-pill-koss — **God of Valor and Protection**, stoic paladin wielding shield and blade.

Harinnil — HAH-ri-nill — **God of Death and Shadow**, fallen and feared, master of ancient dark powers.

This book is printed on paper from sustainable sources managed under the Forest Stewardship Council (FSC) scheme.

It has been printed in the UK to reduce transportation miles and their impact upon the environment.

For every new title that Troubador publishes, we plant a tree to offset CO_2, partnering with the More Trees scheme.

For more about how Troubador offsets its environmental impact, see www.troubador.co.uk/sustainability-and-community